Cinderella Chronicles

By

Alexandria Altman

New Earth Productions First Edition

November 2011

Dedications:

3 Princesses

Cherisa, Tessa, and Adalynn

3 Princes

Logan, Chandler, and Noah

--

Alexandria Altman

"Trying to forget someone you loved is like trying to remember someone you never knew."

Unknown

Table of Contents

"Have faith in your dreams and someday
your rainbow will come smiling through.
No matter how your heart is grieving,
if you keep on believing,
the dream that you wish will come true."

Theme from Walt Disney's *"Cinderella"*

Chapter 1

Atlanta

Weathered, callused fingertips traced the gilded frame's edge, lingering near the artist's name in the lower corner. She grinned at the face in the portrait. "Don't you worry none, Cindy'rella; you'll be prancing' an' showin' off soon 'nough. They's gonna be here anytime now."

Bessie lowered the protective cloth and shuffled to her front porch to wait.

Lightning ripped across the distant sky, shattering the early evening's peace and vibrating the ground. A long, low-toned rumble crackled through the air and recoiled off the earth. "Harrumph!" From the unique sound of the beastly thunder, Bessie knew that more than a bad storm was rolling in and, slowly, uneasily, shifted in her antique wooden rocker. "There's troubles a'comin."

Bessie leaned her head back and closed her eyes, recalling a lifetime of special people she had worked for and for whom she had cared too much. Rubbing her aching, wrinkled, arthritic hands, she chuckled softly. *Uh-huh, what a long time ago. Never did think I'd live to see the day that I'd outlive those people. Even some of the children I raised are gone.*

Unbidden but undeniable, the thought crept to mind: *Why be surprised? The way those white folk did, it's a wonder all of them weren't dead ages ago.*

Chin tilted upward, she inhaled deeply and recognized the sweet fragrances wafting on the misty breeze as the storm pushed itself closer across the landscape. Raindrops splattered on the porch railing, and then a flurry of heavy rain began hammering the tin roof of her large brick home, a drum roll announced the storm's arrival. Bessie smiled, nodded, and rocked a tad faster, glad she'd planned for the tin covering, remembering how, in the good but harder ol' days as a youngster, she always slept better, felt safer, when rain danced on the tin roof of the two-room shack she shared with her mother and three brothers. They'd grown up there the best they could.

She couldn't remember much about her papa, since she was the youngest, just that he'd gotten sick and died. That left her mama to carry on with four children to rear with very few resources. Survival was all that really mattered. *We had to scramble, had to get out almost 'afore dawn every morning, work mighty hard all day, carry home what scraps we could. . . . only ways to get us through those cold winters and hot Georgia summers.*

Bessie's smile widened as rain found its own rhythm on the tin roof. It was a homey, wrapped-in-loving-arms feeling, a rekindling of precious childhood memories when those long-ago rainstorms lulled her into a deep sleep.

Rocking had just about stopped as she slipped further into fond recollections and dreamland when a jagged flash slammed into a warm cloud above the house and struck the ground. The thunderclap nearly jolted her out of the rocking chair and she grabbed the bifocals that had slid down her nose.

"Lordy! That was close." *Whew, you's got to hold on when you's old and no one's around. . . . they's all dead.*

She smoothed her dress and settled against the cushion again. *Best they come on an' not keep an old woman waitin' when it's rainin' cats an' dogs. Hard to believe that a young white boy is coming all the way down from New York City to talk to me. I might be old, but I knows what I knows. They wait until I gets too old to die and too young to live, then they wants to know all about my people. Well, they were my family, my people, an' they treated me good, but I never afore seen the likes of showin' out in all my days, those rich folk were, well, yes'um, they were some kinda crazy.*

13

In the community, Bessie had long been known for clarity and insight on most issues and not ever mincing words.

"Well, might' a knowed they'd be puttin' on airs." Bessie watched as a white stretch limo slowly cruised down her tree-lined lane and carefully pulled up in front of her grand turn-of-the-century home.

She grabbed a napkin to wipe away any trace of the brown liquid that had dribbled down her chin. Snuff wasn't a lifetime habit she was about to break now. The driver got out of the car, splashed through puddles around to the rear passenger door, opened the largest umbrella she'd ever seen, then stood there in the pelting rain, waiting.

Imagine that. They's comin' here to find out about my rich folk. Mighty flatterin'. Bessie tried to stifle a chuckle as she carefully positioned her sensible shoes and thinning legs, pushed up on the seat with trembling hands, and slowly raised herself. After a few seconds, she felt balanced and steady, and began taking short, practiced steps toward the porch doorway.

The chauffeur held the massive umbrella with one hand over a younger, well-dressed man, and slammed the limo's door against the wind with the other hand.

"Ya'll come on! Hurry up now, or you'll be soaked to the bone! It's a big one rollin' in here . . . maybe even a twister. Who knows, this time of year." *Yes'um, there's somethin' blowing all right: white folk nosin' 'round my peoples. Well, I can give them somethin' — my broom to ride back to New York ' a'stead that there fancy car an' private airplane.*

As both men quick-stepped along the walkway, Bessie pushed open the screen door in time for them to scramble up the three cobblestone steps and onto her screened-in covered porch.

"Ya'll come on in outta the wet." Bessie turned and opened the front door, which was secured with several black steel bars.

Both men glanced around, noticed all the barred windows, and hesitated.

Bessie's eyes narrowed. "Them bars are *why* I have a nice home an' nice things inside my home that's smack-dab in the middle of a historic 'lanta neighborhood. My peoples always takes right good care o' me an' my needs now that I gots some years on me. And, ain't nobody comin' through them bars. An' if'n they do, there's somethin' else what's mighty nice too – my Charles Daly side-by-side." Bessie chuckled, crossed the threshold and stepped into the house.

Both men froze in their tracks, wondering if she was joking or serious.

Bessie glanced over her shoulder and stared at the two strangers. *Lordy-Lordy. It's like they's from Mars instead of New York. Ought to know by now that us Southerners stand on our own two foots. Don't 'spect the police to show up in time just 'cause we needs some hep.*

The well-dressed man extended his hand. "I'm Gary Miller from the *New York Times.*"

"Uh-huh, an' I'm Bessie from the ol' 'lanta times. Set yo'self down wherever you want. Bessie's gonna go fetch a coffee tray an' sets it down in here for you gents to hep yo'selves."

Miller glanced around and pointed at an ancient wooden settle against a wall, indicating that his damp driver was to sit there. He strolled around the immaculate living room, studying the unique pieces. He stopped in front of the cloth-covered frame displayed on an elaborate easel. His hand drifted to the cloth's corner, obviously intending to lift and peek while the old woman was distracted. He jumped back when Bessie cleared her throat — loudly. Miller chose one of the twin brocade-covered wing chairs near a drop-leaf coffee table.

Bessie had watched his every move from the kitchen area. *Seems a bit taken with my antiques an' whatnots, don't he?* "You like my things?"

"Uh, why yes, ma'am, I'm fond of antiques. My grandfather in upstate New York was a dealer and owned an antique business. I enjoyed visiting him and learning about the pieces, how they were made, how they were used, what makers mark to look for. He taught me the value of such things."

"Did he now? Yes,um; I can say both families was very good to me, an' still are. They takes good care of ol' Bessie now. Learned a lot too, by-n'-by. I knows the difference 'tween a fancy thing in gold-painted picture frame an' a darkened landscape in a hundred-year-old gold gilded one . . . without havin' to get close enough ta put my sticky fingers on it, too."

Miller's complexion tinged slightly. He glanced at the covered easel in the corner, surprised by the woman's quick candor. Hopefully, it would prove helpful.

Bessie set a silver tray upon the coffee table and pointed to the elaborate silver coffee service surrounded by delicate platinum rimmed, bone china cups and saucers. "Hep yo'self, Mr. Miller, an' your man over there in that corner. Do he want some coffee to ward off a chill from getting wet?" Her eyes narrowed as she watched for Miller's reaction. "Ain't fittin' to forget him."

Miller's eyebrows went up at another sharp critique doled out by the elderly woman. "Uh, no, thank you; we both had coffee in town."

Bessie eyed him sharply. *I doubts that.* "Well, what you want to know? Let's get on with it afore that storm blows us slap all away." Bessie carefully lowered her petite body in the matching wing chair across from Miller and crossed her ankles. *Make no mistake, young Mr. Miller, these ol' joints might be failin' a bit, but the clock upstairs just keeps on tickin'. Keeps pretty good time at that.*

Miller pushed a button on his microcassette tape recorder, set it on the coffee table, eased himself into a comfortable position, prepared to hear what she'd say based upon the questions he was about to ask. He wanted real answers, not rumors, not a puff piece supplied by a publicist in a press kit. "I don't believe in fairy tales and neither do my readers. So, uh, Miss Bessie, I want to know about the tale . . . . 'the slipper and the girl' and whether or not the story is tr—."

"Say what?" Bessie gripped the arms of her chair and leaned forward.

18

Miller's eyes widened, startled by the old lady's outburst. "Well—"

"Don't you 'well' me, young man. What did you say — 'the slipper and the girl'? What on God's green earth you talkin' 'bout? You talkin' crazy now, boy. You didn't come here to talk about the rich folks? My two families?"

"Uh, well, yes and no."

"Make up your mind; yes or no? Don't you go wastin' my time. I ain't got none to spare."

Miller squirmed in his chair. "Well, uh, everyone sort of knows about the families; articles in *Town & Country*' and society magazines, but not much is known about young Drake and his bride. They don't do interviews. They're seen at galas from Atlanta to New York, they're on 'A' lists in Beverly Hills and New York, and they live quite well, mixing it up with the Hollywood crowd.

"So, there's some confusion among the society and industry reporters. You see, Miss Bessie, the young couple is in the limelight, but they don't talk about themselves; they stay in the background; their friends won't talk about them. But they live in one of the most expensive areas — three blocks off Rodeo

Drive. Most young couples can't afford that kind of lifestyle unless they're mega movie stars or were born into wealth. Everyone knows they're part of the rich-and-famous jet set. We know they attend movie premieres in producers' homes and use the MGM jet to fly to New York."

Bessie waved both hands, dismissing Miller's monologue about her young people and their lives, and eyed him again. *Hmm . . . if they won't talk none, young fella, what makes you think ol' Bessie will? You think you're fixin' to trick me into sayin' something? You thinkin' you're gonna win some Pulitzer, maybe, with this tall tale o' yours?*

Miller ignored her rebuff. "We know Drake was born into one of Atlanta's prominent families, but we know practically nothing about *her*. She's been approached, asked to sign with agents, and—"

"What you talkin' 'bout now? Who's 'she'? Who are you talkin' 'bout?"

Miller turned his head to hide a smirk.

"Ally."

The old woman had lost her concentration; perhaps he could confuse her again and she'd blurt out something useful,

20

perhaps reveal Ally's oh-so-secret background. The veteran society reporter showed not one guilty twinge about smearing someone's private life onto the front page of *Variety* or the *Times*. He cleared his throat, grinned and changed tactics.

"Miss Bessie, your Ally has made a strong impression upon powerful people in Hollywood: studio heads, movie directors, producers, agents; the real movers and shakers in a multimillion-dollar-industry. She's gorgeous; turns heads wherever she goes. The Disney, Universal and Paramount studio bosses always invite Drake and Ally to private premieres. It's a very big deal. I'm sure you've heard of those huge, very important companies. Drake and Ally attend those functions like it's no big deal, but it really is."

Bessie's tongue shifted a small soggy wad from one cheek to the other as she studied Miller's expression; she dabbed at a corner of her mouth with a linen napkin and shook her head. "You don't know a pig from a poke, boy, an' you sure don't know my folks, who they is, how they lived long afore they ventured out to your highfalutin Hollywood an' New York. Bet you knows nonthin' about the Piedmont Driving Club, who's allowed in an' who ain't. Why, ugly young'uns with purple spiky hairs an' them shiny bobbles things stickin' outta their eyebrows an' such can't even park our cars. Ha! That there's exclusive. Both my families been members since after The Northern Invasion . . . ever since I can remember. And the family hosts big events over there with dozens of waiters runnin' an tendin' hundreds of big-time guests from the capital an' such. . . . and you sittin' here, all important-like, tellin' me that goin' to some peoples' home to watch a movie is a big deal?" She cackled aloud, patted her knee then wiped her mouth again. "You don't know nothin' 'bout nothin'; nothin' bout the people you come here to ask about. An you sure don't know how many homes my families has or where they's got 'em all tucked away. You're downright pitiful, boy, just pitiful. Full of hot air is all. You come down here all puffed up like you is somebody, but you ain't nothin' 'cause you don't know nothin'. That's downright funny: You thinks my people goin' to some movie show in somebody's house is a big deal. Ha! . . . You sure do get impressed mighty easy 'cause you knows some of them Hollywood folks. You ain't no different from everybody else. You gets up in the mornin' an puts on your britches one leg at a time, just like the rest of us on God's good earth. You ain't no better."

Whew-ee! You're just like them carpetbaggers my ol' granny tol' me about . . . comin' down here a'diggin' through our homes, takin' what weren't hid, hurtin' people, stealin' our chickens an' food, grabbin' everythin'. Ain't changed a bit; want to get something for nothin'.

Stunned by the frail old lady's tongue-lashing, Miller's mouth fell open. "But . . . I thought, uh." He glanced at his
22

chauffeur, hoping the hefty, but graying black man had a quick reply to help calm her down.

Grinning, both of his hands raised in surrender, the chauffeur shook his head. "Oh, no, sir, don't you tangle me in the middle of this here battle of wits; I'm just a driver tonight. I was born an' raised in Atlanta, an' everybody knows Miz Bessie ain't to be messed with. You done dug this hole all by your own self. Think you best stop shovelin' . . . uh, sir."

Miller frowned, held his hands up to indicate he needed a moment to think, to recalculate how to get Bessie to talk about the couple again, or hint at the family's fortune – anything he could print. He poured himself a cup of coffee, added sugar and stirred the brew slowly before taking a sip. "Well, now I'm confused. I was told you knew all about Ally, who she was, where she came from, how she and Drake—"

"Ally? You came here to talk 'bout her and not my boy, Drake?"

Miller studied his coffee cup for a few long seconds. "Let me explain, ma'am. The Hollywood power players tried to sign Ally so they could represent her, to get her into the top movies, but she'd always smile and defer to Drake. He'd be offended, rude, yelled at some people; always said, 'My wife doesn't have to work, I don't want her to work, and she's not going to work!'

"Thousands go to Hollywood every year dreaming about being discovered. They'd kill for an opportunity to have an agent work for them. But the Lanzens . . ." he shook his head, "don't want any part of it. That just doesn't make sense."

Bessie's hearty laughter filled the room. *It don't make no sense, you say? Well, I know the un-kept secret that's a secret.* "Yes, sir, that's my boy! I raised him that away. He's right, too. His wife don't need to work; has everything she could want. An my Drake ain't likely to let Miz Ally out a' sight. A fine looking' woman, an he'd purt-near kill over that woman an' almost has. He got him a jealous streak a mile long an' wide. No sirree, no sirree . . . Miz Ally won't be traipsin' 'round doin' anything that'll take from his time with her. She goes where he goes, and they goes plenty.

"I reckon Miz Ally would make a fine actress, if'n she wanted, but I recall her studyin' on bein' a writer. Drake was involved with the Pac-Man thing an' a monkey thing, an' the movies an' such, an' you know he favors Cary Grant, so I reckon he could be one of them movie star people, if'n he set his mind to it. An' Miz Ally? Well, that little gal could do whatever she wanted. Both of 'em grew up with lots of old money. Old houses, old families, old money. Mind you, young fella, moneys was theirs

24

long afore they set eyes on each other, long afore them big world wars, afore them children been borned. Old money and old-timey family names talk mighty loud 'round here. Uh-huh, yes, sir. People knows. People 'round here called them families a dynasty."

Miller settled back in his chair, studying the elderly woman anew, figuring she'd never guess aloud at the amount of the family fortune, but she knew what old money, decades-long invested money could be worth. Although faded by age and use, her eyes sparked with aggravation when his questions centered on Drake and Ally in Hollywood. He smiled, nodded, gestured, anything to encourage her to continue, to drift into more personal, Atlanta stories. She did.

"So, you see, young fella, with that much money, no end to it, they don't need no Hollywood or New York for entertainment. They's makin' their own movie ever' day."

Bessie leaned back and relaxed a bit. "I got plumb wore out packin' up the ol' Mister and Mizzus; always goin' off to Ireland an' someplace in Europe, an' then my boy off to that fancy millionaire boys' school. Spent my life packin' an unpackin' them bags. Couldn't keep up with all of their whereabouts, their comin's and goin's, to an' fro, an hither, thither an yon . . . always so busy goin'. They'd be home a minute, have some big hoopla,

25

an' off they'd go again. It's a harder job than you might think, keepin' up with rich folks comin' an goin'. Folks weren't happy neither. They'd be carrying' on something fierce, like out of some horror movie, but they were surefire good to me. I mostly raised the young'uns whilst the parents run the roads. And them children did their fair share of runnin', too."

Miller took a deep breath. Time for a different tack: "Miss Bessie, I can tell you were more like a family member. Certainly far more than a servant, or a nanny or a caregiver. I think you were devoted to the family, and you didn't care about how much money they had. I think you were very fond of some of them, and you're still loyal. Am I right?"

Bessie's faded brown eyes brightened. "Yes, sir, I was indeed that. T'weren't no servant. Started workin' for them families when I was jest barely a fourteen year old young'un my own self. Ya might say, we kinda growed up together. I was a mammy to that boy from the get-go. He's my favorite, don't you know. Ain't gonna let nobody hurt my boy. Sometimes, when he was just a little tyke, he'd come a'runnin' to me cryin' his heart out. Cry his'self to sleep many a night; he'd sleep right over there on that maroon velvet settee. Don't want anybody to sit on my settee now that my boy's all grown an' gone. That child felt home with me, an' he could stay here long as he wanted. Yes'um, my boy."

26

Bessie dug into her pocket and took out an antique silver snuffbox, took a fresh pinch, put it between her gum and cheek, then grinned. "I's too old to change my ways now. Reckon I'll be taking in my consumption 'til the Lord comes to fetch me home; better than puffin' on them smelly cigarettes."

Struggling to her feet, Bessie walked to the dining room table where several framed photographs were displayed. "C'mon, look'a here. Don't you think Miz Lanzen looks just like that Lana Turner woman? Everybody thought so. Pretty little thing, Miz Ally."

The napkin swished away a brown dribble from her chin when she grinned at one particular photo. Miller leaned closer but couldn't overhear the old woman's whisper about that photograph. She lifted another photo. "Whoop! This one was mean as a rattlesnake, this one was an' I ain't goin' to tell why, but it was for no good reason. But, well, I can't much blame her none." She picked up another photo and began talking to it and about it.

Miller backtracked to the chauffeur. "What did she say a minute ago . . . that whisper?"

"Sorry, sir, couldn't hear a word from over here; mumbling again, too."

"Yes, she is. Don't have a clue what she said and don't think I'll ask because I doubt she'd tell me, but instinct tells me there's a story behind that rattlesnake comment." Miller glanced at his watch. "I've got to get her back onto the subject." He wheeled around. "Miss Bessie, Miss Bessie, can we talk about the Lanzens some more?"

"Yes, um, I knows you's here to hear 'bout the Prince and the Princess —," Bessie chuckled as she returned a framed photo to the table -"or somethin' like that." She settled in her chair once again and spit into a stained and chipped buffalo china cup. "Drake always thought of himself as a prince, that he had royal blood, and the family's house had those round things what looked like a castle tower, you know. That house looked just like a castle. My little Prince Drake played in those long roundabouts all the time. Scared me spitless most times that he'd go an' fall an' break his royal neck. He even had a purple cape. Oh! Scratch that! He'd be plumb embarrassed, me tellin' such on him.

"Girls would just come to the house, an' he'd be downright rude to them. The meaner he was, the more they'd come back. I reckon he was that away out of spite or boredom 'cause he was really kindhearted. Nobody knew it, but that child carried a deep hurt in his heart. He hid it really well, but being his mammy, I knowed it an reckon I's the only one what could see it plain."

28

Bessie's gaze slipped across the room and over the years; she shook her head. "The Lanzens were gone a lot with their travels. They gave the boy ever'thing he ever wanted - bought that child piles of stuff - they never gave him what he really wanted an' needed the most: was them, their time, an' their love. Bless 'em, the family loved him in their fashion, but just didn't have it in 'em to give the boy any decent attention, not even for one day of that child's life." She shook her head. "A sad thing to watch. A sad thing. Oh, they'd buy him expensive toys, an' hold big to-dos, give him all the wrong things. Sad. I couldn't do nothing to hep the child 'cept pray for 'em all an' go 'bout my business. All that poor child really wanted was pure, old fashion love - the lovin' an' huggin' an' pettin' kind. . . . but nobody could make it happen from those kinda folks."

She sighed, bit her lip, and took a deep breath. "They sent my boy off to one of them there fancy millionaire schools. Like to broke my heart, it did, with him gone from the place for so long. Just too dang quiet without him runnin' an' playin' an' I could hear him laughin somewheres. Too quiet. When he came home, oh, he got busy. Started inventin' things. He was a right smart boy. Lordy, he'd come up with some of the biggest ideas you ever did see, an made lots of money on top of what was already in his trust. Whoo-wee. Lots of money. Money was never enough for none of 'em. Drake earned himself a couple million dollars afore he was seventeen years old. Had one of them long fancy cars, just like you got out there, a long time ago. They all did. Dated them skinny models what's taller than most folks, and some of them talkin' talkin' talkin TV womens. Lordy, even that Trump fella married one, but my boy kept a tight holt on his heart, never fell in love 'til the day he saw Miz Ally. Called her 'his Princess' and 'The One.' He was flat-out head o'er heels."

Bessie smiled and shook her head. "He tol' me, 'The soul wants what the soul wants.' I said the heart wants what the heart wants. But, he just say, 'Nope, mammy, the other way 'round.'" Bessie chuckled softly and spit into her cup.

The reporter's ears twitched as he leaned forward. "Finally! Finally, you're telling me what I want to hear."

"Now, hold on to your horses there, young man. This here's my memory. Some pieces are hard to go back an' fetch. Now, I rightly recall him tellin' me that when he laid eyes on her, his world changed, something deep inside changed. Well, you'd have thought he'd met Queen 'lizbeth herself, an' in a way, he did. He flat said it took him twenty-nine years, but he found what his soul had yearned an' searched for. He come to my house an' I'll never forget it as long as I live and that's awhile, mind you. Oh, was my boy excited, so happy. He said, 'Mammy, it's her. I found her, and I'm not going to stop my pursuit 'til I have her, 'til she's

30

mine.'" Bessie nodded. "Yes'um, that's what he said. An' he done just that – he didn't give up 'til he caught her."

Except for rain pounding on the tin roof, the house was hushed. Suddenly, Miller was on his feet, his hoarse whisper penetrating Bessie's reverie: "Then it's true! Yes! Everything they say about Miss Ally is true!"

"Great day in the mornin'! What are you talkin' about? Yes'um, Drake did capture her, but not in the way you're thinkin'."

"What? Oh, no, no, no; you're not going to drag me through another convoluted story. Are you saying that how they met wasn't like what everyone says, what reporters joke about? Most rumors have a grain of truth, even in Hollywood. Are you saying Ally didn't lose her slipper on a stairway? That's what Drake and Ally says when they're pressed for answers."

Bessie stared at him, mouth tight, silent.

"Oh, come on now, Miss Bessie. It's either a Cinderella story or it's not. Drake either found Ally when she lost a slipper on a stairway or he didn't. Is it a made-up story from beginning to end, a cheap publicity stunt? You've got to admit that it *is* far-fetched, but that's the rumor that's been spread about Drake and Ally."

Bessie's eyes narrowed again as she set her dip cup down with a loud clatter, and straightened her back. "Now, you hush up an' listen here. You ain't gonna sit in my house an' call my boy a liar, mister. I'm here to tell you he wouldn't make up no fairytale about Miz Ally. He don't stoop to any low-down common ways like tellin' lies. He's bigger an' better than that. He's like my own child, an' he loves me like I'm his own momma. If he told anybody he met his bride at a wishin well after he'd dropped in a silver dollar, you'd best not bet a'gin it 'cause my boy don't tell no lies.

"No, ma'am, no. You don't—"

"Hush up! You reckon I'm just some dumb ol' country woman what don't know no better, don't know nothin' about the world, don't know 'bout cheats an' liars? I'm pushing' mighty hard on ninety-three years, boy, an' I learnt a thing or two about the world an' the kind of people in it. I worked at both homes, for both sides o' his family. I raised his momma *and* his daddy, an' they growned up to be fine people. I saw to that. They were like my own. Drake's family may be an do a lot of things I don't 'prove of, but they don't lie to nobody. Best you apologize for that, mister, an' do it quick-like. If you can't, right there's my front door. Get yourself movin' through it!"

Miller stared at Bessie for a moment and took several deep breaths. Obviously, she was upset. He had to fix this problem instantly. "Oh, no, ma'am. I am truly sorry. I didn't mean to insult anyone or call Mr. Lanzen a liar. It's just that we've heard this same old story from too many people for too long, even though it can't be proven or disproven. People want to know the truth.

"This is what we've been told: Ally had attended a major social event and was leaving, going down the stairs toward her limousine. That's when one of her shoes got wedged in the steps. It was one of those fancy, custom-made, clear slipper things covered with jewels – very expensive – designed just like Cinderella's magic slippers in the fairytale. Ally slipped her foot out of it and dashed to her limo to see if her driver could go back and free it from the step. Before the driver could do anything, Drake had already gotten to the stairway, retrieved the slipper, and caught up with Ally.

"Like a scene from the Disney movie, Drake knelt on one knee right there in the courtyard, slipped it back onto her foot, looked up, and said, "'Cinderella lost her slipper.' "

Oh, me . . . Thought I'd heard an' seen it all, but I reckon there's a few surprises yet. This fool's jabberin' 'bout a girl's slipper gettin' stuck, and my boy callin' her Cinderella. Lordy, Lordy. Bessie shook her head, spit in her cup and dabbed at her mouth.

"Well? You say you raised him, Miss Bessie. Is it true or is it gossip, rumors, tall tales?"

Outside, the storm lashed at the roof and blasted rain against the windows. Inside, silence reigned for several minutes as Bessie and Miller stared at each other - an impasse - his challenge, her contemplating, his hopes, her reluctance.

Bessie nodded, got out of her chair, and shuffled across the room. "Bring yourself over here, mister reporter, an looky here. My Drake painted it from one o' his favorite photographs of Miz Ally. She don't even know 'bout it. He asks me to keep it for him.

"You wants to know how Drake found Miz Ally in this whole wide world. Well, here it is, straight from me an' that's straight from Drake his own self: The moment he laid eyes on Miz Ally, he knew he was goin' to marry her." She chuckled. "Said he was 'entranced' – that's what he called it - 'entranced' – an' he followed her outside."

Anxious, Miller helped Bessie lift the protective cloth from the portrait. He almost gasped.

The woman captured in the painting was incredible, as if she had just stepped out of a fairyland fantasy. Long, flowing golden hair fell across her shoulders and cascaded onto a shimmering lavender gown, her hazel eyes gazing into the distance, as if there were a castle only she could see. She held a rich purple velvet pillow in one hand. Nestled in the pillow's center was a tiny Waterford crystal high-heel shoe.

Miller bent to confirm the artist's name in the lower corner: Drake Lanzen. He couldn't contain his grin.

"Yes'um, my Drake painted this here portrait after meetin' her. Told me to keep it safe here in 'lanta 'stead of where that Hollywood riffraff would see it an' say something ugly about his bride, his lady, his dream come true.

"'Mammy'," 'that's what he calls me, you know, 'this is my princess, and you won't believe how I met her!' "

Yes sir, it's all true, but it sure didn't end up like everyone expected.

* * *

"Happiness is like a butterfly which,
when pursued, is always beyond our grasp,
but, if you will sit down quietly, may alight upon you."
Nathaniel Hawthorne

Thus it Begins...

Chapter 2

In the time of myths, magic and mysticism, three planets – Jupiter, Uranus and Pluto – aligned themselves in February 1968 and a special child was born. No ordinary child this: a girl child, a child with unique qualities and incredible gifts, a princess child who would waltz into a fairytale and bring the legend to life.

Louisiana's bayous were frigid, forcing 'gators to seek warmth by diving deeper into the brackish water or to burrow further into their wind-whipped nests. Ice encasing the fallen leaves cracked and shattered as the man's black, highly polished shoes broke through the thin crust on his approach to the old house's veranda. "I don't like this one bit." Brokenhearted, his steps faltered, slipped, stopped, his breath a frosty mist when he looked down at his burden. "Choices vanished with her gone."

Frozen floorboards groaned and popped as his weight shifted upwards, one cautious step at a time. He placed the basket with its elaborate white satin covering a few inches from the screen door, stared down for a second or two. "If there was any other way. . . ." He sighed, long, deep, laid his hand on the covering. "God bless." He shook his head hard, pounded on the door, pivoted, leaped over the porch railing and darted into the thicket near the barn.

Less than a minute later, the screen door bumped the basket as Pearl attempted to push it open. Her eyes narrowed. "Harrumph. Well! Somebody from church must think we can't get to town in this storm and need groceries, momma. There's a big ol' basket out here."

She bent to grab the basket handle and jumped back when the hidden contents moved. "Oh! Great day in the mornin'!"

"I saw that," Violet said from inside the house. "Well, go on, scaredy cat, let's see what Santa brought too late to go under the tree."

Pearl's fingers lifted the blanket's edge and two pink booties thrust out against the sudden cold draft. "Good Lord Almighty, it's a baby!"

"Uh-huh, sure looks like one to me," Violet said, shoving open the door. "Well, don't just stand there, staring. Bring that child in out of the cold."

Pearl sighed. "Now, what in the world . . ." She lifted the baby, wrapping the white satin blanket around the wriggling infant as she cuddled it closer. "Let's see who you are first."

The baby blinked several times in the sunlight, arched her back, kicked again, looked up at Pearl and yawned.

42

"For cryin' out loud. Stop your lollygagging and bring that child on inside before you both catch your death. I'll get the basket," Violet said, her words fell against Pearl's back who was already halfway down the hall with the baby cradled against her chest. "Hmm, there may be a note or something in this fancied up thing."

The wind gusted and several ice-laden tree branches crashed onto the ground. Violet frowned across her yard, shivered, quickly pulled the screen door tight, latched it, shoved the heavy front door closed and snapped on the lock. The wind flipped around, spinning one pink bootie across the front porch and sending it airborne at the edge, swirling it past the sleeping laurels, past the dormant azaleas, past the first live oak until it fell and began to meld into the leaves and rich soil of Wildwind Plantation. The nearby black leather shoe hesitated . . . turned and the man vanished across the icy lawn.

Pearl settled in a kitchen chair, and Violet set the basket within arm's reach on the table. Their eyes locked as unspoken thoughts flashed between them.

Pearl unwrapped the infant and discovered it was wearing a beautiful pink and white satin gown with tiny embroidered roses along the lace-edged collar, cuffs and down the front until they trailed along the hemline. A matching bonnet was too large

43

for a three-day old baby's head, but the delicate roses were perfect.

Violet waved her hand at the blanket and basket. "Reckon it's a girl, with all this get-up."

Glancing around, Pearl asked, "Where's her other bootie? There were two when we found her."

Violet shook her head. "Never saw it. Must have been carried off."

"That's odd, don't you think?" Pearl laid the infant in her lap and studied the child's features, and chuckled softly. "Well now, little one. You have arrived wearing a very fancy ball gown and minus one shoe – well, bootie, but still . . . Now, tell us who you are."

Violet tumbled the basket's contents until her fingers touched something crisp. "A-ha, maybe this will tell us something."

She lifted a scrolled paper that was tied with a pink satin ribbon, quickly slid the ribbon off one end, then adjusted her half-glasses which rested on her nose. "It says, 'Please take care of my baby princess.' Well, I'll be . . ."

Pearl was almost shocked. "No name? Nothing else?"

Violet ran her fingers through her thick silver hair and shook her head. "Nothing. Not a thing. I reckon in that case, it's up to us to decide upon an appropriate name."

"What? Name a child just because we found it on our porch? You've got to be kidding, momma."

"Serious as a heart attack." Violet, who was in her eighties, was an extremely insightful woman. She began to pace the floor and think aloud, a habit when contemplating problems, seeking solutions.

"Delivered to our door. No name. No information. Just our suspicions, is all. Well, as I see it, this is our child now, Pearl. Deliberately placed in our care for an important reason – we were chosen. It's not some random act, or an accident, or just a convenient location to drop off a baby 'cause we're a-ways off the road. Somebody made a real effort to get her here without being seen, in an ice storm, mind you, and no tracks in the driveway so they walked to the house.

"I'm sensing something. This child, her coming here, was predestined. She's different, unique, she's ours, she's supposed to be here, in this house, in our care. Where's that old family album?

If she's one of us . . ." Violet pulled a photo album from a drawer, flipped a few pages. "There! This is it." She frowned at the faded photo taped to the page, her voice almost a whisper. "It's her all over again." She straightened her back. "Let me take a closer look at her." She dragged a chair from the other side of the table so she could sit, pulled back the baby blanket and lifted the fancy gown. Not yet satisfied, she tugged the baby's gown up and over, turning the baby in different directions, as if searching for a birthmark or a sign. Nothing. Flawless newborn skin.

Violet nodded, laid her hand upon the sleeping baby's tiny body, closed her eyes and said a silent prayer. She got up and paced again. A moment later, she turned to stare at her daughter. "Pearl, this is a very special child. I feel her energy. It's strong. Very strong. She almost vibrates with it. Woo-wee. Haven't felt that since I held my granny's hand when I was just a babe my own self."

She studied her hand as if a tingling sensation remained on her palm. "Woo, uh . . . I need to sit back down."

Violet almost collapsed onto the kitchen chair. "Something terrible has happened somewhere. I *Knew* it last night when I heard a hoot owl out in the woods, then a night bird came, probably a crow, and sat on my windowsill in the wee hours, tapping on my window pane, talking, chatting away, trying to tell me something. It was a warning of some sort. I didn't pay it no never mind then, but it was trying to tell me this little princess was on her way to us."

Pearl nodded. "I know, I know. I had a bad feeling last night, too, as if something was missing, that I'd lost something very important, as if part of me had just been snatched away." Her throat went dry and constricted, she tried to clear her throat several times, but it didn't help.

Pearl's grown daughter's disappearance always gripped her throat and twisted heartstrings to the snapping point. Sometimes, Pearl felt melancholy for days when she'd think about her own girl, Katarina. The pain of not knowing where her daughter was, how she was, would almost crush Pearl's spirit entirely, and it always took Violet's understanding and patience to help restore the woman's cheerful attitude. It didn't matter that Pearl's child had left home more than a decade earlier to pursue an obscure career in god-knows-where, the overwhelming pain could wound her in an instant.

Tears welled in Pearl's eyes; she quickly blinked them away. "You suppose . . . Hmm, yes, this is something Katarina would do. The last thing she'd want would be the responsibility of a child. Wouldn't be the first time she's pulled a stunt like this;

she's done it before and the results are upstairs in her bedroom – Jade's talking to her girlfriends on the phone.

"Despite all that, Katarina still flocks together with those of her own kind. A shame. A shame."

Violet pursed her lips and nodded. Katarina was the one child Pearl had raised that hadn't ended up the way Pearl and she had hoped and planned. At a young age, Katarina was bored with life in the bayou and left her mother Pearl, two younger brothers and her grandmother Violet to go wandering the globe, only writing one or two letters home, saying she was going to be famous. Then silence again.

The elderly woman studied the infant's features as the baby dosed in Pearl's arms. "Look here." She slid the photo album across the table to Pearl. Violet hesitated; truth is often hurtful, so she softened her voice. "There's no getting 'round this, Pearl. This here is Katarina's child . . . this is your grand-daughter and my great grand-daughter. Their baby pictures are almost identical."

Pearl nodded, a tear streamed down pone cheek, but she remained silent except for a sniffle or two.

"As for the father, we'll never know if they were married or not. Don't know 'bout you, but I really don't care one whit. It doesn't matter a hill of beans because this precious child is blessed more so than the ones what gave her life, more than that older sister will ever be, more than any others. She was brought home to her family, to her grandmothers where she'd be reared correctly and safely by blood kin. We must rear her carefully, teach her all the things she'll need to know. Whoever brought her here knew that, knew about our connection. Blood always comes first – and last."

Violet studied the child for a moment longer, then peered over the top of her wire-rimmed eyeglasses. "Pearl, we've hit the nail on the head: She's ours forever. Now what do we do?"

Pearl nodded. "Well, we can't keep calling her 'she' or 'baby.' The note said 'princess.' This child needs a real name and, ice storm or no ice storm, we'll need baby supplies from town."

Violet climbed to her feet. "Yes, ma'am, we surely do. Reckon I'll go fetch my books and you think about getting into town before sunset when the roads ice over again."

Within thirty minutes, the infant with one bootie had three names: Gwenievere, which means blessed; Alina, which means princess; and a surname of Starling. All three names carried on the family's lineage and history, yet stretched toward a future embedded in stardust and fame.

Pleased with the results of her quick research, Violet nodded across the table at her daughter. "Perfect names for this special child. I've got a strong feeling she's going to grow into them. too. Besides, we can call her Ally for short."

For a woman of diminutive size, nothing about Violet hinted at a subdued spirit. She was strong-willed and physically tough, intelligent and beautiful with few wrinkles for a woman whose age was counted by decades. A wink from her conveyed she knew an important secret and would only share it with one lucky person, if that person kept it quiet. Well-learned, she had filled the plantation's shelves over her lifetime with books, especially the classics. Plato's philosophies were her favorite dinnertime conversation.

Pearl was blessed with a positive attitude about life, usually finding some humor in even mundane activities, unless she was reminded of her daughter's problems. Almost the same size as her mother, Pearl had large blue eyes and round, flushed cheeks which seemed as if small pink roses had been tattooed on them. Although Pearl was intense and her presence in a room or nearby hallway radiated enough to be felt by others, her gentle voice could soothe troubles as if hummingbirds had settled on a nearby windowsill and whispered them away. Her smile could melt the most hardened heart. If a flock of angels had swooped down from heaven just to save one infant from a freezing front porch, Pearl would have volunteered to stay behind to care for that child for as long as she drew breath.

Gwenievere Alina would be pampered when needed and disciplined when needed. More importantly, she would be taught how to listen, how to detect energies, how to unravel mysteries. All the while, she would be nurtured in a delicate balance of unconditional love, and strengthened in self-confidence and personal courage. She would need to hone that perfect balance to deal with the confusing and magical events and personalities she would encounter as she grew, as her world expanded far beyond Wildwind Plantation and the often dark Louisiana bayous. Her grandmothers, two very ancient souls, became the springboard for Ally's unique universal *Knowing* that caused many to marvel and wonder if she had really been found in a basket on an icy porch, or if that story was just the beginning of a once-upon-a-time fairytale.

* * *

"Just living is not enough," said the butterfly fairy,
"one must have sunshine, freedom and a little flower."

Hans Christian Anderson

Chapter 3

It happened a few weeks after Ally arrived. Santa had brought Jade a Big Bride Doll. Being nine years-old and the self-absorbed older sister, naturally she wanted to play baby dolls with the squirming real one in the crib.

Pearl was busy cooking dinner and had her back turned when Jade decided to dress Ally in the bride doll's wedding gown and high heel slippers. Somehow, the older girl managed to squeeze those doll shoes onto the baby's feet.

Evidently, Ally must have cried for a spell before Pearl realized something was not quite right. She went down the hallway to check and was surprised to find the bedroom door closed, which had muffled the baby's cries. She stared into the crib, almost dumbfounded. The baby was wearing a fancy, wedding gown and white, high-heeled slippers. It might have been quite hysterically funny to some, but it was misguided amusement on Jade's part.

Pearl glanced around. Jade was squatting against the old wardrobe in a vain attempt to hide, but still giggling at the distressed infant lying in a crib, who was kicking her feet and high-heeled slippers in the air and crying in pain.

Pearl pointed a finger at her. "You're in more trouble than you can shake a stick at right now, young lady. Go to your room before I lose my temper. If I were you, I wouldn't come out until somebody comes gets you. Don't want to see your face for a while. Now get!"

Jade tried to swallow her next giggle, and her eyes got wider at her grandmother's terse words. She scrambled to her feet and giggled again.

"Hush up! This is no laughing matter. I can't get these slippers off."

Curious about Pearl's absence from the kitchen and the tone of voice she heard from down the long hallway, Violet stepped into the room. "What's going on?"

"You're not going to believe this, momma, but Jade has shoved those doll shoes onto the baby's feet. I've tried everything I could think of, but the shoes have been on so long that Ally's feet have turned blue . . . and now they're swollen -- badly."

Violet and Pearl conferred and patiently managed to slip tiny drops of cooking oil into one shoe and it finally slid off one foot. The other one was too tight.

Ally's cries of pain and tears nearly broke Pearl's heart.

"Nothing . . .else . . . we can do at home," she said, her voice breaking with frustration. "I'm taking her to the emergency room. Surely, someone there will know how to get this thing off Ally's foot."

Jade was restricted to her room after she got home from school for a week, plus no TV or telephone.

Somewhere in Louisiana's official record of the strangest medical mysteries and occurrences must be a report, along with the doctor's notes, about Ally Starling – a baby who appeared in his emergency room dressed in a long white satin gown and wearing one of Cinderella's high-heel slippers.

Ally was six weeks old when her 'one missing shoe' career officially began.

* * *

Life on the plantation was wonderful. A secure haven where Ally could grow and learn while supported by layers of freedom for her to explore life and to discover her world. Even breakfasts at Wildwind were different. Whenever Pearl cooked pancakes, they were shaped with cookie cutters into trees and butterflies, stars and teddy bears – never anything ordinary like circles unless it was the Man in the Moon or a happy face sun.

Butter was smothered in honey or warm maple syrup. Sometimes, if Pearl was in a hurry to tackle her chores, the little family ate toast spread with homemade jam or jelly from grapes they'd grown in the garden and put up in jars. The best days were when the two grandmothers sat and chatted over their morning coffee, and allowed two-year-old Ally to join them with a fancy teacup of coffee with too much milk and sugar. Sometimes, she was given a mug of hot chocolate with gooey marshmallows on top that left a sticky tasty white mustache on her upper lip. Grandmothers' teasing always made her giggle.

One spring afternoon after her nap, three-year old Ally came downstairs and found the kitchen table covered with beautiful flowers; tiny, pale yellow flowers with a greenish center. Her grandmothers were nowhere to be found. A little flower was in her chair, another one was beside the back door, another on the step outside, then many more were on the family's well-worn path across the yard. Ally followed the flower trail and found her grandmothers waiting for her under the biggest shade tree in the backyard.

Pearl laughed and called to her. "Well, it's about time you woke up. C'mon, slowpoke, we've got a surprise for you."

"Really, Granny Pearl? I likes surprises."

"I know you do. Yes, sweetness; it's a nice surprise, too."

Holding hands, the trio made their way across the yard until they were beyond the tree line and reached the fallow field. "Look what springtime has brought us."

Ally's eyes widened. The normal ragged, unused field of weeds was filled with millions of golden buttercups. Violet, Pearl and Ally picked dozens of the small five-petal flowers, weaving the stems together to make golden wreaths for their hair, and dropping many into a basket to take back to the house.

Violet had Ally sit down beside her to watch how the breeze blew the buttercups into gentle waves and ripples. "Later on, when it's warmer during June and July, the bees will come. And these little flowers will make nectar in the sunshine . . . right . . . here." Violet pulled off a petal and pointed to a tiny spot, a pit, growing near the flower's green center. "Right there. It will fill up with something so sweet that our honeybees can't resist it; they'll take it back to their hive and we'll have honey for our pancakes. Now, isn't that a wonder?"

"Oh, boy," Ally grinned, "buttered'cup honey."

Pearl smiled. "Yes, buttered'cup honey. We'll have to wait for the honeybees to find the flowers and the nectar first. Today,

59

we're going to have a picnic. We're going to watch the flowers and enjoy this blessing while we can. Later on, there'll be too many bees to pick the flowers. We'll be in their way." Pearl selected a nearby shade tree, opened a much-used wicker basket and spread paper plates, sandwiches, iced tea and treats out onto the faded red and white checkered tablecloth.

Ally wasn't ready to settle down. The women watched her run through the flowers, laughing and chasing butterflies.

Another spectacular afternoon was forever etched in Ally's memory.

Later that day, just as the sun began to set, Violet and Pearl led Ally out of the kitchen door and across the yard again, back to the buttercup field, promising her another surprise. They made themselves comfortable on the tablecloth again and waited.

Ally sat still for a long time, at least two minutes before squirming with impatience. "What's it, Granny? There's nothin' but them buttered'cups an' we took bunches to the house an' no honeybees yet."

"Just wait, wiggle-worm. You'll see something soon enough. Just in a few more minutes."

Sunset colors were glorious when they filtered through the leafing trees on the field's far side. It began . . . . one, then another, another further away, a scattering, then a surge.

Ally clutched Pearl's arm, gasped and burst into tears. "Uh-oh. . . . stars fall down go boom." Tears flowed, she buried her face in Pearl's lap and sobbed. "Stars all broke'ted."

"Oh, no, no, Ally, it's okay, it's okay. That's not stars, sweetness. C'mon on, now, look up." Pearl tugged on her until Ally raised her head and sniffled. "See? Look up now. Stars are still up there in the sky."

Ally gradually looked up, peered in all directions and sniffled again. Pearl wiped the child's face with her handkerchief a second before Ally wiped her sweater's sleeve across her eyes and runny nose.

Another tear slithered down Ally's cheek as she stared upwards, blinking several times to clear her eyes. "Stars, oh . . . stars still in heaven." She sighed with relief and grinned. "Okay, I sees 'em now, Granny."

Ally's back straightened as she peered across the field at the unusual scene. "What's it?"

"Insects, little one; a different kind of insect than you've ever seen before."

Ally took a deep breath, her eyes widened as she stared across the huge field. "Insects, Granny? There's sparkles in the buttered'cups. Uh-oh! Looky! Them's in the trees, too!"

Violet and Pearl chuckled. "Those are lighting bugs, Ally. . . fireflies. They always come with the buttercups."

"Bugs an' flies? Bugs that's got flashy lights? Do they bite? Can I see? I wanna see." She scrambled to her feet and ran into the darkened field, arms outstretched, fearless in facing an unknown. A moment later, her laughter and squeals of happiness drifted across the field and filled her grandmothers' hearts with immeasurable joy. "Granny! Granny! Fired flies sittin' on me, so I'm sparkling, too."

Ally saw, caught, and put a half-dozen lighting bugs in a small Mason canning jar Pearl brought along so Ally could watch them closely for awhile before being released. Shimmering bugs tickled her arms and hands, and briefly sat on her fingers, flashing their iridescent glow before flying away. Ally called after each one, telling them to hurry back.

She sat down in the buttercup field and watched as a multitude of fireflies swirled overhead, then gathered closer and closer until they seemed to form a shape in the air directly above her. Suddenly, they flew in all directions. A moment later, they gathered again, hovered, spun, revolved and whirled in a delicate aerial ballet. Ally saw patterns she couldn't explain, but she remembered enough to draw them later.

"C'mon, Ally, it's time to go inside."

"Oh, do we got to, Granny Pearl? I wanna stay."

"Yes; it's getting late. Past your bedtime."

Ally reluctantly climbed to her feet and left the buttercup field.

"Where's your sandal, Miz Ally?"

"Uh, oh. I's berry sorry, Granny, I doesn't know. It cameded off when I danced with the fired flies an' I look-ted for it but it went away."

Violet chuckled when Pearl sighed in frustration. "Might'a known she'd lose another shoe . . . second one already and it's only April."

Springtime always meant buttercups in the field and throughout the house, yellow wreaths for everyone's hair, lighting bugs dancing in the evening breeze, and buttercup honey later in the summer. More precious memories were locked into Ally's heart.

By Ally's third Christmas, Santa brought her a red tricycle and a talking doll. That Christmas week, a special gift was hand delivered. Curious, Ally peered around the doorway at the tall stranger who stood just inside Wildwind's front door . . . an older man she had never seen before quietly talked a long time with her Grandmother Pearl. After he left, both grandmothers took her into the parlor where the decorated Christmas tree still stood and watched as she unwrapped the huge box the man had brought.

Ally gasped in surprise. "Oh, I seen this on tela-bision! Oh, it's wonnerful with tables an' chairs an' other things."

She needed help and a few minutes to lift it from the box: An expensive, very detailed, two-story dollhouse, complete with miniature furniture for every room, including real fabric curtains on the windows.

That one gift became a favorite toy in the months and years to come. After nightly bedtime stories, big hugs and kisses goodnight from both grandmothers and bedtime prayers, Ally would rush to her bedroom.

Not everyone believed her, but Ally witnessed what happened at night after she turned off her bedside table lamp. She would sit up or lie on her tummy and be very still, then watch the wee people slowly come out of their hiding places. Lights came on inside the dollhouse, little people rearranged the furniture, they sat at the tiny kitchen table, rocked in the tiny rocking chairs, opened the dresser drawers and took out clothes, and went in and out the front door. It was fascinating.

Excited about something unusual or new that the wee ones would do, Ally would hold tight to the spindles and go down the long flight one step at a time to tell her grandmothers. She usually found them at the kitchen table, talking.

She peeked around the corner and whispered, "They comeded back, Granny. Wanna come see?"

Pearl sighed. "What came back, Miz Ally? And, why aren't you in bed sound asleep?"

Ally toddled into the kitchen and leaned against her Grandmother Pearl's knees, looked up and grinned. "The wee little people what lives in my dollhouse have comeded back. They turneded on the lights an' they moveded furniture round again an' pushed 'em hard against the walls this time an' they moveded other stuff, too. Wanna come see, Granny?"

Ally hoped her grandmother would say it was nice that the wee ones had returned.

This time, however, Ally's grandmother was a little frustrated. "You know we don't want you to make up stories about your dollhouse, Ally. There are no lights in it. Wee folk can't live there because the refrigerator is too small, it can't be turned on, so there's no food in the dollhouse. They can't live where there's no food, now can they?"

Ally nodded and stood there listening to Pearl and Violet tell her that what she had just seen with her own eyes wasn't real, had not happened. But, Ally knew better. So did they.

It would be at least another year before either woman read stories or told Ally any folklore about wee people, fairies, trolls, or other such beings. They decided Ally had too much encouragement, too much knowledge about such things for someone who was only three years old. After another hug good-night, they sent her back upstairs and to bed.

"How in the world does she already know about tiny people, about fairies living on this plantation since this farm began? Tell me that, please." Pearl flashed an exasperated glance at her mother. "I haven't told her any of the stories handed down through the family. Have you told her anything? How *does* she know all this?"

Violet and Pearl had hoped Ally would grow up to be a normal child who wouldn't ever see such things, someone slightly similar to the older sister. In her heart, Violet knew that wouldn't happen. She had felt Ally's strong energy the instant she laid hands on her when they found her wrapped in white satin on their front porch.

Compared to other children, Gwenievere Alina Starling was anything but normal, even for a Louisiana bayou where the unusual was standard fare and the bizarre was expected.

Violet signed, shook her head. "No, I haven't told her a thing. Shss. . . . she's still on the stairs; standing at the top. Didn't go to bed, the little stinker."

Violet raised her voice. "You might as well come on back down here, young'un, and sit with us for a minute or two, Miz Ally."

Ally smiled and went back downstairs. "Yes'um, I's comin'."

Violet helped the child climb up onto one of the kitchen chairs. "We need to have a serious family conference."

"Oh. Um, yes'um. Have I been bad?"

Pearl took Ally's hand to keep her attention, and looked into her eyes. "No, you haven't been bad, sweetie. I want you to listen to me, though. You, your Great Grandma Violet and I have a secret and we are not going to share it with anyone. It's just for we three. You don't even have to tell Jade. Okay? We are not going to talk about our wee folk to our church-going people on Sunday mornings from now on."

Ally's cheerful face turned to surprise. She looked across the table at Violet, who nodded. Ally's expression showed confusion. "Doesn't grownup peoples like lil'le peoples?"

Pearl bit her lip to keep from smiling. "Many grownups don't understand about little people. They think it's a made-up story about your dollhouse and your wee people. They can't see the wee ones."

Ally frowned. She peered across the room, thinking for a long moment. Her face crinkled as she squeezed her eyes closed, then she blinked several times and grinned. "I know."

"Oh? What do you think you know?" Pearl's gentle voice softened the hard question.

"At church, I sees grownups squish up to make their faces all wrinkley . . . even when they got glasses. An' some close one of their eyes," she covered an eye with her tiny hand, "like this. Know what? When they do, they only see a little bit, so they can't see 'em, our wee people when they get all wrinkley and closes their eyes all tight."

Pearl smiled and nodded. "You're probably right, sweetie. Maybe it's like your puzzles in your toy box. If a piece isn't handy, we cannot see the picture it's supposed to make when it's together. Some people only see the whole thing, or only the parts, or they only see a hole where something ought to be. They don't know what they're seeing at all."

Ally glanced at her Great Grandmother Violet, who winked at her in hopes it would help the child to grasp the idea of 'family secret'. She also hoped Ally understood about most people being limited, that they could not understand the whole of a thing by only glimpsing a part.

Ally squirmed on the chair. "Um, so I can't talk about our wee people now?"

Pearl nodded.

Ally tipped her head to one side. "Okay, Granny. Yes'um."

"Good. We're not going to talk about the wee people outside of our house from now on, either. We know they live here and gather things we drop in the yards and in the barn, and they rifle through the leaves and such, but it's our family secret. Not for anyone else. Understand?"

"Uh-huh, Granny, but I can still watch an' play with them, can't I?"

"Yes, sweetness, you go right on ahead playing. We're just not going to talk about it to anyone else. Go on to your room now and get in bed. It's been a long day."

Ally scooted off the chair, hugged her two grandmothers, then trudged up the stairs again.

Pearl poured herself another class of sweetened iced tea and sat back down. "Momma, you've got to quit spoiling that child so much and telling her things. We don't want her to grow up like Katarina, do we? Or, I hate to say it, Lord knows, but go in the opposite direction like Jade."

Violet waved her hand in the air, brushing off her daughter's concerns. "Don't be silly. Don't you go off on some tangent now. That child won't ever be anything like her natural mother, and she's certainly not like that sister of hers, imagination as dull as dishwater. Whew. Reckon that one's always going to be in the middle causing disagreements.

"Never you mind. You're worrying about something that won't ever happen. I can see past my nose; you need to do the same. I'm not so sure about the father, but I'm willing to bet Ally will be more like him than her mother. Katarina never saw things the way Ally sees them already. At least we know the father was kind enough and wise enough to bring the child to us, to the only safe haven she'd have on this earth. Since he did, I reckon there was lots of talk before he brought that baby here."

Pearl frowned and stirred her iced tea again, making the ice cubes jingle against the tall glass.

"Now, just stop a minute and think about it, Pearl. Babies hear the world even before they're born. They know who cares for them. They recognize voices. I'm positive now the father did care. He cared a lot. Why else would he go to that much trouble to come here . . . in an ice storm, remember? How far did he have to drive on bad roads to get here? We'll never know. But, he wanted her taken care of, protected, loved, taught. That note telling us she was his baby princess, remember? That was no small thing, now was it? I think he already knew she was special. Different. Gifted. Oh, he cared about this child, all right. That's a sure thing. His actions spoke volumes, despite him not writing another word in that note."

The two wise women stirred their iced tea for a long silent moment before Violet said what they were both thinking. "Somewhere, somehow, sometime in the future, she's going to discover who he is and so will we. . . if we live long enough."

Pearl sighed and nodded. "Yes, momma, I see that happening, too, and I don't need my sister Faden's crystal ball to do it. It's just so sad to know I have a dark-hearted daughter who would do such a thing, go 'round having babies but not wanting them. It just breaks my heart, hurts me to my core. I tried to raise Katarina right, taught her the important things in life while I could. But she was so strong willed and stubborn – wouldn't listen, wouldn't abide any rules at all, just wanted to go her own way, no matter what. Can't help it. Can't understand her or what she's thinking, or anybody like her. Not my kind of people, that's all. Don't know where she came from, like she dropped in here from another planet or something. Sad thing is Jade's just like her, too. Cold-hearted, not mean, just cold."

"No blame here, Pearl. Don't go shedding tears all over me about what I said. We have to be strong for little Ally. Ally's soul is growing fast, she sees more things, and she's already getting wise beyond her years. I believe she's feeling energies already, *Knowing* more, hearing more. Jade never will. Like you say, too cold to see or hear what's around her. A shame.

"Now, Katarina is a different story. You can't change what's been done and you can't change a woman's heart when they've decided to take the wrong road. At some point, she'll reach a crossroads and she'll rethink her past doings, and I believe she'll want to come for this child. That's what I fear the most. We must protect Ally from that. We must make sure Katarina or the father never get their hands on Ally. She belongs to us, as long as we're both above ground."

Pearl nodded. "She's not an ordinary child, that's for sure. God only knows where she really came from."

"Shss! Don't you ever talk like that. She's from here – from us – she's gifted, with the same gifts this family has had for decades, maybe centuries. Who knows? That child is gifted, that's all, extraordinarily so. It's been passed all the way down from my great grandmother and probably long afore her; we won't ever know for sure. We're never going to speak about this around Ally. We're not going to tell her a single thing until she's old

73

enough to ask on her own. We'll cross that bridge when we get there and not until. Lips are sealed as is everything else that's sealed for Ally's sake."

Pearl nodded. "Right as usual, momma, but I want to point out the obvious: We're both already old. But, as long as there's breath in me, this child won't go anyplace without me."

Violet tilted her head and placed her index finger on her lips. "Shss. I think I just heard Ally on the stairs."

A second later, a stair tread squeaked. Ally froze: hesitatant, indecisive. She sighed, certain they'd noticed the noise when she had stood up. She slowly began down the long flight, one step at a time for her short legs. She'd been sitting and listening at the top. She was only three and didn't always understand adult conversation, or identify people's names like Katarina or the person they called 'the child's father,' but Ally instinctively knew when to keep secrets, like listening to adults without them realizing. It was another secret she kept to herself, another fireplace story she overheard and remembered, another sensation she had that her grandmothers did not want her to know or question about her life at that time.

It took another fireside storybook, another drink of water, another round of bedtime hugs before Ally was ready to go to bed and stay there.

Christmas was coming and the question of Ally's main gift came up more than once. She overheard them discussing Barbie Dolls, doll houses, doll carriages, another fancy tea set for her lawn parties, but they couldn't decide. They finally called her into the kitchen one chilly afternoon and sat her down in front of the warm fireplace.

"Ally, your great grandmother and I have talked about this long enough. Tell us what you want; another Barbie Doll, a talking doll . . . there's so many nice things for little girls to get for Christmas. What do you want?"

"Really, Granny Pearl? I can get whatever I wants?"

Pearl laughed. "Of course, sweetness. This will be the main gift you'll get from your grandmothers. Santa brings the rest."

Ally grinned, then giggled. "Oh, boy! I only wants one thing: a movie camera."

Blank expressions changed to open mouth shock. "What?"

"A movie camera, Granny."

"But, uh, Ally, you don't even know what a movie camera is."

"Oh, yes, I do. . . I can make pictures with it!"

"Well, I never in my born days. . . ." Pearl shook her head.

Violet's eyes widened and flashed Pearl a 'be quiet' signal. "Well, honey, if that's what you want this year, then we'll try to find one for you. Don't get your hopes up now, you hear?"

"Yes'um, but I knows you'll find one for me. I knows it. Thank you, my wonnerful grannies." Ally scooted until she could slide off her chair and went down the hallway to play.

On Christmas morning, Ally was ecstatic when she unwrapped the special box. Inside was a small, red, plastic camera projector that held cartoon slides. Ally could turn out the lights and the cartoon would show on the parlor walls.

Some nights, the grandmothers would make a snack to bring to the parlor picture show. Ally required their attendance at her shows, along with one or two of her stuffed teddy bears who had behaved nicely all day. Ally would turn on the 'camera' and giggle at the cartoons as they played across the shadowy walls of the old plantation. It certainly wasn't a silent picture show because Ally provided the dialogue for each cartoon, sometimes changing the story since the last time that cartoon was dancing across the wall.

Magic came from the small red box. Ally was hooked on make-believe, on pictures coming to life on walls, on stories – especially those that sprang from her own imagination, which moved, changed and grew almost larger than life. She knew it was just a matter of time before she would make magic happen all the time, using bigger cameras and larger stories that everyone wanted to hear.

Time. Ally just needed enough time.

* * *

"I think at a child's birth, if a mother could ask a fairy godmother to endow it with the most useful gift, that gift would be curiosity."

Eleanor Roosevelt

Chapter 4

"Come, child, wake up." Pearl's whispered breath gently washed across the little girl's face. "Uh, something . . ."

"Hmm? Oh, no, Granny, I wanna sleep some more."

Pearl tugged on the pink and white checked quilt that Violet had hand-sewn for Ally's bedroom. "Get up now, child. Something wonderful has been going on. Reckon angels been here. You'd best come see. Get your slippers, child."

"Angels?" Barely awake and rubbing the sleepies out of her eyes, Ally slowly rolled over onto her tummy, and slid off the tall mattress that was tucked between the massive wooden pillars of the antique four-poster. "Real angels, Granny?"

Pearl waited, watching out the bedroom window while Ally found her slippers under the bed and her thick, fuzzy, warm robe. "Ah, they came once before to bring us a wonderful gift – you. It's something I haven't seen in a month of Sundays. Get a wiggle on; fog's lifting. Hurry, child."

Ally clutched Pearl's hand as they stood on the east veranda and the child shivered in the cold air. Barely four-years old, Ally snuggled against the woman's knee and peered through the dense fog, wondering why her grandmother was excited — nothing was out there but layers of heavy mist slowly moving through the trees. Red-streaked gold clouds slowly dissolved while dawn gradually, silently, pierced through the live oaks.

"Look there, child." Joyful tears filled Pearl's eyes.

Ally shivered a little, and then gasped with surprise as the shimmering garden revealed itself. A jeweler's treasure chest had emptied itself onto the trees and ground, sprinkling crystals onto everything below. Millions more clung to the grand ladies as Ally called the magnificent live oaks that lined the narrow drive from River Road to the front of the house. Overgrown laurels and myrtles surrounding the old home and against the outbuildings glistened in the crisp air. Spanish moss shawls, which draped the ladies' outstretched arms, seemed embedded with clusters of diamonds when the sun crept over the horizon, then treetops, then sliver shafts of sunlight burrowed wedges through the branches to dance among the sleeping rosebushes. The almost-secret bayou world Pearl and Violet shared with Ally that stretched to the Mississippi River was encased in a rare ice storm.

"Ohh . . . stars fall down. . . . just like the fired flies. You said angels, Granny Pearl. I don't see angels."

"They've done been and gone; can't see them now, child. My own granny told me that when we get a coating of ice that looks like diamonds got sprinkled into our trees, it's because angels flew through here when we weren't looking. Wherever their wings brushed by, they left diamonds behind.

"All this glory only lasts a short time. Vanishes right before your eyes. I wanted you to know, to see it for yourself. And, I want you to remember what a piece of heaven – a real fantasyland – looks like. I want you to recognize it, if you ever see it again. Mayhap you will. God willing, mayhap you will."

The winter wind, like an invisible whisperer, rustled the scattered leaves about Wildwind Plantation's grounds. Crystals clung to twigs and branches for only an hour or two before seeping into the leafy amber carpet.

That afternoon, Ally crunched through the earthbound bronze rainbow, a kaleidoscope of gold, crimson, russet and ginger-tinged maroon leaves that lifted, arched and swirled in the breeze off the Mississippi River.

Untainted and complete joy bubbled up in nature's child as she smiled, twirling arms outstretched, stirring a multicolored gauze cape around her of varying shapes that rose to form a leafy protective shield. She laughed aloud and pirouetted again and again, leaves lifting, darting, swirling until they clung to her moist clothing and long, now-damp, goldilocks. Dizzy, she stumbled and fell onto a soft mound of leaves, still laughing. Rolling over onto her tummy in the lush, musty dampness, she noticed a silver thread among the crystals that laced directly across a leaf.

"Uh-oh. What's this?" She reached to touch the leaf, then gasped when a tiny creature, muddy brown with green splotches on its lower body with smears of yellow up higher, darted out, stopped, stood up and stared at her, then blinked a few times before scampering under the nearest big leaf.

Quickly up on her knees and shoving leaves aside with both hands, she searched with curious excitement for the tiny thing that had escaped. Nothing. It was gone.

She remembered her special books and the stories told by her grandmothers in front of the fireplace about woodland fairies. The books said fairies never allowed a human to see them, but she was pretty sure she had just seen one. Where did it go? It certainly wasn't a lizard or a frog or any other forest critter she found and played with almost daily. It had stood straight up on long legs and looked at her. She hunted though the leaves mounded around her knees. Not a trace, but she found the leaf etched with the silver trail.

"Here's tiny footprints. I saw you, I really did." Ally wondered if it was a him or a her, then decided it didn't matter. "I knows you're here somewhere."

Trying not to crumble the edges, she gently tucked the leaf into her jacket pocket, planning to add it to the other treasures kept hidden in her room.

Chin snapped up. Pearl was stepping out onto the side veranda about to call her to lunch. Dusting off her hands, she glanced around the leaves and twigs again. "I'll be back to find you another time."

Knowing a secret is so much fun. She giggled aloud and skipped through the leaves, scattering them in all directions, touching several of the huge trees and calling each by their very-private names, reminding them how much each was loved.

Far above, the naked trees stood stark, condemned to wait unprotected for the full blast of winter's fury to fall upon them. Ally slowed to a walk and sighed, suddenly saddened by the thought of the trees' increasing misery. The leaves she played among were their clothing, and now they stood stripped of their glory. The child hated to see layers of ice weighing down the branches, and shuddered every time a loud crack rippled through the chilled air. The splits and rips reminded those living in their protection that another fragile limb had shattered as it hit the ground. Even though Pearl tried to explain it more than once, Ally simply could not understand why the weather could be so cruel at times. These trees were alive, were special, she loved them and didn't like seeing them shivering, encased in ice.

Ally hated winter and what it did to her friends, her trees. Her trees were tangible elements in her life. They watched her play and kept her shaded when she was hot. They also had their own secrets, just like humans. Ally felt the trees were alive and watched over her.

She knew the trees felt the warmth of summer and the hurtfulness of winter storms. Winter always dampened the child's spirit and made her sad. Winter changed everything, turned her usual happy and sunny world dismal and gray. In the bayous, trees crowd against each other, contending for every sliver of solid land they can find in the soggy ground. Ancient live oaks shade many of the narrow dirt roads and long driveways that lead to most of the old plantations from the Mississippi River. Ally could care less if old Mr. Winter ever came again. Well, almost . . . except for the snow.

Snow. Oh, how she loved the snow. She loved snow ice cream so much. When it snowed, she and her grandmothers went outside carrying the largest bowl they could find, each one armed with a huge dipping spoon. It took time to carefully scrape off the top layer to get spoonfuls of the cleanest snow underneath without scooping up grass and leaves. Each spoonful was plopped into the big bowl. They'd get tickled as they competed to see who could get the most the fastest and hurrying before the snow could melt – scooping, dipping, deliberately bumping into each other, laughing – then rushing back to the kitchen in a footrace.

Pearl pulled a chair across the room from the kitchen table so Ally could stand on the solid seat to reach the countertop where she could help. Attentive, Ally watched every move to learn the secret to creating the special treat. Pearl poured sweet milk and vanilla flavoring and lots of sugar into another bowl, then gave Ally a spoon to stir the mixture until it was silky smooth. Next, Pearl drizzled it over the giant mound of snow, gently lifted and folded, lifted and folded, over and over, telling Ally why it could not be rushed.

Ally shifted her weight from one foot to the other, anxious for Pearl to say it was ready. Ally was convinced they made the best snow ice cream in the whole world, and wanted to get the first bite. She'd sneak a spoonful whenever Pearl wasn't looking. One time she ate too much too fast and gave herself a bad headache, but she didn't care – she got the first bowl of snow ice cream and that was like winning a prize.

86

Violet fussed at her for being silly and freezing her brain. Ally never understood what she meant by that because her forehead felt like it burned, not froze.

Winter meant snow and snow meant Christmas. This was the hardest time of year for Ally: Waiting. Waiting for Santa, waiting for the much-needed snow. Santa needed snow so his heavy sleigh could land on the old roof without breaking the shingles or any presents tucked in his bag.

Ally would stand on one of the chairs at the kitchen door to look out the window near the top and watch, watch for hours, watch until her little legs grew tired of standing, until her eyes grew weary. From her lookout, she could see towards the dark woods and the tree line. From atop that chair, she could see the first tiny snowflake drifting on the breeze. Waiting was the hardest, yet always the most exciting time in winter. Pearl and Violet understood why Ally was determined to stand on that old, wooden, high-back chair until the child's legs ached, until her eyes were ready to close, waiting for one snowflake, waiting for the snowfall, waiting for Santa and his sleigh to arrive.

Occasionally, they'd get on to her about standing there for so long and tell her to get herself on down. Pearl sometimes said, "A watch pot never boils." Ally never knew what that meant either. She had never heard of a watch pot or knew if it ticked and chimed like the tall case clock that stood on the stairway landing. Besides, she wasn't watching for a pot to boil, she was watching for snow, for the first tiny snowflake, the first flurry, for Santa, for her mother, perhaps for her father.

That part she'd be quiet about, wouldn't reveal her secret – maybe later when she was older – but for now, she simply watched for her parents in silence. She knew for sure Santa would deliver them just in time for Christmas, but remained hush-hush about her deepest wish, never saying a word to her two devoted grandmothers. They did have some strange sayings and expressions sometimes, like freezing her brain or a watch pot that never ticked. No telling what they'd say if she told them her secret, about her watching and waiting for parents to arrive with the snow just like Santa's elves.

Pearl often invited her two sons, Frankie and Clark, Ally's mother's younger brothers, to come to Wildwind on weekends. They arrived with their guitars and played music while Pearl and Violet cooked a big dinner. Ally hoped her mother would hear them playing wherever she was, and would come home to be with the family. She thought it was a shame her mother missed all the fun and excitement when Ally's two uncles came to visit. Ally loved music and performed for her grownup relatives. She practiced singing a couple of times with a mop or a broom in the bathroom where no one could hear. A wonderful echo bounced off the bathroom's tile walls and made her little voice sound even better and stronger. She was positive her two grandmothers and uncles would clap their hands and cheer if they could only hear her sing the perfect song without missing a word or a beat.

Usually, Ally and both uncles stayed in the parlor playing guitars and singing while the grandmothers were cooking dinner. Every once in a while, her uncles stopped playing and sniffed the air, then talk about how those two women could cook. The wonderful fragrances of a traditional Cajun dinner drifted throughout the old house, down the hallway, into the parlor and they could hardly wait to dip a giant spoon into the huge, bubbling cast-iron pot of jambalaya and ladle their own bowls to the brim. Red beans and rice, hush puppies or cornbread, and sometimes a massive pile of steamed shrimp on the table made family dinners a feast fit for a princess, her two brave knights and her fairy godmother grandmothers. Those wonderful smells promised empty tummies would be filled to overflowing, and the love shared at the table filled Ally's heart.

Ally was always excited when her two uncles came for a visit. Her grandmothers and they made her feel a part of their music. On several evenings, Ally ran upstairs and brought out one or two of her beautiful party dresses from her wardrobe. Sometimes, she scampered all the way up to the attic. She'd either get a party dress or one of the many costumes Pearl had sewn.

Those were very special dresses. Ally was the biggest fan of fairytales in the world. It was easy to figure out why: Living a fairytale book life wasn't as complicated as living in a world filled with a terrible aching loneliness. Ally's books gave her a fantasy life that was far better, far easier than the one she lived.

Pearl had sewn a particular dress that looked exactly like the one worn by Snow White. She had copied it from one of Ally's books; a crisp white skirt topped by a blue blouse with narrow pin tucks and fancy short sleeves. Ally put it on and instantly felt transformed into Snow White. She could bring the character to life in a matter of seconds, acting out every scene that was in her fairytale book.

Sometimes, she performed just for her two grandmothers, and always for her uncles when they came to visit. Ally wanted to give Snow White a family, an evening of fun since Snow White only had the Seven Dwarfs to entertain her. Ally felt as if Snow White and she were a lot alike – both were waiting waiting waiting, forever waiting.

One evening, she wore the Snow White costume because she was in a happy mood and wanted to sing a particular favorite song. She prompted her uncles on how to play it, then began singing, "Just Whistle While You Work," giggled and marched around the parlor trying to imitate the dwarfs and sing and whistle all at the same time. She couldn't stop giggling, but when she finished the song, she bowed to her uncles' wild applause and cheers.

Pearl and Violet heard every sound from the kitchen. They shared a keen look which softened, grinned and shook their heads.

Pearl sighed and picked up a wooden spoon to stir the sautéed onions, chopped garlic and bell peppers again. "Well, I reckon all that's in her blood. She can't help performing for anybody. All they've got to do is sit still long enough."

"Hmm . . . or being a busybody, telling others how they ought to be doing something," Violet added, then chuckled. "Listen to her carrying on, telling the boys what to do."

"Yes'um. She's still way too little and doesn't know who she is . . . but we do."

They winked and laughed, knowing the truth.

Ally craved entertaining everyone with her costumes, loved hearing them laugh and hearing praise for her performances. No matter what they said about the others, the Cinderella story was her favorite to perform. For a child, it seemed it took longer for Pearl to design and sew the new, larger Cinderella costume than all the others in the collection. The new one would be a white satin ball gown with a sky blue sash.

At seven years of age, Ally just wasn't old enough to have much patience. She wanted something new to wear sooner.

Ally had glimpsed it once: An old cedar steamer trunk in the attic – a place Ally was forbidden to go due to the old mansion's third floor being damaged and unstable. Pearl said one of the hurricanes that had barreled up past New Orleans decades ago had pushed a huge tree limb through the wooden shingles. Before the roof was repaired, other violent storms had pounded on the roof and rain poured into the house, the flooring had soaked up most of it, so had gradually deteriorated.

Both grandmothers said the old floor was so fragile that if Ally stepped on the wrong spot, it could crack wide open like an eggshell.

Violet leaned close, squinted her eyes, and lowered her voice to a raspy whisper. "I don't want to scare you too much, but that old floor could open up wide enough that you'd fall right on through . . . all the way down to the bedrooms, maybe even under the house."

Ally's eyes widened. "That sounds terrible."

Violet nodded. "It surely would be. Best stay out of there." She hoped a stern warning would keep the child out of the attic and safe.

Not likely. Not Ally. She feared few things on the earth and an old wooden floor wasn't one of them. The warning only managed to create an aura of irresistible mystery and intrigue that lingered around the room and in Ally's imagination.

Some things are too tempting for children. That attic and all the mysteries it contained couldn't be ignored. Ally imagined hidden secrets in the attic and that old trunk, and she desperately wanted to see everything inside. Curiosity set in and wouldn't let go. All she could think about was what wonderful treasures must lie behind that old locked door.

Ally had climbed those creaky stairs many times and had sat outside that door to stare at that ornate metal lock. She had tried every key she could find to open it, and remained undaunted when the keys failed to get the job done. She simply went in search of another key, and another and another.

The attic could be a cool hideaway, a place she could go to escape her grumpy older sister. She could be alone to read, to play, or just to think. How does one get into a locked room that had no key?

One morning, when Pearl and Violet would be gone on a short journey, meaning all day – it presented a whole day for Ally to concentrate on the locked door question. She brought the kitchen knives, scissors, long nails, and anything that looked like it might open the lock, to the attic door and tried them all. No luck.

But, while snooping in Pearl's jewelry box, Ally found a sizable hatpin. It looked as if it might just work. She climbed up the long, twisted stairwell again, so excited that she was sweating. Ally stuck the hatpin in the antique lock's hole, twisted and poked, and Snap! Oops! The hatpin broke in the lock! Click! The door opened.

The moment she stepped into the attic, dust rose and she began to cough uncontrollably. She tried to be quiet so she wouldn't alert her grumpy older sister. She carefully began walking across the ancient planked floors Pearl and Violet had warned about. Each step made a loud crackling sound.

Ally tiptoed to the window where sunlight was shining through, and pushed the curtain to one side. Then turned around and peered into the shadows. In the corner was a large black trunk; scattered about were a few chairs, odds and ends of furniture no one wanted, a few books, outdated lamps, a broken wooden rocking horse. Nothing special.

Her eyes were captivated by a large, rounded-top steamer trunk. It took a lot of strength to lift that heavy round lid against its rusted hinges, but she finally got it up far enough to peek inside. With a pleased grin, Ally gave it one more push and managed to lean the top against a wall.

Ally gasped for air. Dust flew out and floated up into her nose and mouth. She waved her hands around trying to push the dust motes away, and turned her back for only one moment before looking. Nothing except old dresses, a few old nylon slips that went beneath dresses from way back when, and some undergarments.

Ally carried them as if they were spun glass figurines, and carefully laid them on the nearest discarded rocking chair that had a broken armrest. She lifted one more thing and discovered a small hoop petticoat – a most wonderful find.

Then she lifted an age-yellowed linen cloth. Beneath it lay a beautiful ivory dress with delicate embroidery, fancy lace at the throat and long puffy sleeves with more embroidery on the cuffs. Ally instantly knew it wasn't an ordinary dress. It was elegant, maybe a ball gown.

There was also an album of black-and-white photographs. She looked at them, thinking perhaps there was one of a great-aunt or someone who had owned all of these garments. She moved a few more items of clothing around, and found a pair of shoes.

Lifting the shoes out of the gloomy trunk, Ally discovered they weren't just any old shoes. These were silver and very fancy with tiny silver beads sewn in designs all around the fabric. They looked as if they had never been worn.

Ally loved shoes. She simply couldn't leave them there in the dark, in the musty old attic – they needed to be rescued. She carefully put everything back into place — except the hoop skirt and shoes — and closed the trunk. She tucked them under her arm, tiptoed back out of the attic before she was caught, and quietly closed the door.

She rushed to her room, excited about the hoop skirt and silver shoes because she played dress-up with her costumes. The shoes would go with those wonderful Cinderella and Snow White gowns, two costumes she wore when acting out her favorite fairytales.

The shoes fit perfectly, only a few sizes too large. They sparkled in the light. They were the prettiest shoes ever and were for grown-ups, not for seven-year-old girls. Ally was thrilled. She knew these shoes were important, so kept them hidden and only brought them out to play with when no one was around.

She put on the hoop skirt and got her Cinderella costume out of the tall wardrobe. It was a slight struggle, but she wriggled into the pieces and turned around in front of the giant mirror that would tip downward . . . surprised and pleased. *Voila'*! She looked exactly like Cinderella with such a full skirt.

Later, she went downstairs to show her two grandmothers and uncles in the parlor. They clapped and laughed as she spun around and around to show off her wide skirt.

A few days later, Pearl made Ally a wand, saying it really wasn't magic, just a pretend magic wand. Ally was disappointed it couldn't perform magic tricks, but understood her grandmother couldn't always do everything.

It would be months before Alley learned the trunk safeguarded her Great Grandmother Violet's private pain.

Pearl had been cleaning Ally's room one day when she discovered Ally's secret. When Ally came home from school, Pearl made it clear that it was time for Ally to reveal how she had broken into the attic, how she had found the trunk, and how she had found the fancy silver shoes.

Pearl patted the bed next to her. "C'mon up here and sit down, Ally, and I'll tell you about these silver beaded shoes.

"They are a special memory treasure. Your Great Grandmother Violet was to be married wearing those shoes after her first husband, Thomas, died. Someone she truly loved proposed to her. These were to be her magic wedding shoes – but he was killed in a war. When he didn't come home, she put her wedding dress, trousseau, and these silver beaded shoes into the old cedar trunk, covered them, and closed the lid on her dreams of a different future instead of a life as a young widow with children. The wedding dress and shoes haven't been out of the trunk since that day."

"Oh, Granny, please let me keep the shoes. I promise to care for them. I know they are special."

Pearl allowed her to keep the shoes.

"Oh, you know everything, Granny. Do you really think I'll grow up and marry a prince someday – for real?"

It was a serious business question, especially when it came to Ally's prince and castles and fairytales.

There was a twinkle in Pearl's eye, which hinted that she already knew the answer. "Yes, dear one, you will grow up and marry a prince. But, before the prince comes along, I mean the *real* prince, you'll have to kiss many frogs and maybe one toad."

"Euw. Kiss a frog? Ugh. Do I gotta, Granny? That'll be awful if I got to kiss a toad. That's worser."

Pearl's tone of voice changed, she grew more serious. "Not just frogs and toads, Ally. You need to be aware that many things out there are not as they seem."

Even at the young age of seven years, Ally realized Pearl was talking about something other than kissing frogs. "You sound funny, Granny Pearl. Feels scary."

"Not scary, child. I mean for you to look out for the darkness, Ally. Just because something has a pretty coat of shiny new paint on it does not mean it is pretty underneath. It could be rusted or worse. Such as, well, a good-looking prince as you may dream of may come along and appear to be a prince on the outside, but on the inside, he is dark and rusted, which would mean that he is no prince at all.

"And, child, sometimes we are drawn to the very thing we cannot have simply because it is not of us or of this earth.

"It is because of curiosity, child, and young folks are curious – especially you, Ally, being such a sensitive child and wanting answers to all those questions in your head.

"Heed my words – listen! – take what I say seriously: If you ever find yourself caught in a mousetrap, any trap, wiggle out as fast as you can and move like a lightning bug – run! Run and don't look back. Never look back. Keep going forward."

Ally studied her grandmother's face for a long moment, seeing the concern and love in her eyes. "I promise I will, Granny. I love you." Wrapped her arms around Pearl's neck and held on tight until Pearl gently pulled away.

Ally wrapped the precious shoes in a clean, soft cloth and placed them in the wardrobe's corner. She'd find her special prince and marry him while wearing those silver shoes, unless her feet wouldn't fit. For now, she would be Cinderella and would dance at fancy balls in the fairytale world she had created on the old plantation.

* * *

"It hurts to find out that what you wanted doesn't match what you dreamed it would be."

Ralph Waldo Emerson

Chapter 5

There wasn't much to do in that small bayou town. Ally attended a small private academy. Most of the children lived thirty minutes away or longer from Wildwind. They had something Ally didn't have: Fun-loving parents who did everything with them, activities her two grandmothers couldn't do with her due to their age. They tried when they could, but not having a young mother and a father was depressing for Ally, especially whenever one of the children asked where her parents were. She simply didn't have an answer; not a clue where they were beyond what Pearl had told her.

Sometimes, cruel children laughed and made fun of her, chiding her at every opportunity. After being bullied all day, Ally would step off the school bus and run home in tears, upset for days.

Sometimes, other children were friendly and treated her nice because her parents weren't around. They seemed to understand what it was like to be lonely, to be without parents.

It was always an extreme, bouncing from one emotion to another, depending upon what other children said; they either broke her heart or made her think they understood and felt sorry she was alone in her emptiness.

No one was around to play with every day. The only children her age who were nice lived too far away. The others, the mean-spirited ones at school, called her names like 'weirdo,' since she didn't live with her parents, and teased her for living with 'old ladies' – her two beloved grandmothers. They also thought it was strange that Ally didn't have lots of brothers and sisters, and didn't go to all the places they did.

Going places was a problem. No matter what, Ally didn't ever want to talk about Pearl's driving skills. Pearl never drove very far and Ally understood why even when she was still young. That was the main reason Ally rarely asked to be driven anywhere. The only place Pearl drove to that she felt comfortable was to the doctor's office or the grocery store in town. Occasionally, Pearl went shopping for Ally, but mostly she ordered items from the Sears & Roebuck catalog or other clothing catalogs.

Since there were no parents to take her places, Ally learned to escape the old plantation in her own way: Books. Once a week, the public library's book mobile came to town and parked at the corner near the end of the plantation's driveway. It would be there for three hours, bringing the entire world beyond Wildwind into Ally's hands and heart. Ally was ecstatic on those days. She was always early, waiting anxiously at the corner, waiting to be first to climb the steps into a magical place of other worlds. She could check out five books for the week; she always wanted fairytales. She carried them home to read and for Pearl to see the clothes in the pictures. She hoped Pearl saw something she liked and would sew another costume for Ally's collection.

Books were and are magic. They made Ally feel exactly like whatever she read and that she was the main character in the story. She floated along with Tom Sawyer on the river raft, played on the playgrounds with other children from around the world, she toured France, and went scuba diving with dolphins.

It was magical when her imagination let her step deep into any forest with fairies and goblins. Reading made her dull life sparkle.

Early one evening, Pearl looked at her mother, Ally's great grandmother Violet, and said, "That child has always got her head in those books. I don't know if it's a good thing or a bad thing."

Filled with wisdom, Violet smiled. "Now, Pearl, you let that child be. Let her run wild with her imagination. She's got to go somewhere with all that energy and spirit she has. I have never seen so much energy bottled up in one child."

Pearl looked at her ancient mother and sighed long and deep.

Violet's grin widened and she shook her head. "I don't reckon either one of us would have lived this long if it wasn't for that child's enthusiasm and passion for life. Just look how old we are, Pearl. She keeps us young with all her tall tales."

"Hmm, tall tales is right. You know what they say: Life is just energy. Ally's got enough for the both of us. Look at her right now, thinking she's hiding at the top of those stairs again."

Pearl spoke much louder. "You might as well come on down, Miz Ally, and share one of those nighttime stories with us. We might as well dream right along with you."

Ally giggled, suddenly excited. She tried not to stumble as she ran down those tall steps to tell her nightly stories, the ones that appeared in her head from nowhere. Sometimes she would act them out as well, as if she were in a play. She was happy they wanted to hear her tales. She would bound down the stairs as fast as her little legs would allow, her arms outstretched to welcome her beloved grandmothers into her engrossing and all-encompassing world. She lived in the best of all possible worlds surrounded by undying love and wisdom.

Such memories lived on forever in Ally's heart and soul. Many years later, she remembered laughing with pure joy as she rushed down the stairs on oh, so many nights of her childhood because her great grandmother knew her so well and encouraged her to embrace all of life's possibilities. The older woman's eyes would twinkle as if she lived through some of those marvelous book adventures right alongside Ally – that made each story as real as their next breath.

Violet's latest Plato reading and thinking was usually discussed over dinner, and she patiently explained so little Ally could understand. Ally, who was barely tall enough to reach a sink faucet, quickly grasped in-depth thought as well as any high school student. Classics were stacked and shelved all over Wildwind and were rarely ignored – copies were dog-eared from being read and re-read.

Ally's stable home life and knowledge, which was learned from true wisdom that was as old as life itself in the specific personages of her two grandmothers, told her she was born *Knowing*, that she had the *Gift of Knowing*. There was very little anyone could say that Ally didn't already *Know*.

Knowing is a blessing. Sometimes it's a curse.

* * *

Ally understood *The Wizard of Oz* story, about Dorothy being raised by her Auntie Em, about not having a mother around. That made them almost alike. Her mother wasn't around either, and she was reared by two older women – a double whammy. Ally didn't have a Toto. Her grandmothers wouldn't allow a dog, but she could have a cat. Oh, my, a familiar was all too real. Ally always had a cat or several cats that listened to all her secrets and kept them, too, never telling anyone.

Ally couldn't help relating to fairytale books. Each one seemed to apply to her life in some way. As she grew, she played their characters and recreated their worlds in her smaller world – she brought them to life. She disliked the fact Snow White didn't have any friends except the Seven Dwarfs, so Ally had special fun dressing and pretending to be Snow White. She also loved scooting about in the woods and imagining how Snow White lived in that story.

When it came to *Alice in Wonderland*, or in this case, 'Ally in Wonderland,' it was a natural thing to have rabbits around. It seemed Ally usually stepped or fell in to and through a large hole of imagination to see what was on the other side. She played hostess at many dress-up tea parties under the trees in the backyard with her cats, dolls and teddy bears, and an occasional curious bunny as a special guest.

Ally may have lived near a bayou on an old southern plantation, but she inhabited the wonderful world of fairies and secret prince toads, red birds and giants, elves and trolls, and everything her magical kingdom offered. She brought each character to life, gave them new adventures, let them visit her, live in her bedroom and in her play yard. They came to her tea parties where she served cookies and pretend tea, and told them wonderful stories. Sometimes, they told her stories. Ally was certain her favorite characters were as real as she, and somehow, by some magical way or a wicked witch's curse, they had gotten trapped inside her books. She helped them escape from the gilded pages for a while.

Ally was positive she was doing them a favor until a special day when she discovered the complete wonder of Cinderella. It was all over for the other fairytales. Her little heart fluttered like a butterfly. She saw herself in the woods, looking for the handsome prince, knowing that someday in real life she would be just like Cinderella. She hoped she wouldn't have mean stepsisters and housework and other horrible chores to do. None of that part of Cinderella's life sounded good at all.

The real princess Cinderella would grow up to become was wondrous and brilliant and gorgeous – just like Ally dreamt she, too, would become.

Ally was certain she would have a castle just as Cinderella had, and she, too, would find a dark-haired handsome prince to marry. She, too, would have birds flying around her head, singing. And she, too, would have the best fairy godmother in the whole world. Ally knew her mother, who had certainly left her by mistake, would someday find her, would wave a magic wand to make all the hurt go away. She hoped her father would show up as well. If he didn't, it wouldn't matter because Ally's True Prince would be the one person on earth who had the one shoe in the world that would fit only her. He would carry her away from the mean stepsisters and hard housework; he would marry her and take her to his magic kingdom. Someday everything would be perfect. Someday, she and her Handsome True Prince would live happily ever after in a beautiful castle on a hilltop.

It was a fact: Ally considered herself Cinderella. Cinderella had left the fairytale book to live through Ally so the two of them, as one person, could find their True Prince. Ally felt this with every ounce of her being, more than all the characters she had ever related to before. Cinderella fit her perfectly, just as Cinderella's glass slipper had fit her perfectly.

More shoes would enter Ally's life and her future because she loved shoes.

Ally's life journey as a modern day Cinderella began when she was three years of age, pushing hard on four.

* * *

Ally decided she was going to be an actress. After all, as an actress, she'd have the chance to live in the world of some of her favorite fairy tales. She practiced early and late, practiced in the house and in the yard, practiced until she was almost perfect. She practiced her songs, her two uncles played the music, she put on her little plays, and her grandmothers always cooked the best dinners. The grownups were her audience in a home-style dinner theatre.

Once in a blue moon – maybe once a month – a friend named Susie spent the night at Wildwind. They dressed up in Ally's costumes and pretended fairytales had come to life in her bedroom. But her friend could never be Cinderella; that role was forever Ally's.

The long hot nights were intertwined with dreams and reality of a time when everything was good and the world was perfect. Ally's make-believe world was carefully, thoughtfully, built and fortified piece-by-piece.

She often thought about her mother and what the woman looked like. Ally envisioned her as very beautiful since her two grandmothers were beautiful, and they were wise, talented, very smart and witty. If they were all that and so was she, then Ally's mother had to be all that, too. She wondered if her mother was a natural blonde, like she; if her hair was very long like hers; if she smiled a lot; if she dreamed of castles and fairies, if she liked Barbie Dolls, if her mother liked playing dress-up as much as she.

Ally was sure a real prince had seen her mother, had instantly fallen in love with her, had ridden his white horse into the yard and had stolen her away – that *had* to be the real reason she had left Ally behind. Maybe an ugly wicked witch was holding her mother in a castle dungeon somewhere. Ally planned to break her free with the help of her little friends in the fairy kingdom. All the birds and little creatures would travel around the world searching until they found her, then they would fly back to Wildwind and tell Ally where her mother was being held captive. All Ally's fairy friends and the smallest woodland creatures would go with her to help bring about a daring escape. Ally planned it carefully and knew it would work. First though, she had to discover where her mother was being held.

Ally also thought of her father, wondering if he was a tall, dark and handsome prince; if he rode big white horses; if he was like her and wanted to be famous one day; if he wanted to make wonderful stories come to life in movies as Ally did with her little red camera. Ally would paste her drawings together and imagine the words they would say; maybe he dreamed about his characters or made them up like Ally always did and maybe he would put them together, the pictures and the words. Even if he was a real prince, he *had* to be missing her somehow as he built sand castles on a far away beach somewhere. He would stop building long enough to listen to conch shells whispering stories of ancient sea gods and mermaids, of Ally waiting for him to return to fetch her.

Ally knew he had to think of her from time to time, and knew he had to wonder what she must look like; if she was growing up pretty; if she looked like the woman he loved once . . . maybe still did.

He would come get her one day, she was sure of that. Maybe he would come on his white horse and tell her how they had gotten tired of traveling, how he stopped in a far away land until he could get another horse . . . and that's why he couldn't get back until now, until that day, that hour, that minute. Ally knew he would have boxes filled with photographs to show her two grandmothers and her, and they would hear all the stories about each one.

Ally wished on too many stars for her mother to call or come to get her, or for her father to call or come get her. She would often ask her grandmothers where her parents were, what they were doing, why were they gone so long. Pearl would try to hide the sad expression when she sat down to tell all sorts of stories about what could have caused such a long delay, tell anything to make an innocent little girl feel better about her parents not being there. Pearl knew Ally knew she made up the stories, but it didn't matter then or now. Her stories gave Ally brighter rays of hope that her parents really loved her, but just couldn't come get her that day, week, month, year. Pearl always gave the child something to hope for.

Ally could never understand why she had parents who had gone far away for so long, but looked forward to Santa Claus and Christmas because surely they would come this year. She knew when they saw her, they would have many presents just like all the other parents had for their children.

Summers became longer, so did the winters, then a birthday would come along, and this was the year they would come get her, then next year, then the next. Ally was always so sure of it because she wished on stars and at the secret wishing well in the back of the plantation. Surely, the Man in the Moon and all the stars heard Ally's deepest wishes. Even though she wanted her parents to come get her, she decided she wouldn't go

116

anywhere without her two grandmothers – they would come, too.

Another birthday came and went, so did another sad, disappointing Christmas with Ally standing on the chair, watching out the door for the much prized snow, or staring at men and women holding their little girls' hands in the stores, or laughing as their children played on the carousels or stood in line to speak to Santa. Even though these things filled her with a special joy for those lucky little girls, her heart sank deeper and deeper into despair. She didn't understand what was wrong with her, why her parents didn't like her at all, why she had so many flaws that they didn't want her to be near them. Ally always brushed her blonde hair one hundred times every night to keep it long and shiny. She always kept her bows tied and her dresses clean as much as possible, hoping to look really cute for the big surprise when they showed up at the house.

Wherever they were working and wherever they were living, it was taking forever to come back. She was certain that no matter how long it had been, people didn't ever forget their baby girl. Or could they? Was that possible? Could anyone just forget about their little daughter, never think about Santa's presents or birthday cakes or Barbie Dolls or other baby dolls when they saw other little girls someplace? Maybe Ally had a baby sister or brother somewhere, someone other than the grumpy, resentful,

117

older sister she did have who disliked Ally and didn't like to even speak to her. Maybe she would find the younger ones one day and they would search together for their parents. Ally was so full of hope and faith, so positive that the stars and every forest creature and bird she talked to and played with would surely help get a message to her parents – even if they were lost on the other side of the world.

Sometimes, she would sneak out of the house and go into the woods to search for her prince. She expected him to come riding up on his white horse and carry her off to his castle somewhere.

Springtime and summer were the best part of the year. Ally would get up early, throw on some clean play shorts and matching shirt or a little sundress – and a hat – and leave the house. Ally had to have a hat. Every little Southern Belle In Training must have many hats in different colors to match the outfit they wore that day. It was very important, and Ally was a typical little Louisiana Southern Belle who had to have a hat. It didn't matter if it was a fancy straw sunbonnet with artificial flowers and a long ribbon or a cloth baseball cap, a hat was an important part of what she would wear for the day. She pulled her long hair up into a ponytail, then over the baseball cap's strap in the back. She knew it looked cute and bouncy because her grandmothers said so. That made it true.

118

There was one more very important thing for a little Belle: She had to have a small basket or water pail to use for a lunch box. She never wanted to carry a tacky metal one unless it had Cinderella's picture painted on it. She needed a good basket because she would be gone for a long time, busy with serious business, so she needed to carry a snack or a lunch.

When she stepped out of the house and headed toward the woods, she knew she would be gone until her grandmothers looked for her. Fairies were in the woods, she suspected other things were there, too, but went anyway. She usually took a peanut butter and grape jelly sandwich to entice fairies to come out from under the leaves, and to feed bugs or worms or whatever came her way. Something always did.

When she packed the lunch basket, she needed to remember one particular thing: A long straw to get worms out of the ground. That chore took a while. It was easy to find tiny worms holes, but it took longer to beckon them out.

There were always hungry rabbits in the woods that were fascinated by Ally's presence, but very shy. They stayed at a distance and peeked around trees to see what she would do. They knew they'd get a few breadcrumbs if they waited long enough; so did the birds. Ally would have conversations with birds, telling them which direction to fly to next in their search for Ally's mother and father. A time or two she saw a snake in the grass, usually tiny garter snakes, never big scary snakes, but they weren't friendly like other creatures. They just slithered past, in a hurry to go someplace to hide again.

After talking to everything, she sat under a tree and talked to the tree or whatever was hiding in the grass or behind a bush. That's when she would eat her sandwich or cookies and enjoy a private picnic.

One day, Ally walked further into the woods than usual, and discovered a small chest under an oak tree. It looked old, similar to her lunch pail: A rusted silver metal with odd designs on the top and sides. Alley thought someone must have forgotten their lunch pail a long time ago.

Ally's chin snapped up. A slight inland breeze wafted past her head. Ally's nostrils twitched and flared at the strong repugnant odor. It was more of a damp river bottom smell than the sweet summer sunshine that normally stirred through sugarcane fields and corn stalks. A second breeze brought dampness that changed to a bitterness, changed again to a stagnant marsh and long-growing mold. "Whew . . . that's stinky."

Her attention returned to the little chest just as a flock of birds erupted from the treetops, swooped down and flew

120

straight at her. She ducked a second before they flew past her head, squawking loudly. Ally wondered what could have caused them to abandon their afternoon nap in a favorite tree. The birds flew on, darting and weaving around the trees and branches until out of sight.

Several bunnies ignored her as they scampered past in a straight line, barely dodging around her feet. Odd they hadn't run in circles. She watched as the bunnies dove into a thicket.

Crickets and cicadas hushed. Butterflies vanished. No tree frogs croaked. No breeze stirred the leaves. Forest creatures had folded in on themselves in preparation for something out of the ordinary. Another strong breeze. Ally sucked in her breath in a tiny gasp, too apprehensive to move another step, trying not to gag at the stench.

A hard thump – a concussion – reared up from the earth and jolted her feet through the dirt and the forest floor's thick mulch carpet. The ground shook a little a second time, leaves shuddered when the tree branches whipped back and forth. Ally instinctively squatted, pivoted on her toes when she heard a loud crack and a grumble behind her.

The ground shook in a slow, definite rhythm.

121

Ally cautiously stood and looked around before taking another step toward the treasure chest, wondering what could have made such a scary sound or that smell. Perhaps it was why the birds and bunnies had run away. Perhaps it was a mean person, or Big Foot, or the Swamp Monster, perhaps one of the ogres her grandmothers said were outside when they heard strange sounds late at night.

She looked up in time to see the trees in the distance shiver and a flock of blackbirds fly away, squawking. Something was there. She thought she ought to hurry. Something must be very big and strong enough to shake entire trees. She took a few steps closer to the chest as quietly as she could.

A loud grumble, a guttural rumble. Ally stopped. She *Knew* what it was.

There she was, alone in the woods and too far away from any house, field or pasture to call for help. She crouched again and watched as the intruder stepped into a small clearing.

It hesitated, lifted its massive head and looked around. It was almost as tall as the live oaks: A huge human-like creature dressed in sagging, ragged clothes that were a haphazard mixture of browns and tans and greens, the shirt was torn, shaggy and uneven around its hips. Dingy-gray Spanish Moss clung to its clothes, long strands of kudzu caught around its feet trailed along the ground, twigs and leaves were gnarled in its stringy brown hair. Its long arms and meaty fists swung freely from the wide shoulders.

The twig beneath Ally's sandal snapped.

It twisted around and looked in her direction. No beard covered its massive jaws or trunk-like neck, or the snarl on its lips.

It must have heard or sensed someone was near. It scanned the woods . . . it saw her. "Agh!"

Its small dark eyes narrowed, its forehead wrenched into a deep frown, and a low-toned growl rippled through the air, then soared into a high-pitched screech that could have shattered glass.

Ally wanted to cover her ears from the horrible sound, but she was too afraid to flinch or move.

It bent, shoulders hunched closer to the earth. It spun, the shirt flinging out behind, then a shoulder smacked into a tree, sending a loud crack from the impact resounding through the woods.

Within seconds, it vanished.

Still crouching, still holding her breath, Ally felt every step the giant took as it pounded its way across the solid ground.

Ally shook her head. *No, no, no. It can't be true.*

She had frozen in place, gasped for a quick breath, too scared to scream. She knew she was too deep in the woods to run away. It would be impossible to get very far before the big thing's long legs could catch her. It was the first time in Ally's life she ever felt the inner trembling that accompanies real fear. Within seconds after the thing vanished, Ally's fear escalated to panic. She knew it could have gone in any direction, it could have circled back around, it could have hidden behind a clump of trees somewhere along the path she had to take to get back home.

Her heart pounded stronger as she thought about Dorothy and Toto when they were being blown around in the tornado and had to face the Wicked Witch. She looked down and saw she was wearing her brown sandals – not magic jeweled red slippers. She could not click her heels together and be home in an instant.

She told herself she could not scream. Oh, she'd better not scream. She'd better stay as quiet as possible, as small as possible, lean tight against a tree and not move. She rightly thought if she screamed or made a loud noise, it could hear her. It could still be out there, just a few yards away, it could come rushing toward her any second and snatch her up inside one of its giant hands and trap her. Perhaps it hadn't run away after all. She knew she could not escape if it wanted to come back to get her.

The old silver chest was still sitting on the ground beneath the big tree, just a short distance away. Perhaps the monster wanted to come back for the treasure chest. She figured it belonged to the tall man-like creature, or giant, or forest troll, or whatever it was. She tried to take a deep breath that smelled like good earth, familiar forest, and to think clearly.

That was a real giant – just like one in my fairytales.

It had human features, but it wasn't hairy like Big Foot that her Great Grandmother Violet spoke about when they heard noises in the woods at night.

Then she remembered a story in a book about a giant that took a little girl and buried her under a tree where she played in the woods on a swing her grandfather had made for her – never to be found again.

Tears filled Ally's eyes. She didn't want to be buried under a tree. She didn't want to be lost forever. She wanted to go home, to curl up in the safety of her Granny Pearl's arms. The more she thought about it, the more frightened Ally became. Her little hand shook, tears filled her eyes, but she wiped them dry with the hem of her sundress, and bit her lip. Somehow, the scared little girl conjured up the willpower and determination of an adult. She decided she wasn't going anywhere without that small treasure chest.

She listened. A cicada made a tiny noise in the distance. She looked around and pushed away from the tree and crept forward one step at a time until she reached another tree, then another, then quick-stepped across the remaining open ground to the oak tree. She glanced around, quickly bent, grabbed the chest, and backed up against that tree and listened.

Everything was quiet except for the smallest of forest creatures, the rustle of dried leaves as a nearby mouse searched for a new hiding place. No grumbling or ground shaking. Maybe the giant was gone. She held her breath, stood still and listened longer. The birds hadn't returned, no bunnies scurried in the leaves, no squirrels jumped from branch to branch, no twigs snapped. Ah, she heard a tree frog in the far distance. Silence again. That was even scarier. The forest creatures were still afraid, too.

She waited and listened, could smell trees and sunshine again. As soon as she felt the coast was clear, she ran as fast as her little legs could carry her to a small overhang and hid there. She concentrated on her breath and tried to stay calm. There was only a little more open ground to run across, then through a small patch of trees to another clearing that stretched around a bend. If she ran as fast as she could, she would be out of the woods in a few more minutes. Maybe it wouldn't find her once she reached her own backyard again.

Ally took a deep breath and ran. Her sandal got caught on a tree root and she fell face down in the dirt, her basket tumbling out of her hands. She held onto the silver chest as tight as she could. She took a deep dusty breath and struggled to her feet, grabbed the basket and ran again.

Her heart was beating so fast from exhaustion and fear that her chest really ached; her ribs and side began to hurt. She had to slow down a bit, but ran on. She was too frightened not to run. She glanced over her shoulder to see if the giant was coming up behind her, and fell again. Scrambled to her feet while she looked all around. She couldn't see anything that looked like it was looming high above or among the trees, but it wore colors just like the forest. She wasn't about to take time to look closely at every tree.

Ally was panting by the time she reached the fallow field of buttercups, ran straight through the flowers, ignoring the buzzing honeybees. She reached the property line and jumped over the bottom strand of barbed wire fencing that marked Wildwind's backyard. She was home. She was safe. Or so she thought.

There stood her grandmothers, Pearl and Violet, their arms folded across their chests, concerned expressions on their faces. At first they seemed relieved to see her, then their expressions darkened.

Big trouble.

"Ally! Where *have* you been!?" Pearl's voice was high pitched, her words clipped. "Been looking for woodland fairies again, have you, child?"

Ally tried to catch her breath so she could reply. "Well, no, uh, yes'um, . . . ma'am . . . not really, Granny."

"Good Lord, child, there's dirt all over your sundress, leaves in your hair, your beautiful red hat is hanging down your back, and you've got fairy dust all over that little face of yours."

"Uh, fairy dust, Granny?"

"Yes. Sprinkles of sparkles just like you've been playing in the woods with fairies."

Ally glanced over her shoulder to make sure the giant hadn't followed her home, wasn't standing just beyond the nearest trees, wasn't peering at them as they stood in their big backyard. Ally moved closer to her grandmother and shifted around to the other side so she could watch for movement in the woods.

"Granny, I did see a fairy today. . . . an', an', there was a big ol' giant in the woods, too, an' I saw him for a little bit but I saw all of him an' he was really big an' mean lookin' an' he even scared the birds an' bunnies an' they ran-ded away an' I fell down but I brung his treasure chest back with me. See?"

Pearl shook her head, but smiled. "Slow down, child, slow down. Oh, got his treasure chest, did you? Hmm, well, what makes you think it's the giant's treasure chest?"

"Um, well, um, he was kind of mad an' growled an' maybe stomped a little an' he didn't smell good, kinda stinky, an' I run'ded very fast to get home, Granny Pearl."

Violet's eyes narrowed in a frown, recognizing fear on the child's face. Their little one was watching the forest, expecting

129

something, expecting anything any moment. Violet wheeled around and carefully scanned the tree line before turning back. "Nothing's there now, child. Don't you worry none, but that's not a good thing, Ally. Did you really take something from one of the giants?"

Ally's lower lip pouted when she nodded. "Uh-huh."

"Well then, they'll be very angry and there's no telling what they'll do. You'll have to take it back to them, child. You mustn't ever take anything that doesn't belong to you, even if it belongs to a forest giant."

The corners of Ally's mouth turned down in disappointment. "Uh, do I have to?" She sighed. "Well, uh, I reckon, but maybe it was a gift from the fairies, Grandma."

"Oh, Ally, where do you get all of this nonsense?"

Surprised, Ally looked up. "Well, you, of course, Granny Pearl. You told me."

Violet laughed and pointed her finger at Pearl. "She got one up on you there, Pearl. I don't remember teaching her about any giants in the woods. Not giants, no, never about giants. But woodland fairies? Of course, I have. There's fairies and giants and trolls – we know all about them; not many giants, though. Well, I reckon they all must hang out together in the woods, don't they, child?"

Pearl shook her head at her mother and Ally. "If you two don't beat all."

Violet tipped her head to the side and smiled. "Now, Ally, I bet you ate your picnic, played a while, got tired and fell asleep under an old oak tree. And, I bet you had a dream about a giant. I doubt a giant was really in those woods, Ally."

"Well! That helps me out a lot, mother. First, you admit to telling her all about fairies and such, then go telling her there's no giants in our woods when we all know there's something out there. We just don't talk about it. Hmm! Our little one here will be running off to school soon and you'll be to blame when she tells her teachers and classmates about giants and fairies and all that applies, are living in our woods. Maybe a little Plato thrown in the pot for luck as well."

Ally looked from one grandmother to the other, finally relaxed and giggled. "Yes'um, split apart. We all are split apart, like clams on a half-shell that are scattered out to sea. An' these humans bean-in's were just all sad an' lonely an' lost, lookin' for their other half. Sometimes bein' so busy not noticin' an' *Boom!* they were right there in front of them the whole time."

131

Violet smiled down at her and nodded. "Well done, Ally. Very good indeed. You remembered Plato and quoted that very well."

"Yes'um, Grandma Violet," Ally said, grinning. "I do like that story. You told me that one."

"Well, yes, I did. That has a bit of validity behind it."

Pearl grumbled. "Hog wash!" She swung around and began walking up the hill toward the house. "With her sundress all dirty and torn from that barbwire fence, trying to jump over it. And we're out here calling until we're hoarse from yelling, looking for Ally in Wonderland in the woods."

Ally always laughed when they called her 'Ally in Wonderland.' They made her feel like an adventurous child for sure.

'Ally in Wonderland' was only one title the two grandmothers had given her. Another one was 'dirty child,' because she sat on the ground a lot, especially whenever she went into the woods to talk to the birds and creatures, telling them where to search for her mother and father.

Pearl glanced over her shoulder to make sure Violet and Ally were following. "Just look at that dirty dress. Harrumph! Bet she was clicking those brown sandals together, thinking they were magic, were ruby red slippers, and she was trying to find a way out of the woods when that giant and other scary things were chasing — . . . . Oh! Now wait just one minute!"

Pearl spun around. "Your feet, Ally. They're filthy. I thought you were wearing sandals. Where's your sandal?"

Ally looked down and wriggled her toes. "Uh, well, I doesn't know, Granny. I fall'ded down runnin' so that monster giant couldn't catch me an' bury me under a tree so I reckon I ran'ded out of it an' left it somewhere. I's berry sorry, Granny." Ally turned around, looked at the tree line, hesitated and sighed. "Okay, I go find it."

"Oh, no you don't. Come back here, young lady. It's just a sandal and you've come this far barefooted. Well, one foot barefooted. We'll find it tomorrow."

Relief spread across Ally's face.

Violet shook her head and took Ally's hand as they slowly walked behind Pearl toward the house. "If Ally did see a giant, the monster we've heard scratching about in the yard at night and making the neighbor's dogs bark, then she probably *was* wishing she was Dorothy, wishing and hoping a storm would blow her on home. Isn't that right, child?"

Ally nodded. "Uh-huh, yes'um."

Both women chuckled. "If this keeps up, I'll have to buy her two pair of the same shoes and sandals every time we shop. She keeps losing one of them."

Violet looked down at Ally. "You *are* the adventurous, wonder child, aren't you?"

"Yes'um, Grandma Violet. How'd you know I was thinking 'bout Dorothy when I was scared in the woods?"

Violet's eyebrows lifted, her forehead wrinkled slightly. "Yea, I often do wonder why and how I do know these things."

Although still young, Ally thought it was odd and almost scary that her two grandmothers seemed to know exactly what was in her mind. *How do they know what I'm doin', even when they can't see me, even when we're far apart? That's almost as scary as the giant, or the wolf in the Little Red Ridin' Hood story.*

When they reached the house, Pearl washed some of the dust off Ally's face and gave her a drink of cool water. "That's better; I can see you in there now. Go on upstairs and take a nap. You look sort'a peaked."

"Yes'um." *Runnin' from giants make me peak-ted.*

* * *

"Wake up, child," Pearl tugged on Ally's quilt. "Come on. Dinner's on the table. You wore yourself out in the woods today. Time to get cleaned up and eat. We need to talk about the chest you brought home."

Pearl started back downstairs, stopped and called again. "Get up now, child."

Oh, boy! Strong energy. Violet had taught her about energy, how to feel it in the air. *Uh-oh, they's some kind of mad.*

Ally pushed off the handmade quilt and slid down to the floor from the tall mattress of her four-poster bed. She knew she had to answer their questions, so reluctantly drudged down the stairs to the kitchen and peeked around the doorway.

"Ah, there you are; about time. Just where have you been, Little Miss Riding Hood, with your red bonnet on today?" Pearl asked in a stern voice.

"Oh, um, I went in the woods with my lunch pail an' some cookies an' I found a treasure chest an' I c'lected four-leaf clovers an' some pretty little stones with sparkles in 'em an' put them in my basket, Granny. Wanna see?"

"Slow down, child, catch your breath. You were a busy little bee, weren't you? Come here, honey." Pearl plucked a few twigs from Ally's tangled hair and untied the sash of her sundress. She noticed the scrapes on Ally's knees. "Hmm, and how'd you get hurt?"

Ally looked up, puzzled. "I tol' you I fell'ded down." She sigh. "Well, I ran'ded when the giant grumbled an' stomped on the ground an' went the other way but I figured he might come back so I ran'ded as fast as I could an' I tripped over some ol' dumb tree root or something stickin' up an' spilled everything an'— "

"Whoa! Slow down, child. You fell running away from the giant you saw in the woods?"

"Yes'um. Splat. Got dirt all over my nice dress, too an' then got it torn-ded when I jump'ded over that ol' wire fence 'cause I was runnin' hard an' . . . an' . . . well, hmm, that's all."

Pearl and Violet shared a concerned, knowing glance across the table. Violet sent a 'be quiet for now' signal and Pearl nodded.

"I see, Miz Ally," Pearl said. "I want you to get a bath so you can eat dinner. We'll take a good look at those scrapes after you scrub off the grass and dirt. Then I want you to get to bed early. I'm a little upset with you, young lady."

"Yes'um." Ally drudged upstairs, hid her treasure chest in the clothes wardrobe, took a bath, gently rubbed her sore knees, and tried to wash her long hair. She put on her pajamas before trekking downstairs so Pearl could tend to the scrapes. One look told Pearl she had to wash Ally's long hair again, then comb out two cockleburs and some tangles.

Ally ate her dinner in silence, then went to bed . . . until she was certain everyone had settled in for the night.

That's when curiosity got the best of her. She crept out of bed to open the giant's old treasure chest to see what was inside. Empty. She sat on the floor for a long time, thinking.

The next morning, Pearl and Ally walked into the woods to return the treasure chest to the exact spot where Ally had found it the day before. Pearl was relieved there weren't anything resembling large footprints.

"We may be in time, child," Pearl said. "Perhaps the giant hasn't come looking for it yet. You need to remember this day, child. Always remember you cannot take anything that doesn't belong to you. We must respect each other. Respect the fact others have their property. It doesn't matter what size they are, a small person like you or a giant."

Ally's lower lip pouted a bit. "Yes'um, I reckon."

"How would you like it if someone took your Cinderella ball gown without asking you first?"

Ally gasped. Her eyes widened at the thought of losing her most prized costume. "Oh, no, ma'am. I wouldn't like that one bit."

"Exactly. The ball gown is special to you. That's why you can't take something from someone else. It may be something special to them. Do you understand it now?"

Ally stared into the distance for a brief moment, and nodded. "Yes'um. I better write a 'I'm sorry' note an' put it in the chest. Would that make him feel better?"

Pearl tried not to smile at the child's purity of thought and innocence in an attempt to gain an imaginary creature's forgiveness. "I think finding it here when he comes back will be enough. Let's go home now."

"Yes'um."

Ally glanced over her shoulder as they walked away. She planned to return in a few days to see if the chest was still there, and grinned. The chest was empty when she opened it, so she decided to put something inside, one of her treasures: A sparkling white crystal that looked exactly like a chunk of snow that would never melt – it was magical – something very rare in the Louisiana bayous.

Ally's face brightened with her secret plan as she watched a small flock of birds flying around. That's when she saw her sandal, its leather strap caught on a tree branch.

* * *

Playing Barbie dolls with Ally's older half-sister Jade was always fun until the day both grandmothers went to town to shop, leaving the big sister in charge.

Jade wrapped a huge towel around Ally's shoulders so she could play beauty shop. Ally's natural blonde hair was long, slightly past her shoulders, full of curls, swirls and waves. Jade decided to give Ally a new style, a new 'do,' as she called it. She described it in such a way that it sounded so pretty. Jade dubbed it a "Barbie Do."

Ally was only about four- or five-years-old, so it didn't take much for her older sister to convince her that what she was about to do was too good to pass up. She combed and brushed Ally's hair, then leaned close. "It's going to look just like my Malibu Barbie!"

"Oh, I can't wait," Ally replied.

Jade had been to the wishing well. She wanted to be a beauty shop girl, to cut hair, and to do makeup on people. That day, she even put makeup on Ally and the little one felt so grown up, pampered and pretty sitting on the tall kitchen stool.

Out of the corner of Ally's eye, something flashed silver – a pair of thick-bladed scissors. They came from nowhere. A second later, Jade was tugging downward and cutting Ally's hair.

Ally gritted her teeth, but wishfully, and optimistically, remained silent. *I shouldn't be nervous. Jade has done this many times with her friends. She knows how to do this.*

Ally was wrong. Ally was Jade's first customer.

140

When Jade finished with the Malibu Barbie Do hairstyle, it was as short as a man's hair after he walked out of a barbershop. Ally looked down and screamed when she saw all of her blonde hair lying on the kitchen floor.

Mad was not a close enough word to describe how Ally felt. A much stronger stock from the lexical cabinet was called for in this case, but being very young, she didn't have a key to the cabinet. All her pretty, blonde locks were gone – she was ruined.

She gasped and sobbed, shuddering at the thought of ever leaving the house again as she slowly climbed off the stool. Her trembling fingers brushed along the sides of her head, stopping, flinching. Silent tears filled her eyes as she gasped for air, for control. She certainly didn't feel like a Barbie doll now. Ally ran down the hallway and stared at herself in the bathroom mirror. *I look just like Ken.*

The only 'do' Ally got that day was a 'Jade-Do.' Tears and cries echoed against the bathroom tile for a long time.

Lo' and behold, when the two grandmothers returned and saw pitiful little Ally crying her eyes out and her lovely hair piled on the kitchen floor, they literally chased Jade down with a switch from the bushes. She got it big time for making such a mistake. Restriction for Jade to her room for a week wasn't near long enough, as far as Ally was concerned. She would have preferred she would stay out of her sight until Ally's hair had all grown back.

Eventually, a perfect opportunity came along for Ally to get back at Jade, to get even for all her meanness. Sometimes revenge, even if delayed, tastes sweet. Ally merely had to wait until boyfriends started calling on Jade.

One hot July night, Jade's boyfriend, who was better than good looking, came over. His name was Eddie, but everyone called him 'Fast Eddie' because he had the fastest car in town, and he had Jade, the most beautiful girl in town.

Ally's big half-sister thought she was so slick. Fast Eddie would come over to the plantation and they'd go smooch in the parlor in the far, dark, right-hand corner of the house where Granny Pearl couldn't hear a sound or see a thing.

Ally knew what they were up to. She'd run down the hall, burst into Granny's bedroom, grab her arm and tell her to wake up fast. "Jade's kissing up a storm downstairs . . . in the parlor. You know, those long, long smoochie, loud ones. You better hurry, Granny Pearl."

Granny Pearl was as old fashioned and traditional as anyone in town. She certainly didn't put up with that sort of goings on under her roof.

Ally would get tickled with herself, thinking she was really smart for getting Jade in trouble. Jade thought Ally was asleep upstairs because she always tiptoed into Ally's room and peeked in to make sure. Ally pretended to be sound asleep. The moment she left the room and shut the door, Ally slid out of bed and sneaked down the stairs to watch her and her boyfriends. It was fun to get Jade into trouble after all the things she had gotten away with. Anyway, it was always hard to sleep with an older half-sister, who was bossy and played loud music that she and the boys danced to – like The Beatles. Who could sleep with that going on downstairs?

Granny Pearl always put a quick end to Jade's kissing evenings. Granny Pearl would go into the kitchen, grab her stiffest broom, and burst into the parlor. "Jade! Get your bony butt up to bed right this minute."

Granny would wheel around and scare the daylights out of Jade's latest boyfriend. "And, you . . . you young whippersnapper! If you know what's good for you, you'd best get your fanny out my door and you'd better stay away from this plantation or you'll be riding my broom home. Am I making myself clear? You understand me, young man?"

After a few dozen 'Yes'ums' and backing toward the door, the boy could usually escape Granny Pearl's broom. Jade would be so embarrassed. Granny was so old fashioned at a time when it seemed all the other parents were cool about their daughters having boys come to their house. But not Granny Pearl. Boys couldn't be in the parlor with Jade unless Granny Pearl chaperoned them herself.

Ally's half-sister never knew she had been out of bed and spying on her almost every time. Well, Ally guessed she does now.

* * *

"Every man's life is a fairytale
written by God's fingers."

Hans Christian Anderson

Chapter 6

St. Francisville was a small town, but it wasn't cut off from the entire world. Once a week, the big blue bus, the Book Mobile from the county library, would rattle down the highway and stop near Wildwind's driveway. Ally was always the first one in line, shifting her weight from one foot to the other, too eager to stand still. It was as exciting as Christmas when Santa arrived. Oh, how she loved books and pictures of faraway places. She planned to travel all over the world to visit each one someday, and relished all the different places and longed to meet all the different people around the world.

Ally would check out as many books from the big bookstore on wheels that her small arms could carry. Of course, the librarian would only allow five books a week.

She always ran home to show off her newfound treasures to her two grannies. She usually bounced through the front door, yelling for them. "Come see what books I got this week!"

Granny Pearl would shake her head. "Oh, child, for cryin' out loud, why not just get one book a week and read it?"

"But I do read them all."

Granny Pearl knew better. She knew Ally could only read one or two, and only turn the pages and study the pictures of each book of those she didn't have time to read. Ally always planned to read those she had to skip.

Books were and are magic. They made her feel like whatever story she read, that she was the person in the book. She hung out with Tom Sawyer on the river raft, she played on the playgrounds with other children from around the world, and toured France and went scuba diving with dolphins. It was so magical when she could step deep into any forest with the fairies and the goblins and the elves. . . . and even the ugly hairy trolls.

The scariest was when she met one of the giants in front of a huge old live oak tree. Even years later, Ally would swear it wasn't a tall tale when she met that giant. At that point, both grannies became a little concerned. They didn't want her to get too deep into the mystical forest with giants. Ally didn't want to either, but she could and did go everywhere and anywhere with all her wonderful books.

Granny Pearl looked at her mother, Ally's Great Grandmother Violet. "That child has always got her head in those books. I don't know if it's a good thing or a bad thing."

Violet grinned. "Now, Pearl, you let that child be. Let her run wild with her imagination. She's got to go somewhere with all that energy and spirit she has. I have never seen so much energy bottled up in one child."

Granny Pearl looked at her ancient mother and sighed long and deep.

Violet just grinned and shook her head. "I don't reckon either one of us would have lived this long if it wasn't for that child's enthusiasm and passion for life. Just look how old we are, Pearl. She keeps us young with all her tall tales!"

"Tall tales is 'bout right. You know what they say: life is just energy, and Ally's got enough for the both of us. Just look at her right now . . . thinking she's a-hiding at the top of those stairs."

Granny Pearl spoke much louder. "You might as well come on down, Miz Ally, and share one of those night-time stories with us. We might as well dream right along with you."

Ally would get so excited to come running down those steps to tell nightly stories, and sometimes she'd act them out as well, as if she were in her own play. She'd be so happy they wanted to hear her tall tales. She'd come bounding down those stairs with her arms outstretched to welcome her beloved grannies into her engrossing and all-encompassing world. Ally knew she lived in the best of all worlds.

Such memories will live on forever in her heart and soul. She remembers laughing with pure joy and merriment as she rushed down the stairs on so many nights of her childhood, and laughing because her Great Grandmother Violet knew the child so well and encouraged her to embrace all of life's possibilities. She lived through some of those marvelous book adventures with Ally . . . and that made each story real and unforgettable.

* * *

Men must not check reason by tradition,
but contrariwise, must check tradition by reason.

Tolstoy

Chapter 7

St. Francisville was like most Louisiana communities. Whether Cajun, Creole or Caucasian, everyone had at least one stranger-than-usual relative, just like the Carry Bradshaw character said in the television show 'Sex and the City.' Ally's family was really no different than their neighbors, except for one unusual extra element: there were two witches in the immediately family at the same time. Even the locals thought that wasn't merely strange – it was bizarre.

Ally may not have known about witches, but she could sense a person's energy by the time she was three. Even if she didn't know what it was or knew enough to give it a name, Ally could tell when there was powerful negative energies emanating from some people. Some people can see and interpret the hues in a person's aura. As she grew older, Ally could delve deeper: She could hear their thoughts and the beat of their heart.

The family's first witch was Pearl's daughter-in-law.

This particular woman visited Wildwind more than once. She always brought special treats like candy or cookies and ice cream for the girls. That wasn't as wonderful as it sounds on the surface; it made her visits scarier for young children.

She was middle-aged and her stringy, jet-black hair hung all the way down her back. If she wanted, she could even sit on it. Her complexion was very pale, even her arms and legs. She was almost white, like a porcelain doll or a white wax candle. It seemed if she ever walked outside and stood in the summer sunlight for a few minutes, her skin would begin to melt. Thinking about that happening was terrifying to the two youngsters. The woman swept into rooms, her long dark hair swinging back and forth, her small, dark brown eyes darting around, quickly taking in everything and everyone. Her steady gaze sent chills up and down some people, and it seemed she could glare a hole right through anyone, especially a child, who would usually cringe.

This woman looked and acted as if she had just stepped right out of 'Hocus Pocus.' Her presence even made many adults uncomfortable.

When she arrived, Ally always felt a strange fluttering in her tummy. When the woman approached, her little hands would tremble. Ally and Rachel would sit to one side in the room and watch every move the woman made.

Ally wasn't old enough to watch horror movies on television, that was definitely never allowed by the grandmothers. She knew very little, nothing really, about witches or what they were, what they could do, but whenever this woman came into the house, Ally grabbed onto her big half-sister and squeezed her hand tightly.

Jade made matters much worse one day. She leaned closer to Ally and whispered, "She's a witch."

"What's a witch?"

"That's an evil woman who wants to put you in a pot to cook you and eat you."

Ally gasped and gripped Jade's hand even tighter. As a small child, maybe only four or five years old when she first began observing this particular relative, Ally's fears increased as the woman attempted to get acquainted, to be nice, to be a family member. She came across the room and bent low to speak to the girls.

Ally's eyes widened when she saw the woman's long chin and nose, and her dark, piercing eyes up close. The child could not help staring at the woman's stringy black hair that was completely different from Ally's long blonde ponytail.

"Hello. My, my, my . . . such pretty little girls we have here," the woman said. "How are you?"

155

Silence. Ally kept a tight grip on Jade's hand, but wanted to back away.

The woman smiled. "I've brought ice cream this time. I hope you like chocolate. It's in the freezer in the kitchen. Why don't you go help your selves? Jade can reach it. Cookies are on the table."

Ally shuddered. She was convinced Jade was right: This woman was a real witch, one who probably had left her broomstick out on the veranda before she came inside. Ally suspected the treats, like cookies and ice cream, were really bait. The woman was there to fatten them up, and then capture them; she really wanted to put them in a pot and eat them.

Ally backed up against the wall. "No, uh, hmm, no, ma'am, I doesn't like ice cream no more," turned and ran into the hallway, skimmed the corner, and headed toward the stairway.

Jade giggled as she watched Ally skedaddle across the shiny wooden floors, and then followed her up the stairs. Ally went as fast as she could. The two of them ducked into a hiding place where the pale woman couldn't find them.

On one visit, the woman spent a great deal of time searching for the two girls. She even went upstairs, calling their names, searching and saying she wanted to visit and to give them more ice cream. Ally shook with fright, but the two girls stayed quiet while the woman looked in the wardrobes and under the beds. She looked everywhere, but she didn't find them that time.

Childhood memories are both fun and scary, and there's a tinge of fairytale to them, too. Reconsidering these incidents, Ally thought it may have sounded silly and stupid to some people, but she had been convinced that the family visitor was a witch. There was no reason not to believe her older half-sister.

What is even stranger is that although extremely frightened of her, after a few years, Ally couldn't remember the woman's name.

The other witch in the Louisiana family was Aunt Faden, grandmother Pearl's sister. Faden was a good witch, if there is such a thing – a white witch.

Ally was very young when they began going to Faden's house to visit. She was a lovely woman, slightly older than Pearl. Faden was shorter and a slightly overweight. She wore her hair in a short neat style, and she always wore lipstick and had the kindest, sweetest smile.

Neither Ally nor Jade ever felt threatened around Faden, and never thought she would give them poisoned candy or stick them in a pot to cook and eat them. But there was no doubt about it – Aunt Faden was considered to be on the strange side, even by experienced Louisianans who knew how to judge such things.

There were always a few odd happenings amongst Ally's blood kin, her blood relatives, just as there were in most longtime families that lived in the area. Few tales were told about those who had merely married into the family, but Ally always listened for hints.

Odd happenings seemed to occur more often around Aunt Faden, or to people around her who had displeased her in some way. She was a constant source of bewilderment by her close relatives, who, after a lifetime, were quite accustomed to strangeness. Even in the deep bayou country, Faden was an oddity.

Aunt Faden's house was located way off the road in a swampy area surrounded by much deeper water. Many times, if the water was high, it covered the road to her house, so the only way to reach it was by boat. Pearl kept a little rowboat tied to a tree and pulled onto the higher ground near the road where they would leave the car.

Faden lived in a wooden house painted red, a house that spooked Ally somewhat. Pearl, Jade and Ally would visit Aunt Faden in the early afternoon. It was always an adventure.

As a child, Ally thought it was fun to take a small boat to her great aunt's house. They could float right up against the steps and tie the boat to one of the posts. Since the house was built on stilts, they had to climb about ten steps to the little landing to reach the entrance.

It was a whole different matter after the sun went down. They had to row the boat back, and that was always very creepy, not only with frogs making loud noises, but other unusual noises as well, noises they weren't used to at all. Unidentifiable odors wafted across the water. Something howled in the distance. Something splashed very close to the boat. Something else shook tree branches high above them. They only had a small lantern to light their way back to the road and the car. Fog could get very thick, too. The youngsters always worried they would get lost among those giant cypress trees.

Ally never could understand why they had to leave the house at night — why her Granny Pearl insisted.

Wrapped in a quilt or a blanket, she tried to stay warm in all that dampness while Pearl and Jade rowed the boat toward the car. Since Ally was too little to row, she sat in the bow so she could act as lookout for what was making all those scary, strange swamp noises, and to tell her Grandmother Pearl if they were about to ram into a tree. Ally was positive alligators followed them on every trip back and forth across the water. Every child from the youngest age in Louisiana knew about alligators. Ally feared a hungry alligator would suddenly lunge up out of that black water and drop into their little boat to grab one of them for a meal. She always dreaded that black water, where something like a Loch Ness monster or worse was hiding, waiting until their boat got close enough to seize and then it would pull them all under.

Ally was certain of one thing: Granny Pearl loved her sister Faden, but would never spend the night in that red house. Instead, the little threesome risked the black water and the things hiding in it to get back to their car. That told Ally there were many secrets at Aunt Faden's than just the scary ones in the water.

Obviously, Pearl knew more about kind, sweet, Aunt Faden than Ally could see or comprehend at her young age. Ally never felt negative energy while at Faden's house, but she did recognize there was something negative present that she could not name.

Faden always had the most delicious-smelling food cooking on the stove. It was a warm, inviting home with pretty furnishings, mostly antiques. And, she made the best desserts; always a wonderful selection of cakes and pies were waiting on the kitchen counter. The girls had a hard time deciding which one to eat first.

There were some telltale signs that Aunt Faden could have been something other than a bad witch, or a white witch, or a fortune teller.

Faden would take a glass of water, tell a person to take a sip, then peer into the water for a long time. She would see things no one else could see. She would tell great stories about what she saw in the water glass.

Tea was much more fun. Faden brewed loose tea, straining most of the leaves out as she poured tea into their teacups. Afterwards, she told them what shapes she saw in the leaves left in the bottom of the cup, and what those different shapes meant.

That always amused Ally and Jade because they didn't know any different. The two youngsters thought everyone had an Aunt Faden who read tealeaves. Actually, almost everyone in the community had at least one family member who read tealeaves.

161

If Pearl wasn't looking, Faden would take out a deck of playing cards, shuffle them, and tell the girls their futures.

One time when they made a trip to see Faden, Jade had a wart on her finger. Aunt Faden said it was from frogs. She burned a matchstick, blew it out and quickly made a cross over the wart.

"Take this back home with you, Jade," Faden said. "Bury the match in the backyard and the wart will disappear in a few days."

It did.

Pearl would get onto Faden for doing these things, as if she was doing something wrong. Pearl was against some of Aunt Faden's "doings," as she called it.

Rattlesnakes, frogs and lizards were part of Faden's remedies for some illnesses or conditions, so were different herbs that she grew. People from miles around came to her house for those old remedies and healings and maybe tea readings.

Faden was a pretty lady who hugged and kissed Ally and Jade, and fussed over them at Christmas and other holidays. She seemed normal to Ally, except for using a few old healing remedies that she called "the natural way" and which seemed to work. Perhaps she'd be called an herbalist today.

As Ally got older, she didn't see Faden very often, and couldn't convince her grandmother to go visiting. Pearl said there was some black magic going on, and she did not approve of her sister's strange and peculiar ways.

"What she does sometimes just ain't fittin'," was all Pearl would say.

Pearl was a firm believer, a strict, go-to-church, Bible-reading woman. Even in her youngest years, Ally realized her grandmother was special, and was proud to be with and around her. She knew that Pearl felt in her heart something negative was going on at Faden's place, but wouldn't tell anyone any details.

Louisiana is like no other place on earth. It has its own strange and atypical ways; a world that exists within another world. At the same time, it is the most beautiful and serene place a person would ever want to be. It's where people can create and exist, insulated within their own private world.

* * * *

Wildwind was a large manor house which needed many hands to help keep it maintained, and to help rear the two young girls. Cicely and Ellie, the family's housekeepers and caregivers, attended to much of the work and looked after Jade and Ally. The girls' great grandmother Violet was almost ninety years old and still sharp of mind, and even though Violet was physically strong for someone her age, she and Pearl could not do everything the big place required. Violet still performed all of her own personal chores, but the heavy and time-consuming chores were turned over to Cicely and Ellie.

Sometimes Ally could sit nearby and hear Cicely and Ellie just going to town in the plantation's kitchen. They'd be sweeping and mopping those wide plank pine floors and talking up a storm.

Cicely always seemed to be first to jump on something Ally had done or said, never letting up a minute. Ellie would join right in, enjoying the things Ally said, the child's stories and antics.

"Lord, Lord, that Miz Ally's gonna be something when she grows up," Cicely said. "That child got more spunk and sassiness to her than I've ever did see in all my days of workin' for the folks on all these here plantations."

Ellie would just laugh. "Yes'um, you is right about that. Woo-wee. Trouble ain't even seen trouble till Miz Ally gets out in the great big ol' world."

"Girl, you ain't even a-foolin'."

"What you think she said to me, just the other day, Miz Cicely?" Ellie asked.

"Ain't no guessin'. Ain't no tellin' 'bout that child. She's something else, I'm here to tell it. What'd she tell you?"

"Miz Ally came a' runnin' an' carryin' on, hollerin' for me. 'Miz Ellie, Miz Ellie,' she done yelled. 'Come quick!' she says. 'I made my decision.'"

"A decision? What kind of decision, 'bout what?" Cicely asked.

"Ally had her little fingers just a-twirlin' those long curls, you knows how she does, and she looked up at me all bright-eyed an' bushy-tailed, an says, "I's goin' to Hollywood an' gonna be a movie star."

Both women laughed aloud while they worked.

"Well, now, I sure didn't want to hurt that child's feelings. She'd get all pouty an' all, so I played right along, don't you know. So, I says, 'You is, Miz Ally?' " Ellie chuckled.

"'I am,' that child told me. She says, 'I thought long an hard today at the wishing well. I can read an dance an write an all of that,' Ally says to me. Then she say, 'You know I can act good. You seen me do my plays here at the house in my room since I was little.

"'So, I've decided. I'm gonna grow up an move to a big city, an I'm gonna do my training like Jade wants to do. Jade says she's gonna be a beauty shop girl. Well, I don't want no beauty shop. I reckon the best place for me would be Hollywood. What do you think 'bout that, Miz Ellie?'

"Woo-wee. What's do I think? I told that child, 'Well, I reckon you'd make a right fine movie star, Miz Ally. I's better get to work now a'fore your granny gets after me.'"

Cicely and Ellie laughed up a storm at Ally's dreams more than once. Then Cicely would quiet down for a minute and shake her head. "The funny thing is that the child is serious. She's just liable to do that, if she sets her mind to it. Ain't a bit of tellin' what Miz Ally's gonna do, but I'd bet money on it, if I had some, that she'll do somethin' big-time, that's for sure."

The two would laugh at Ally and her dreams, and her stories about talking to fairies in the yard. Ally never could figure why they thought she was so funny when she was just a little girl with big dreams.

*****

"Life itself is the most

wonderful fairytale."

Hans Christian Anderson

Chapter 8

Turning off the county's two-lane asphalt highway onto the half-mile dirt drive to Wildwind's main house was always an abrupt change. Within a few feet, one felt as if they'd been swallowed up, spun around, transported by a time warp to a different level of existence. Civilization's harsh noise and stench instantly faded, almost blocked at the pavement's edge, replaced by an innate peacefulness and heady fragrances of honeysuckle and lavender that drifted on cool, gentle breezes. A private world. The grannies explained that it was the threshold.

The old carriage-wide drive curled beneath a thick canopy of ancient weeping willows along both sides of the road, willows with tendrils so long that they swept back and forth in the slightest breeze; massive fans dueling against the summer heat and humidity. Near the end, the narrow roadway curved so that the overhead trees formed a living green frame around the two-story main house in the distance.

Re-entering this solitude from the tense and strained outside world was truly mystical. Ally knew it was a privilege to live there, that it was far superior to many others, that the trees along the entranceway held tightly to the memories of those who had come and gone, and they still held strongly to the witnessed secrets; revelation to a human wasn't possible. Ally knew her

171

secrets would be concealed for several lifetimes, just as her ancestors' confidences were safeguarded there for more decades than she could count. The air, the branches, the soil promised her so.

As a small child, she played alone among the trees, talking to them and to the forest creatures that lived in the well-established domain. Her conversations probably sounded silly to those who might have overheard, but Ally was a child of nature: pure, simple, innocent, untouched by the world's brutality.

Ally and Pearl often walked the long driveway, watching for forest creatures, Pearl speaking about the family's history and the old plantation. They stopped often, speaking gently, enticing the creatures closer. Animals and insects seemed to answer by making strange noises, or a squirrel would drop a pine nut at their feet, a delicacy it had gathered from a forest evergreen, perhaps deliberately sharing.

Cardinals were special. One spring afternoon, Pearl stopped Ally in mid-step. "Shss. Look over there. See him? He's on the log under that blooming tulip poplar way off the road. He's wearing his brightest colors right now, wants to look handsome so he can catch a wife. Whenever you see a bright redbird, turn your back and make three wishes. And, if you turn back again and the redbird is gone, then the wish will come true."

Ally grinned, turned around, took a deep breath and cast her wishes. Wishes were a huge part of Ally's life.

Ally's great grandmother Violet taught in other ways, teaching her of the Great Spirit honored by the Hopi, the Navajo, ancient Anasazi and other native nations, telling her reverence for the earth transcends manmade cultural barriers. Violet wove in the Cajun and Creole ways, reminding her that they, too, were Ally's inheritance. Violet also spoke of her own nature spirit friends.

Both grandmothers taught her about Knowing, a special gift granted to many of their blood kin, mostly the women. They told her the great light would appear when a person was ready to receive it, there was no particular day; and once it went inside, it always stayed, unless driven out by the person.

One afternoon on the porch swing, Violet lifted Ally's chin with a gentle finger. "Look at me, child. I want you to hear this and remember what I tell you."

Ally blinked hard and nodded. "Yes'um."

"From the moment the great light enters into a person, you, you must listen to it at all times – no matter where you are or what you're doing. You must stop, be very still so you can feel it and hear what the great light tries to tell you. The great light only speaks the truth. And, it speaks directly into your heart and soul."

Ally's eyes got wider. "A voice talkin' inside?"

Violet placed her hand on Ally's chest and smiled. "Not exactly a voice, but you will hear the words. Don't be frightened of it, child. You're supposed to hear it and you're supposed to have this gift. The great light comes when it thinks we're ready and goes right inside here," she tapped Ally's chest with a wrinkled finger, "right inside your heart."

Ally received her great light when she was five years old.

She wasn't thrilled when she first saw it. Actually, it was a bit frightening. It looked a lot like a Casper the Friendly Ghost cartoon when it floated across the bedroom toward her. She was snuggling on the bed with Pearl during bedtime stories.

"Well, look there. It's okay, honey," Pearl said. "You're old enough now."

Ally nodded and bit her lower lip, still unsure. Great Grandmother Violet also said she and Pearl had received the great light when they were very young, too. Ally wasn't completely convinced. She burrowed closer into Pearl's side and squeezed her hand tightly.

The light came closer and silently hovered over them, pulsing, brighter for a few seconds then slightly darker for several moments, and then the pulsing became faster.

Ally squinted from the glare as the great light grew intensely bright. It moved closer until it was exactly on top of her, floating, almost within reach of her fingertips.

Ally cringed. "Granny . . . "

Suddenly, *Zap!* It streaked downward and went inside Ally's midsection. Vanished.

"Oh! Oh . . . it tickles all over. Oh, I feel all sparkly, now." Ally looked up at her grandmother. "It feels glittery in my tummy." She smiled and laughed, jumped up and bounced on the bed, shaking Pearl until she laughed and finally stood or she would have been bounced off the mattress.

"This is fun. I wanna go tell Grandma Violet that I'm lighted now. Can I, please?"

"Of course you can. Get down from there before you fall down. She's downstairs piecing together another quilt."

Only afterwards did the real Knowing set in, just as Ally's Great Grandmother Violet had described. Only afterwards did Violet and Ally spend hour upon hour in the front parlor or sitting on the veranda swing, talking, questioning, answering hundreds of Ally's questions, Ally learning, Violet telling what she believed Ally could understand at that time, at that age.

Violet also revealed details in the ancient healing wisdoms of the ages, and tried to pass on the knowledge for Ally to use in her lifetime. Fortunately, Violet and Pearl could repeat the lessons and expand on them for many years until Ally knew almost as much as they.

In the far rear acres of Wildwind Plantation was an old covered well, probably dug sometime in the early 1800s, the household's main fresh water source. Pearl wouldn't allow Ally to play there when she was young, fearful the child could fall into the old well. As Ally grew older, Pearl told a different tale.

One day, Pearl took Ally aside and became very serious. "Listen here, child, if and when you truly want something really badly, you need to peer down into the water at the bottom of the well. Stare into the water for a long time, concentrate and hold your breath. You may see things. That's when you make a wish."

Of course, Ally understood this was something special: she had her own private wishing well. Most likely, her wishes were different so they would be granted.

By the time Ally was almost six years old, she had developed a nightly routine. She would curl up on the wide window seat in the old estate's parlor, pull a light blanket or quilt up to her chin, nestle against a throw pillow, and listen to the night birds sing. She stared out the window for hours on end, a calming habit she developed while she watched the stars sparkle as they flashed between the silhouetted trees. Everyone knew the first star that came out at night was the one they could wish upon; to close their eyes tight and make a wish — it was always the very first star.

Star light, star bright, first star I see tonight,

I wish I may, I wish I might, I wish this wish comes true tonight.

Whether it was only a silly superstition or a true something, Ally didn't care at all. The nightly ritual was important: her wish must be entered into the star system before it was too late, before all the others cast their wishes, before their wishes were granted and hers were overlooked, and before the Fourth Watch. That was a big secret. She knew about it as she sat and thought about her serious wishes as a five and a-half-year-old.

* * *

Great Grandma Violet was getting very old now, almost ninety. She only made one full quilt a year, slept longer and insisted on taking an afternoon nap or she'd be more fussy than usual.

Going back to the grand scheme of life about wishing on that first star, Ally loved to stargaze and wondered what floated so high in the heavens. What were the stars, really? Were they souls snatched up into the heavens the second they left earth? Would her beloved Great Grandma be caught up high above the clouds? Would she when she died? Were all those stars lost loved ones looking down at those still on earth? Were they keeping watch over those they'd left behind? On a larger scale, were all those stars new worlds waiting to be explored? What an adventure that would be. Ally's imagination ran wild.

Granny Pearl would usually come into the parlor, and say, always too loudly, "Miz Ally, it's way past your bedtime. So, when you are through with your stargazing and dreaming of some foreign fairytale land, do you think you can get your hair combed, your teeth brushed, and yourself up to bed before you've dreamed yourself right into dreamland on that bench?"

Ally's forehead wrinkled in thought. What was it about old people, especially Granny Pearl? Did she have a hidden crystal ball in her brain somewhere? How did she always know what Ally was thinking? She could stand there, look at the child and say exactly what was on Ally's mind. Talk about strange and superstitious. Now, that was one thing Ally did not miss out on as a young child, especially growing up with two grannies, who were really old and filled with wisdom far beyond their years. It was like living in a real *Alice in Wonderland* or maybe in *Charlotte's Web*, a benevolent spider's web.

So, Ally grew up telling herself to think twice about everything: *Be careful what you think in this old cold house; one tiny twitch of a thought in her little head would alert both grannies in a heartbeat.*

Ally loved Wildwind dearly; so did Granny Pearl and Great-Grandma Violet. They had a perfect world hidden deep inside an even larger hidden world.

* * *

"Fairy tales are more than true;

not because they tell us that dragons exist,

but because they tell us that dragons can be beaten."

G. K. Chesterton

Chapter 9

Jade graduated from school, left to attend beauty school and married a rather nice looking guy named Matt, who always beat Ally playing basketball. Jade eventually bought a beauty shop of her own, hopefully, not doing Barbie-Do's on anyone.

For a while it was the funniest story on the planet when someone told about their growing-up incidents: the Barbie-Do, about her cutting off most of Ally's hair when she was a gullible five-year-old, and the fancy wedding dress and high-heel slippers shoved onto her feet as a newborn. No wonder Ally grew up thinking of herself as a princess or Cinderella.

Some sayings are true: be careful what you wish for, and you can't ever go back home. At least not always, and especially if you look down a well and wish to grow up really fast and move away from a small stupid little town, which turned out to be not stupid at all, but you don't know that at the time. Kids will be kids, and think like kids.

After Jade moved away, both grandmothers were Ally's to enjoy by herself and she enjoyed every minute. By then, she was tired of wishing for her parents to come. She stopped watching for the first snowflakes, stopped asking her grandmothers about her missing parents, and stopped casting wishes into her wishing well.

St. Francisville only had two traffic signals, most of the roads were two lanes, and many streets that turned off the main highway immediately narrowed to one lane wide. Residents didn't need big strips of wide asphalt to know where they were heading; they could get there blindfolded. Life was simple and quiet. Heavy traffic rumbling or bumper-to-bumper vehicles, sirens blaring away on police cars or fire trucks weren't normal happenings, so the residents were rarely bothered by noise or inconvenience. If and when anyone ever heard a siren, they knew instantly something terrible was happening.

Not many visitors stopped in St. Francisville, mainly people just passing through – until all the news articles and TV shows about ghosts – that's when things changed.

Christmas was a warm and inviting time. The townsfolk strung up multicolored lights on the antique poles that resembled the nice, softly lit, green-tinted globes ones in the French Quarter of New Orleans. Giant plastic snowflakes hung from the traffic signals and across the narrow roadways in several places.

Everyone in town volunteered to help decorate the city's huge Christmas tree, which was set up in the lush park of the city square. Folks gathered around and sang Christmas carols, and then someone would flip the switch to turn on the tree's lights. There were always the loud 'oohs' and 'ahhs' from the crowd, and squeals of excitement from the children. Santa Claus's workshop was always at the corner in front of the Dollar General store where Saint Nick waved and greeted the little ones, and listened to their wishes. So did their parents.

Night air drifting inland from the riverside brought unique fragrances. People could hear the loud whistle on the ferryboat coming to the downtown levee. People from the small town across the river, Old Cypresses, would unload their cars on the St. Francisville side. It reminded everyone that no pretty little 'how-town' was this. It was a great, an old-time, classical yuletide Americana. After the cars from Old Cypresses unloaded, cars on the St. Francisville side loaded to cross to the other side.

Everything was in balance, reason, with moderation and consideration, as even and as comfortably predictable as a stopwatch, which was a reassuring counterpoint to the sharp spark of clinging and cloying mystery that otherwise hung over the bayous.

Most small towns in the Louisiana bayous prided themselves on the old plantations that still worked the land. Many still claimed a wagon-wide strip of dirt that touched the riverfront, a holdover from days when ferries plowed the Mississippi, carrying the plantations' crops of rice and sugarcane to markets in New Orleans or Natchez, some cargo eventually made it to Europe. Everyone knew everyone else living along River Road, the lifeline ribbon connecting one old homeplace to another. Creeks ran in every direction, which kept the land fertile and moist but were usually occupied with water creatures. There's something to be said about the Deep South, especially Louisiana, where there were many dark, looming secrets floating in its muddy waters and deep black swamps. Massive cypress pillars thrust skyward toward promising scraps of sunlight, pushed ever higher by the tortured, twisted, gnarled trunks embedded in the slow-moving brackish water.

Even the air had a distant, somehow remote and alien smell to it, clearly announcing *Yes, this place is very different.* So were the people. Everyone seemed guarded, watchful for what people both knew and didn't know but suspected. Ally felt it, too. Everyone lived under the spell of superstitions, curses, and fantastical creatures such as Big Foot and the Swamp Monster some said was kin to the Skunk Ape of the Florida Everglades. Ally never saw any Big Foot tracks in the bayou mud, but always kept the possibility in the back of her mind – she might encounter the giant of the woods again, and might not escape next time.

There were quite a few dark nights, nights without any moon at all, that she and her two grandmothers would be reading in the front parlor, and they'd hear howling or loud moaning and groaning coming from the nearby woods. Pearl always said it was only wolves.

Ally cringed. "Werewolves, Granny? Do they really eat people?"

"No, there's not werewolves out there, child. Just plain ol' wolves wandering around."

Violet disagreed. "Now, Pearl, that racket is that big, old, hairy monster out there again. He's hungry and looking for food."

Ally cuddled closer against Pearl, who would scold Violet for saying such things. "Now see what you've gone an' done. Just hush up. You're going to scare the daylights out of this child. There's no such thing out there!"

Pearl would get up and walk off, kind of in a half-amused mood, but Ally usually felt a tingling in the air on those occasions. Oh, there was something big moving around outside all right. She didn't know what it was. She thought about it and decided she really didn't want to know.

Some youngsters in St. Francisville had a difficult time distinguishing the real and comfortable from the unreal and the unsafe. They needed time to grow and time to gain experience before they'd instantly recognize the potential in a dangerous situation. Sometimes, they came face-to-face with it before they were ready.

Real vampires look human, act human, but aren't human. If someone gazes into a vampire's eyes for a long time, the person could get caught up in the vampire's ability to lull them into a trance-like state. They'd be in deep trouble and not even know it.

Pearl warned Ally what to watch for, to be aware. "You can glance, but never, never look into their eyes. Never stare in a stranger's eyes too long, if at all – ever! Who knows what might peer back."

One evening, Ally and her friends were invited to go to the local drive-in theatre to see a movie. It was the first time Ally ever went to a drive-in movie theatre . . . and her last.

She was excited about the special treat. She climbed out of the car and walked into the concession stand for popcorn and a

Coke. She set the box and bottle on the counter so she could take the money out of her wallet to pay for the snacks, and felt something weird near her. Something pressuring, staring. Something with a strange heaviness.

She looked up and saw a dark-haired, older boy about seventeen on the outside, but who seemed much older on the inside, who was staring at her.

Ally glanced around. No one else was in the concession stand. Her eyes trailed back to the boy, into his silent stare. She couldn't move. Frightened, she was suddenly nauseous. Looking closer, she realized his hair was coal black, his complexion pale as chalk. Her gaze drifted to his face. The pupils of his eyes were huge and solid black, and his eyes had a glazed-over look about them as if he would be more comfortable working at the county morgue instead of a theatre's concession stand.

Something Pearl told her clicked in Ally's mind: *He's a vampire. He's trying to frighten you into not moving. Get out.*

Ally struggled with her wallet and put a dollar on the counter. He never spoke, never blinked, never glanced away, even when he took her dollar and slid the correct change toward her. She looked at his pale hand, his thin tapered fingers, his too long, almost pointed fingernails and the fingertip that rested on the dime, holding it against the countertop.

Again, Pearl's voice echoed in Ally's memory: *He's trying to implant his thoughts into your mind. Get out. Now.*

Ally looked up at him and frowned. The boy smirked at her before taking a step backward. She grabbed her dime, pivoted on her toes and left. Once outside, she ran to the car and scrambled inside, and locked the door.

It was one of her scariest moments since seeing the giant in the woods. She tried to catch her breath, and glanced at the movie screen in the distance. The little girl in "The Night of the Living Dead" had just torn off a man's arm and was gnawing on it as if it was a giant chicken leg. Ally's friend sharing the backseat with her first gasped at the sight, then giggled with nerves.

Ally cringed and shuddered, turned away from the screen. The movie was twice as scary now that she had seen a real, living, breathing, undead working among the living in the drive-in theater. He, it, sold her some popcorn and a Coke, but she was too nervous to take one bite. She handed the snacks to her friend.

Ally turned her back on the horror film and watched out the rear window, fearful the vampire boy may have followed her to the car, would sneak up on them, overpower everyone and have them for dinner.

She tried to tell her friends and the older teenage driver about the vampire boy, but they came to see a scary movie, paid money to see it, were already scared, so no one believed a word she said.

Such environmental awe, mystery and classically gothic pageantry and spectacle were part of the normal backdrop of Ally's life as she grew into a living, breathing Cinderella.

In a world surrounded by and founded upon ancient secrets, Ally slowly came into her own individual awareness. Circumstances change. Within time, she could only stop and listen, remember the words spoken by her beloved grandmothers. She practiced and was able to hit replay in her mind and hear her them speaking to her, softly, slowly, repeating their Knowing, their knowledge, their wisdom. It was a mental exercise Ally began in her adolescent years that would prove helpful in the years ahead, long after she lost both grandmothers to age and illness. This special gift allowed Ally to communicate with them by remembering details of their advice, their words, their warnings – they said they would be there for her in the future and they were right. Their wisdom never left her. Even while still a youngster, Ally often tried it on for size to make sure it still fit, that it grew and strengthened as she grew. Just to hear a tiny whisper of their voices guiding her through the challenges she'd face as a teenager and young adult was a treasured gift and godsend.

* * *

"Obsessed by a fairy tale,
we spend our lives searching for a magic door
and a lost kingdom of peace."

Eugene O'Neill

Chapter 10

Once a year, almost everyone in town participated in what the city officials and volunteers called a pilgrimage. It was really a reenactment of everyday early life in the bayous.

St. Francisville residents dressed in nineteenth-century-style clothing and made all sorts of Cajun and Creole dishes and desserts. There were handcrafts and paintings on display and for sale, and, believe it or not, even stuffed alligators and fried frog legs. It wouldn't have been complete without the locals' favorite: a spicy crawfish boil with new red potatoes, corn on the cob, and pounds of andouille sausage for an extra kick. Even years afterwards, it doesn't take much to stir up the imagination of those delicious fragrances floating over the entire city . . . dozens of giant pots boiling along the riverfront, newspaper-covered tables of steaming crawfish, locals laughing and telling jokes on each other in French and broken English spiced with dollops of Cajun and Tabasco, people dancing to the music performed by several bands, and visitors taste-testing from the tables as they walked around carrying plates piled high with the annual feast. People from all over the United States came to watch, to buy homemade crafts, and to get their fill of the local crawfish and frog legs. It was wonderful.

Of course, the locals would take the visitors on tours of all the community's haunted plantations and mysterious bayous to see the wildlife. Residents gladly gave them a glimpse of how the Cajun and Creole people lived in the swamps and big farms that are called plantations to this day. Most everyone grew up knowing histories of the plantations because they were intertwined with commerce, marriages and families.

Ally was pleased to be getting a bit older, at twelve and three-quarters, and definitely feeling frisky because she was pushing hard on the big official 'teenage thirteen' door. It was a crazy time, and the townsfolk loved it, she included.

Ally was now old enough to work as a tour guide at the Lily Down's Plantation. They actually paid her to wear a lovely long dress with huge hoop skirts. It was impossible to sit down while wearing that dress. She felt like Scarlet O'Hara wearing it, and even imagined herself like Scarlet, holding onto that four-poster bed with her ol' nanny pulling and yanking on the strings of the corset until Miss Scarlet squeezed into that tight get-up. Ally thought perhaps she needed one of those corsets as well. After all, Miss Scarlet caught Rhett Butler. Maybe in those days he was considered good-looking, but now it would have to be someone much more adapted to her likes and dislikes, the modern times.

Sometimes, if some cute teenage boy tourist stared at her, she blushed, obviously feeling foolish wearing that gown. All-in-all though, it was fun. There was no school during the day, lots to eat and see during the night. It was one giant festival for an entire week. Everyone looked and acted as if they were living in another century. Tourists couldn't get enough of the townsfolk: the way they dressed and spoke in a mixture of Cajun, French and English, and offered their wonderful food and peculiar handicrafts for sale.

Some brave tourists usually asked about the darker tales, tales of voodoo practiced by the slaves from two hundred years ago, but, mostly, they wanted to know about the haunted plantations. The bravest always wanted to spend the night in one. Many owners of the old plantations were operating bed and breakfast businesses in their homes.

Ally found it odd and curious that so many tourists wanted to step into those spooky homes for fun. All the people who harbored strong ideas concerning what went on inside the ghostly manors believed as much as the locals knew, and only as much as the tourists were told. They believed everything. Mostly, the locals told it wrong. They kept up the fiction for the prying public, but not the way most people might imagine. In truth, there were far *more* ghosts around than the residents ever revealed.

Ally grew up with ghosts. They weren't strangers to her, but almost daily visitors. She knew exactly what ghosts looked like and knew what ghosts were because her grandmothers taught her about spirits. Her grandmothers wanted to make sure Ally was never afraid. They said a ghost couldn't hurt a live person, that ghosts are only replays or re-enactments of the things or events that happened before the spirit-person left the earth, before they died.

"If a woman baked bread everyday at a certain time," Pearl explained, "then it's a good chance after she's gone, her ghost may still do this same thing."

Whether people believe or do not believe, it doesn't matter. Everyone who grew up in the Louisiana bayous knew about ghosts, and they were a normal discussion topic at the dinner table. Folks spoke about who died and whose ghost someone saw. Details. Everyone always wanted to hear the details.

One evening at dinnertime, Pearl said one of their neighbors saw the Headless Horseman go by, gallop around the corner. Of course, Pearl and Violet wondered aloud about who may have died that afternoon. Regular conversations during dinner in the South's deep bayous often centered around who was dying, who died that day or week, and who saw one of the recently-dead carrying on as usual. It was normal.

Ghosts or no ghosts, what was real, what was tangible, was strange enough.

Some strangeness required exploration by a young adventurous girl, who was officially entering her teenage years in a few weeks.

Thirteen. A number to be reckoned with. It seemed to represent remembering ghosts and Goths and legends of the old bayous' deep swamps and it was a constant subject of conversation when you are thirteen and live in Louisiana. It seemed every child's home was haunted, friends' homes, grandparents' homes were haunted, or someone somewhere lived in a haunted house. For thirteen-year-old girls haunts were cool and were the main topic of discussion. It was almost like an adult conversation where a young person could be bad without really being bad. That was when young girls could tell secrets about all of the haunted areas, who sees the ghosts, and what and which ghosts haunt so-and-so and how often. Details. Details were important.

At almost thirteen, Ally decided she needed independent transportation. She asked for and got a 10-speed bicycle for her birthday. She was thrilled because it gave her a newfound freedom to move around by herself, not attached to an old-fashioned minded grandmother. She could move about the community with a few trusted friends and discover areas her grandmothers never took her to see. That provided several interesting adventures with her new friend, Davie, but she found herself in a bit of trouble because of an innate sense of wonder and curiosity.

Ally and Davie, whose family was involved in oil production, was her first real boyfriend. He liked her far more than she liked him, but he was fun to be with and liked to explore the town as much as she. Every girl at school and around town liked him because he was the richest boy in the entire city; horses, motorbikes, a swimming pool were his everyday playthings. He taught Ally how to swim, had a neat sense of humor, and gave her a different birthday gift: a watermelon.

On the morning of her thirteenth birthday, Ally made a special trip to her private wishing well in the far back of Wildwind. She decided to make a wish for good fortune during her teenage years. That old well was a solid, reassuring touchstone of comfort. Many years later, Ally recounted the serious wishes that were cast into the well's depths, and realized something remarkable: something powerful was there because most of her wishes had come true.

200

There was plenty of opportunity for her to find and know her roots in the small town. There were, of course, wonderful good times as well as scary times. Ally was curious and it often led her straight into trouble.

With or without someone tagging along, thirteen was a serious age to go adventuring down by the old Low Water Creek Bridge. The bridge was only a few feet above the surface; whenever the creek flooded, the bridge was under water. Both grandmothers forbid Ally to go near the place, but she was determined to see it for herself. She and some others planned to meet at a certain place at a certain time on their bikes, and go exploring. Only Davie showed up.

Everyone in town said real witches lived in the old house on the far side of the creek, and they'd been there for years. It was only one of the local tales. Brave to a fault, Ally and Davie decided to check it out firsthand. They left their bikes on the town side, carefully stepped onto the bridge, and slowly crossed to the opposite side of the Low Water Creek. No one in the group ever dared to go there before. They were very disappointed when they didn't find anything suspicious.

Within another year and another birthday, Davie began hanging out with a certain girl at school. That didn't bother Ally too much because he wasn't much of a true boyfriend in the first place. She did miss their bike rides together, though.

Another local tale was about three witches who supposedly lived in a house on an old back road. Ally rode her bicycle past the property almost daily. It was set so far back and so much lower in the woods that people could barely see the structure without leaving the road, without stepping onto the property.

Huge trees almost hid the building, overgrown vines and hedges nearly covered the old place. The only things visible were a rusted tin roof and a small section of a cracked, whitewashed wall that was aged to a dirty brown. There were tall windows on the stone house that seemed to go from the top of the room to the floor. People said it was a "century home," meaning it was probably a hundred or more years old. It looked like a place where witches would live. Very creepy. How could anyone live there? At least anyone who was not a refugee from a classical Gothic H. P. Lovecraft tale of corrupted locals peering queerly from curiously angled windows, under weirdly sloping gambrel roofs.

There probably wasn't much more than a narrow footpath from the road to the house; no driveway. It was a very large structure, judging from what was visible from the road. An ancient sign that read BEWARE dangled from an old pole and blew back and forth in the wind like a weather vane. It made a crinkly-rasping noise — a scary enough warning for most people.

According to the locals, no one was brave enough to walk down the footpath to to see inside the house, to see if anyone was dead or alive. It was private property and plainly stated, DO NOT ENTER. Also according to the tale, anyone who went in there to check on the occupants was never seen again.

Every day when Ally rode her bike past the entrance, she only thought about: *don't ever go there, especially on a full moon night, or on All Hallows' Eve.*

That place was a definite no-no. Whenever Ally asked, Pearl always said, "There are lots of goings-on there. Stay away." Ally believed her. It was a place to avoid. She knew her limits. She knew what to stay clear of, where not to go. After all, this was Louisiana where most people believed in dark tales, some experienced dark tales, some survived dark tales, and some even practiced dark things. Ally had already seen enough weird people up close, one or two could have been a witch, one could have been a vampire, and ghosts moving around the old plantations in her neighborhood – she didn't want to add more to her list.

"All in all," as Pearl said, "there are tales and then there are . . . tales."

To Ally, there just seemed to be more in Louisiana than anywhere else.

"We must teach our children to dream

with their eyes open."

Harry Edwards

Chapter 11

Tales, tall or otherwise, voodoo, vampires and haunted plantations are all part of Louisiana's history. Ally never dwelled too hard on any of it, keeping it hidden safely away in the back of her mind until one afternoon when curiosity got the best of her.

Since she rode her bicycle all over town, she could generally find herself in the right place at the right time. Ally learned a great deal by sitting off to the side in the shadows, staying quiet, trying to be as small as possible, and listening to the grown-ups as carefully as she could.

One day, she found the town's leading ladies sitting on the veranda of Mrs. Cotton's popular café, planning the upcoming pilgrimage. Ally got herself a cool drink and settled into a corner to wait, knowing it wouldn't take long before the ladies' conversation turned serious. The women were gently debating whether or not the Myrtles would be listed on the tour that season.

They all knew Ally, and they knew she kept secrets. They also knew Ally's grandmother Pearl knew each one of them and all their secrets. They didn't dare shoo Ally away.

One elderly lady said the Myrtles had plenty of tall – wrong – tales about a slave woman and a lethal birthday cake. She said the truth was much sadder because of so many natural deaths from sickness, especially yellow fever, over the centuries. All the women agreed.

Almost everyone in St. Francisville knew the Myrtles began just like most of the other plantations; hundreds of acres planted in sugarcane and rice. Farming with hurricanes blowing through and destroying crops almost every year wasn't an easy life.

Ally's ears perked up when one older lady said her great-great-grandmother kept a diary and kept track of the news of the day. The book and family stories were handed down through the generations.

Everyone in town knew the basic history: David Bradford built Laurel Grove in 1796, but he didn't fetch his family until 1799. Bradford practiced and taught law there, and a student, Clark Woodruff, married Bradford's daughter Sarah Mathilda. When old man Bradford died, Woodruff managed the place for his mother-in-law, Elizabeth Bradford. Woodruff and Sarah Mathilda had three children: Cornelia Gale, a son James, and Mary Octavia.

They were living there when the yellow fever epidemics struck down someone in almost every family in the region. The mother, Sarah Mathilda, died on July 21, 1823, the son James died about a year later on July 15, 1824, then the girl Cornelia Gale died two months afterwards. The mother-in-law, Elizabeth Bradford, died there in April 1835.

Ally shuttered. She had heard some of those tales before, but listening to how all those deaths came so close to each other made chills run up and down her arms. All the ladies reckoned Mr. Woodruff needed to get away from the place after losing most of his family, and that's why he sold the place to Ruffin Stirling.

They talked about Stirling remodeling the house, making it much bigger, and changing its name to the Myrtles before he died four years later, in July 1854. Ruffin's eldest son, Lewis, died of yellow fever a few months later, in October 1854.

Worse of all was that five of the Stirling's nine children died there. That bit of news made Ally sad: eight – so many children died in the house. No wonder she heard so many children's voices. Yellow Fever swept through the black families as well; everyone had losses; everyone grieved.

Sadness was everywhere in that house, locked into the very walls. It even explained some of the noises Ally heard coming from the old house and grounds when she was walking on the dirt road between the two properties.

According to that old diary, Ruffin Stirling's widow, Mary, gave the Myrtles to her daughter Sarah and her son-in-law William Drew Winter before she died in December 1865. The War Between the States devastated the South. Mr. Winter was bankrupt by 1867 and had to sell the Myrtles. Somehow, his wife Sarah managed to buy it back two years later.

Death struck the place again: On January 26, 1871, an unknown horseman came riding up the road and called William Winter out onto the veranda, saying there was some business they needed to discuss. Winter was shot and killed on the porch. The murderer simply rode off.

Ally almost held her breath when she learned about the murder. It explained why she heard a horse gallop up and down the road in the afternoons when no one was out riding. It also explained why she heard a loud bang once in awhile.

The lady with the diary said the widow, Sarah Winter, probably died of a broken heart in April 1878. Everyone agreed, then someone said she was only forty-four years of age. Ally thought forty-four was really old. Sarah's mother, Mary Stirling, died two years later. Ally figured that woman must have been ancient.

The place changed hands several times between 1880 and the 1970s, when it was owned first by Arlin Dease, then by James and Frances Kermeen Myers.

One of the newer ladies to the community asked about the rumors, about all the magazine stories and television shows, and about the Yankee looters who were killed at the Myrtles. Several ladies laughed, saying most of those rumors were fanciful tales made up to impress people, and was like similar stories around town to attract customers for the bed and breakfast businesses. The lady with the diary was very matter-of-fact: no slave's ear was cut off, and she never poisoned a birthday cake with oleander leaves, and everyone in town knew the homeowner was a very pious gentleman.

The group admitted that a later owner, Frances Myers, claimed in 1987 she was sleeping in a downstairs bedroom when awakened by a black woman wearing a green turban and a long dress. Ms. Myers said the black woman was standing beside her bed with a metal candlestick and lit candle in her hand. The ladies decided this real ghost was probably the shadowy figure captured in a much-publicized photograph of the back of the house.

Ally curled up tighter, staying small and silent in the porch shadows, pondering those tales. She realized there was a lot more to the Myrtles' history that was next door to her Wildwind. She thought about each story and decided most of the cries she heard whenever she was on the dirt road between the two properties or visited the Myrtles were probably people grieving over their loved ones who died of yellow fever. At least nine children died there, so mothers and fathers, maybe grandparents, would cry, too. Ally just wished the baby's cries weren't so loud all the time. At least it explained the galloping sounds, the gunshot, and seeing a man crumple on the side veranda. Ally was always glad to see him get up and walk away. Some of the adult ghosts drifted along the porches where they sat and rocked in the rockers, but some came into the bedrooms and watched Ally's friend and her during their sleepovers. Ally didn't like that part. The older ghost children played under the trees in the yard, the younger ones played in the old nursery. One of the children or an older spirit rocked the baby cradle for a long time. Ally was sympathetic, but wished the baby would stop crying all night — it kept her awake.

Of course, it was impossible not to think about any of the old tales whenever the ladies got together over afternoon tea to

212

talk about the stories they heard or their own memories of being inside, or of what went on in the deep bayous. Ally always wanted to know what happened because she loved history, especially about her bayou home. She wanted to know everything. It was like taking someone's advice not to think about a purple ostrich with orange stripes. Now, just how well did *that* go?

Since it was next door, Ally knew the Myrtles Plantation well. It was named for all the crepe myrtles growing there. It was a graceful, two-story design, a white home with large green shutters and big door-sized windows. The veranda stretched from one end to the other across the front, and, as was often the case with such homes, down the sides so the windows could be opened to allow breezes, and for people to sit and cool off in the shade. Dormer windows were on the second floor.

Many shade trees, crepe myrtles and live oaks, which weren't scary at all, filled the yards. The house looked quite normal.

Ally wasn't afraid of any ghost. She had seen them, heard them, and dealt with them since a small child. Having ghosts about was normal.

Many people said that perhaps it was just the Myrtles growing older and the building settling deeper onto its foundation – nothing to be too scared of, right? *Wrong!* When it came to this particular old home, nothing was normal. As a youngster, Ally found the Myrtles a real challenge because of all the noises, and the things she saw.

A new family took up residence, but rumors were they wouldn't be there long; no one ever stayed at the Myrtles for long. Even if they owned it, even if they planned to farm the land, families would eventually establish alternative living quarters elsewhere in town. Stories of the old home's being haunted were true — the haunts just weren't the same ghosts popularized in articles and television programs. Ally saw and heard the real ones.

Ally was one child in the community who always tested the waters. Growing up with two wise grandmothers who saw it all and knew it all taught her not to wander very far into the unknown, or into the woods alone, especially after she saw the giant as a very young child. She knew not to search out the witches or the vampires. It was best to leave them be, whether anyone else thought they were real or not. Ally Knew. Leave them be.

Just the name, the Myrtles conjures up many fond and uneasy memories. That old place was almost in Wildwind's backyard – the properties were adjacent. A small dirt road joined the Myrtles property to the Wildwind's property. According to numerous magazine articles and even television shows of so-called paranormal investigations, the Myrtles was supposed to be one of America's most haunted plantations – actually, one of the most haunted in the world.

Ghosts were one thing. Vampires were another big to-do, not only in New Orleans but in every other bayou area. It was said they hid in the bigger cities so people wouldn't discover them – they blend in easier in crowds, especially sitting in corners of dreary barrooms. Modern vampires, people said, hung out in the famed nightclubs of old New Orleans where many curiosity seekers spend hours listening to music. Some of those tourists or hangers-on were never seen again. Also creepy, but also true. They simply vanished.

The famous author, Anne Rice, wrote bestselling novels about vampires. Rice was always a main character of the Mardi Gras parades each year, riding in her trademark coffin, of course.

This was a traditional time. Everyone participated, and wore costumes. Some people chose something graceful, like a queen or Peter Pan or other fanciful characters, lots of glitter, lots of feathers, lots of color and shiny beads.

Ally was always Cinderella, escorted by her prince of the moment, or month, or season. She was finally fourteen-years-old, almost fifteen, so she could attend the costume balls. Everyone lived their favorite fairytale or fantasy at Mardi Gras. Some came as swamp beasts, and some came as characters from Camelot or Shakespeare. People were always expensively attired and attended huge parties hosted by wealthy people who tried to out-do each other with the most lavish buffets scattered over numerous patios, lots of servants, and several bands playing. Even the state's governor hosted some of those elaborate parties. Tradition.

Mardi Gras: mysterious times. Ally always wondered if, beneath the costumes, people attempted to depict who they really were in their souls, or if their costume depicted who they wanted to be. It was interesting and fun to guess about the people's choice of costumes every year. Of course, Ally was always Cinderella in the production.

For a Louisiana resident, it was the best of times. Students got out of school for the week. They went to the parades and most of the fancy parties. It was a fun time, if they remembered to stay away from the places frequented by vampires.

Those in their mid-teens were allowed a little more freedom, they could hang out in groups in town, go to movies together, and the girls enjoyed sleepovers with their girlfriends. Neighborhood boys would sneak out after dark by climbing out of their bedroom windows, and hightail it to their girlfriend's house. They'd toss small stones against the girl's window to get them to open it, hand them a flower, a card, or a handwritten note.

That made a different and difficult problem for the girls. They had to know exactly who was on the outside of their house long before they'd open their window. The girls learned early on to know to whom they opened their window. They were warned never to open their window at night if a young man came calling . . . they could be opening it to the Darkest of the Dark. Everyone knew vamps roamed at night, but so did the cute, brave boys who would sneak out to risk being out after dark to steal a kiss through an open window or to hand-deliver a special note.

It was romantic. Innocent. Dangerous.

* * *

"Children are the living messages
we send to a time we will not see."

John W. Whitehead

Chapter 12

Word quickly got around town that a new family had bought the Myrtles Plantation. Ally hadn't seen or met the new owners, and it was almost time for the next school year to start. The town gossips said there were a boy and a girl about Ally's age, who would attend the same school.

Joch Van Fanshau was a handsome young man whose family moved from France to buy the grand old estate. He and his twin sister, Janelle, lived with their parents – a happy family. Perfect. Right? Well, that remained to be seen.

It only took Ally three seconds to spot the young man from France. Students at St. Martin's Academy wore uniforms. Drab khaki-color slacks and pale blue shirts for the guys made every boy look alike. Girls wore blue-on-blue plaid skirts with a white blouse. It was easy to dress in the mornings because no decisions were made, but students felt dull and ugly, especially Ally, who craved vibrancy.

The moment Ally saw Joch coming around a corner at school, she lost her breath. She didn't notice the ugly khaki slacks or the plain blue shirt. All she saw was a tall, dark-haired guy with a floppy hairstyle, who brushed by her on his way to a classroom. He glanced at her with a strong sense of what's called 'knowing.' Ally's breath left her lungs in a gush of disbelief.

All the girls at school who weren't going steady with someone almost passed out from hyperventilating while staring at Joch. It was obvious he wouldn't be unattached for long, as each girl would be out to win his affections. And, oh, how Ally hated to admit it even to herself, but she daydreamed of him during class. He even looked like drawings of the Handsome Prince from her favorite fairytale, *Cinderella*. Perhaps Joch was a real prince. Since he practically lived in her backyard, Ally planned to walk in the woods behind Wildwind more often, quite often, like a lot, perhaps several times a day.

Ally wouldn't lock eyes with Joch, only a quick hard glance, just long enough that she stopped breathing. She wasn't about to act as if she was interested in him, or like the girls who were drooling over him. How boring. How ordinary. Oh, no, she was going to let all the silly girls fawn over him — they were always so glamorous and languid, something she never pretended to be. Ally planned to be disinterested in the French prince. *Why?* That was just her attitude then. She did not want him, if he was not truly for her. But Ally could feel his presence without looking in his direction when he walked past her to go to his next class.

Ally was ready to pack her clothes and move to France. She had no idea there was any boy anywhere on the planet who looked like Joch. But, Ally's viewpoint was limited since she hadn't ever been anywhere outside the Louisiana bayou.

She realized she needed to get out more often and farther away. Shortly after Joch walked down the hall, she saw a stunning girl, tall, dark hair, very tanned as if she was a born sun bronzer coming up the hallway. The girl looked almost identical to Joch. Here were two newcomers, a clan of gorgeous people who looked alike. Ally wondered how many more were going to walk through the door.

All the girls giggled, whispered and made eyes at the boy from France, the teacher introduced them as twins, Joch and Janelle, as new students at the private academy and asked the students to introduce themselves after class.

Ally complied. She introduced herself to Janelle, and told her she lived next door to the Myrtles and would be happy to befriend her, tell her about the neighborhood, spend time together. All the other girls gathered around the French Prince, giggling. He seemed to be a bit uncomfortable, grabbing onto his top shirt button as if to loosen it a bit. After school, Ally walked swiftly to her car, determined not to be among those slobbering over him.

Joch wouldn't have noticed, but most of the boys were taken with Ally/ There were plenty to choose from, any one she wanted. Ally knew it wasn't because of her looks – it was charm and wit. And fairy dust. There was a magical, inner glow, an 'illumination' her grandmothers said, about Ally.

Pearl always told her, "Shine your light." Ally knew exactly how to shine, but she was saving it for a rainy day.

Several days went by and she only had the first class with Joch. Her friends only talked about which one was going to get the French Prince, and were curious why she hadn't made a move.

"I'm not interested."

"Hello?" Leanna said. "That's impossible. No woman alive wouldn't be interested, Ally. What's wrong with you? Don't want competition?"

"Yeah, something like that," Ally said, then smiled.

Somehow Ally managed not to let the world know she was falling for the French Prince just like everyone else.

How could she hide that inner light when her feet wouldn't stay on the ground when she was in the same room with him? It was worse lying in bed knowing she only had to walk out her back door, into the woods apiece, across the yard to the back of his house and up to his bedroom. She was tempted to get goggles and sit in a tree.

Ally was certain Renee' would get Joch anyway. Renee' was model tall, pencil thin, had long, shiny brown hair with natural highlights, tanned, perfect legs, and she enticed every boy until they were hers and then she dumped them a few weeks later. Christa was another beautiful girl, an oversized blonde, who wore her skirts a little shorter and her tops a bit tighter than everyone else, and who always unbuttoned the extra button and let every single guy know she was ready and willing.

These two superficial divas were Ally's cheerleading teammates. Yet Ally remained self-confident. She never worked to get attention – it flowed to her naturally. She knew she only had to be patient. In the meantime, phone numbers and personal notes went flying back and forth to the French Prince, who seemed enchanted by all the attention. He smiled when he opened the notes, but Ally never saw him put one in his pocket. They were left on his desk, either accidentally or by design.

Almost a week passed and Ally hadn't introduced herself or spoken to him. Time to take that walk in the woods that joined the two properties. She was merely walking along when he literally ran smack-dab into her. He came to a sudden stop a second before knocking her down.

He stood there, shocked to find a pretty, young blonde walking on what he thought was his private road. He straightened his shoulders and got a little huffy and arrogant. "I am so sorry, but I did not expect to run into anyone on my property. I run every day, and thought this was our property."

Ally didn't expect a rude introduction. "You're right. It *is* private property, but it's *my* property that you're standing on."

He caught his breath. "What?" He leaned over to take a second look. "Oh, I recognize you now. You're the girl in my classroom who ignores me."

Ally laughed. "I really don't think you have to worry about being ignored with Jessie, Alicia, Renee', Christa and other girls trying to occupy your time." Ally stepped back and nodded. "It seems to me you're fitting in just fine here, 'France Boy.'"

Joch chuckled at the joke, then formally introduced himself with an apology. That was when their eyes locked. He took hold of her hand for what seemed to be an eternity. She was suddenly breathless, light-headed, as if her knees weren't going to support her. It was in that very moment she realized what was happening, and quickly snatched her hand from his.

"Yes, it's, it's, nice here, and I think, you'll love, uh, I mean, like it here." Ally's cheeks turned crimson because the words wouldn't come out right. Embarrassing.

Joch stared at her as intensely as she stared at him. They both felt as though that moment in time was, well, *was.* What else is there to say when one runs into a prince on the back road of *your* home, in *your* forest, on *your* trail? What else is there left to say? Either way, it was obvious, and the romance between them ignited like Fourth of July fireworks.

Ally and Joch laughed at each other and suspected where it was going.

"France boy? What is up with your attitude?

Ally apologized. "How could you notice anyone ignoring you, with all the girls giving you their phone numbers and asking if you were going to the prom? Which one of my cheerleader friends did you choose to take to the prom?"

There was a boyish grin on Joch's face as they walked along. "I haven't yet. I hoped you might ask me."

"Yea, right, Joch. I don't ask guys to proms. I wait for my own invitation."

"Well, I understand from talk in the boys locker room that the quarterback of the football team asked you to the prom."

Ally shook her head.

"Really? What about Bentley, who owns the big cattle ranch? He certainly has a thing for you."

Ally laughed. "Yeah, Bentley is very cute and maybe, but no."

" 'Maybe, but no?' Is that suppose to be an answer?"

"Yes." She laughed again.

"Oh, I see. You're going to keep me guessing, aren't you? I don't know all who there is yet. So, ah, Ally, let me ask you a question: yes or no."

She waited with anticipation. "Okay."

"Have you chosen someone to go to the prom with, or are you dating someone from another school? Am I way off-base, period? Maybe you have a boyfriend in college or something?"

"Boy, you French boys ask a lot of questions, don't you?"

"Yes or no."

"Yes and no what?"

Joch had a puzzled expression. "You are such a mystery girl."

"Okay. No, I don't have a boyfriend," Ally replied. "I sort of had one, but it was one-sided. And, yes, he goes to another private school in Baton Rouge. We've been friends for a long time, but he wasn't for me. I recently broke it off.

"As far as the quarterback goes, yes, he asked me to the prom and so did Bentley."

"Which one did you choose?"

Ally giggled and wanted to keep him in suspense longer, but couldn't. "Neither."

"What?"

"That is what I said."

"Do you plan to attend at all?" Jock asked.

"I certainly hoped so."

"And you are going without a date?"

Ally frowned. *What was this Frenchman doing? Was he trying to ask her to go, or not trying to ask, or had he decided to take another girl?*

Ally stopped in the middle of dirt road and looked up at him. "Why? Were *you* planning to go alone?"

Joch grabbed Ally's hand. "Not if you will do me the honor . . ."

Ally was happily stunned by the elegant way he asked, and became flustered. She didn't want to ruin this event in her life by blurting out a simple word, 'yes.'

Despite her head spinning, she managed to mutter, "I would be honored as well to do you the honor to go to our prom."

Ally frowned. *Uh, did I say that right? The words just tumbled out sideways.*

Joch smiled. "Is that a yes?"

She laughed. "Uh-huh. Yes, I mean."

230

"You really do have a problem with yes and no, but it's kind of cute."

He was still holding Ally's hand. "Oh, sorry, I didn't realize I claimed your hand, mademoiselle."

Ally's nerves were too far gone by this point. "I have to go now, Joch." She scurried toward Wildwind, turned back and asked, "See you tomorrow, Joch?"

"Same place, mademoiselle."

Ally stopped running and looked back.

Joch bowed, his hand across his stomach with his other hand extended out to one side.

Ally found herself in a living dream. "Yes, Joch; here, tomorrow after school, same time."

What made her run? Ally didn't know, but felt she needed to get away to catch her breath and think.

School came early the next morning for Ally because of a short night with little sleep. First period class even felt different. All of her friends were adoring Joch, but he only looked at her across the room. She smiled back. It didn't take long before everyone saw the rainbow-colored electricity that streamed between the two.

After class, Janelle said, in front of everyone, that Jock had asked Ally to the prom. She asked if Ally would come for dinner that night to meet their parents.

Nothing more was said. No friendly banter, no comments, but there were many disappointed expressions. Joch was shy and it was several days before they acted like a couple.

After that, Ally's friends disappeared and the whispering behind her back began to get louder. Ally ignored everyone but Joch and Janelle, who became her new best friends. It seemed she lost her girlfriends because she 'betrayed' them by falling for Joch and he for her. Petty.

Days became shorter and the evenings longer as Ally spent most evenings at the Myrtles Plantation. During the summer, she and Janelle became close friends, and Ally stayed many a night at the Myrtles with Janelle and, as typical teenagers, they sat up half the night talking and giggling. Ally was close to her prince although she was a bit frightened by the ghost baby's loud cries at night, and the scary portrait of a man whose eyes followed people around the room. There were other noises in the house, and lights went out on their own. Ally girded herself to be strong, refusing to let ghosts frighten her away.

Ally and Joch spent romantic evenings together, she learned a great deal more French than the Cajun she had known since birth, and Joch learned about Louisiana customs, vampires and ghosts. They shared hayrides, cruises on river boats, watched moonlight dance on the Mississippi from the ferry landing, and toured historic plantations. Ally helped Janelle get past a spirit that disturbed her personal objects and a very scary moment when one of the ghosts locked her bedroom door.

As Fate would have it, theirs was a short-lived romance. There came that time, like every other time before with every other family that tried to live at the Myrtles, when it was indisputably time to leave. There was a business in France. They had had more than enough of Louisiana. They missed their huge manor house, and their much nicer ghosts. They made up their minds, packed up and were ready to leave.

Joch and Ally said their good-byes, knowing in their hearts they'd never see each other again. They clung to each other in a long good-bye kiss and many tears, standing in the same spot on the little private road where they first met.

Ally was so angry with herself. She had cast numerous wishes in her private well for a prince, but hadn't wished for him to stay. Oh, they promised they'd find each other when they got older. Joch said he'd come for her. She said she'd wait. They said their last good-byes and looked back at each other through tears one last time as his family urged Joch to hurry.

The family fled back to France and Ally pined away in her room. She wished her grandmothers could console her with their wisdom and love, but they weren't able to stem the pain. No one could.

School friends slowly warmed up to her, saying they were sorry it didn't work out. Beneath the surface, they seemed bitter and kept their distance, seemingly enjoying her pain rather than consoling her. Most forgot Ally could tune in to their energy, she Knew they were laughing behind her back. One even ventured to think that if she couldn't have Joch, it was a good thing he went back to France. Ally avoided her from then on.

Although Ally won the prince's heart, it no longer mattered. Ally's heart was in France with Joch, and his heart was with her in Louisiana. She didn't want her heart back; she wanted him. France was a universe away from the bayou.

Letters rushed back and forth, came and went for months, then gradually faded to a trickle. Joch invited her to come be with him and his family, to finish her education in Europe, but her duty was to her aging grandmothers then. She was willingly tied to Wildwind. Letters from France slowed, then quit. Ally couldn't understand why Joch hadn't written with his new address or had called. Many months later, Ally's half-sister Jade confessed to hiding Joch's letters whenever she visited their elderly grandmothers.

Somehow, Ally felt in her heart Joch hadn't forgotten her and knew he'd never forget her. He'd always remember the jog he took one day and ran into a beautiful blonde in the woods, who called him "French boy." He'd recall the plans they made of being together for eternity just like the New Orleans vampires that live forever.

Ally's heart and spirit grew stronger when she learned Joch wrote to her after all. She was more determined than ever to lay a solid foundation for her own successful future on her own terms. She would be free to travel, to find him in France or wherever he was.

Dreams haunted Ally, dreams of the crying baby at the Myrtles, ghosts moving things, galloping horses and gunshots, of holding hands with Joch and walking in the woods.

Young love is fool-hearty and carefree, without worries. It is pure, natural and unscathed with time's cruel embrace. It is true in every manner of its being, in its awareness of every thought and breath and touch, and is as special as the first snowflake that falls on a couple's first Christmas together, the first realization that true love exists in the heart of the adored person. That is when time itself stops and lets the whole world see two people shine in one light.

Her grandmothers told her more than once they believed she'd grow up to marry a real prince, but it would not happen for many moons. Ally felt it was already many moons, but her prince had flown away with her heart in his hand.

All Ally could do was cry and grieve for what she lost, had hoped for, had wished for. Gone. Joch and her dreams vanished in an instant. Even as a young teenager, she knew she must create her own happiness. Somehow, it would be up to her to find and make it on her own. Alone.

* * *

"The future lies before you, like paths of pure white snow.
Be careful how you tread it, for every step will show."

Anonymous

Chapter 13

Unless there was desperate need, no one ever wanted to go to a particular ancient rice plantation in a bayou outside of New Orleans. Notorious for an old woman's mysteriousness and uncanny accuracy at predicting peoples futures, only those brave enough to deal with the fright she stirred in their soul would make the journey through the forests and swamps to reach the old house.

Slithering marsh creatures and alligator gar large enough to swallow a bait bucket patrolled the murky tannic water that rippled around the cypress trees and higher land. Isolated by design, the property's dank air burned nostrils, Spanish moss veiled every tree branch, and alien noises emanated from the dense, untouched woods. People were warned to stay in their boat until they could step onto the pier, or in their car along the dirt driveway.

Blistered by summer heat and lashed by storms, the main house's walls had nothing more than a memory of ever being whitewashed. It was an unfriendly, unwelcoming face of a building, but still the desperate came – nothing could keep them away. For some, it was the only solution.

The weathered board-and-batten house looked abandoned but wasn't. The screen door hung at an odd angle from one hinge, a breeze blew it open and let it slam, as if someone came and went from some long ago day. Salt-laden grime coated every window from decades of seaborne storms, trash and yard debris littered the porch.

Overgrown hedges scraped both sides of Ally's car; anything, animal or human, could easily hide only a foot away. She touched the brake pedal and slowed the car to a crawl. "No, no, no. . . . I don't like this place one bit."

"It's gonna be okay," Cheree replied. "My aunt said it was scary on this side, to drive 'round back."

"Hmm . . . okay, but one wrong thing and I'm out of here."

"Yeah. Me, too."

The long driveway guided vehicles from the highway around the main house to a rear clearing where numerous cars and pickup trucks were parked. The backyard was completely different compared to the front, perhaps a deceptive move to eliminate the weak of heart early on. A white picket fence separated the old mansion from the crowd assembled in the busy yard and parking lot. Algae-covered stone benches were under the mature trees, birdbaths were scattered among the blooming flowerbeds, honeysuckle clambered over the wild blackberry bushes, its fragrance filling the air.

The honeysuckle kindled a childhood memory of Wildwind summers. Ally's grip on the steering wheel relaxed a bit. She and Cheree were surprised to see so many people waiting to see the elderly lady known by the only name she proclaimed to have: Sara. People from miles around sought her, similar to a pilgrimage for the young to set their life's course or for the older ones to rationalize their past.

A shanty, nothing more than planks of rough, gray-weathered barn wood nailed together snuggled against a tree line behind the dilapidated mansion. Ally parked the car, the two teenagers chose a stone bench and looked over the crowd. Mature Cajun women with babes hanging on their hips, pretty young Creole women, and several men were there. Everyone patiently waiting in the humid New Orleans weather was fanning himself or herself with anything they could find. Sweat, from either the heat or nerves, dripped off everyone. It was probably one-hundred degrees the day Ally and her friend waited for two hours for their turn. The stifling heat was getting the best of everyone who wanted to hear what the ninety-three year-old legendary oracle had to say about them, their future, their chance at happiness in life, or worse.

A woman, who seemed to be in charge, gave individuals and small groups of people instructions and signaled them when it was their turn. She walked over to Ally and Cheree and lowered her voice.

"Glad y'all could come see Miz Sara. You been here before?"

The girls shook their heads.

"All right then. Here's what you gonna do. Open your mind, prepare it to hear the unexpected when you step into the darkness. There'll be one lit candle on a small table. It will be the only light in there – there's no window. Sara will be in her rocking chair in the corner. She's ancient, so sometimes her voice is very soft. Listen with your ears and your heart.

"When you step inside, follow her directions, don't say a word and don't give her any information; no details. When she tells you to leave, get up and get out of there that minute. She's old and doesn't have time to dillydally around with folks. She can be gruff at times, so do what she says when she says it.

"Understand what I'm telling you?"

They nodded, but the instructions gave Ally the heebie-jeebies. "What does she use, Tarot cards, a crystal ball, read tea leaves? How can she, if it's dark?"

"Miz Sara don't ever touch any of that stuff." She turned on her heel and approached another group.

According to local legend, the old woman had the extraordinary gift of seeing into one's future without any device whatsoever.

"You know what's really scary 'bout all this," Cheree asked and answered in the same breath, "there's no magic involved. It's all from her, from her mind, from whatever source she taps into and understands. That's what she tells people."

On this one day, Guinevere Alina and Patricia stepped into a shanty and walked through the threshold of time. Little did they know that their lives would never be the same.

Far more than rumor, decades-old legends held that Sara herself was similar to the fairytale about an old woman who lived in a shoe. As improbable as it was, Sara's main house, outbuildings of sheds and barns, and the shape of the driveway completed the design: from high above, the property was shaped exactly like a shoe.

Ally instantly felt at home with anything that had to do with shoes. Already convinced she was a modern day Cinderella, Ally thought running headlong into another fairytale was almost normal. There were times when she suspected that, instead of being born, perhaps she had stepped out of a fairytale and was living the adventures of the real Cinderella – her life, even as early as her teen years, seemed to play out as such.

Ally's Cinderella adventures were never dull, never a boring moment. Strange and wonderful characters presented themselves just as they did for Dorothy as she skipped down the yellow brick road. Ally's 'road' turned out to be a dirt one that led to a small shanty in an old lady's backyard.

The girls thought it was odd Sara did all her seeing into the future in that shanty. It wasn't more than a tiny shack barely large enough for four people to be inside at the same time – if they stood.

The crowd thinned somewhat and the woman in charge of the proceedings wandered back to tell them more. "Miz Sara sits in a rocking chair in one corner and there's a white candle beside her."

"You told us that already," Cheree's lips tried to form a smile, but trembled.

The woman stared at her for several long seconds. "You done now, missy?"

Cheree nodded.

"Good. About four feet away from Miz Sara is a small wooden chair. That's where you're going to sit down. She never touches anyone and you don't touch her. She never talks very long, so listen carefully. That's about it for now." The woman walked away.

"Whew . . . she's some kinda friendly," Cheree shook her head. "I asked my aunt about something I'd heard. Sometimes, this ol' Sara lady sits and she'll have her few thoughts without saying anything, not a word, to whoever is in there with her. According to my aunt, Sara saying nothing is the scariest part of going inside."

"Why? That doesn't make any sense," Ally replied.

"Well, legend has it that if you take a chance on seeing her and she says nothing – if she sits there for a while but don't say nothing and asks you to leave – it means there's nothing to tell. Your life is over. You haven't got any future at all. You're done."

"Oh." Ally sat back and considered that prospect. "I'm sure it would be a shock to anybody to be told their life was over.

Why, they might not make it all the way back home before something awful happened."

"That's exactly what my aunt said. Ol' Miz Sara's silence is a bad omen, the worse there could be."

They stared at each other for a moment, both thinking about leaving even before seeing the old woman. Everyone who was milling about or sitting around the courtyard whispered back and forth, as if it was sanctified ground near some church. They, too, were probably frightened of not what Sara would tell them, but if she had nothing to say at all.

The two young women concentrated on studying the people who were about to step inside and then noticing any changes in their expression when they came out. Some changes were dramatic, others were not, while still others were pale, as if the breath had been yanked out of them.

Most of them came out without an expression on their face the girls could easily read. They had gone inside the shanty very human and had come out completely drained, stiff, stunned, a robot. They stepped back into the bright sunlight, blink a couple of times, then rush to get across the parking lot to their car, ignoring the people who still waited, never saying a word to anyone, never laughing or giggling, no humor, no crying. Obviously, they had been struck by something strong.

This was serious stuff.

Finally, it was Ally's turn. She was a bit afraid of what she would hear or wouldn't hear. She was more than a bit skeptical because she had never cared for psychics, card readers or fortunetellers. At seventeen and reared by two older, wise women who had their own *Knowing*, and who had passed that gift down to Ally who had her own *Knowing* since she was four years old, Ally was not about to be fooled. She steeled her heart before she stood, before she began walking to the shanty, because she did not appreciate anyone 'strewing their knowledge' on her, as Demi Moore's character said in the movie, "The Butcher Wife."

Perhaps it was her imagination, but Ally's two grandmothers began whispering in her ear, saying they never approved of hoodoo magic. It didn't feel like hoodoo magic to Ally. It was a comfort, more like a wise older woman who was much like her own beloved grandmothers, who were blessed with *Knowing* and with wisdom. That was the only reason she had decided to come with Cheree, and to see if Miz Sara really had the gift, the Sight. Some people had such gifts. If those gifts were used in the right light, in correct ways to help people, then it was never harmful.

Ally allowed herself to feel the energy in the area, if it was positive or negative. There was nothing negative or bad near the house or the shanty. It felt right in her heart. That was her logic in learning what old Sara would tell her, if anything at all.

Reading tarot cards, peering into crystal balls, reading palms and such things were out of the question. Ally's grandmothers had taught well and long from her earliest days that all the power and wisdom one needs comes from within one's self, from one's soul, to listen to what one's heart says – it may be a small voice, but it is real – pay attention and listen closer.

"You're next." The woman pointed at Ally.

Uh-oh. Suddenly, Ally was full of doubt about taking her turn.

Cheree's slightly twisted smile had traces of fear and nerves. "Go on."

Ally gathered her courage as she approached the shanty. Butterflies flitted about in her stomach, then a ladybug landed on her arm, to rest, to take a ride, perhaps to go along on a new adventure. Everyone knows ladybugs are a good luck sign, so Ally let the insect come along.

When she slowly walked across the shanty's threshold, she felt a hint of a cool breeze in the summer's late afternoon. It was as if she was being transported into something new, yet ancient.

"Good evening." It was a woman's soft voice from a dark corner. "Seat yourself and be quiet. No talking."

Flickering candlelight indicated movement, so the woman really was in a rocking chair. Ally squinted into the dimness as she fumbled in the darkness to find and lower herself onto the wooden chair. In a few seconds, her eyes began to adjust and she could see the woman's outline, then saw the old woman's eyes were closed tightly. Ally couldn't tell if the woman could see her, if age had nearly blinded her.

For a brief moment, Ally was frightened, ready to jump and run. Time felt as if it raced onward, spiraling, she could hardly breathe; silence dominated the shack other than the creaking of that antique rocker.

Ally caught her breath. *Oh, crap! I'm one of those with no future.*

The old woman began to speak slowly, saying odd things Ally didn't understand. "You will not marry the blond-headed fellow."

Ally was surprised. She *was* going steady with a young man who had blond hair . . . engaged to be engaged sometime in the future.

"You're going to meet a brown headed fellow with five letters in his name. His middle name is the same name as a town," she said. "He'll be very tall, have dark wavy hair, and he'll be the most handsome man you ever did see. You'll fall deeply in love and will marry . . ."

Silence stretched into the darkness.

"No! It won't happen. . . ."

"What? What won't happen?"

"Don't talk. Be silent, girl.

"The marriage . . . it won't happen. He'll be killed in a car accident; tragic."

Instantly on alert, Ally's back straightened. She already didn't like this woman, and suddenly got a second case of severe heebie-jeebies.

"Ah, but then your life will turn a major corner. I see you in a large room . . . dressed up in fine clothes and jewels. . . . and a big diamond and running with a rich and famous crowd."

Ally was astounded and gasped.

The woman wasn't through. "You're going to meet kings and queens, and you'll be known by many people. You'll have a huge following . . . after you cross over a large body of water and marry into a family that's almost royalty.

"Oh, oh . . . but then you'll be entrapped and sad, but you'll finally escape this man and his life. It'll be many years before you find true love again. Ah, but when you do, it will find you. This new love will have something to do with bells.

"Three exactly. One bell will be far away; an ancient clock that hasn't chimed in almost a hundred years. That bell will suddenly chime three times when you're near it. You'll be dealing with a man, involved with him, but nothing else.

"This other man will be a dark prince. There'll be other dark princes on the horizon." She gasped slightly, took a deep

251

breath, leaned forward and almost hissed a warning. "Guard your heart, child!

"The second bell will be of a French native origin. There'll be a dark-haired woman. You'll meet her in an uncanny way and she'll be in the company of an old black man. This is a sign of good fortune."

Ally's mind was spinning, but the old woman took another deep breath and kept on with seeing into Ally's future somewhere, somehow.

"The third bell is a blue bell, and this too is in a far away land. It is of an ancient origin and will have something to do with your career. Don't you *ever* forget the blue bells! There's some magic in them . . . and there's magic in that far away land. Don't you forget."

Ally tried to grasp everything the woman said, but details began to jumble in her mind. She took a deep breath, thinking the woman had gone as far as she could or would.

Not so.

"There's one other thing . . . the man who falls in love with you will be living far away, and he'll also be very well known . . . as you will be. You two will have a long and happy marriage."
252

Her head lifted slightly as she stared through the darkened space. "Good-bye. Leave now."

It took Ally a second or two to find her feet, the floor, gravity, breath, the door, and to stumble into the blinding sunlight, confused and mystified about what had just happened. Ally could not help wondering what in the world that strange woman was talking about. None of what she had said made any sense to the young girl.

The stunned expression on Ally's face gave Cheree second doubts about stepping through that doorway to take her turn. Ally walked toward the shady bench and sort of collapsed. Cheree tugged on Ally's arm, then harder a second time before she came to her senses.

"Are you okay?"

"I think so, but I feel like I've been in a Star Trek episode, Scotty has just beamed me up, flipped a switch to transport me to a different planet, a different Earth."

Ally leaned closer and lowered her head. "If I were you, Cheree, I wouldn't go in there. That woman is freaky. She gave me the heebie-jeebies. Nothing she said was right . . . except that I was engaged to a blond guy."

Of course, Cheree was too curious. She had to go in to hear from the old woman. She stayed in the shack for only a moment or two, not near as long as Ally had been.

Cheree came out as if she had been shoved into an automatic car wash and had come out on the wrong side of the dryer, her hair almost brushed backwards. She rushed across the yard, grabbed Ally's arm and pulled her to her feet.

She frowned, her face almost contorted, and her mouth was drawn tight. "Let's leave!"

There was a strained, disturbed look about Cheree. She was as alarmed as Ally about their readings, or predictions, or whatever anyone called it that Sara performed.

It was a long drive home to St. Orleans. Both of the girls rode in silence all the way. The car radio had been turned on, but the volume was low; noise would clutter their already overloaded minds. It was as if they had lapsed into a trance-like state, trying to comprehend what the ancient black oracle had detailed . . . music would have been too much for their spirits to handle.

Having that unique experience with a true 'future teller' wasn't spoken about between the two friends, not in the days, weeks, months or years that followed. Even stranger was that details diminished from Ally's mind almost as fast as the woman had spoken them . . . then, over time, those words faded into mist until . . . until the day she came face-to-face with reality.

"Even miracles take a little time."

Cinderella's Fairy Godmother

Chapter 14

In a house filled with classics and dinnertime discussions based upon various philosophies by such notables as Plato, it wasn't long before Ally had outgrown her fickle and foolish girlfriends, dull classmates and mediocre instructors. Despite private school and excellent textbooks, she found them repetitive and boring. She tested out of high school at fifteen and entered college.

Her great grandmother Violet was very old now, well into her first one hundred years, she didn't work on her complicated quilt designs as often, and seemed to sleep longer and take afternoon naps more often than before. However, in quiet weekend conversations she gave Ally many secrets on how to cope with the trials she would face throughout her lifetime.

"I'm leaving a treasure behind in all the knowledge I've passed on to you," Violet told Ally one afternoon, "and a bit of magic to use as you get older."

It was late February and ugly winter clouds were showing up almost daily. Violet was one hundred and six years old, but still doing most of her own personal chores. At breakfast one morning, she sat her coffee cup down and peered across the table at her daughter, Pearl. "I'm ready to venture on."

Pearl called Ally at college and broke the news. Ally instantly understood Violet was ready to leave the planet, ready to die, that she had finished whatever she had set out to accomplish and was ready to move on to the next level.

Just thinking about losing Violet made Ally grief stricken. She had to ask the elderly woman to stay. Ally had spent her entire life learning at Violet's knee, then at the kitchen table, the veranda swing, at the parlor fireplace. Violet could make up her mind to do anything, including deciding exactly when she would die. If she was really leaving, Ally had to go home, climb those stairs, enter that bedroom, force herself to tell her great grandmother good-bye. She packed for the hardest journey and event of her life, left the campus within the hour and headed to Wildwind.

Ally hugged her Grandmother Pearl and climbed those wide stairs. She opened Violet's door a tiny sliver and peeked in. Violet was in bed, sleeping peacefully. Ally stepped inside and closed the door without making a sound, not wanting to awaken her, but needing, craving, to awaken her, to hear her voice.

Violet looked fine, like an angel sleeping on a cloud, but Ally knew in her heart the elderly woman was going, slipping further away. She had no other choice. She dropped to her knees next to the bed to awaken Violet, tapping her gently on the shoulder. Nothing. No reaction. Ally laid her hand on Violet's shoulder and shook it slightly.

Violet jerked. "Goodness, child. What's wrong?"

She raised her head a little, blinked and looked at Ally closer. "It's a very late hour, my dear. I didn't know you were home from campus. What's wrong? Are you okay? You're not sick, are you? Oh, you're here for me . . . what's on that curious mind of yours?"

Ally was trying to hold back her tears, but couldn't speak a word. Her fingers grasped the bedspread and held on tight. She didn't know what to say except to blurt out a plea. "Please, Grandma Violet, please don't go. Please stay. I cannot help Granny Pearl like you do, and she is sick with her heart problems.

"I'll be so lost if you both leave me." Tears cascaded down Ally's cheeks and she trembled, and finally burst out crying, burying her face in the bedspread in grief.

Violet sat up in bed, grabbed Ally and pulled her closer. "Oh, Ally, my precious one, I'm not going very far."

Ally gasped and sniffled, and wiped her wet face with her sleeve. "But there are so many existences. Where do you think you will go? Where do I look for you?"

"Oh, I'm going to venture out into the land of wonder just as you're doing now, Ally. There is a much bigger world out there for you to discover. I know you'll have many adventures. You'll get married, have children and grandchildren, and you'll live to be old with your family, just as I have with you.

"Then, one day, there is nothing else to do. You have no more work to do. You'll be old and tired, and you'll also want a new body because yours just won't work anymore and you hurt. Look around, my precious girl. No one my age is still alive. They've all gone on. You get lonely because there's no one left to share memories with. I've stayed this long because of you, to have you on a solid footing.

"I've done my job. Now, I must go rest up somewhere for another grand adventure. I have had one here . . . I reckon there's nothing left to do now.

"I'll always watch over you. Watch you finish college, start your own business, and I'll be there in your dreams when you call for me. It's my destiny. It's time to go."

Ally shuddered. "I hope and pray it won't hurt when you go."

"Oh, no, it won't hurt one bit. I'll just go to sleep. You take all your memories, put them into your mind . . . and smile. God takes care of the rest and carries you to a beautiful place.

"Death is a new beginning, you know. I'll be young like you, Ally, young all over again, and I shall be young forever.

"Know this: Death is only a doorway and it's a long journey into other worlds of light. Oh, we'll see each other again, and we'll always be together. It's not the end. It's just a different beginning.

"Your Granny Pearl will stay as long as she is needed. Don't be sad for me. Know that I am young again and happy," Violet winked, her age-old signal to Ally that she was sharing a special secret, "and I'll be traveling across the starry skies."

Ally stared at Violet for a long moment and blinked back her tears. Her lower lip trembled as she tried not to cry again. "Okay, I'll watch for you in the starry skies, but—"

"No buts," Violet said firmly as she hugged Ally tight. Then she sent Ally off bed just as she had done a thousand times over the years.

Ally couldn't sleep, positive Violet would leave that night. It worried her so much she awakened Pearl. They cried a moment and laughed at what Violet had said about being young again, and never getting old since she was so very old now.

Pearl wiped tears from her eyes and tucked the damp handkerchief in a pocket. "I know Grandma Violet will leave during the Fourth Watch."

"Huh? What's that? I remember hearing that phrase from you both."

"It's the wee hours between three in the morning and sunrise. Calling it 'the fourth watch' is a holdover from the Roman Empire when soldiers changed guards at the gates, especially in Jerusalem, and on all the watch towers. It was a good way for everyone to know the time, too. It fits right in with several Native American plains nations. They put sticks into the ground on the east side of their house, and write their prayers on strips of cloth or ribbons or length of leather, and tie them to the sticks.

"During the Fourth Watch, God Himself, the Great Spirit, comes sweeping across the earth bringing the sunrise, He sees and reads the peoples' prayers and perhaps grants the wishes and prayers. That is when she will to go – with the sunrise. She'll wait until then, and she'll start her journey at the same instant God is traveling through here. Knowing her, she'll try to catch up with Him."

They both chuckled.

"I will miss her so much."

"Me, too, girl . . . me, too. I've never lived a day without her, and you only missed the first three days of your life."

Ally spent as many hours as possible with her Great Grandmother Violet before returning to college Sunday afternoon.

A month passed quickly and Ally had almost forgotten about Violet traveling to her destiny place. One Saturday morning, Pearl asked Ally to awaken Violet for breakfast because she hadn't come downstairs as usual.

Ally went upstairs calling her name. No answer. She walked into Violet's room and saw her lying in her bed, smiling, her hands crossed on her chest . . . and she was gone.

"Oh, no! Grandma Violet, no! Wake up! Wake up!"

Pearl appeared from out of nowhere, suddenly behind Ally, pulling her into her arms, and they cried together. They held onto Violet for a little while and talked to her, thanking her for all the treasures and wisdom she had given them, and wishing her a good journey on her next adventure.

"See, my precious girl . . . she made it to the Fourth Watch after all, exactly like she wanted."

Ally had a very sad year and so did Pearl. They missed Violet so much, missed the flow of common sense, wisdom and knowledge she had instilled throughout their lives and the household. Despite being out of sight, Violet remained a constant positive force in Ally's life. It was many months before Ally could smile again, and a year or two more before she could enjoy a birthday, even though Violet wasn't there to help make the cake and light the candles.

Ally managed to attend her college classes and still be in and out of Wildwind often. She watched Pearl get weaker, slower, more dependent upon help. Pearl's heart was giving out. By the year's end, she knew it was almost time for another destiny place journey during another Fourth Watch sunrise.

Late that winter, Pearl needed surgery. She came through it fine, the doctor said she was recovering nicely and all was well.

Pearl came home from the hospital, said she felt okay, so Ally spent the night with a girlfriend to catch up on local news. In the middle of night, a telephone call awakened them. A stranger said he was an emergency medical technician and that Ally needed to come home right away. When she arrived, fire trucks and an ambulance were in the driveway. Ally's heart sank. She knew Pearl had not waited for the Fourth Watch or sunrise. Pearl was too impatient to begin her adventure, so had left early without saying good-bye.

The pain of losing the two most precious people in her life remained the deepest hurt Ally carried, one that would barely heal. She was alone except for a cold-natured, married, older half-sister, who found fault and didn't want her around. Distance between them suited Ally perfectly.

Her entire world of 'Ally in Wonderland' revolved completely around two ancient soul grandmothers, the old plantation, the mysterious bayou, elves and fairies in the woods, storybooks and costumes, and at least one giant, a treasure chest and a sandal caught on a branch high overhead.

Ally made the arrangements, dealt with the attorney and the Realtor, and finished college two months later. It was heart wrenching to pack and store her grandmothers' cherished antiques, but she managed – she had no choice. Ally would reclaim those material treasures later, after she recovered from losing the spiritual ones. She had to leave her only known world. Options had vanished before her true prince had ridden into her life on his white horse.

Ally had no idea her wishes would travel in the winds of time all the way to a larger place, a place far away from any family or anyone she had ever known. Pearl always said, "The proof is in the pudding." Ally believed it now.

It was a shame Pearl had told Ally the truth about the wishing well, about wishing on stars, about wishing with her back turned to the red birds. Both grandmothers always said 'be careful what you wish for'. Now, Ally could quickly add 'because wishes *do* come true.' For years, she had wished for adventure and to find her true prince, but she hadn't expected she would have to leave her familiar world of Wildwind to begin searching among strangers.

* * *

"A heart that loves is always young."

Greek Proverb

Chapter 15

Ally never thought about the black future teller's predictions again or told anyone what old Sara of the bayou had said. It simply slipped from her memory completely, until – *until* – one day after she had made a new life for herself elsewhere. She came face-to-face with reality and her future: a stranger in her apartment building's hallway. She accidently ran 'slap-dab' over him, as her Granny Pearl would say.

She had been in a hurry, rushing down the stairway while trying to slip her arm into the coat sleeve as she turned a corner. *Bam!* She ran into a man and literally knocked him down. She stumbled, lost her balance, and landed on top of him.

They rolled as one. Ally had never seen him before and now she was lying next to an unknown man who was on the floor, they were eye-to-eye, almost nose-to-nose. She was stunned, mesmerized, embarrassed, frightened and unable to utter one intelligible word. She gasped; he was the best-looking man she had ever had seen in her life.

Ally laid there, not ready or willing to get up. Several long seconds passed before either one had enough breath to say anything. Ally pulled in some air as her cheeks turned crimson with humiliation. "I, I, uh, I'm so sorry." She fumbled around and scrambled to her feet.

He stood and they both laughed at their situation, introduced themselves, and waited in the hallway for some reason, simply staring at each other.

"Collin," Ally repeated his name, tasting it on her tongue for the first time.

Ally forgot the universe existed. Time stopped, noise stopped, movement stopped. Her breath seemingly left her body and she felt as if it would not return for a long while.

Then it hit. The vision suddenly flashed in her mind clearly: The dark shanty in the bayou, the old black woman's voice returned for a brief moment: 'You will not marry the blond-headed fellow, but will meet a dark, wavy-haired man, who is the best-looking man you have ever seen.'

Ally's pulse quickened, slowed, quickened again. She couldn't remember anything else the woman had told her years earlier – she wasn't supposed to recall.

She was officially engaged and getting ready to marry the 'blond-headed fellow,' her best friend Cheree's brother, Beau. Ally thought, had believed, had been convinced she was in love.

272

"Where are you going?" Collin asked, snapping Ally's attention back to that moment, that place.

Ally stared at him, unable to remember. She thought there was no reason to go anywhere, completely content to be in the hallway, standing by his side. She shook her head.

"Coffee? I'm going upstairs to fix some coffee. Would you like some coffee?"

Ally never drank coffee, but today she was a coffee convert. "Yes, thanks."

He extended his hand to help her take off the tangled short, white fur coat and held it while she gingerly climbed the stairs on her wobbly knees. He led her to his friend's apartment where he was visiting.

Ally watched every move he made as he prepared the coffee maker and set it to brewing. He wore light colored, tight jeans and a white shirt that showed a hint of his flat, tanned stomach and his muscular arms. His dark brown hair was wavy enough on the sides that also fit the curve of his exotic jaw line, and long enough in front to flop into his face. He could have been a male model peeled from the cover of a Harlequin Romance novel. He had the body of a Greek god.

Ally was mentally in another world, suddenly deliriously happy, floating on a cloud circling the planet Venus.

He said his name was Collin, middle name, Lafayette. "My parents tell me there's a nice city in Louisiana called Lafayette."

That detail spoken by the future teller Sara came back to Ally's memory for a brief moment, but slipped from her mind just as quickly as it came. Traffic noise stopped. Ally's pulse slowed. She couldn't remember anything else the woman had told her years earlier – Ally wasn't supposed to recall. She was distracted by the obvious, by the most handsome man she had ever seen in her life. She was amazingly happy just waiting for the coffee to brew.

The man's walk, every movement made Ally breathless as she watched him. She had never encountered the erotic stirrings she felt at that moment. Far from the tacky women in New Orleans, the 'throw 'em down strangers' or the well-known, but at that moment, she didn't care if the sun ever shown or if she ever left the building again. She licked her parched lips and discovered she was lusting after a man she had met only moments before.

What the hell is wrong with me? I've never felt this way before in my life.

Ally had been intimate with her boyfriend. Okay, but no fireworks. He was a great guy, but at that moment, watching Collin move or lean against the kitchen counter as he watched her, she couldn't remember the very-soon-to-be-ex-boyfriend's name.

This may be a one-night stand . . . or a one day stand. Oh, my God. What should I do? I can't believe I'm thinking like this. Unreal. It's a good thing he can't read my mind, or he'd think I'm one of those street walking ladies of the evening type people. Oh, my God.

The stranger eyed Ally's low-cut pink blouse and form-fitting beige jeans. She looked good; a healthy glow about her and in perfect shape from working at a fitness center as an aerobics instructor.

They talked for hours about nothing of importance, both just satisfied to be in each other's company. Ally looked out the window, surprised to see the sun was going down, astonished she had spent the entire afternoon with someone she had just met, but had felt so comfortable with to talk. It was as if she had always known him, yet discovered she was also physically drawn to him. He was the first sexually desirable man she had ever spent any time with, and she fully recognized her own desire to become physically intimate.

At that time, she was officially engaged and getting ready to marry the 'blond-headed fellow,' who was Cheree's brother Beau. She thought, believed, had been convinced she was in love, but suddenly, since the accidental run-in with the good-looking, dark-headed stranger, she was in another world, deliriously happy.

Ally was too honest to go through with a marriage to Beau that wasn't blessed, wasn't true. She broke the engagement, spent time with Collin, and fell deeply in love.

Within three weeks, Collin was a fixture in Ally's life. They shared each other's apartments, moving back and forth as if the units were merely an annex of the other. Employment changes many months later made it possible for them to move to Florida, leasing an older, isolated, beachfront home, and made love under the moon and stars.

This man was a modern day romantic Don Juan. They would go out and dance until dawn, staring at each other. Time only existed for them. They walked hand-in-hand, watching the water drift out to sea, slept many nights on the sand by the ocean just staring up at the stars that had been flung into the sky for them alone.

Was it too good to be true? Not to Ally. It was her lifelong dreams come true. Every wish for her true prince that had been cast into Wildwind's wishing well had been granted when Collin entered her life. It seemed they had been together for all eternity and had been blessed by the gods to spend eternity together. Forever was a reality. So entranced by one another nothing else could exist except dancing in each other's arms, midnight walks along the beach, sleeping under the stars.

Of course, they were getting married. They had made plans on what they would do and places they would see until they were a thousand years old.

Life was perfect.

Almost as important were the nights they went into town to the clubs to dance. They moved as one, never missing a step, bodies synchronized and blending so smoothly that other couples left the dance floor to watch their performance.

Even after many months together, they still adored each other, still wined and dined several times a week, still danced at friends' weddings, danced at home, in the kitchen, on the beach, wherever and whenever the mood hit them.

Women obviously lusted after Collin, attracted to his great looks, his easy-going attitude, his witty conversation, and his rich laughter. Whatever star system Collin had fallen from, it had to have been where they created the perfect male.

He was the man she would marry and they would spend the rest of their lives together. She had never had this feeling before, or thought of love in such a fashion. It was as if she was living in a dream bubble. It was just the two of them. They were the only two people who existed on the planet. After three wonderful years, they decided to make wedding plans. Ally knew in her heart this was the right man, the right time. She was ready for a lifetime, a forever, commitment.

One evening, they were sitting on the sand watching waves rolling onto shore.

"I don't want to get old," Collin blurted. "I don't want to get all wrinkled with age. I don't want to ever look or feel like an old man. I'll have to leave at thirty."

Ally was amused, then confused for a moment. "Oh, don't be silly. You won't be all wrinkled and old. Even if you are, I will be too. We'll look alike."

Collin's lips tightened closed and he remained silent.

Ally frowned, thinking he was just being vain because he was so handsome, and decided not to say anything more about his odd sentiment about his looks changing as he aged.

One night, lying in his arms when the glow of the full moon washed across his face, Ally heard a strange sound outside and propped herself up on her elbows to listen. A galloping horse.

Ally's Great Grandmother Violet often heard a galloping horse that would portend an imminent death. Ally shook her head. She gripped the lightweight coverlet when a dark, shadowy figure moved across the bedroom wall. Tears welled in her eyes and flowed down her cheeks.

No! Not the Headless Horseman of the Louisiana bayous! How could he find me here? No! He will not take the love of my life from me. Not now, not ever. If he does, then I must go too. I cannot live without Collin. Not ever!

She rolled over and looked into Collin's face. Death. The vision was clear.

The next morning, Ally kept that vision and information to herself, and handed him a cup of coffee. "You would never, *ever* . . . in this life leave me, would you?"

Collin sat the cup down and grabbed her tightly. "No, Ally, I will never ever leave you. Eternally, I'll be with you. We are one, Ally, and soon we'll be married. But, right now, this very minute, even as we speak, we're already one."

He kissed her. "If I ever *had* to leave, I still won't leave you. Even death cannot separate us, Ally. We'll always dance, and I'll always be wherever you are."

Ally smiled and kissed him again, turned and poured herself some juice. *Okay, he just said it. He's leaving. Where? Why? He's not sick, is he? He'd tell me if he was sick.*

She grasped the glass tighter, steadying it with both hands because she was trembling. Juice splashed onto the countertop. She heard the horrible words echoing in the deepest part of her memory. *No! It can't happen!*

The words spoken by the old black woman came almost too late: 'The marriage . . . it won't happen. He'll be killed in a car accident; tragic.'

Ally stared across the kitchen counter at him. With Collin by her side, she felt whole, complete and loved for the first time far beyond anything she had ever dreamt possible. Collin was her perfect match, making love was endless and perfect, Collin was the life force that coursed through her veins.

Almost without warning, the anguish of abandonment gripped her, the sickening sensation she had once endured while waiting for her birth parents to arrive with the first snowflakes. Her knees felt weak. She gripped the countertop's edge.

No! I won't let it. It's just a bad memory; remembering them never coming, that's all. . . . Maybe it's Joch, my first love in school, taken back to France. That's all it is. . . . Maybe it's losing my aunt. This just can't be real. It's just insecurities. He could never leave. He won't ever leave me. He breathes, therefore, I can . . . because he's my life.

She watched him. Nothing else was said.

One of the Los Angeles studios called about a movie Ally had worked on earlier, asking Ally to return for additional work. Ally was hesitatant to leave.

"You need to go, angel," Collin said. "You're destined for stardom, so go. We'll move to L.A., so you can work in the movies instead of just being a fitness queen."

Ally smiled at him.

"It's your calling, Ally. It's your dream, angel. You're my angel lady; please do this for me, for us."

"Are you sure? Is that what you really want me to do?"

"Yes! Of course. Do it for me."

Ally sighed, relieved her biggest fan supported her ambition in the entertainment industry one hundred percent. "Okay. Great. We'll go, Collin. We'll fly out tomorrow."

Collin nodded slightly, apparently thinking about other matters. "C'mon, angel girl, it's time for us to go to sleep."

The next morning, Ally got ready for the trip and noticed he was sitting, waiting. "What's up, Collin? You're not packing anything."

"Work, angel girl, just work problems. You'll only be gone a couple of days. C'mon, it's almost time to leave. You'll miss your flight."

Ally stared at him.

No, something else was wrong. She felt it. She felt him.

They drove to the airport and he insisted she get on the plane. Ally was excited about going, but still worried about leaving him.

"It's only a few days, angel girl. No worries, no fears. I'm always here." Collin kissed her, his lips touched her sunlit hair and brow, then he kissed her good-bye.

Everything went well in L.A. with casting for a movie, and it was time for her portion of work. Suddenly, she felt sick. It was around two o'clock L.A. time, perhaps five o'clock in Louisiana. She was slightly dizzy with a strange headache; felt nauseous and asked to lie down for a moment. She made her way to her dressing room, stretched out on the sofa, closed her eyes, and instantly dropped into a deep sleep.

She giggled when Collin showed up wearing a black tuxedo and she saw she was wearing a bridal gown. Their wedding day. The reception had already started, others were dancing in the ballroom, eating cake, toasting the happy couple, smiling and laughing. Ally and Collin moved to a small portion of the dance floor so they could dance slower, closer to each other. He held her tighter than ever before – almost hurting her. She looked up into his loving eyes and smiled.

Collin began to rise, his feet were off the floor. "You're so funny, Collin. Such a prankster. How are you doing that?"

Ally smiled at him again, and looked down. Her bridal gown had vanished. "Collin, my gown's gone! It's a green dress. Stop! You're rising off the floor. You're going higher. What's happening, Collin!?"

He leaned forward and kissed her, tears streaming down both of his cheeks. "I love you. I have always loved you. I will always love you."

Collin's feet slid out from under him until he was horizontal in midair. He held onto her arms but began to rise higher.

Ally screamed. "What's happening? No, this can't be happening!"

Her heart seemed to rip from her chest, her breath turned to pants as oxygen left her lungs, her muscles froze as Collin's grip slid down her arms, past her elbows, to her wrists, until he finally released his grasp on her fingertips. His link was broken and he floated further away where Ally couldn't reach him to pull him back. She followed him across the dance floor to the open

French doors where the white curtains rippled in the breeze. Collin slowly floated out the door and Ally awoke.

"Oh, my God! Where is he? I smell him. His aftershave. He was here! I know it." She ran a hand across her cheek. Her face was wet.

"Oh, no, no, no. He's gone. Oh, God." Ally sobbed and gasped for breath, then jumped to her feet and ran onto the sound stage. "A phone? Quick. I need a telephone! Please, somebody; a phone right now."

"What's wrong, Ally? You're confusing me." The movie director frowned at her.

"My fiancé is gone. He died just now. When I went to sleep, he came to tell me good-bye."

The director shook his head. "That's impossible, Ally. You've been in there less than five minutes. That's not long enough for anyone to go to sleep, or to have a nightmare."

She stared at him. Someone brought a telephone, she fumbled with the push buttons, but couldn't reach Collin; no answer at home. She called her friends, his friends, and his co-workers all afternoon. No one could tell her anything. Ally caught a flight back the next day. Nothing. No one knew where Collin was or where his family lived. Ally only knew his family lived in another town.

She called local hospitals, she asked about wrecks. Nothing. No information. Ally sat down and turned on the TV to catch any news. All she saw were graveyards and tombstones. Collin was sending her a message. She was ripped apart. He was gone. When? Where? How?

She moved like an automaton, barely sleeping, barely eating, for two or three days, she lost track. She finally found his parents' phone number in some paperwork, and they told her Collin had been buried that day. They said there had been an automobile accident in a rainstorm on his way to his parents' house; his car had gone out of control when he crossed a bridge. Collin had rarely visited his parents. Perhaps he intended to tell them good-bye also.

A police officer and chaplain came, told her it had been a very bad accident, that the Corvette had almost disintegrated on impact, that the emergency rescue crew pulled body parts from the wreckage, but there was too little to positively identify the deceased victim as her Collin. They were sorry for her loss, then left.

She was crushed, could not breathe, could not comprehend simple things people said.

One of Ally's Great Grandmother Violet's silver wedding shoes, the ones she had never worn, was in Collin's Corvette. Ally had been taking it to shops to find a complementary dress for her own wedding ceremony. An antique silver beaded slipper never worn . . . a second time.

Ally sank deep into a depression. Collin was gone. She couldn't force herself to drive to the other town, to go to a grave that held him locked in its depths. She couldn't accept him leaving her – ever.

Life had dealt Ally another blow that time. All of time could never mend the immense loss, the extreme pain . . . not until Collin found his way back to her. Ally couldn't accept the death of her prince. It was eleven years before she could muster up the strength to face the bitter and brutal fact: He was gone, dead – forever may come but it would be without him by her side.

Being the perpetual Cinderella, Ally automatically thought of Romeo and Juliet. Perhaps Romeo had not drunk poison after all. Perhaps it was a magic potion and he was only in a deep sleep. That meant he would awaken one day. Ally, too, would be asleep; one day her true love would come kiss her and just as

Sleeping Beauty had, she would awaken. She would discover it had all been just one long nightmare. It was already true, already happening. He came to her almost every night, he visited her and they waltzed by candlelight, and walked on the beach under the stars. Their lives were still alive in Ally's dreams.

It wasn't necessary for her to walk into a cemetery and gaze at a tombstone for proof that her true love was dead and gone. It was impossible to accept that he was in that coffin, in that grave, beneath that headstone – the body dragged from the wreck could never be positively identified. Anyone could be in that grave, beneath that stone. No, it wasn't necessary for her to see with her own eyes. It could not be he. Ever.

No. Ally's subconscious chose to keep him alive through a romantic dreamscape where they danced on the waves of time. It became obvious that the things told by the old black future teller had entered Ally's mind, but had become disjointed, bits and pieces, and only one tiny sliver at a time was revealed.

Collin was the one true love of Ally's life. Where could she go after losing him?

It would be a long time before she remembered other parts of old Sara's predictions, and those, too, came to her in a blur and disjointed. What was to come would be far more interesting than what she had already lived through. . . another unbelievable and strange saga.

Gradually, Ally understood that we humans are not supposed to know our future. As she explained it to herself and friends, if we truly knew our future, it would affect almost every decision we made. Of upmost importance is that we would be unable to appreciate the day-to-day joys of life and the people around us, if we already knew what every moment of our time on earth held. If we did know in advance, we would miss the dance.

* * *

"One shoe can change your life ..."

Walt Disney

Chapter 16

Ah! 'If the shoe fits,' they say. In Ally's case, the shoe did fit because, of course, it was hers. She compared her life to Cinderella's – it was like a fairytale, but she had lost the silver beaded slipper and the prince of her dreams. She couldn't linger there. It was time to move on.

It would be years before she would meet the handsome and debonair prince she had yearned for as a teenager and young woman. However, before it could happen, she would grow up, learn a lot more, leave the beach house and its memories, and say a final good-bye to her hometown.

It was too sad to stay where she had once been so happy with her fiancé Collin. She knew she couldn't return to live among the haunted plantations and vampires of New Orleans and the twisted memories of St. Francisville. She needed to move to a place that offered more opportunities – a larger city with tall buildings and lights and action. She packed up and left the past behind.

Of course, Jade thought Ally shouldn't move far away, claiming she wanted her half-sister closer. Ally tried to explain that her dreams were much larger than the small town attitude and imaginations she had grown up with, but could never accept as her own. None of her dreams could ever come true if she stayed there.

Ally considered many things and decided where to begin her next adventure: Atlanta, Georgia. Her family called her 'Miss Scarlet' and teased her, wondering whether, instead of a prince, she'd meet her own Rhett Butler. They were all sad to see her go and they worried about her, but knew she was smart enough to do well no matter where she lived. She felt confident it would be a good move.

The car was packed and she was ready to leave, letting the car roll forward slowly as she gazed a final time at each glorious live oak in the yard where she had played as a child. It was where she had searched for fairies in the leaves, and the oaks' outstretched arms had sheltered her precious Wildwind home for decades. She knew she'd miss the trees and her home's serenity and security – her new life would never be the same as what she had at Wildwind. Ally straightened her back and drove out the gate, onto the highway, and then drove through her hometown one last time. She really did wish it and the people well. Her final thought as the car rumbled onto the gangway and the ferry's deck to cross the Mississippi that would take her into a new world and life was of Joch. He was her first prince, and she thought how she had been convinced she would never see him again. Now he was a fading, happy, childhood memory. Then

Collin flashed through her mind again. It was time to move on. Ally was grabbing adulthood with both hands, and laughed aloud as the ferry pushed off from shore.

* * *

"Every child is an artist.
The problem is to remain an artist
once they grow up."

Pablo Picasso

Chapter 17

Sunlight streamed into the car windshield, making it difficult to read the markers along the interstate. Squinting despite sunglasses, Ally could barely make out that her exit was only about twenty miles ahead. There were so many cars, medium size trucks and giant 18-wheelers all rushing in the same direction in multiple lanes of traffic – nothing like it would ever be built in St. Francisville – and the beach was almost as quiet.

Ally's grip on the steering wheel tightened and she clinched her teeth. *Better get use to this traffic. You don't really have a choice in the matter. There's going to be lots of traffic in this new way of life.*

Usually the loudest night noises in St. Francisville were crickets – an endless chatter, and Ally had grown accustomed to waves constantly washing ashore to lull her to sleep. Jaded big-city dwellers who visited both those places were reassured at night by the mechanical whirring of police helicopters, or cops in emergency vehicles chasing down suspects. They might even be unnerved by the curious absence of a tumultuous city's white-noise background, or consider the comparative silence quite unnatural.

Noise on the interstate entering Atlanta was an assault on Ally's ears – deafening – especially the huge trucks rumbling alongside her at 65 miles per hour.

Oh, good heavens. I haven't been gone a whole day and I'm missing my quiet little hometown. It ought to be nothing more than a smoky haze now, with mile upon mile separating me from my past. What am I thinking? Pay attention to the traffic, to the exit signs, to anything. Get a'hold of yourself.

A tear rolled down her cheek, and she quickly brushed it away.

Oh, I knew this would happen. The whole way here I've been happy to get out of that little town and now look at me! Well, I haven't even made it to the Holiday Inn exit yet and I'm all of a sudden struck with tears and missing home, and even thinking about my half-sister and missing ol' Miss Cotton's café. Oh, It'll be just my luck – I bet there's not one decent place in Atlanta that makes beignets.

Ally planned the locale change a month earlier, and had chosen Atlanta because that was where Margaret Mitchell had written 'Gone With The Wind,' the most famous and well-read book in the South and one of Ally's favorites. Ms. Mitchell had done just fine for herself, and that inspired Ally to choose

Atlanta. She was determined to write the next great American novel, and knew if a great author like Ms. Mitchell could make it, so could she. Atlanta was a city ripe for the plucking, and that's exactly what Ally intended to do. She set her cap for it and smiled.

A few more long sweeping highway curves down the hillsides, and a fast-growing trepidation about the cars zipping and darting in and out of lanes had her grasping the steering wheel with a white-knuckle grip. Traffic was almost overwhelming the closer she drove toward downtown, and began to worry this adventure was a big mistake. She considered taking any exit, turning the car around and heading back home.

She glanced across the lanes of rushing traffic and gasped at the stunning sight of Atlanta's beautiful skyline; lights had begun to flicker on in the tall buildings' windows. It was getting dark, either from the sun going down or from a thunderstorm rolling into the area.

She glanced at the dark clouds. *Maybe someone up there is just laughing at me and thinking: Let's brew up something and send scared little Dorothy back home.*

"You just go right on ahead then, dern you! Why not! Brew up my worse nightmare: being struck by lightning where nobody knows me. Why not swirl me up by some twister!? If that happens, just let me wake up back home in my bed like Dorothy did with little Toto tucked under my arm. Do that and I swear I won't leave St. Francisville ever again!"

Ally gritted her teeth and shook her head. "Can't be thinking of my childhood now, remembering the good ol' days of growing up, of making Miz Cicely and Ellie laugh. Oh, it's funny, all right. If they could see me now in the big city – one day out and crying. Oh, good heavens! I've got to grow up right this minute. I can't be scared away from my own future."

Suddenly, a fast-flying contraption beyond description rudely and abruptly invaded her field of view, snapping her out of the dazed and confused illusions about home. The huge yellow vehicle was doing about a hundred. It zoomed ahead, passed a car on the right, then jerked back into the same lane. Drivers on both sides drifted further away from the yellow accident-en-route-to somewhere that kept on going. Ally slowed down for a minute to allow some distance between it and her.

Whew! Glad I wasn't in that madman's way.

Ally promised herself that she'd quit reeling and reflecting on the past. It was too late to go home again; she was already inside Atlanta's City Limits. She remembered being so young and little, of being excited when given permission for sleepovers at a friend's house. They'd have a lot of fun until it got dark and it was bedtime. Bedtime. All she wanted to do then was run home as fast as she could, jump into her own bed, pull the covers over her head, curl up and sleep where she was safe, where her Granny Pearl was just down the hall and would come chase off any monsters. Today, Ally missed that safe bed where nothing could scare her too much.

Good heavens. . . . What's wrong with my ears? Oh, no! Not again.

Whenever Ally's ears bothered her, it was a sure-fire sign someone somewhere was speaking her name and rattling those lips. It was exactly as her Great Grandma Violet always said. She was 106 when she left this world and she was always right, and even had understood and explained Plato.

Oh, I know what it is.

About now, Jade was talking about her, very likely in that smart-alecky vein, something akin to: 'She just knew it.' Ally could hear Jade's words reverberating through the air, the beloved big half-sister's voice betraying her, scolding in that childish sing-song voice, "Ally's a big scaredy cat. Can't even spend one night away from St. Francisville. She's nothing but a big cry baby."

Ally could clearly hear Jade laughing loudly, and then her voice dissolved into unrepressed giggles, literally basking in her smug comfort of joy without shame. 'Watch Ally, she won't be gone no time at all. She's afraid to stay by herself and she's even afraid of the dark. Bet you didn't know that. And, she's never been on her own 'cept for a short time. I bet you money-to-nothing she'll be coming up that drive any minute, saying she hated that big old city and couldn't find a job. She'll have an excuse, but she'll be back anytime now – just you watch and see!'

God knows, I know my half-sister. I know exactly what she's thinking at the time. Granny Pearl was right. I was born with the gift.

Both Granny Pearl and Great Grandma Violet had the Knowing, and they had many other gifts, too. Ally inherited quite a few from those two gifted and insightful old women. One day, Ally would learn to appreciate those heirlooms of the mind and senses, but today wasn't it.

Ally looked out the car window again where the tallest buildings, the likes of which she'd only seen in magazines, waited in the twilight. Atlanta looked a great deal like the photographs of New York City at night, a massive city all glittering with excitement and beckoning newcomers. Both cities had only been toured through the many books Ally had read and almost memorized.

Ally changed lanes twice and took the next exit marked 'Downtown.' She drove right through the middle of Atlanta, tall buildings on both sides of the street, and then drove past the famous, huge Coca-Cola Company complex. Further away was the Holiday Inn sign glowing green in the distance. She pulled to the curb and looked around.

A small tear streaked down a cheek as Ally's two blessed grannies came to mind. She missed them greatly at that moment. Their love and wisdom would be with her forever and would grow stronger over the years. But, that evening, they were certainly with her, taking her back down memory lane where she was embraced by their love. They were with her as she entered a strange and unusual place to which she had never been – an adventure. Those days at Wildwind were the good times. Little girls grow up. Ally had, now she was finally on her own in a big city – only slightly lost.

A smile touched her lips. *I am going to marry the most eligible and handsome prince in this town.*

Oops! The Fairytale had officially begun.

The last thing she wanted was a new life in a new city while thinking about Collin and the complicated history, even Joch from her academy days. Every girl has a first love, but not for long. Perhaps even the true love of a prince. But, if it doesn't work out, she pulls herself together, regains her spark and self-confidence and lives on. So be it. Collin was hers for a while, it was wonderful, but that was the past – she had to live in today's world. Today, tonight, this minute, this new beginning – It was the start of her new life.

It's funny how life just doesn't work out quite as planned. Hard to understand. Why can't we meet the man of our dreams, guys like Collin, get married and live happy ever after?

Life just doesn't work out as simply and as straightforwardly like that for anyone. At least, in her twenty-something years, she hadn't seen it happen with even one person she knew. Sad.

Ally knew she was intelligent, ready and willing to change the course of her life. No more mourning Collin, no more small-time towns that had nothing to do and not even a decent promise of something to do in the near future.

This is my new beginning, starting at—. she glanced at the clock on the dashboard. *Well! How odd is that? It's one-eleven – 1:11. This is too funny.*

"One . . . one . . . one. This means something." Ally told herself she'd just made the first decision of her new life, and looked at the clock again.

Ally remembered a lot about numerology, and was really into it, studying it at one time. Eleven. The number was one of her lucky numbers, and so was the number one, which has a very special meaning; Granny Pearl's birthday was on January first. And, Granny Pearl was the first baby born on New Year's Day.

Ally giggled. "This is getting more exciting. I feel luckier than ever because I arrived at a new destination at such an exact time."

She laughed and spoke her mind aloud so all the universe could hear her at exactly one-eleven, which was three added together and her other lucky number.

It all made perfect sense to her now. She thought back to the books and her beloved Grannies. *They're here giving me a sign. There's Granny Pearl's Birthday. Eleven is my lucky number. Add them together and they make three, which my two Grannies and I used to joke about, calling ourselves the threesome or three stooges. And, three is a triangle, which is lucky.*

Chills ran up and down her arms while thinking about how everything in the universe can line itself up to give people little signs and road maps to life in general. . . . useful if they paid attention when the signs and details were revealed.

It was late and she was tired from the long drive. It was time to find the Holiday Inn and rest instead of sitting in the car talking to herself and doing numerology.

She smiled. *There's power in numbers.*

She glanced around and decided it was definitely a strong sign that things in this city were going to go excellently. She knew in her heart that both of her beloved Grannies were there somehow – in spite of being gone from sight, they were there in spirit.

* * *

"This is a work of fiction. All the characters in it, human and otherwise, are imaginary excepting only certain of the fairy folk, whom it might be
unwise to offend by casting doubts on their existence. Or lack thereof."

Neil Gaiman

Chapter 18

The night Ally met her 'prince,' she was a naïve young woman out with her girlfriends for a night of fun. She never suspected her entire world was about to change.

Life is all about choices when we come to a split in the road. Depending upon whether we go right or left, it really doesn't matter. Neither is a right or wrong decision. If we take what some consider the wrong road, it's only a lesson in life we're supposed to learn anyway. If we choose what some consider the right road, then life is good and we have earned and learned lessons. Either way, we move up for our rewards.

Looking back, Ally knew why she chose the wrong road. It was definitely the wrong road in many ways, but now that she'd made that mistake, she felt she could help other women make better choices. She intended to help awaken women who thought they had the world by the tail just because they landed the "rich and handsome prince." Not until it is too late do you make the same discoveries she'd made. Ally thanked God she hadn't ended up like some of the famous women who made the same mistake. There are women with millionaire husbands who would rather have their wives murdered or kill them themselves rather than let the unhappy wife leave. The wife really is a piece of property to them . . . and those husbands don't depart easily with their acquired property.

Atlanta was very big and a great place to start her new business. She settled into a cozy home in a nice neighborhood with great schools. It was the perfect place to live out big dreams. Little did she know at the time that she was turning dreams into reality. That's life and how it runs its course. Life is one gigantic playground sometimes, and we do set our own stage.

Ally had always wondered about the people who rode in those long white coaches, she was obsessed with limousines, but never knew why. She just knew her heart raced when they would pass by – it gave her a rush. The women would step out of the vehicle wearing lovely long gowns and the men always looked fantastic dressed to the nines. It was exciting. They were having fun and going to great places. They looked and felt like kings and queens for the night. During prom time, the young girls were Cinderella for that one night, wearing their gowns and riding in their white coaches.

It didn't take a rocket scientist to tell Ally how she could wisely invest her inheritance from her grandmothers and from the sale of Wildwind that would provide a secure future. The perfect business? Cinderella's Coach. She bought five, stretch, white limousines. Oh, there was a lot of competition in the

Atlanta area, but she felt confident and knew she was selling dreams for the evening, not just another expensive ride for the night. How? Ally knew exactly how to market a dream.

Inside each limo was a red rose for the ladies and a boutonnière for the gentlemen. If the man didn't want it, they could simply leave it in the limo. Rose pedals were scattered inside, gifts were waiting for the lady or the gentleman, and very special gifts were waiting for those couples bringing their babies home from the hospital. Every limo and every client received something extra to make their ride unforgettable.

Ally's business card reflected the dream coach experience waiting for each person. She worked at making sure people remembered her and her company's special services, and it paid off. It didn't take long before she had a huge client list and Cinderella's Coach moved into the number one slot of limo services in Atlanta. Word had also gotten out to celebrities who came into town, and her client list of rich and famous grew swiftly.

There was plenty of money and her life was great. Of course, every young female wants a handsome prince to share her life. Granny Pearl always said, "Ally, you never know what's around the next corner." She was right.

Ally and her girlfriends were having a night on the town. They were business women, always busy, always working, and rarely had time to just get together to enjoy each other's company. For some reason, this particular night felt good. It was warm and the sky was clear – stars peeked out just to watch Ally and her special moment – as if they knew something different was about to happen. It was almost as if a private council was sitting in judgment; three men in white robes with long white beards, sitting behind a long white table surrounded by twinkling stars, planning and calculating. That's how she envisioned this whole thing, this serendipity event. Perhaps not planning each step along the way, but she thought they sat and watched, and did a bit of stirring . . . then they'd sit back and watch what happened. As you can imagine, this was one of those magic nights. Those bearded men got a big kick out of watching Ally. To this day, Ally would often look up and consider those three bearded men up there, watching, especially when something magical or mysterious happens. Ally would stand still for a moment, watching the clouds, waiting for a break. "Okay, you guys!"

That night she was dressed to the nines in a slinky, yet classy black dress . . . and clear candelas slippers. Her blonde hair was down, long and shiny. She had that special female glow – you know the one. We all have our good and bad days and moments.

On this night, she looked great and knew it, felt it. A bit vain? Perhaps, but everything was right in her universe and it aligned entirely on her. Beauty and confidence radiated.

Ally's friends really looked great as well. They popped open a bottle of champagne when they got into the limo and off they went for a night of female bonding, of catching up on each other's lives, and business successes. They were also like wildcats on the prowl. They knew they had the upper hand with classy looks and a white coach. They'd done it before: If a good-looking male was lucky enough to be seen and if voted to be worthy of consideration, he might be allowed to come along for a ride on their magical night. Yes, the champagne did help to feel pretty and confident.

Their first stop was a favorite nightspot country club. They really weren't into country and cowboys, but all types of males were usually there. After a few drinks and a couple of dances with some semi-interesting cowboy hats, it was time to move on to another playground.

That's when something unusual happened: A man, who looked out of place and extremely well dressed, walked over to Ally, grabbed her hand, bowed slightly, lifted her hand to his lips and kissed her hand. He softly spoke the King's English as he leaned over her hand.

315

She was shocked. That sort of thing might have happened in an earlier time or maybe in a romance novel, but in this day and age men just don't do that anymore. It was as if he had stepped out of another time and suddenly appeared. He wasn't dressed like anyone else there, and he didn't look like anyone she had ever seen before. Ally was taken aback for a moment. Her friends were tugging on her arm since they were already walking toward the exit, Ally the last to follow. On her way down the wooden steps to the limo, her heel of her shoe became stuck in the crevice of the wood planks. She was so close to the car, she simply stepped out of the high heel and stepped into the backseat of the limo, and was about to ask the driver to see if he could figure out how to retrieve the stuck shoe.

The instant she got into the seat and looked out the still open door, there stood the green-eyed, dark brown-haired, mysterious stranger . . . kneeling. "Cinderella has lost her slipper," he said in a husky voice.

He reached down, cradled Ally's foot in his hand, and gently slipped her high heel back onto her foot.

With a dazzling smile, he said, "You ladies have a wonderful evening." Stood, turned and vanished back up the stairs into the dark.

Ally's girlfriends all laughed about her shoe and called her 'Cinderella' for the rest of the night. They teased her, asking why she didn't get his name. They all thought he was handsome, were certain she'd never see him again. They all said she should have invited him to join them for the evening, the least she could have done was get his name, and certainly hadn't handled the situation correctly. They gave her a hard time for hours.

Ally didn't feel the same. She wasn't certain what she felt at the time, but knew that guy was not from around town, as Granny Pearl would say. There was something very wonderful and strange about him. Oh, well, the night was young and Ally was going to enjoy it. She put him out of her mind for the evening.

The alarm went off way too early the next morning; maybe she should have blamed the champagne instead of the clock.

Also too early, the doorbell began to ring. She opened the door to a huge, almost embarrassing, display of roses. Two men ran back and forth to their delivery van, bringing in dozens after dozens of roses. Ally tried to stop them, saying it was a mistake of some sort, that she wasn't dating anyone, and didn't know anyone who would do that sort of thing with so many flowers.

The little guy stopped long enough to say, "Well, ma'am, you musta have one rich admirer is all I gotz to say. But dat man sent a big card."

Ally was confused. There wasn't any space left for another vase in the house. She opened the lovely beige card with embossed butterflies.

"I didn't know dreams were real or came to life, but it wasn't until I saw you in the pale light walking by and I reached out and kissed your hand that I knew, and I mean I knew the moment I looked into your eyes that you had somehow stepped out of my dreams into a living, breathing human being. Now I believe in dreams, because you were my dream, but now that I know you really exist, you must accompany me to dinner tonight. I will have a car pick you up at five o'clock. Drake"

She immediately called her friends. They were astounded over the flowers and the card, which didn't sound like the rehearsed, well-delivered lines most guys use. It all seemed genuine. Ally was skeptical about going out with a stranger; of course, her friends talked her into risking it. They planned to secretly follow in another limo, in case she was in any danger or left the car and needed a safe ride home. She finally agreed to go. Before the day was half over, her doorbell rang again: A special delivery of a huge box from Niemen Marcus. Inside was a beautiful, black, lacey dress with a bit of silver trim on it and it was just her size. How does a guy know these things?

Never in Ally's wildest of dreams could she have made up this man! Her friends helped her get dressed and right on time, a well-dressed, black gentlemen knocked on the door. Parked out front was a two-toned, older model, very luxurious Rolls-Royce limo, something seen in the movies that was right out of old, elegant Hollywood. He escorted her to the car, and poured a glass of white wine for her before gently closing the door. In the back seat lay one perfect white rose.

As they drove toward a private airport, she asked the driver, "Where are you taking me?"

"Oh, Miss Ally, it's a big surprise Mr. Lanzen has set up for you," he replied. "And I can't even spoil it. But I can assure you Mr. Lanzen is doing this one up right. He's quite taken with you, Miss Ally. You don't have to worry none or be afraid. Everybody in this town knows Mr. Lanzen. He's good folk."

That was somewhat comforting as she was already about to crawl out of her skin with nerves. The driver helped her out of the car at the front edge of a red carpet that had been unrolled to a private jet.

Drake Lanzen stood there, awaiting Ally's arrival. As she walked down the red carpet, she wasn't sure if she felt like an idiot or a movie star. She definitely wasn't sure about this first date with a stranger, flying away on a private jet.

Oh, God, You've got to watch out for me tonight with those white bearded men up there because . . . I am not sure about this escapade.

Drake took her hand and led her aboard the jet that was decorated like a hotel suite with cushioned white leather seating, a private bar and a TV. As they took off, he popped a bottle of Dom and toasted them and their first evening together.

"We're going to New York for dinner, and then to the opera," he said. "I promise to have you home by midnight in Atlanta."

Well, she certainly couldn't say 'no' at thirty-thousand feet in the air. Inside the airplane, the lights were dim and Nat King Cole softly sang in the background. Drake sat holding her hand and staring into her eyes and saying very little. It was as if he already knew her or had known her forever from some other time. Ally did most of the talking because she was so nervous.

The dinner was superb and the opera was captivating. Ally's first opera experience. Now she understood the saying about people either love opera or hate it. She was surprised that she felt so comfortable with this mysterious stranger. She truly was amazed and in awe of the whole evening. They laughed and talked on the way home. His driver was waiting when they landed, and Drake did no more than bow, kiss her cheek and hand when he said goodnight. She was home by midnight as he promised.

Ally's friends couldn't wait to hear all that had happened and the strange thing was he had not asked her to go out with him for the following evening. Naturally, she thought she would never see him again. The very next day, a letter was hand delivered, stating the time he would pick her up for our next date.

What a different character. She had never known anyone quite like Drake Lanzen. He let her know all of his intentions in writing beforehand, and had them hand delivered. Weeks went by and then months, they saw each other almost every day or night, laughing until dawn, and going on strange and exciting adventures. She had never been romanced like that before. She had never read a romance novel, but now could write several. This was the most captivating, sexy, mysterious man in the universe and they got along famously. Ally began to think he was right; maybe she was made just for him and maybe she did appear out of his dreams. Now she was in a whirlwind where she wasn't sure what was real and what was fantasy.

* * *

"A dream is a wish your heart makes..."

From Cinderella

Chapter 19

She returned home at midnight as promised after her date with the millionaire prince. The moon was starting to peek its way through a misty fog that had draped over a velvet black, starlit night. She took a last look at the magical sky, watching the stars brighten one by one, and thought of the evening she had spent with a complete stranger. Thoughts rushed through her mind as a distant wave drifting back out to sea.

With slippers in hand, she slowly climbed the stairs, laying the one white rose on a shelf near her bed, a shelf which held her most precious memories of things she had collected along the way.

Thankfully, she had no meetings to attend the next morning. She could fall into the huge, white, four-poster bed, slide between the pink satin sheets and soft, white, down comforter, grab all the fluffy pillows around her and sleep half the day away.

She had dropped the lovely dress to the floor – just that and nothing more – too tired to even think about pajamas or hanging up the expensive Bob Mackey dress. All she wanted to do was sleep. Sleep is a funny thing. It's something you cannot do when you have plenty of time to do it. Sometimes, the opposite happens. Instead of sleeping, she tossed and turned, and thought about the night and the strange events that had taken place in a city far from Atlanta, a city so far away that they flew there by jet just to eat at a fine Italian restaurant.

The night danced around in her half-awake, half-asleep mind while she continued to toss and turn, not realizing sleep had overtaken her tired and frail body, and had transported it back to a scene, a place in a time where she had known the prince before.

Suddenly, she seemed to be floating. She looked down and found herself in another era. The dress she was wearing was from a time of exquisite elegance. It was of a deep maroon satin with full puffy sleeves and a fitted bodice. She couldn't remember how she had gotten there or when, but knew she was in a room awaiting someone to join her. Who was it? Where had she been taken? Was she really taken somewhere else? Was it the present? the past? From all she could remember while floating on that deep wave of sleep was that this did not appear to be the reality she knew, that she could grasp, that she could trust as secure.

Ally heard footsteps approaching from behind, felt someone lean down and kiss her neck. She instantly recognized the scent, recognized the touch. It, and he, were all too familiar.

"He's back once more," she heard herself sigh. Her heart began to beat rapidly, and she could no longer catch her breath.

He moved slowly in front of her, but she could only see part of him because of the light shining from the brightest of night candles, and the full moon, which shone through the shear pearl-toned curtains that hung across the open French doorway.

He reached out his hand and she heard music playing an old familiar melody, one from long ago. His attire was from a period she had known before. His scent was also intimate in her memory. She felt the essence of his scent rush through her senses as he took her hand in his.

Perhaps the half-empty wine glass in front of her may have something to do with the lightheadedness she felt. He gracefully extended his hand and she nervously slipped her small hand into his. It immediately warmed to her touch.

Silence. Words weren't needed. Just powerful memories of a yesterday, which had traversed into the present. Somehow, this handsome prince had come to claim her in the midnight of the full moon's embrace. True love knows not death, nor time, nor space, nor limitation. It moves within a dream state, fulfilling its duty to once again live through an unknown present reality, a dimension which it can slip through unchallenged.

With inviting enchantment they danced quietly to a waltz only they could hear, as silent and as soft as the night air that had blown the long pearl-colored drapes until they billowed across the open French doors.

She knew she had been there before. She had danced this dance to the same music in the misty candlelight before. She watched a full moon come closer and closer as the curtains changed shape and swayed with the wind billowing in the breeze of the midnight air.

This was so normal, comfortable, and the clothes were fitting because it was a favorite dress. The man who had delicately swirled her around the large stately manor was so familiar. She had resided in this estate at one time.

No words needed to be spoken. He pulled her close, sweeping her into his strong embrace. Although she felt him peering down at her, she still had a problem making out his face and eyes. She must have been heavily intoxicated, either from the wine or simply from love itself. The winds of time swooped her up and took her flying through the air as if she hadn't a care in the world. Time and space seemed not to matter at all.

Though merely in a dream, she was awakened by a reality that only existed here, at this one moment in time. Although a bit confused, she didn't mind because she was in the arms of a man who was taking her on a trip from a distant but continual frame of time where time stood still, where nothing mattered but them. Romance was of sweet night air and breezes of rain coming in that swept her to the ocean's waves of sleep when it washed onto midnight sands.

Finally, she could see. She knew him. She recognized her fiancé Collin, her prince whom she will soon marry, her one true love who visited her night after night. She could not understand how she could reach him or he reached her, but it doesn't really matter because her state of mind is non-existent now. She did not care how or why.

It is all about the moment. About Collin coming to her, summoning her to their secret place where the last dance goes on nightly. She did not care to awaken from this dream that is so perfect, yet so unnatural.

Why does he not speak? Why doesn't she begin a conversation? She knew she had danced with this man hundreds of times before. This was a one-of-a-kind affair where no one ever need know it even existed. It was all about the dance. It never was about anything but the dance.

All that mattered was the look of love in his eyes. As she gazed deep into his dark brown eyes, she saw beyond all reality into a timeless escape, and she chose not to even take a moment's breath if it meant this might end.

Trying to hold on to a moment in time, dancing with this man who could not speak a word, nor could he ever be seen in the light of day, it slowly dawned on her how he had come to be here. Such a memory was more than she could fathom for this moment that was timeless, a time that seemed to be only fragments of fleeting memories, slowly came to her intoxicated senses: This could not possibly exist anywhere but in her dreams.

She had never lived in this house, nor had hse ever really lived in this time, but as memories began to come into focus, she thought of a time and a man where everything was a dream and every dream was of a time that never really happened, never really existed . . . except under the illusions of red wine and late night full moon romance.

Soft music drifted on the air in the background where scenes of another time were a vision in her mind as she danced with a man from that earlier time. . . . when love was there with her, filling her, telling her of a Shakespearian play of two lovers who had to play roles at some part of their life in time.

She could smell the rain and feel the sand, and she watched the stars as she held tightly to the one love with whom she had hoped would come again and again. They danced from the time when he existed for a brief moment until she looked down and saw her beautiful maroon dress had turned to green and his Romeo suit had turned into a common black suit. Collin gently leaned down and placed a damp kiss upon her cheek and brow, and whispered that he must leave, that he loved her and would forever. Then his feet lifted and he drifted upwards and began to float away from her reach. Tears ran down her face and she sobbed. She knew that although her prince was asleep in death he would still come to this place, this manor, to dance with her and show her his true love, even if it could only be for a little while. He floated further out of reach, out over the ocean until she could no longer see him or feel his presence.

Daylight blasted into Ally's bedroom and she sat up screaming his name, then realized she was awake, that it was only a dream . . . . the same dream again and again.

Sitting in the middle of her bed, shaking, crying and confused, Ally tried to catch her breath from the strong re-occurring dream of the man she dearly loved, the man who had suddenly arrived in my life and who was taken just as quickly, never to return except through her dreams. Somehow through the sands of time, Collin would often come back to dance the night away in the ocean breezes where she could touch him and feel him and dance until dawn with the one man she would always love, but never could have because of time's cruel joke . . . and a rainy night that had swept him away.

This dream always left her confused and emotionally exhausted. She had never really come to grips with the death of her beloved prince, her fiancé Collin. He could only come back to her in this dream, a dream in which she welcomed night after night. It was always more intense when she was tired or preoccupied with business matters and other things going on in her life.

No wonder she dreamt of her lost love tonight of all nights, with flying to New York, the opera, the beautiful dress, the wine and champagne, and a renewed hope of a romance. All of these things were so similar to the time she had spent with her true love. They all made her think somehow and in some way, this was Collin coming back.

The dance – it was always about the dance – and romance. A once in a lifetime love that was too good to be true. Now it was a faded and distant memory that only came to visit in order to help her move forward in time, not back.

She had to let go of this dream. One day she would dream of a new prince who was real, at least alive, and dance until dawn while having a real conversation and while wearing clothing from the present and not the past.

If last night's date was any indication, then this handsome, very sweet stranger had come to sweep her off her feet.

Ally came to the conclusion that it was time to move on. She certainly was tired of that dream and having a romance with a man who had been long gone. Love, they say, never dies, but the living have to remain and go on, move forward. She had to put this dream behind her. She made up her mind right then to try harder to forget all about Collin . . . and would begin by never saying his name again.

Drake was going to be her new prince!

In her mind, the dream would never die, but it needed to fade into a cloud of mystical lands where dreams go to never return. There had to be such a place where she could send this dream. She had to get a new one. And, she was almost sure Drake would keep her occupied.

Oh, my god! She laid back down on the bed and a smile brightened her face. How she met this new Prince Charming, was, of all things, once again through a shoe, a slipper. How could she have possibly gotten her shoe stuck in the stairs? No one had ever done that before. Why couldn't it have been one of her girlfriends who had walked down those same steps only a moment before? Why is it always her who gets into these unusual shoe situations? It had happened her whole life. Her sister shoved that doll's shoes onto her feet when she was just an infant. Was she cursed by some magical talisman formed into a shoe? Is her shoe fetish the result of some nightmare haunting her past? After all, her life seemed to be about shoes, or at least one shoe at a time and they always seemed to get her involved in the most peculiar situations, no matter what color, shape, or style.

What is it about shoes? What is it with her? None of her friends had unusual situations that she knew about. They had normal lives and situations. What was 'normal'? Perhaps real and 'normal' were on backorder when Ally was created.

The telephone ringing broke her thought process. She had a sneaky feeling it was a certain good-looking man, hopefully telling her he would love to do the all-night flight again sometime soon.

She stumbled out of bed and searched for the phone, only to be disappointed that it was the dry cleaners reminding her to pick up some late laundry she had forgotten. That disappointment turned to joy when I discovered an invitation was waiting on the other side of her front door. A special delivery. Boy, did this guy have a certain air of mystery about him or what? He couldn't pick up the phone and ask her out like most guys do. Instead, he sent it through special delivery.

It was a private note that left her with a happy smile on her face. She drove down the road humming, knowing tonight would be a special occasion. This time it would not be on a private jet, but in an entirely private dining room rented just for them, to which I would be whisked away by his private driver for another evening of the unexpected with her new charming prince.

Thinking back for a moment, the dance began to fade to a place where dreams floated. Dances are timely . . . in time where they belong.

A new chapter had begun in Ally's life. Whether it involved dancing, she didn't know, but whatever this new chapter held, she was going to make it her new dream.

* * *

"Mirror, Mirror on the wall,
Who's the fairest one of all?"

The Wicked Queen

CHAPTER 20

Ally's next private jet trip took her to New York and a surprise: A huge engagement ring from Harry Winston's. Drake proposed marriage under the stars while they rode in an open white carriage through Central Park. It was a fantasyland. She accepted after a few seconds hesitation. She'd lost her breath. She simply couldn't believe this fairytale was really happening. She was marrying a millionaire prince who was deeply in love with her.

The blaring alarm clock awakened her. *"Oh, my God!"* It was all a dream, but it was too surreal, too vivid. She sat straight up in bed, shivering with nerves, and yanked the covers up to her chin. That dream was too close to reality to be comfortable. She had to think about this entire situation before she could face a busy workday. This dating Drake thing was getting too complicated too fast.

Why would Harry Winston's even enter her head? She'd never been in that shop before. She'd heard of it, but hadn't had the time or even the inclination to window shop in New York. Owning and supervising a successful business with numerous employees takes time to keep it successful. Oh, a magnificent engagement ring – any ring – from Harry Winston's would be exceedingly nice, but that kind of gesture wasn't the sort of thing

Drake would do. Or would he? She hadn't known him long enough to make any sort of judgment. Drake had certainly been extravagant in the different methods to show her a good time on their dates, and it was obvious he was accustomed to freely using any level of money on any whim or desire. He relished spending his money on fun activities and seemed to enjoy including her in his plans.

Proposing marriage while on a carriage ride in Central Park? Oh, my gosh – that was just too over the top, too much, way too much, uh, too Cinderella. Drake would and could go all out in a big way, but not on a carriage ride; too ordinary, too overdone, not his style at all.

Besides, they had only been dating a few weeks. The degree of seriousness she had dreamed about was too soon for a man of his status and character. For all she knew, he may not even be the marrying kind. Most wealthy men weren't. They're professional playboys, only want to be surrounded by beautiful women, to have one or two clinging to their arm showing off, to travel the world, play the field with different women, come and go as they wish, and answer to no one. We all know or have met that kind of man. It's best they stay single rather than leave a trail of a dozen broken hearts.

Whew! That was too much to consider before getting a cup of coffee. She needed to clear the cobwebs. She climbed out of bed, grabbed a robe and headed downstairs to the kitchen, almost thinking aloud: That dream was one of those where your imagination goes wild and plays tricks with your mind. That's especially true in the early stages of a relationship when something trivial could be misinterpreted, when every little gesture or whispered word can make your heart flutter or crash, and you think you're in love. And, you're so excited you want to run out and rent one of those huge flying contraptions and have those magical words 'I'm in love' scrolling and blinking to broadcast your feelings across the sky for the world to see. Ah, yes . . . love. Sweet, wonderful, never have a doubt or a care L O V E. Why not let the whole world know you are in love?

When all that happens, most of us don't realize the rest of the people on this planet are convinced you are an idiot, that you've lost your good mind, and no one, not even a most devoted friend, absolutely gives a flying flip about your love life. . . . mainly because they're either wrapped up in their own love affair, or they're still horribly bitter over their own 'love bug' that flew out of their coo-coo nest, or it was smacked down and squashed, or it got stuck between 5th and Main Street, or was vaulted into the ether – straight off the planet into Only God Knows Where Land.

The worse kind of message is when you see a decorated car going down the road with "Just Married" scribbled on the windows, fenders and trunk. It gets worse if the newlyweds are practically sitting in each other's lap and they've got those sickly plaster-plastic smiles . . . it's as if they'd had bad collagen jobs, as if their photo was used for a toothpaste commercial, or they'd been models in a "Got Milk?" magazine advertisement.

The rest of the world that hadn't been lucky in love sees those love-sick couples, sigh and say, 'Look at those dumb idiots!' The unlucky ones have traveled down that road before and they know the lousy survival rate of marriages today. . . . it's less than fresh meat at a cannibals convention.

By now she finished her second cup of coffee, but haven't reached a decision about that strange dream. Was it merely her imagination playing tricks again, was her subconscious sending a storyline for another book, or was it echoes of lessons learned at my grandmother's knee of what was truly important in life? Well, she remembered the movie 'Notebook,' where love lasts forever and the two people die together. Then there was the famous quote in 'Notting Hill' when Julia Roberts' character says, "Some people really do spend a lifetime together." Ah. . . . perfect, right? Sure, if you can find that special person.

Well, for Ally, she saw love like the characters portrayed by Meg Ryan and Tom Hanks in Nora Elfron's mega-hit film 'You've Got Mail.' The story gets off to a rocky start with overwhelming competition, then sadness when a boutique book store's influence on several generations of young readers comes to an end, but it still brings the lead roles together – their souls and personalities, more or less, match – and Ryan's character begins writing her own children's books. It works. It's perfect.

Ally just kind of goes with the flow like Meg Ryan's character, just hoping a real life Tom Hanks shows up who also happens to own a massive bookstore in the heart of Manhattan. Oh, if only . . . .

No, that's so not true. The truth – Ally's truth – is stupid. She wants the whole fairytale, thank you very much! She wants the magical True Prince to come galloping into her life on a beautiful white charger, flags flying, trumpets sounding, drums beating. Her True Prince will be tall, have dark hair, glorious eyes, and he'll be carrying the one slipper that will only fit my foot because it is the one I keep losing. Her True Prince will try it on her foot and of course it will only fit her, and he scoops her up onto his horse and they ride across the valley toward his castle on a hill in the distance. Ah, perfect.

Coffee hasn't helped. She still doesn't know what to do about that strange dream. It left her more confused than decisive. She laid back down, thinking about all those crazed ideas and images when there was a loud, weird noise downstairs. She was on her feet, rushing down the steps, around the corner, through the doorway, and there's her faithful cat trying to open his own food can. That's a desperate little hungry beastie and it made her feel absolutely awful that she forgot all about him. Sadly, it wasn't the first time.

Ring. The phone's sudden jangle startled her and she almost dropped the cat food can. It's the new someone. Drake wants to fly back to New York for a special evening.

Uh-oh. . . a nervous shiver at the timing of his invitation. Maybe now is the right time to come up with a good excuse not to go, just in case that big diamond is calling her name from the Harry Winston jewelry display case. Ally wasn't ready to consider an engagement ring after that strange dreamscape. Drake pushes, really wanting her to go with him.

"New York, Drake? Are you sure you want to go back to New York so soon?"

Drake was a man who didn't like to ask the same question twice or to repeat himself. There was a pause. "Uh, yes, honey," he replied in a soft, yet curious tone. "New York; I thought you loved New York, Ally."

"Yes, New York is always a good idea. . . .

"But . . . I hear a but coming," he said.

She couldn't help but laugh at that one: Never 'heard a but coming.' We both giggled for a moment.

She sighed. "No buts, I promise. When do you want to leave? Where are we going? What time?"

Drake immediately cheered up, his voice changing from melancholy to his usual sexy baritone. Even his self-confidence returned.

Oh, God, I was still thinking about that dream. Sometimes my dreams come true and sometimes they don't. I thought about the details. This was the same man who had dated famous super models and actresses. She was none of those types of women; not famous, not a supermodel. However, she's a wise and successful businesswoman.

At that point, she wasn't sure if Drake was her real prince, if there was a shoe, or if the shoe would fit. She was quite fond of the few other men she was dating at the time. One or two had some well-delivered lines as well . . . maybe, just maybe, a man like Drake needed a bit of good ol' fashioned Southern competition. It might bring him down a peg or two off his high horse.

Uh-oh. "Okay, Granny Pearl, that's you talking, not me, but you're putting your words of wisdom on me and in my mind."

Ally sat quietly for a few minutes, trying to think this through. Yes, it might be bad timing to talk to her blessed Granny Pearl long after she'd left this earth, but she was always her touchstone, sheltering fortress, font of practical knowledge and universal wisdom. What would she tell her to do now? Ally knew what she would tell her: "I think this man Drake is a great catch, too big of a fish to throw back in the water." Somehow, she got the feeling Granny Pearl disagreed.

Even though she had doubts about Drake, Alley was having way too much fun flying around the country in luxurious company jets, being wined and dined by a man of his status, which was very close to a prince. It was about accurate. Drake claimed his family's lineage had been traced back to royalty. And, of course, she didn't doubt it for a moment.

Ally finally backed out of her shoe closet after finding the perfect Cinderella slipper for a special night in New York with

Drake. She really hoped they were going back to the opera. After her first experience, she discovered she loved it a lot despite a previous attitude that she wouldn't like it at all. She quickly learned opera was a love story in motion. It was Romeo and Juliet, Colin and her, and yes, of course, opera was a powerful emotional and soul-moving performance.

Collin? Did she just say Collin? She'd been in the closet too long. Drake Lanzen. She had to give him credit for introducing her to opera. What is wrong? She promised herself not to live in the past, to live in the present, in the moment, to enjoy life again.

Actually, Ally was excited about going to New York. After all, how many young women get to go out with a millionaire 'prince' on such amazing dates in a private jet all the way to New York? How many are romanced like a princess? Very few, that's for sure.

Besides, Ally had just about lost contact with her girlfriends over all the romance with Drake Lanzen. They were blindly jealous of the attention he gave her, the imagination he invested into making their dates special, and showering her with flowers and small tokens.

Her girlfriends' dates usually consisted of going to the local Hooters for beer and chicken wings while their boyfriends stared at waitresses wearing too-short orange shorts and low cut, thin, white, tee-shirts with owls printed on them. Oh, *right . . .* how fascinating – *not.* Ally shook her head. *Save me from such mundane 'fascination.'* If they were really lucky, the girls went to a Ruth Chris Steakhouse in Buckhead, but that only happened on special occasions, like a birthday party or to celebrate a promotion.

She was late coming home from the office. She'd had just enough time to literally jump into a tiny black dress and heels, and then refreshed her makeup before the doorbell rang. Drake must be there already. She wondered how long she'd really sat on the closet floor holding a pair of shoes. She'd been swept away by memories, back to a time which wasn't favorable to remember. While in the closet, one white rose had fallen from the top shelf, slipped from the pages of a special book where she kept many of the pressed white roses Collin had given her over the years.

The doorbell rang again, long bursts, then short bursts, again and again. She could detect anxiety in the chimes. "Okay, okay! I'm coming, Drake!"

She opened the door to a six-foot, five-inch tall handsome man with thick, brownish hair. His smile gleaming down at her was as wide as the Atlantic Ocean, his eyes twinkling with happiness. He held a single red rose in his hand.

"Oh, thank you. How sweet of you." Ally took the rose, accepted his arm as he helped her down the front steps and into the limousine.

Dom was poured into rose-colored flutes to celebrate the night ahead – one that Ally certainly wasn't expecting.

There was something different about the cool, collected and enchanting Drake Lanzen, a different air about him, a gleam in his eyes like a kid at Christmas, a kid that had crawled under the Christmas tree and unwrapped a present when no one was looking. Of course, no one could know about his surprise, but at the same time it was obvious he was excited, dying to tell her. He wasn't very talkative, but he held her hand tighter than usual. A lot of kissing was going on.

"Whoa, there fella, what's up with mister kissy face this evening?"

Drake really didn't like the terminology 'kissy face' so much, but he was so amorous that she had to reapply her pink rose lipstick twice before they reached Love Field Airport where the private jet waited.

The night was cool and a bit of fog was rolling in, but it was still a beautiful evening. As they got out of the car, the driver called out, "Oh, Miss Ally, you forgot your rose."

"Leave it there," Drake replied, "she has more waiting for her."

She glanced up at Drake, but before she could think of a retort or a question, she had stepped into Drake's plane. It was filled, decorated with roses – pink, all pink – very different for Drake to choose pink because he was a red rose guy all the way.

As long as they weren't white roses, Ally was okay. White roses would always be Collin. He had said his love for me was as pure as white snow and as true as white castles among the skies over the oceans. Ally had no idea about the white castles . . . yet.

Okay, something was certainly up, but Ally was afraid to ask.

Drake grinned his happy, wide grin again, poured more champagne, sat down and was silent. He fastened their seatbelts and told the pilot to take off. Within minutes, the plane was zooming off, headed into the sky.

This time the background music was an old love song by Frank Sinatra. Ally suddenly felt like she was in the middle of an

350

old Hollywood movie, maybe back at home in a dream and hadn't awakened.

"Drake, I think I have a clue about what this night is about," she said, "and I'm going to tell you ahead of time. This is so not fair. What girl could resist all of this, the roses, the champagne, plane trips, and the restaurants in five-star hotels?

"But, look here, Drake . . . if you think this is going to be the night we sleep together, well, you, uh, I just want to say before you waste any more money on me, I am *not* the girl you want to waste money on for that kind of thing."

Drake laughed, took her hand, and looked into her eyes all frisky and bushy-tailed. "Oh, I'm sure of it! Ally, if I was looking for a woman to sleep with, do you think I'd have to go all-out like this? No, I don't think so. Too many women in line for that kind of thing, when a man comes from where I come from. That's why all the roses and wining and dining with you.

"Ally," Drake slowly took both of her hands, looked at her for a long moment in silence. He took a deep breath. "I am in love with you. I have been since the moment I laid eyes on you. I am so confused how a woman like you, Ally . . . your beauty, your style, and grace have not been swooped up long ago."

Ally's mind spun, then quickly moved to Collin. She glanced away from Drake's gaze. He gently cradled her chin in his hand and turned her face back toward him.

Oh, my God. Now I'm thinking about that strange dream. It's true. He's going to take me into Harry Winston's after all. Oh, God I think too much. . . . .

"Drake . . ." She tried to stop him before he went much further and she would be forced into a decision of saying 'yes' to a proposal that she couldn't quite say 'no' to.

"Ally," Drake once again got her attention, "I want you to know something. From the very first moment I looked across the room and saw you, and you glanced my way, it was like a bolt of electricity had gone through my heart. It was something I never felt before with any woman.

"You have a powerful spell on me, milady, and I cannot seem to break it. You have a special gleam in your eyes that takes my breath away when I look at you. You have a certain charm about you that's like an elixir to me. I'm intoxicated without drinking when I kiss you, and I am breathless without you."

Oh, my God. . . . Ally's throat constricted until she thought she'd cry. She fought back tears. "Drake, . . . breathless without me, Drake?" *She had never, in all her life, heard such a line, not even in a song.*

"I don't know what to say, Drake. Ii is all so fast and so unexpected – so sudden."

Before she could say anything else, he put his fingers across her lips and kissed her – long, passionate. Magical.

At that moment, Ally felt something for the first time in a long time. It was as if her heart suddenly started beating again after losing the man she thought was her True Love. *Oh, my goodness. I'm feeling the night's magic, feeling his spirit, or she'd had way too much champagne.*

"I don't know what to say, Drake."

"Ally, don't say a word."

The pilot signaled them to fasten their seatbelts. It was as if the flight had been extra fast or she had experienced a time warp, was missing time. Many words and emotions had been crowded into that flight time. She was truly caught up in the magic of it all.

A white coach was waiting for their arrival. That indicated Drake planned to take her some place special. Ally sighed, and silently thanked God it was already dark, so all the jewelry stores in Manhattan were closed at that hour.

Drake didn't give her a ring on the airplane. *Off the hook.*

But now hearing the 'I love you' part, Ally knew some sort of ring or tribute was not far behind. Tonight was all about the romance of their special evening. They were driven to a renowned hotel restaurant that overlooked Manhattan and enjoyed a fabulous dinner. Somehow, she had been able to rid her mind of all those pre-engagement ring dream jitters. Perhaps she would take them up again on another evening and another time.

While they were in the private dining room, violin players strolled in and began a serenade, a medley of famous love songs. Drake reach across the table, set her wine glass down, took her hand and then pulled her onto her feet. They locked into one another and began to dance.

"Drake, I had no idea you were such a great dancer."

"Sure I am, and I can also play piano by ear. I hear a melody and can reproduce it with very little trouble. Actually, I'm quite an excellent painter, too."

"Painting? You mean you are an artist as well?"

Drake grinned down. "Ally, I can paint your portrait. And, as far as you know, I have already painted your portrait."

"Funny. . . . that's funny." Then realized she had thought out loud. "How could you paint me, Drake? If you did already paint me, what would you paint, I might so boldly ask?"

As soon as the words left her mouth, she wished she could pull them back into her mind. She so wished she hadn't asked because Drake stopped dancing, pushed her back to arm's length, then sat her back down at their table.

He pulled a tiny box out of his jacket pocket. The box was oblong rather than square, a shape too weird for any type of ring. But, the box was gold with silver strings holding it together. He placed it in her hand. It was quite heavy.

Oh, my God. What could this be? Ally's hands trembled slightly as she opened the box and folded back the edges of delicate gold tissue paper.

It was a tiny crystal slipper.

Ally was astounded.

"It's from Ireland," he said. "I had some engraving done on the foot. It says . . . Be My Cinderella."

Drake immediately began to speak about an out-of-town business trip to Ireland and how he had come across this slipper while shopping in a small village. He said as soon as he had seen it, Ally had flashed into his memory, how she had lost her slipper that first evening when he saw her, how he had knelt down at the limousine, and without thinking about the words in advance, had blurted out: 'Cinderella has lost her slipper.'

"My heart spoke to me," Drake said, "and it said that this was Ally's slipper. You must have it."

He said the trip to Ireland was shortly after meeting her, then he had painted her portrait with this tiny slipper and this moment they were now living.

"For that painting, I had placed the slipper on a royal purple pillow and set it in your tiny hands." Drake cleared his throat. "I envisioned you as in forever, as my true princess.

"Ally, this is your engagement ring."

Drake knelt at Ally's feet. "Will you marry me?"

Oh, my god. What man on this earth goes all the way to Ireland and finds a Waterford crystal slipper in some little shop, and then uses it to propose marriage instead of bringing out the usual engagement ring that's hiding in their pocket? Oh, not Drake Lanzen. He was unique among men.

"Yes, Drake . . . I cannot say no to you, so it's a definite yes."

Violins began to play again and they danced again. Magic.

They left the restaurant and went for a carriage ride through Central Park. Then they returned to the limousine and headed back to what she thought would be the airport. But surprises weren't over. They met a man who escorted them to a store, unlocked the front door, and they shopped for a diamond. It was Tiffany's instead of Harry Winston's that was in Ally's dreams.

"Winston's made my mother's ring," Drake said as they walked through the doors of Tiffany's. "I prefer here."

Ally didn't choose her ring as Reese did in the movie 'Sweet Home Alabama.' They were escorted through the store to a special place in the rear. There was a locked case behind a vault. Inside, loose diamonds were displayed on black velvet.

Drake looked at many diamonds, viewing them closely. He picked up one, looked at it for a long moment and finally said, "Ah," as he laid it in Ally's hands. "This is the one. This is the lucky diamond for a princess like you. It has magic. Feel it?"

Ally was astounded by his words, but more surprised when she held the stone. She, too, could feel it. Her hand tingled and she knew her heart had to be smiling.

At that point, they carefully selected the mounting, the platinum, the band width, and exactly how they wanted this one-of-a-kind diamond to be set.

After the transactions were completed, they left Tiffany's long after normal business hours in Manhattan. They climbed back into the limo, poured fresh flutes of champagne and headed back to the airport. The ring Drake selected for Ally to wear forever was a really large diamond. It must have cost a fortune. Money was nothing more than printed paper to Drake. She wished she had mentally zoned in more clearly on what was happening at that time, but she was still in a state of shock at what had occurred that evening in New York, of being carried away by a tiny Waterford crystal shoe, a display case of diamonds and being told, 'Choose one.' *Oh, my God, what a fantasy come true.*

Soon they were in the airplane with our seatbelts fastened. She had heard thunder rolling in the distance as they had gotten out of the limo and had climbed into the aircraft. The pilot assured us there was nothing to be concerned about. Not too long into the flight, the ride began to get a bit bumpy.

Oh, dear. Ally had been told there was nothing to worry about, but this storm had brewed up from nowhere and they were flying right through the middle of it. Ally's grandmothers were trying to get through to her mind, too, but she wasn't thinking of Granny Pearl, or my Grandma Violet – not even Collin, who had died on a stormy night.

Ally could only think about being at thirty-thousand feet above the earth in a jet that was rocking and rolling. *Oh, that's great; just my luck: one tiny crystal shoe, one huge diamond, one prince, and the flippin' plane goes down in a storm.*

She had never cared for thunderstorms at all. She was always frightened as a child when bad weather slammed into the bayou. It doesn't take long for any child to learn that hurricanes damage everything they think is solid and safe. She gripped the seat and anxiety must have shown on her face.

Ally wasn't tuned in to the message the bad weather had delivered; she hadn't heard what the storm was trying so hard to reveal as the airplane pitched and rolled: Rocky times were ahead, I was headed for a stormy relationship, lightning strikes, lightning does not strike twice, Drake was not going to die, they were both in the storm.

Her mind wandered in different directions. Drake held on tight and it was obvious that he had gotten scared. It was really bad as objects were flung onto the floor, then into the air and back to the floor within seconds. Suddenly, it was calm. The plane stopped rocking and rolling, and the pilot's voice came on the intercom. "Sorry, folks. It's a smooth ride the rest of the way."

Whew! After Ally recovered from her terrible fright, they drank another glass of champagne and celebrated their engagement.

"Now we only have to face the wicked witch," Drake said with a smirk.

What? Ally was quite shocked by his statement. *Oh, great, here comes another surprising fairytale in this life as Cinderella. I'll have my own personal wicked witch? Oh, God.*

"Well, pray tell, Drake. I'm about buzzed anyway with all that champagne and the scary roller-coaster ride in your airplane. I guess I'm about up for any ol' weird story you've got to tell me now. Go ahead. I'll try to hold on to my sanity. What's next?"

Drake gave me a funny look and shook his head. "It's my mother, honey. She is, uh, so different and always has been an odd woman, and I love her more than anything but—"

"Uh-oh . . . *but*? Here we go with 'buts' again."

". . . my mother has always wanted me to marry late in life. Well, I am almost thirty and I've respected her wishes. Please don't take this the wrong way, but she is one of those control freaks you hear about, one who wants to pick out their son's wife, just like in the olden days. She has always tried to pick my women for me, the ones I dated, and potential wives. . . . all because of her uppity Driving Club friends' daughters were so-and-so daughters from so-and-sos family. I think you know what I mean by picking out my friends and girlfriends.

"She wanted me to marry so many different daughters of her friends, and you know me, well, I mean you don't, but, Ally, before you I was the original playboy. I could care less about getting married, having a wife, being tied down. I was having too much fun and frankly, I never saw myself tied down to one woman. I'd date one in Atlanta, date another in London or France when I was in Europe, and some Hollywood actresses when on the West Coast, and a model here and there. Nothing serious because I never considered any of them as serious contenders. That's fact.

361

"Wealthy men, even some independently wealthy women, really don't get married until late in life. You being a woman probably don't understand this. Women just think differently than guys and—."

"Whoa! Hold it right there, Mister Lanzen, before you get too carried away with your high n' mighty own-self. You're beginning to sound exactly like that Carol King song."

Drake laughed and started singing 'You're So Vain.'

Ally grinned at him. He settled down and continued to explain how he had grown up.

"No, I'm really not that vain at all. I love my dad so much, and my mom of course, but I saw quite a bit of things I couldn't rationalize as a child. My God, Ally, when you are a child, you don't like to see your family go through fights and split-ups. As a boy and even now as a grown man it does something to you. My parents split when I was ten and then my mom got remarried within six months – *only six months!* – married my dad's best friend, who was more wealthy than my dad. My dad loves her to this day – he'll never get over it.

"I swore when I was just a kid that I'd never get married, never, all because of what I saw my parents go through, and what my dad is still going through. I never wanted to fall in love, never planned on it except for one of two nights."

Drake turned his head and tried to stifle a giggle. Ally thought he sounded a little coy and was surprised he didn't blush. How cute.

"My mother is a hard woman even though she's beautiful and smart. She has some strong beliefs and issues, and she sure doesn't mind throwing them on anyone or anything that crosses her path. In other words, she's going to be simply pissed off because she didn't handpick my bride. She's sick in that way."

Ally felt that she must have turned pale. "Oh, no... so, what you're saying is that no matter what, she won't like me."

"Uh, well, yes. She's never liked any woman I've ever dated."

"Oh, God. This is going to be a mess."

"I mean, no, Ally; she'll love you in time, but that's what it will take – time. You will have to grow on her, and she will simply have to get over herself. So, don't fret any over it because it will eventually pass. . . . sooner or later."

Drake's wide grin returned briefly. "Besides, I don't care. And, my dad and my stepdad will adore you.

"The main one who seems like my real mom is Bessie. She raised me. It was always Bessie more than my mother for everything a kid needed. My mother was always traveling around the world, going here, going there, going everywhere. Even when she wasn't traveling, she still wasn't around for me. Too busy.

"I couldn't keep up with their travels because I had school and private tutors, and special accelerated classes for gifted students. I always felt my black mammy Bessie was my real mom. She was the one who cooked for me, tucked me in at night, told me stories, set up with me when I was sick, and put up with my misbehaving when I was bad or bored, and was there for me when I just couldn't stand to hear my parents arguing for hours. I could always run to her and she'd make me feel better. And, there were always hugs and warm cookies and ice cold milk in her kitchen. She was like an angel to me when I had no one else. . . . no one.

"I love Bessie and she already knows about you, Ally. And, well, I have something of yours that's very special that I leave in her home."

Ally's head had quit spinning and had merely slid into a numbness that was spreading throughout her body. All this was just too much to comprehend at one time.

Okay, now there's a second mom I have to deal with, too? Oh, God. "Okay, Drake, and what would that special something be?"

Drake started to smile, and changed his mind. "No, not yet. Another time and place."

She thought their next plane trip to New York would result in another huge surprise. She had agreed to marry a millionaire prince who was deeply in love with her. What else was there? She didn't need to know anything else.

Or did she?

* * *

"Let no one deceive another or despise anyone anywhere, or through anger or irritation wish for another to suffer."

Buddha Dhammapada

Chapter 21

A few days later, they were en route to Drake's home. Ally held onto her nerve as best she could. She was about to meet her soon-to-be in-laws. Excited? Oh, yes. Finally, she was going to have a real mother-in-law, and since she'd never had such a relationship before, she could hardly wait. After everything Drake had said, Alley was more nervous than excited.

Over the past few days, Drake had also told her many wonderful stories of his childhood, not just the heartache of his parents' divorce. He told her of growing up in the marvelous old Atlanta mansions, of traveling the world, of the family's collection of Renoirs, Rembrandts, Picassos, and an aviary that contained rare birds which cost a million dollars each. Ally hadn't been reared in abject poverty, but as far as she knew, million dollar birds didn't nest or fly around in Louisiana bayous.

Drake talked on and on about his parents and Ally's mind drifted into other realms. There was something different about the stories Drake told, and it just didn't sit right. He kept going on and on, and it began to sound like bragging. Well, he did have an awful lot to brag about: Born with a platinum spoon in his mouth instead of a silver one. Ally tried not to think so sarcastically, but anybody who brags too much never sits right in her mind and it also made her uncomfortable. And, yes, Ally admitted that sarcasm was a downfall.

"Ally, did you hear me? Hey! Earth to Ally."

She blinked and realized Drake was still talking about the birds. The limo pulled up to the main gate and Otto stepped out of the gatehouse as the driver lowered the window.

"Good evening, Mr. Drake."

"Good evening to you, too. Buzz us on through, please."

"Yes, sir." Otto grinned, stepped into the doorway and pushed a button. The heavy, yet ornate iron gate began to swing open. When it had cleared, the driver moved the limo up the hillside. Tall antique lights lined the landscaped drive; Ally didn't remember seeing them earlier, and she was still thinking about the family having a man to stand there, waiting to push a button to open their gate when someone wanted in or out.

Oh! Well, hello Ally. He's there because of all those million dollar birds Drake keeps talking about. If someone stole just one, they'd be set for life. The aviary held twenty-five of those rare birds. Wow. Okay, things were beginning to take shape in her mind, becoming clearer.

Drake said tennis was Mr. Lanzen's hobby, so Ally wasn't surprised to see lavish tennis courts. She imagined half of Atlanta could drop by to watch the matches from the numerous scattered patio tables. She looked forward to playing on that court herself.

The first time Ally had seen the house it was after sundown and a huge party was going on. This time, the sun was shining and she could see exactly how massive the house really was. Her eyes widened and her pulse began to race – not excitement – fear! Ally wasn't marrying into a family with a little bit more than the usual Atlanta wealth. This family was a dynasty.

She gripped the seat and stared at Drake when he said, "This is home."

"No," she replied softly, "this is more like the Ritz-Carlton."

"Oh, Ally, don't be so melodramatic! It's just one of our homes. My parents have chalets in Switzerland, in Hawaii, and, well, all over. They just buy a home wherever they're traveling. It's really no big deal."

'No big deal'? You've got to be kidding me. Ally suddenly felt like Dorothy in The Wizard of Oz and the twister had just lifted

me off the ground. She wanted to click her ruby red slippers together and swirl herself and Toto back home.

The limo pulled around the huge circular, manicured driveway and the driver stopped. Ally was still gripping the seat.

Drake sensed she was nervous. He gave her an assuring peck on the cheek and grabbed her hand. "It's okay, honey. You just have to pray my mother likes you."

Was he joking? Suddenly, Ally's heart began to throb and she felt sick to her stomach. A million butterflies started fluttering and circling inside her and were pounding on her insides to escape. Why was she so nauseous? Drake's warning was loaded with such intensity and bluntness that she instantly and instinctively knew he wasn't joking. This visit was far more than an introduction. She had every reason to be apprehensive. She wanted to stay in the limo, but Drake took her hand, pulled her to her feet as her head swirled a bit. Her eyes refocused on what lay ahead. They were standing at the front door. *Oh, Lord...*
.

Drake rang the bell to his parent's home. How odd. In Louisiana, family pulled around to the rear, opened the back door, and shouted, 'Hello, the house!' as they stepped inside.

The massive hand-carved door slowly opened and Celli, the maid, smiled. "How do you do, Mr. Lanzen? Please do come in. Would you please wait here while I tell Mrs. Lanzen you're here."

Once again, Ally found something was pretty strange: The maid announced their son's arrival? For some unknown reason, she heard Granny Pearl's voice; the lyrics of Reba's ballad, 'Here's your one chance, Fancy, don't let me down.'

Mrs. Lanzen stepped into the foyer. "Drake, darling, how are you?" She hugged her son, leaned back and looked at him closer, smiled and nodded.

Then she turned toward Ally. Cold eyes. Looked her up and down. A formal handshake. Frozen smile. "Well."

Ally felt doomed.

They followed Mrs. Lanzen down a long hallway and passed a dining room with a table long enough for a king's court. Ally tried not to be obvious that she was in awe of the home. They walked through a huge living room that led into a smaller sitting room.

"Sit and let's chat," Mrs. Lanzen said. "I will have Celli bring us tea."

Ally's back straightened. *Oh, yes. . . . let's do have tea. I'll have something to do while being inspected. Deep breathe. Don't think aloud. Don't jump to conclusions. Smile. Oh, Lord.*

She took several deep breaths, tried to quiet her Cajun spirit, and tried to go with the flow of the moment. Mrs. Lanzen and Drake made idle chitchat, then suddenly, the woman focused her full attention on Ally. Dark eyes gleamed across the tea table and bored into Ally.

"Soooo, . . . Miss Ally, . . . however in the world did *you* meet my son?"

Drake knew his mother intended to put Ally on the spot, to deliberately make her feel uncomfortable. He leaned back on the sofa and tilted his head, watching Ally maneuver through his mother's verbal joust.

Although still slightly nervous, Ally was an experienced businesswoman and not an ingénue. She was ready for this grilling. She decided to reply to the woman's cold questions in the same manner as she asked them. Ally studied her expression when she told the older woman the truth. "Actually, Mrs. Lanzen, Drake followed me until he caught me."

Drake laughed, and Mrs. Lanzen glared at her son.

Rapid-fire questions flew: where did she come from? what family would that be? what does her family do? did they leave Ally a dowry?

"Oh, yes, ma'am, I have had a dowry since I was seven years old," I replied. "I got it for my birthday."

Drake muffled a giggle. "No, honey . . . dowry." Then he changed the subject, thank goodness.

Ally's mind cleared for a second. *Oh! She didn't ask about a diary; she meant an inheritance.*

Mrs. Lanzen poured herself another cup of tea, and looked at Ally's ensemble again. "Did you go to finishing school in France?"

"Oh, no, ma'am, I finished school in Louisiana."

"They don't have finishing schools there, Mom," Drake added. "Ally is from Louisiana. She grew up on a nice plantation with her grandmother. And, that sums it up. She had a great upbringing."

Oh, that was very humbling. "Thank you, Drake."

"Well, you are very pretty, Ally," his mother replied.

Oh, my God, a compliment. "Thank you."

Mrs. Lanzen was a very beautiful woman. Her blonde hair looked like woven silk, her complexion was flawless, and she was trim and tall. But, she was unsettling in a dark, mean spirited way. Somewhere along the line in her life, something drastic must have happened to make her view the world and people in such a negative way.

As Ally watched her, it was obvious the woman's finishing school didn't create many lingering niceties for her to use later in life. She was brutally cold, and the looks she shot across the tea table at Ally were right out of the 'Witches of Eastwick.' Her distrustfulness, evidently, had turned on full force. It wasn't hard to figure out she did not like Ally, but Ally doubted the woman would have liked an angel, even if she'd flown in the door with brass wings. This new family relationship was going to be a challenge and not fun at all.

Mrs. Lanzen wore an astounding diamond ring. It should have been in the Tower of London and guarded by the Black Watch as part of the Queen's royal jewels, or in Elizabeth Taylor's collection, or a museum somewhere. Ally hadn't known diamonds were ever found that large. The woman's bony finger looked as if it could barely handle the weight, and Ally assumed she probably had painful arthritis in those protruding joints.

The trio continued with inconsequential chitchat with the tea. Celli popped in wearing her right-out-of-the-movies perfect maid's attire and checked to see if they needed anything. Mrs. Lanzen would just wave her away as if she was nothing. Ally felt sorry for poor old Celli.

From somewhere in the mansion, a floor clock's deep chimes tolled the hour: five o'clock. Suddenly, Mrs. Lanzen's head snapped upward, she seemed extremely excited, grinned and rubbed her hands together. "Drake! It's five o'clock!"

Drake also got excited.

What, pray tell, goes on here at five that's so exciting?

Mrs. Lanzen looked at her diamond wristwatch, turning it in different directions. "It's a minute *after* five already!" She picked up a small silver dinner bell and rang it, and began calling in a loud, cold voice. "Celli! It is a minute after five! What *are* you doing?"

Celli rushed into the room carrying a silver tray of cocktails. "I am so sorry, Miz. Lanzen. I'm on my way."

"Ha! You know that five o'clock is cocktail hour. How long, Celli, have you worked here . . . twenty-five years? Then you ought to know what to do by now. You may go."

377

Cocktails were delivered every twenty to thirty minutes – a fresh pitcher of cocktails, not just glasses. Ally certainly couldn't keep up with Mrs. Lanzen or Drake's drinking. The more Mrs. Lanzen drank, the nicer to Ally she became. Perhaps the pitchers of cocktails wasn't a bad thing after all.

As Ally continued speaking, she addressed her as Mrs. Lanzen, and she raised her hand. "Oh, for heaven's sake," she said in a snobbish tone, "call me Doodle."

Doodle? What kind of a nickname is that? Ally sighed and thought about it, and decided she wasn't going to ask what the name may mean, where on earth it came from, or who had given her that odd tag?

'Doodle' asked about Ally's two daughters, Nicollet and Terrin. Ally couldn't stop a smile from touching her lips. "I had them when I was very young, and we've literally grown up together. They are the only family I've ever had beside my grandmother and great grandmother, who were very elderly ladies. I can't possibly imagine what my world would be without my beautiful girls."

Some people may not agree about having children at so young an age, but everyone has their own unique timing. It worked out for Ally and was exactly what she needed in her life.

Doodle's upper lip curled in disgust as Ally spoke of her daughters. She told Doodle she had finished high school almost two years early and was in college when she met and married her first husband.

Mrs. Lanzen took a completely different tone.

Mr. Lanzen came home and stepped into the parlor to join them for cocktails. He was about five-foot eleven-inches tall, with a thin, very reserved-looking expression. He gave the impression that he didn't enjoy life, he was merely participating in it because he had no other choice. He shook Ally's hand when they were introduced, sat down in what she assumed was his favorite chair, opened a small brass box, and pulled out what appeared to be a huge pricey cigar. She watched him as he carefully cut and lit it. He was a man of character, one of whom you could tell preferred to live in his own little world.

Doodle's endless, aimless, chatter faded into the background as far as Mr. Lanzen was concerned. She tried to include him in the conversation, but he was content in another world of his own making. It took a moment to rattle him enough that he would speak, but it was rarely more than a few words. He immediately returned to his newspaper.

Apparently, when Doodle drank, she talked to be talking, to hear herself talking, as if her voice confirmed she was still on the planet. She drank and talked until she became loud and boisterous. Shortly afterwards, Drake was ready to leave. Ally had been ready to leave for quite some time.

Drake had wanted to tell his mother the news of the engagement, but it seemed to be the wrong time.

As they left the estate, the sky was turning dark and ominous. It seemed later than it actually was, and Ally was mentally and emotionally exhausted. She felt they had been inside at the Lanzen mansion for an eternity, her answering questions, trying to be social, trying to be friendly, trying to be liked. It had been an effort. Being inside the place was definitely one those instances when a little goes a long way. . . . a long, long way. She needed a nap. Obviously, Drake loved his parents, but it was a strange, different type of love; not a typical mom and pop story. Children and family issues seemed an intrusion into their separate, high society world and lifestyle. Ally wondered if given enough time, facts about Drake's relationship with his mother and step-father would unfold and she would understand and appreciate how they lived.

Drake asked about her feelings, thoughts and impressions about his parents. For a few minutes, he tried to play the uppity

380

son, but it didn't last long. He had had a few drinks and was feeling sentimental . . . eager to tell her more.

They pulled into the driveway perhaps thirty seconds before it began to pour buckets of rain. Thunder roared and lightning pierced through the dark Atlanta skies. They dashed inside and Drake went straight to the bar to pour himself a drink. He brought her a glass of Merlot and seemed restless. The smile he had worn during the visit with his parents had vanished. He was very serious, and paced the room for a few minutes before turning to face her again.

"Ally, I guess you need to know about this family, especially if you're going to be in it." He sat down by the fireplace, lit a cigarette, and told her to get comfortable.

"Walter Lanzen is one of the most respected men in Atlanta, not to mention one of the most powerful," Drake said. "Walter comes from Old Money and with it came Atlanta Road Construction, one of the largest companies in Georgia. I don't need to tell you how much just one month's profit is in road construction. That's just the beginning."

Drake took a long sip of his drink and shook his head. "There's major Coca-Cola stock, stock in everything you can imagine. It would take a whole book to describe all Walter owns and is involved in. One thing is for sure: the state doesn't name the ritziest and oldest historical section of town after someone unless they owned a sizeable portion of that town.

"Furthermore, Walter gave one of his mansions to the state to be used as a historical society. His accountants simply wrote it off one quarter. That explains Walter Lanzen, and that, Ally, is the man who'll be your father-in-law."

Ally stomach rumbled and another weird feeling came over her. She felt as if she was marrying the Prince of Georgia and the king would be her father-in-law. Maybe her childhood fairytale about being a real life Cinderella wasn't going to be so far off the mark after all.

"I'm not done." Drake climbed to his feet, went to the bar and refreshed his drink. "My mother also comes from Old Money. She was one of Atlanta's most prominent society girls; the usual coming out debutant balls, cotillions, charities, all those functions. She was a member of the Driving Club when she met Walter. He fell in love with her the moment he laid eyes on her. My mother was very beautiful; stunning when she was young. She and Walter made quite the pair in the Atlanta social scene."

Drake wandered back to the fireplace and sat down. "Their combined wealth exceeded most peoples' wealth in many states.

They were known worldwide and their photographs were in many magazines. So, without me boring you to tears all evening long, that's the bottom line on who my parents are."

He tipped his glass and drained it, climbed to his feet, refilled Ally's wine glass and made himself another drink.

"You need to know that life is going to be very different now that you're becoming a Lanzen," he said from the bar. "Also, you'll need to get involved with the ladies of the charities; you'll represent the Lanzen family to deliver donations, photographs in the newspapers, that sort of thing. That's what you'll do as a Lanzen lady. My mother will tell you all about it as she gets more involved and reorganizes your life and schedule."

Ally was almost trembling at that point. She had already passed the uneasy stage about his mother and stepdad and their high expectations. She still felt confident they would learn to love her in time. Little did she know then what she was up against with this family. They didn't like their own children, much less anyone else. For that matter, Alley wasn't sure they liked or accepted themselves.

She had her work cut out for her with the wealthiest and most prominent family in the South. Ally assumed it was the double-edged sword spoken about in Louisiana. Time would

383

reveal more about the family, and her road would lead her to wherever her heart carried.

"Men fear death as children fear to go in the dark..."

Sir Francis Bacon

Chapter 22

Ally and Drake spent some quiet evenings together, both of us working during the day. One evening Drake asked her what was so sad in her life.

She pondered his question for a moment. "Why? Do I appear sad to you?"

"Honey, don't answer a question with a question because you know the answer."

"Yes, Drake, I do know the answer. I'm wondering why you ask."

"As much as you try to hide it, sometimes you fade away. There's a faraway look in your eyes – as if you are a million miles and century away from here."

Ally knew before she got too deep in this man's life that she owed him an explanation. "Yes, I guess I do from time to time. There's a reason I escaped to Atlanta."

"Escaped or ran?"

"Well, both. I was in love. I had found him, the man I wanted to spend eternity with."

"Eternity, Ally? That sounds like you're from a different time."

"Yes, I guess I do, but it wasn't me who was from a different time; it was the man I fell in love with. I've thought about this: I really believe he was from a different time because of a re-occurring dream I have.

"I was involved with a man who was somehow in the wrong time era. I cannot explain it, but I can tell you what happened. We were engaged to be married.

"The ceremony was supposed to be held in three weeks. I was shopping for my wedding gown and planned to wear silver beaded shoes I had found as a child. They were my great grandmother's wedding shoes that she never wore because he died. I had shown them to my fiancé; and he thought it would be special to wear them since my great grandmother never had the chance.

"We had been running errands in town when it began to rain. He took me home, I kissed him good-bye, got out of his car, grabbed what I thought were my slippers and ran into the house before I got soaked, but I only got one slipper. I thought I had dropped the other one or left it in my fiancé's car. I ran outside to see if it was in one of the mud puddles. I couldn't find it, so figured it must have been left in my fiancé's car."

Drake had patiently listened to every word, and nodded agreement.

"I was in California doing some business with a film company, and would wait until I flew back to retrieve the slipper. Collin, my fiancé, could have found it in his car. Something made me ill and I had a bad dream about him floating away from me. I just knew something was terribly wrong. The whole thing wasn't right. Phone calls weren't answered, none of our friends knew where he was, and I couldn't find anyone at home who could tell me anything.

"After I flew back, I got in touch with Colin's parents. They told me there'd been a terrible accident on old Highway 40 by the bridge. They said it had been bad weather; rain. Colin was going over the bridge a bit fast, and collided with another car at a high speed. He was in the car when it went over the bridge railing."

Tears welled in Ally's eyes, but she kept talking, trying not to cry. "When they pulled him out of the crushed vehicle, very little was left. I was devastated. I couldn't bear to use that bridge where it had happened. I couldn't go anywhere for a while. I had been heartbroken when my high school sweetheart went back to France, but death? That was different, so impossibly final.

"I was very young and it was difficult to comprehend. I was crying uncontrollably on my bed when I rolled over onto something: my great grandmother's silver slipper. I picked it up and screamed. One slipper. Collin had the other one in his car when he crashed. All I had left from Collin was a promised ring, a promised lifetime – the love of my life was gone forever – and one silver slipper.

"I could only take it one way: losing my first love as a teenager, then my great grandmother's slipper and my fiancé' in one blow . . . there was nothing left for me there. I had to leave, get out of that small town. That place felt cursed for me somehow. I had to leave the bayou where I had grown up.

"I wrapped the silver slipper in white linen and I returned to its hiding place in the trunk in the attic. It was where it belonged . . . never to be worn by a bride on her wedding day."

Tears spilled from Ally's eyes. She wiped them away with her sleeve and gritted her teeth to hold back the sobs. She looked across the sofa and was surprised to see tears had welled up in Drake's eyes.

"I wish I hadn't asked that question. Oh, darling . . ." he said as he wrapped his arms around her shoulders and pulled her closer. "I'm so sorry."

Drake got up, went to the bar and poured another glass of wine and something for himself. "You're not going to believe what I'm about to tell you." He sat back down.

"You're not the only one who had a last encounter with their first love. My first real girlfriend and I had a fight because I had to work at the last minute. We had made plans to spend Labor Day weekend with friends on the lake. She was really mad at me, but I had to work. I kissed her good-bye and she left in one of our friends' cars. They were boating on the lake, just like always. Something happened and she drowned. I had sent her off alone with friends and she never came back to me. Snatched out of my life, and I wasn't there to prevent the accident. I felt guilty for a long time."

Ally stared at Drake and realized they had both endured tragedies years before that were still open, painful wounds. Memories of lost first loves are often etched deep in some souls; only another saddened soul could completely understand. They hugged and cried, their tears gradually dried, and then she managed to laugh when a mouse dashed and skidded across the living room floor, leaving tiny, wet footprints from the storm.

"Marriages are made in heaven,
But so are thunder and lightning."

Unknown

Chapter 23

Ally had always wanted a fairytale wedding. Hasn't every girl?

There's always a favorite movie with the incredible, fantasy wedding scene where some young girl somewhere whispers to herself, or says it loud enough for her 'intended' to overhear . . . 'Oh, if only I could have a fabulous wedding like that.'

Well, once again Ally's life turned into a Cinderella movie. Looking back now at the strong influence the Cinderella story had in her life, she realized how strongly she related to that character and her circumstances. Neither of them had parents in their daily lives – real parents like the majority of children and teenagers had as they grew up. However, Ally had something unbelievable that none of the other children could even dream of: She was blessed with a Fairy God Grandmother and her grandmother was just that. Granny Pearl was magical in every sense of the word. She believed in fairies and said they lived in her flower garden. Pearl also said she often talked to them.

One day when Ally helped in the garden, Pearl knelt beside Ally and quickly scanned the plants and leaves. "Ally, if people are really quiet and tune into nature, they can all see them."

Ally and Pearl talked about the fairies several times over the years, and Ally learned her grandmother fully expected her to listen and to hear the fairies that lived in her garden and for her to hear and see the others that live in gardens everywhere. Ally grew up looking for those fairies whenever she found herself in any garden. She could almost feel them watching her as she walked along pathways, looking at the landscape designs.

Granny Pearl had a great life on her plantation. She had found and married her True Prince and was in love with him right up until the moment he slipped into heaven.

"Ally, there *are* real princes out there," Pearl had said, "and you can and do find them. Sometimes, you will find yours when you least expect it, when you are busy doing something else. But, you will know him. Your heart will tell you. You will recognize your prince when you meet him.

"But true love isn't always an easy ride. Sometimes, we are forced to travel down some bumpy roads in life before we come to the road we are meant to take. Be watchful that you are where you are supposed to be.

"Here's another important thing for you to know: beauty is a double-edged sword. Your mother was very beautiful, and you, Ally, are even more beautiful than she was. That can be a blessing

396

and a curse. So, you must choose wisely when you grow up. You need to be patient and wait for your Mister Right, your true prince to appear. More importantly, you need to wait for your heart to recognize him, to sing loudly that he is your true prince."

Well, there Ally was . . . in Atlanta living a daydream, a million miles away from reality, thinking about everything Granny Pearl had tried to teach her.

Oh, my God . . . it's my wedding to my True Prince. There's so much to consider and to do. But, I want a small wedding that has a big flair. Uh, did I say that right?

It was going to be her personal day. She really didn't have many blood relatives and certainly didn't want every stranger in Atlanta showing up for free food off a buffet table. The more she thought about wedding plans, the more she got excited.

The telephone rang: It was Doodle. Why was she calling? What a surprise when she asked Ally to join her for luncheon at the famous Driving Club. Ally was almost in shock, but accepted her invitation. She went to the closet and selected the nicest daytime dress instead of a business suit she would normally wear to the office. She had never been to the Driving Club, and now she was going to lunch there. She'd be able to see for herself what all the fuss was about. She laughed aloud when it dawned on her that since she owned a successful limo company, she should arrive in style. That's exactly what she did.

Ally certainly wasn't rich, but she had done quite well with the limousine company, and enjoyed that distinction voiced by many in the business world; even a few longtime members of the Atlanta Chamber of Commerce considered her a success, even if they also thought she was on the too young side. Ally was pleased with the lifestyle she had created for her two daughters and herself. They had a nice house, nice furnishings and cars. She could afford to send her two precious girls to private schools where they received the best education in safe environments. She thought about all she had accomplished in a short, very busy, intense couple of years since moving from St. Francisville. She straightened her back and realized she was quite pleased with herself. She certainly did belong at the Driving Club.

The expensive stretch white coach pulled up to the club's door. She didn't move. *Oh, dear Lord, what am I doing here?*

Her driver turned around to look at her over his broad shoulder. "Miz Ally, don't you go being nervous now. This here place is just a place on Atlanta's map, a fancy place for sure. But this is your life now. You go on in there where you belong."

Oh, how she needed those words at that instant. She had tried saying them to herself for hours and almost believed them, but to hear someone else actually say them was like frosting on a cake – so sweet.

This was the next step in her life and she had worked very hard for those accomplishments, surely Doodle would be able to see that too.

The maître 'de met Ally at the door and escorted her to Mrs. Lanzen's table. She got up and shook Ally's hand as if it was a business meeting. Little did Ally really know about this luncheon or this woman.

"We have lots to do and very little time to plan this event. I have spoken with Drake this morning and asked him to pick a later date so we would have plenty of time. I will have Wanda, my personal dress designer, call you this afternoon to set an appointment so she can take your measurements and start on your gown. We'll have the fabrics flown in from Paris.

"Here, look, Ally. I picked this out for you. It will be perfect and I thought you could have peach and white for your six bridesmaids' dresses. Here are photos of the dresses which will complement your gown.

"I will have Barton do the color and flower arrangements. I'm still not sure about which jeweler we'll use. We will arrange for the pastor at Peachtree Christian Church to perform the service. He is quite wonderful. I'm sure the organist and choir will be available to perform whatever we decide."

As Doodle continued, Ally was appalled at the thought of the woman assuming she could make these extravagant plans without consulting her or even telling her she was making plans. They had just met, and yes, Drake and she planned to get married in six weeks, but she had already thought about the wedding day to her prince. Ally knew exactly what she wanted: a small, quaint ceremony with only very special people to witness them taking their vows, perhaps in a quiet place somewhere in the Smoky Mountains, perhaps a chapel in Gatlinburg, perhaps in an open meadow or in the forest near a stream. She hadn't decided.

"Ally? Ally, did you hear me? We have to get our announcement to the newspapers in two days so it can be published in time, and the invitations must get to the printers as quickly as possible."

"What? I haven't even digested the part about a dress designer yet, and you're talking about newspapers. Why? Drake and I aren't celebrities. His family – you – are the wealthy

Southern society people, not us. Our wedding doesn't have to be a public spectacle."

Color drained from Doodle's face, and she crumbled the linen napkin in her fist. "Ally! What *are* you thinking?" she said rather indignantly. "This is my son's first wedding. All of Atlanta's society will attend, the press will send society reporters and photographs to cover it. We cannot forget to alert *Town & Country* and *Southern Living* magazines, either. They will want to send reporters, too."

Oh, no, let's not forget those, Doodle.

She had the entire wedding already planned. Ally felt like throwing up and couldn't even think about food. She had lost all interest in the Driving Club and lunch. She felt she had been thrown into a huge castle's icy dungeon and her wicked stepmother was locking the cell door. She was making her plans for Ally's wedding ceremony. At that point, Alley wasn't even sure she would attend. Her wedding had become cold and impersonal, and no longer felt like love, but a massive publicity stunt for the Lanzen dynasty.

Ally had always thought mother-in-laws were there to help, not make life decisions for people. She wondered if Mrs. Lanzen thought Ally was incapable of making her own wedding plans. Maybe she thought Ally was just a dumb blonde. This was all about her, not Ally or her son's wedding. To her, it was a social event where she would play hostess; Atlanta's party of the year. She was using Ally and the wedding as an excuse to host a huge soirée and garner a massive amount of publicity for herself.

She didn't know what to say to Mrs. Lanzen, or how to handle the situation. It was like going shopping for your dream home and the Realtor telling you she had already picked it out, you didn't need to bother looking, here's the address, and you could move in whenever you wanted.

This scheme may have worked in the olden days, but not now. Ally excused herself from the table and from lunch. Mrs. Lanzen had noticed Ally was very pale but hadn't bothered to ask why. Ally told her she wasn't feeling well and had to go lie down. She ran out of the fancy Driving Club in tears.

The driver easily saw she was more than upset. "Oh, Miz Ally, what in the world happened in that place? You must talk to Mister Drake about it. Those rich folk do some flat-out weird things, an' I take it this mighta been one of them weird ones." He handed her his handkerchief to dry her eyes.

Ally appreciated his kind words, but she cried all the way home anyway. What was supposed to be a happy occasion certainly hadn't turned out that way.

Morning came earlier than usual . . . to the sound of the doorbell ringing like there was a fire. She ran down stairs and looked out the peep hole. There stood Drake, nervously shifting his weight from one foot to the other, obviously more than a little anxious to come inside.

Oh, no; he'd have to be half-blind not to notice these red eyes from crying herself to sleep. Darn.

She opened the door. "Well, mornin' . . . come on in and make yourself comfortable. I'm going to take a shower." Turning away, I dashed back upstairs, grabbed what I needed and let the cold shower trickle down my face.

What am I going to say to Drake about his control freak mother? He's a momma's boy. He's going to defend everything she has said she plans to do for our wedding. He's going to think she's just trying to help. Oh, this doesn't feel right.

Ally thought she had to change her way of thinking, to think of her just helping out. *Can I do that? . . . With a straight face and my mouth closed? For how long? For the rest of my life? When would it end? Oh, dear. . . .*

What about her own family back in Louisiana? Doodle wanted her to forget her family and who she was, her heritage. Ally didn't have much of a family left at this point in time – her sister had her own life and was busy raising a family. There really isn't anyone who would stand by to support her dreams and wishes about her wedding day to her prince.

Ally sobbed in the shower, crouching in the corner, trying to figure out how she could deal with these complications. She wished for the hundredth time that her mother or Granny Pearl were by her side, but this wish wasn't going to come true; there was simply no one. Of course, there were Ally's two girls, but they were young, and it seemed they were her only forever friends. She truly felt alone in the world. How she wished she could rub a magic lamp at that instant and her very own fairy godmother would suddenly appear and wave a magic wand to right all the wrongs.

Granny Pearl's distinctive Southern accent came to her ears and into my heart: "Get yourself up out of there, Ally, right this minute. And you dry those tears. You aren't alone. You never have been and you never will be. You are far tougher than this problem. You go right on ahead now, and you do as you wish – it's your wedding, not hers."

All of a sudden, Ally felt her woman power come back full force. She held her head higher and went on her way.

Mrs. Lanzen continued with her massive wedding party plans, with all the publicity and inviting more than half of Atlanta's high society. Ally tried telling her she wished she would stop, to let Drake and her have a quiet, simple wedding.

Doodle's face paled and her lips turned into a snarl. "Oh, no! That won't do! That's unacceptable!"

She screamed and yelled horrible things at Ally, calling her just a 'plain and simple country girl without any class or breeding'; she did not understand why her precious baby boy wanted to marry a dowdy country bumpkin in the first place, she'd never live it down. Her insults went on and on, and made Ally's head spin. The woman was desperate to make her son look good. Ally would get some attention, but the wedding was all about Drake and his family and his parents' position in society.

"This is how it is, and you, you little piece of nothing, you'd better get used to being in the background, of being invisible, never seen and never heard."

That was to be Ally's place in this family? Ally was sure that's exactly what Mrs. Lanzen hoped. She was certain her son would soon see Ally as she described, a pitiful nothing without talent or brains, and he would move on to someone of his mother's choosing. She said Ally should get out of her son's life, expect nothing from the family except scorn, and if she had any intelligence at all, she would reconsider this marriage.

Mrs. Lanzen wasn't finished: "If you do marry, I hope and pray it's a very short-lived one!"

Ally's heart fluttered in her chest and she held her breath. How could any one person on the planet be so cruel? She had always gone out of her way to be considerate of everyone. She was very happy to be marrying Drake, not because he was wealthy, but because he loved her very much and she was his choice of all the women in the world. He told her many times that she was his princess and he made her feel like one as well.

Why did there have to be a wicked witch in their lives? Why couldn't this woman accept Ally and be happy for them? Ally could already tell Doodle was going to do everything in her power to make her life absolutely miserable.

That night Drake came to Ally's house with yellow roses, my favorite. "Go get dressed, honey. Mom is taking us out for a special dinner."

Ally's heart sank. How could she tell Drake about the way Doodle had talked to her earlier that very day? The last thing she wanted to do would be to eat dinner sitting at the same table with the wicked witch. Ally so hated feeling that way about her future mother-in-law, but it was the truth.

She had no choice. She had to get dressed and go with Drake. She sobbed the whole time as she tried to put on makeup. She studied the clothing in the closet, knowing that no matter what she wore it would not be good enough, classy enough, expensive enough, to suit Drake's mother's idea of proper style.

Drake and she held hands and sang songs on the way to the restaurant. They were the happy couple, or so it would appear. They walked in holding hands and all smiles. Doodle glared at Ally, then smiled and hugged her son. Drake and Ally continued to hold hands tightly under the table, as any soon-to-be married couple would.

"Really, Ally! Can't you wait until you get home to paw all over my son? It is quite embarrassing, you holding Drake's hand under the table. I know everyone here. *Please!*"

Her remark was confusing and upsetting.

She began telling Drake what a lovely chat she and Ally had had earlier, and how they were getting along famously with the wedding plans. . . . the plans they were putting together. She turned in her chair and stared at Ally. "Aren't they . . . *Miss* Ally?"

Ally was breathless. She couldn't believe the woman was pretending everything was fine between them. She was trying to make Ally lie to Drake, to agree that what she said was true. She was making herself look like the perfect mother-in-law. Ally's head spun. She was caught in a fairytale that had turned into a living nightmare. Oh, if only she could awaken soon.

Ally had never been abused or treated in such a manner as that. She was confused about how to fix the problem without hurting Drake's feelings about his mother. This was horrible and she had had enough. It had gone on long enough. She couldn't tell Drake the truth while they were at the restaurant at a table with his mother staring at her. Ally swallowed hard and took a deep breath. It was time to take matters into her own hands.

Ally's hands trembled, but she was ready.

Drake knew Ally was upset about his mother's plans for a massive wedding, and suspected she was ready to call off the whole thing. That was exactly what Doodle wanted, but Ally was determined to deny her any more pleasure at Ally's expense. She was going to marry her true prince her way, without inviting the wicked witch to witness the event. Ally decided Drake and she would elope.

Drake knew his bride-to-be was serious. He finally decided he, too, had had enough of his fiancée being so unhappy and figured it out. He knew his mother all too well. She was spoiled, always got her way, and had a controlling personality. He had seen it all his life, but this was different. This was his new life, his wedding, his bride, his own family to worry about, and it was his responsibility to make them happy. Drake was done with listening to his mother's twisted truths. It was time to please Ally. Elopement was the perfect answer.

One of Drake's friends owned an exquisite hotel off the South Carolina beach. He called and reserved the honeymoon suite, but didn't tell Ally. He did tell her they were going to get away and spend a few days in Myrtle Beach. It sounded like a great idea. She wanted nothing more than to escape Atlanta and the wicked soon-to-be mother-in-law.

When they stepped into the suite, Ally knew she was getting married. The Flamingo Paradise Hotel had decorated the rooms with dozens of pink and white roses; a beautiful white dress was laid out on the bed; a card with a note said that her precious girls were already there waiting for them to arrive. That made this day perfect.

Ally's daughters helped her prepare for her special day.

A chilled bottle of Dom and icy bottles of Coke for the girls were delivered to her room. The wine tasted slightly off, but Ally thought it was just her nervous stomach and excitement.

At sundown, they walked out of the suite's sliding glass doors and stepped onto the sand. Flowers and tike torches were scattered along a pathway that led closer to the ocean. A pastor waited. Beside him stood the handsome groom, Ally's true prince, wearing a white suit. It was perfect. Ally couldn't believe Drake had secretly pulled this off. The wedding was private. A few curious bystanders walking along the beach stopped for a moment before strolling on. After the ceremony, Drake and she toasted their marriage, and had a midnight cruise aboard a yacht. Ally finally had her prince . . . and it was only the beginning.

The next day, they climbed aboard a private jet and flew to Orlando and Disney World. It was a fairytale honeymoon dream to be in Cinderella's castle as they repeated their vows in the castle's keep. The two girls were flown in, too, and had adjoining suites. The whole family enjoyed a week in Disney World. It was living a fairytale.

Then reality struck. It was time to return to Atlanta and face the angry wicked witch.

* * *

"I wonder if I've been changed in the night?
Let me think. Was I the same when I got up this morning?
I almost think I can remember feeling a little different.
But if I'm not the same, the next question is,
'who in the world am I?
ah, that's the great puzzle!"

Alice Through the Looking Glass

414

Chapter 24

The elopement did not go over well with Mrs. Lanzen. It made her even more angry with Ally. Sadly, that wasn't Ally's intent, but after all it was *Ally's* wedding, Ally's fairytale. God knows she had her own wedding ceremony, and she could only imagine that it had turned into a three-day extravaganza. Ally wasn't quite sure what Mrs. Lanzen's wedding was like, but from the outside looking in, it certainly didn't seem to have anything to do with love. Ally would never say Doodle married Mr. Lanzen only for money because she certainly had plenty of her own to start with. Maybe it had something to do with acquiring the most prestigious title in Atlanta's social circle. It seemed titles were of far greater importance in the Mid-South than it was in the bayous.

Mrs. Lanzen had nothing to say to Ally after the marriage ceremony. That was absolutely okay with Ally, even a preference, since the things she would have said would have only been nasty. For that matter, she had very little to say to her son, too. Odd.

Drake said he thought they should move away for a while. "I do business all over the world. We can live anywhere. The girls only have a couple of months left in the school year, so we can get them transferred and enrolled anywhere we want."

Ally thought if they moved away from the family tension, it would be the perfect time and solution.

Drake and she thought for a few days about where they would like to live. Ally was thinking about Florida because she loved ocean and the weather, the casual lifestyle, and so did the girls. Since Ally was a writer, it would definitely be a serene and calming place to create novels. South Carolina was also on their list because it was nice, too.

One afternoon, Drake came home early. "We're moving to Beverly Hills."

Ally almost choked on the cracker she was eating. "But Drake, Beverly Hills is for movie stars."

He began to laugh. "Yes, it is, honey, and we look like movie stars, so that's where we're going. I certainly do enough business in that industry."

Ally wasn't sure about such a drastic change. Perhaps Drake was joking.

Beverly Hills? Just saying those two words made her recall a friend Jodie and how they had spent time when they were only seventeen. Jodie and she thought of themselves as really beautiful. After all, they had won every beauty contest under the

416

sun, taking turns on which one would be the first runner-up. It seemed every Southern would-be beau was always asking them out. They simply thought they belonged in Beverly Hills. It was a funny thought, but not for long.

When Ally turned twenty, she and Jodie, along with their husbands and children loaded up the SUV like the Beverly Hillbillies and off they went to California.

Ally had never been anywhere except Louisiana, Georgia or Florida on vacations. Jodie and I convinced their husbands they were going to be movie stars because they were so beautiful. They believed us. It seemed as if they drove almost a week to get there, and they did it with very little money.

There's always problems when you travel, but they added to the potential of things going wrong. Some of them smoked a little pot back then, and they wanted to be sure there was some left when they reached California; two full bags were in the car.

Little did they know they would pass through a huge border station through Mexico. They automatically assumed they were checking people for drugs. Why else would officers stop everyone? They were about ten cars back when all at once, reality hit and someone screamed, "Oh, Lord! We have two bags full of pot, and we are going into Mexico."

Ally's husband said, "Yeah. I heard when they put you in jail for drugs here they never let you out. And, hey guys, we have our kids with us."

Ally's heart began to pound. They were all freaking out about this time. Jodie said, "Let's hide it in our bras."

The guys said they could hide some in their underwear.

"No," Ally said, "they have dogs up there and I'm sure they're trained to smell pot."

All four of them were sweating as they got closer to the border. "We don't have much of a choice here, and we're running out of time. We're going to have to split the two bags . . . and . . . eat it."

Everyone groaned.

Finally, Jodie said, "You're right."

They ate one bag of pot and thought they would throw the other baggie out the window. No! Someone could see it. The guys ate the other bag full. Then they tried to wash the dry stuff down with Coke-Cola, and ate some mints. Voila' . . . the evidence had vanished just as they pulled up to the station check.

Ally was driving. She rolled down her window and the border security guard leaned down. "Have you got any fruit?"

"Huh? Excuse me, sir?"

His tone of voice got louder. "I said, have you got any fruit?"

"Fruit? You're looking for fruit?"

He leaned back, frowned, took a deep breath and his voice went up two decibels on his volume control: "Are you hard of hearing, lady? I said fruit!"

"No, we don't have any fruit."

"All right then. You can go on through."

There was complete silence in the car. This had to be a joke. They had just eaten two hundred dollars worth of pot, and the officials were looking for fruit and not illegal drugs. They were in too much of a shock to laugh, and felt like complete idiots.

About thirty minutes down the road, Ally began to feel sick to her stomach. So did the rest of the crew – really sick. Ally was so sick she couldn't wait to get to a rest area or a regular bathroom. She pulled over onto the highway shoulder, jumped out of the car and ran for a bush for the first time in her life.

They all looked like Cheech and Chong, trying to find bushes. They were also throwing up. Basically, the ill effects of the pot erupted from both ends, and they had turned a greenish color.

Oh, my God. Were they going to die out here in the desert? They gave the word 'high' a whole new meaning that day.

Their upset systems went on for two days, making it a very miserable trip to Los Angeles. Each one lost about ten pounds in two days. One good thing came out of that disastrous experience: none of them ever wanted to see pot again. They had made it to L.A. where Jodie and she enrolled in acting classes. It only lasted a few weeks when they ran out of money and went back home.

That was Ally's big L.A. story, her teenage and young adult dream that came flooding into her mind at the words 'Beverly Hills.'

"Ally . . . Ally . . . you listening to me or not? You've drifted away like on another planet."

"Oh, I'm sorry, Drake." She wasn't about to tell Drake that pot story.

420

"Sooooo, honey, what do you say?"

"Beverly Hills, huh? Oh, Drake it would be a dream. Let's do it. Let's really do it."

About a week later, Drake and she moved into the Beverly Wilshire Hotel. Much later on, Ally recognized that their suite was the one used for the movie 'Pretty Woman.' They stayed there before the movie was filmed.

A special elevator key took them up to the penthouse. When they reached that floor, the elevator automatically stopped and the heavy door opened right at that suite. Dumbfounded, Ally said, "Oh, my God, Drake, honey. Are we having another honeymoon night here?"

Drake laughed. "No, honey, this will be our home until we find a house."

"But, that could take a while."

He put his hand over Ally's mouth to keep her quiet in front of the bellman. Keeping Ally quiet was a task. Holy cow. Ally was in the middle of Beverly Hills in the biggest suite at the Beverly Hills Wilshire Hotel. She ran though the suite with excitement.

"Drake, this ain't nothing like the Red Roof Inn. Are you sure they're going to let us stay here?"

"Ally, honey, calm down. It's just money."

"How much money do we have? Is there enough to stay here?"

He looked at Ally as if she'd gone insane. "Okay, Ally, contain your excitement."

"Oh, my God. Drake! You've got to come see this bathroom. My whole family from Louisiana could fit in this shower and tub."

"Honey, I have a meeting to go to. Make yourself comfortable. Someone will be up shortly to unpack us."

"Drake, you mean they unpack our suitcases and put our clothes away?"

"Yes, that's what I said. I'll be back by six. Just meet me in the lounge downstairs and we'll go out to dinner. And, Ally, I want you to look great."

Ally's mouth almost split from smiling. She was in heaven. She ran into the bedroom and bounced on the bed. That's what she did when excited as a kid. She really didn't think or feel she had grown up much – while jumping on the bed. That's when the maid walked in.

Oh, yes, Ally felt like a complete idiot.

The maid smiled. "Having a good time, Mrs. Lanzen?"

She quietly managed to get off the bed and tried to contain herself. She was curious about what the maid would do. She watched her unpack the clothes, put them neatly into drawers and hang them in the closets.

Ally was still excited. "I'm staying here."

The big black lady looked at Ally and said, "Yes, ma'am, I assumed that."

She waited a moment and said, "I'm moving here, too. I think I'm going to be a movie star or something."

She turned and looked at Ally again. "Honey, with your looks, you're probably right."

"I need a really pretty dress to wear out tonight. Is there a J.C. Penny's here, in walking distance?"

Her eyes widened. "A what? Honey, this is Beverly Hills. They ain't got no J.C. Penny's in walking distance here or a Sears, neither. If you can afford this room, you need to head on over to Barney's. It's right next door."

"Oh! Okay. Thanks."

Ally walked into Barney's and excitedly said to the saleslady, "I'm living next door at that big hotel, and I'm going to dinner tonight."

She had a strange expression on her face. "Can I help you?"

"Yes, a dress. I need a really pretty dress that will knock my husband's socks off."

She sent Ally into a dressing room and came back with what Ally thought was a strapless dress. She didn't think it was all that pretty, but figured people dressed like that in Hollywood. It was awful tight around her top. She walked out to find the sales clerk. There she stood with a beautiful white lace satin top.

"Excuse me, ma'am, but this dress is way too short and tight on me up top."

"That would be a skirt," she said, trying to hide her laugher.

Once again, Ally felt stupid. Ally had had money and nice dresses before, just not like this fancy design. Ally was nervous, so she tried to play it off as if she knew it was a skirt all along.

After awhile the clerk brought over a beautiful dress that was a delicate black lace on satin. It fit perfectly and looked like a million bucks. The price on it was $3,500.00, but Ally didn't have that much in her purse; only a couple of hundred.

She smiled and said, "That's fine. We will charge it to your room."

Ally thought her husband would kill her if she paid that much for one dress, but what the heck, she needed a dress right that minute and didn't have a car to go to other places to shop. She really didn't know where to go at that point.

Wow, what a dress it was and what a store. She decided to definitely go back to Barney's. Ally went back to their hotel suite, rearranged her long blonde hair, and got all dressed up. She went downstairs to wait for her husband in the bar. One look at her took his breath away. Money for the dress wasn't a problem at all.

The next day, Drake took Ally shopping. Their first stop was Chanel where he bought purses in many colors, including designs by Louis Vutton in all the latest colors. Now that she had purses, it was time for shoes. He bought practically every shoe in Beverly Hills. No one back home would ever believe this wild shopping spree; it was something only seen in the movies. Ally truly felt like a princess. She never dreamed she would be shopping in Beverly Hills, or spending thousands of dollars on purses, shoes, sunglasses and belts. It was insane. But, after she thought about it for a minute, she guessed she'd need these things since she was going to be a movie star.

Drake left every day to attend meetings at movie studios. Ally learned how to shop for clothes that fit her shape and style, got a suntan, got massages and facials in fancy spas. And was thrilled to have her hair cut and styled by really good-looking, famous, hairdressers.

One day, she was going up in the elevator. At the rear was a huge security type man standing beside someone who looked familiar, who was wearing a mask over his nose and mouth. "Oh, my God," Ally whispered to herself. It was Michael Jackson. He was staying at the same hotel. Ally wasn't star struck, but she never thought she'd be on the same elevator with such a mega star as Michael Jackson.

Once she felt she looked presentable to people in Beverly Hill and was positive Drake's socks would stay knocked off when he saw the clothing she'd purchased, she went house shopping. She found a rather odd-looking Realtor, who was very nice but sort of reminded her of a space alien.

When Mr. Jones picked her up, he asked what she was looking for in a home. "Oh," she said, "I'm pretty much a princess and I'm going to be a movie star. So, I think I need a castle."

He laughed for quite a while. "You and I are going to have a good time house shopping. You are quite funny."

Ally didn't understand what his comment meant, so she stayed silent.

"So, young lady, what kind of house are we looking for? What price range?"

Didn't he hear me? "I said, I need a castle."

He studied my face and eyes for fifteen seconds or longer. "You're really serious."

"Yes. I know of a castle that's in the Hollywood Hills. The price is about thirty million. My husband said to find what I wanted. So, let's at least take a look at it."

Jones explained music videos for the Pop Artist Prince were filmed there; a few horror movies, also. They drove up a long, winding, very scary road that seemed to go straight up the mountainside. The road was so narrow that only one car could use it at a time. Ally held on for dear life, hoping they wouldn't meet another vehicle – there was a huge drop off that went straight down into a canyon. She gripped the seat tighter, more accustomed to living near flatlands and bayous instead of mountains.

At the top, they drove up to two huge iron gates that looked like something right out of a Dracula horror film. Beyond the gate was a real castle with peacocks strutting around the lawn, a mote filled with water surrounding the mansion, and a real drawbridge to cross. Wow.

This can't really be happening. But it was real. It was a huge, beautiful, wonderful castle. . . . just like in her dreams, down to the red velvet period furnishings throughout.

The Realtor said, "You know what? This place even has secret passages and a dungeon."

Dungeon? Suddenly, Ally didn't feel well. Something was wrong; déjà vu hit hard. She felt she had been there before, perhaps in another time. Somehow, she knew this house, every room, every inch – and it felt bad everywhere. She was overwhelmed by a sense of dread. A dungeon? Maybe she had been enslaved in the dungeon ages ago.

Jones said, "Well, is this your castle? Is it what you were expecting?"

When she looked at Jones, her mind pictured him there, in that long ago time as well. Maybe he was Renfield. He sure looked like he could eat a fly or a bug.

Terror suddenly came over her and she had to get out of there as quickly as possible. "Mr. Jones, let's go. I'll think about it."

As they drove away, she glanced up at the street sign: Wonderland Drive. *No, no, no! This must be a dream. I couldn't possibly conduct business from there.* When she would call a potential client and gave them the address, they'd think it was a joke and hang up. She could hear it in her head already: 'Hi, my name is Ally and I live in a castle on Wonderland Drive in Beverly Hills and—'

Click.

She nearly yelled. "No, Mister Jones, no!"

He looked at her as if she had gone crazy.

Of course, the man couldn't know her thoughts. She took a deep breath and tried to remember her upbringing, her manners, and to lower her voice. "No, Mister Jones, I couldn't possibly live here . . . on Wonderland Drive . . . in this castle. No, no, no."

"Okay, okay, calm down, lady. I'll take you to see some nice homes in the flats of Beverly Hills."

They looked at houses everywhere. She and Drake had been at the Beverly Wilshire about eight weeks, and it was time to make a decision on a home and she did. Three blocks over from Rodeo Drive on Crescent and Sunset was the perfect home. They bought it and moved in. It had a beautiful landscaped yard, an Olympic size swimming pool, cabanas, two hot tubs and a tennis court on one side. They hired fulltime butlers, maids and a limo driver who lived in the guesthouse.

That was her new life. She was that rich . . . but wondered what happened to her dream of being a movie star.

* * *

"There are as many nights as days,
and the one is just as long as the other in the year's course.
Even a happy life cannot be without a measure of darkness,
and the word 'happy' would lose its meaning
if it were not balanced by sadness."

Carl Jung

Chapter 25

Every fairytale has a dark side. It's a little too late when you discover something you don't quite understand.

Jones had worked out a deal with the sellers on the home in Beverly Hills, the paperwork was done and Ally and Drake were almost completely moved into the house. The Realtor was almost like a friend now, since Ally had spent about two months with him looking for their new home.

Jones had asked her to have coffee with him the next morning. Since her husband was busy, she invited him to come over. As they sat and chatted about the area and places she and Drake could go to dine and places they could go as a family, just simple chit-chat, Jones looked at her with a very perplexed expression on his face.

He wanted to say something, she could tell. "Okay, Jones; what's bothering you?"

"Very perceptive of you," Jones replied. "Yes, something certainly is bothering me."

"Okay, tell me what's bothering you."

"Well, Miss Ally, it's that castle. When we were up there you were so thrilled. It was your dream to buy a castle. Every house I suggested, the ones in the Multiple Listings of the area, the ones you read the descriptions of and studied the photographs, well, you said they didn't look enough like a castle. When we went to look at a real castle, you were beside yourself; so excited. Then you became ill. A horrified look came over you and you went pale. You just ran out and asked me to drive you away from there as quickly as possible.

"As far as I know, you don't have any friends here. I think I'm the closest thing to a friend you have in California. It's driving me crazy. You've got to tell me. . . . what frightened you so much?"

Ally frowned, then fidgeted in her chair, dropped her coffee spoon into the saucer, got up, paced, and then looked out the tall glass window. She reminisced to Atlanta and the Lanzen mansion, her eerie mother-in-law, and the similar ghostly pasts Drake and she had in common. Tears welled in her eyes.

"I'm sorry," Jones said. "Please don't get upset. I just want to help. Sometimes it helps to talk through something, to talk to someone you don't know all that well so you can hear a different perspective."

"I don't know. Maybe it would help if I talked about everything. Drake and I got married quickly, like three months after we met. It was a whirlwind romance. He fell madly in love with me and the next thing I knew I was married. I can't even remember saying I do or I don't. . . .

"I feel guilty for marrying him since . . . now, I don't even know if I even like him, let alone be in love with him. It happened so fast. I was going along with my life, happy-go-lucky, working with my own company, no troubles, and here he came."

She sat back down at the table and shook her head.

"From the first evening I met him, my life changed drastically. I felt swept away with flying here and there, with expensive gifts almost daily, roses delivered, and on and on. Then things changed and I felt trapped. He never left my side; he even managed to get rid of the man I was dating, and was insanely jealous over minor things.

"Somehow, he gained control over me, a level of control I still cannot understand. I couldn't tell him no. He told me he had waited for me all his life, I was his, and he was going to save me from something.

435

"All of a sudden, my friends weren't around, my business was gone, and before I knew it, I was on a small island off the coast of the Carolinas saying I do. I think I may have been intoxicated or drugged.

"I awakened with a giant engagement ring and wedding band on my finger. I tried to escape and get the marriage annulled, but he has a very powerful family. I couldn't.

"I finally came to the realization that my home was sold, my limousine company was sold, and all the money I had in the bank was in his name – it became *our* money, not mine, and he had the only key, account number and password.

"I was moved into a mansion with his family. There were security guards inside on the grounds and they were outside the gates, too. Maybe my father-in-law was afraid of robbery or a family member being kidnapped and held for ransom; I don't know. Maybe they were just very paranoid because they had all that wealth. It doesn't matter; I was trapped inside with all their other possessions.

"The entire family was like a bunch of walking dead, demon-possessed people I had never met before. I had only known their public face, not the real people, the real personalities. Finally, I got my own house, and that's when I got

436

deathly ill. He could have poisoned me, I don't know. I just wanted out. The doctors said I was going to die, so I was running out of time.

"I wanted out even if it meant my death. I regained my health, and now he has me here. You asked about the castle. When we were there and you mentioned it had a dungeon, I pictured myself in it. At that moment, I realized exactly what had happened to me.

"I care for him. He buys me everything I want. But he's like an owner and I am his pet, a possession, not a wife, not an equal."

"My, my," Jones shook his head. "I think I know what's wrong."

"You do?"

"Yes; this man has all the money in the world. He saw you and he claimed you. Many rich people don't know a thing about real love, or right and wrong. They know the devil and the devil's ways, and they take what they want. Those Atlanta people sound like a lot of the people here in Beverly Hills. Money is their god.

"You were an unsuspecting victim. He swooped in and grabbed you before you knew what hit you. That's what I think happened. He grabbed you up and express-trained you to the altar before you could stop and think. Now he has you locked away behind his castle walls."

Ally's complexion paled. *Oh! Like Rapunzel . . . he's got me just like Rapunzel was trapped. Why hadn't I realized that before? Oh, dear.*

"There are many women in your situation right here in Beverly Hills; rich men with beautiful wives that they've chained down. It's like a demon lover."

"A what?"

"Never mind, Miz Lanzen. I hope you'll take my advice. Play it cool. Live and act as if you like this man, and when he isn't looking, get out. Go as far as you can, and hide out if you have to. But once you get out, never look back."

Ally took a quick breath. *Oh, my God, that's almost exactly what Granny Pearl told me: 'run and never go back.' If I did go back, I could end up like Lot's wife in the Sodom and Gomorrah story.*

"Now, it's just my opinion, but I think that man stole you. He's probably an evil man. His parents sure sound like they were bred that way, too."

Ally nodded. "I don't want their money. I just want away from all of them; out of this marriage!"

"Well, I can relate to the wanting out part, but you won't get out from under a green-eyed monster until he's ready to let go. A woman like you? No, he won't let go easily."

Ally had to think more about the situation. Drake was a man accustomed to extreme wealth. Although she had lived with him for a while, there wasn't a bit of telling what all he really sold, besides his many inventions and other things, to get that wealth.

Jones shook his head. "I don't tell many people this, but I'll tell you: I see into people, into their souls, usually through their eyes. When I met him, I saw something in those green eyes – I saw it and I know what he is.

"That's why you got so sick. You're nothing like that. You're a good soul. I'll pray that God will help get you free. At first I thought you had married into a wealthy family, to a wealthy inventor, just for his money."

Ally frowned. *Not entirely true; I married a millionaire, but in the bargain I married a spoiled mama's boy, too.*

"I'm not one-hundred percent positive of what," Jones said, "but he's something that's not wholesome. I've seen similar things over the years while working in Beverly Hills. There are many reasons not to get involved with some of the rich people around here. Some are all right, I guess, but some of them are really messed up.

"You've got to trust someone sometime. Tell me the story and we'll figure out a way for you to get away as soon as it's possible. I swear I'll be a trustworthy friend and will keep watch as best as I can."

Ally remained calm, trying to think back and remember about Drake's mother and stepfather, and her sudden ill health. Ah, what happened in Atlanta might be a good clue.

She told Jones it began in early September, about three months after she married Drake. They decided to move out of the Lanzen mansion and get their own home somewhere in Atlanta.

Mrs. Lanzen was still angry over the fact Drake and she had eloped, which had denied her from hosting the party of the century. That was the only thing the wedding meant to her anyway. Ally knew it was going to take time for Mrs. Lanzen to get past the marriage, the disappointment, and that she would be reeling for a long time. What made the situation worse was another fact: They had to stay at the mansion for a few months. They stayed until Drake saw it was impossible for her to stay a moment longer.

Although it was nice living in the mansion on the large estate with beautifully landscaped gardens, Ally couldn't have been more thrilled than to move out. There were secret gardens that led into very secret gardens, and walking paths that twisted and turned through groves of well-groomed hedges and trees. One walking path would go on and on, turning and turning, and somehow people would end back up where they started. It was a huge flowered maze.

There were private tennis courts, and private sitting areas with lace-looking white iron seating near beautiful waterfalls. There was a serene sort of haunting beauty about the whole atmosphere. There were very private courtyards, also. Ally was sure it was designed for the many parties the Lanzens hosted. People could scatter and roam the gardens and grounds. The pool area was equipped with cabanas, a guesthouse, and even a private pool for the guesthouse.

There was a large staff to maintain the pools, another crew to care for the gardens, tree surgeons and landscapers, flower-garden groomers. Ally had no idea how many employees there really were on Lanzen property.

If a person looked up and saw the large estate house from any part of the grounds, it too looked haunted – it inhabited the hillside in its own sense of time. Inside were different halls and rooms that went nowhere, plus other rooms that led to secret places. Most of the furnishings came from the era and region of Louis XVI. Many interior areas were permeated with deep reds, oranges and dark woods. There were large furniture pieces that belonged in a castle some place, any place other than a modern home.

The mansion was always quite dark. There was not much light in or from any area of the home. If there was light coming through the windows, the shades and drapers were pulled to keep the home dark. It was more than just normal protection of the priceless paintings, which could never have sunlight strike the canvas.

None of the Lanzens went out much on their property. Mr. Lanzen stayed at his downtown Buckhead office, while Mrs. Lanzen slept most of the day, when she wasn't having beauty treatments done somewhere. She didn't worry about coming downstairs for anything. Her private maid brought her coffee, breakfast, or anything else she needed.

It seemed a shame to have such a beautiful place and never go outside, but the family stayed inside in dark rooms and slept.

Ally roamed the gardens and walked the paths, played on the tennis courts, and swam in the pool regularly.

It was extremely eerie to be outside wandering the grounds and look up and see Mrs. Lanzen's watching her, peering down with a half-hearted evil grin. It was as if she hated Ally being there, even though Ally rarely saw her.

On sleepless, windy nights Ally loved to roam the large halls when everything was quiet and everyone was asleep. She would hear strange noises that did frighten her a bit and she'd tell Drake about it the next morning, He'd just laugh and growl like an angry ghost as if it were funny. "Why? In God's name, why do you roam around all night, Ally?"

"I love strolling through the marble-inlayed hallways, and looking at the artwork on the walls. It's works that usually you would only see in a museum."

"You really don't know a lot about this house, do you?" Drake said.

"What was that supposed to mean? Are you saying this house is haunted?" Ally wasn't afraid of a few ghostly shadows. She grew up in Louisiana where almost every home had its own ghosts in residence, even Wildwind and the Myrtles that was next door. He never answered her question.

Drake stayed down in the home's lower level and played his grand piano at night. He played by ear and was very good. But he played dark, sad, heavy music which sounded like it was from another era. Ally had never heard anything like it, not before and not since. It was not anything that would be considered romantic or relaxing. The strange melodies were like being trapped in a perpetual episode of "Dark Shadows," with Barnabas himself lurking about.

Ally never understood why everyone there was always so doom and gloom; laughter never filled the hallways or any of the rooms; making any noises and talking loudly or even audibly across a room was frowned upon, and even the servants wore rubber soled shoes and even said, "Shss!" if she made a noise accidentally. The Lanzens didn't like any disturbances, as if they could really hear anything from their perch on the third level.

She was living in a home of the dead, with the dead, with Mrs. Lanzen watching her every move and giving her evil glares. Ally became very uncomfortable and finally begged Drake to move out of that cold mausoleum. Of course, he didn't understand since he felt they had every convenience there, and had grown up in that strange atmosphere.

Ally wanted her own home, away from the noises and the weirdness, away from the Lanzens who acted very bizarre, as well as all their fighting. There was never a serene or happy moment, they were always arguing. She lived there long enough to know there were a lot of dark secrets in that home. She didn't particularly think it was the home being haunted – it was the family in the home. The home just felt sad; it needed light and happy people.

Ally strongly believed people make a home what it is and the home supports it.

She and Drake moved into a pretty, two-story home with lots of windows for sunlight, and great light fixtures. She finally got to decorate her own home. Now she could live normally like most people. She didn't have to worry about a dark looming character staring at her all the time.

Now she could live normally. *Did I say normally?*

It wasn't long before Drake began to hear noises in their new home, noises that Ally didn't hear. He had nightmares, waking up screaming. He would be furious at Ally because she didn't see or hear what he had seen or heard.

However, Ally began to get sick. Her feet began to swell. A few weeks later, her hands and all her joints became swollen. She had always been very healthy and athletic, but now no one knew what was wrong.

At that time, Ally became frightened for her health, for the first time in her life. Along with everything else, Drake began talking to some unknown entities in his sleep. He said, cryptically, that they had followed him, that they were there in the house. Ally didn't know who 'they' were, but she began to hear things and to feel very uncomfortable, and was afraid to be left alone even during the day.

It was the first week of December. Doctors said Ally was dying and they had no clue why. They said she would be dead by Christmas – three weeks. She couldn't believe what was happening to her. She felt it was someone else's life, not her own. In the meanwhile, her husband kept coming up with strange inventions, making more and more and more money. Money flowed into the bank accounts.

Ally prayed a lot. She prayed for a miracle healing. She realized something was wrong and it had nothing to do with her. Whatever was making her sick unto death was not her doing.

Drake did nothing except drink and drink and dream and have screaming nightmares, and talk to strange beings in his sleep. It sounded as if he was possessed by some demon.

When Ally tried to get answers from his family, they said it was all her fault, not their precious baby son or brother. But, Ally had noticed those same characteristics in his brother, his sister, and his mother. No one was happy. No one ever smiled. They stayed in the dark, as if they hated sunshine. They never wanted to go out during the day.

As for Ally, she stayed outside on her front porch in the more lighted areas as much as possible. She decided she had to leave, even if it meant dying somewhere alone. She was frightened for the first time in her life. What were these people?

They held secret family meetings, to which she was never invited, that lasted until late into the night, sometimes until dawn. Drake imbibed lots of liquor all the time, every day. By the grace of God and a lot of praying, Ally began to heal, but there were still strange happenings around their home and in their home. They started staying at hotels a lot and staying away on any excuse.

During the three months they lived in that mansion, Ally was deliriously sick more than half the time. She told Drake she wanted to move somewhere, anywhere, perhaps even away from Atlanta. Drake finally told her his mother hated her because she had married her son, she had taken him away.

Then Drake asked her what she genuinely thought about moving away. He said moving away wasn't going to go over big with his mother, and if there was someone I never wanted to be on the bad side of it would be his mother.

Ally thought and pondered: Mrs. Lanzen hated her already. She couldn't do anything right in her eyes anyway, so why should she try? There was never going to be a friendship, or anything close to a healthy mother/daughter-in-law relationship. She decided to refuse to live her life being miserable under Mrs. Lanzen's thumb, or under all the weirdness that existed in the Lanzen mansion.

She made up her mind: Ally would leave, go somewhere – she didn't care where as long as it was away from there, the house, the Lanzens, and her husband who was becoming more of a stranger than a friend. She already felt she had married something "unnatural," as Granny Pearl would say.

Drake had to make a decision: his wife, or his mother, who had babied him to death all the years. It was time for him to grow up, to be on his own as an adult, to be with his new family, to make a new start, and hope that what Ally called 'the weird' would not ever follow him. Drake wasn't ready to show her the truly weird or his other side, nor was he going to tell her the truth about the family or the house just yet.

There are family secrets and then there are secrets. There are secrets Drake would carry to his grave.

Ally was in deep now. She had to stay with the program, so to speak, because she was getting ready to settle into her new home on the West Coast. Although things weren't as they seemed on the surface, and fun was probably only lingering in memories along with her sanity, she had to make the best of it for now. She knew one thing: Somehow, someday, there would be one moment, as Jones said, when she could escape the Dark Prince.

* * *

"Life is full of beauty. Notice it. Notice the bumble bee, the small child, and the smiling faces. Smell the rain and feel the wind.
Live your life to the fullest potential, and fight for your dreams."

Ashley Smith

Chapter 26

Rain poured out of dark Los Angeles skies and thunder roared – both rare occurrences in Southern California. Drake was withdrawn and not as animated as usual as they made their way down the twisting, winding Hollywood Hills road. No chitchat, no romantic music, no laughter or gossip, no talk of the people and party they had just left. Whenever Ally tried to talk to make the drive home shorter, he yelled, "Stop! I need silence now."

Ally already knew everything she needed to know, so she shut up. He was a far cry from the romantic, perfect, fairytale prince he had portrayed himself to be while at the party. When they stepped into their vehicle, Drake instantly turned into a cold, estranged, non-caring and almost non-existent being. Early on in the marriage, he tried to hide from her who he really was. But, as Granny Pearl always said: 'It all comes out in the wash.'

When Drake Lanzen came out of the wash, he was like a Tasmanian Devil.

Ally could hear her grandmother's voice: 'A fool and his money.' When money becomes someone's god, there's no longer any fun living with that person. Nothing excites that person, and they cannot look forward to anything. That was how Ally felt living with her husband. Within weeks of moving into their new home, he had turned into a sort of devil, and the devil was fully loaded. She no longer wanted to be a part of his world. She didn't want any more diamonds, clothes, trips to exotic places – she didn't want anything. But, she did want out. She was desperate for something money couldn't buy.

From the outside looking in, people would say she had the perfect fairytale life and the perfect fairytale world. She had it all: A young, good-looking, rich husband, a mansion in Beverly Hills, maids, butlers, and all the money she could ever spend. Even today, it sounds too good to be true, but guess what? That's a warning sign in itself, isn't it?

There's an old saying: Nothing is what it seems.

Ally felt like Rapunzel. Every night she stepped out onto the balcony of the twenty-five-hundred square foot master bedroom suite to peer through the smog layer in hopes of seeing stars in the sky. She wished upon those stars and dreamt of getting away. She was living a dream, but why couldn't it be with the special prince she had dreamt of all her life, the one she believed she had married?

How can you have it all, and not have it all at the same time?

Ally was very confused about life in general. Looking back over her earlier years all she could think about was how happy she had been with Collin, a guy who didn't have anything. Somehow, it never mattered that they had nothing of high value except a bright future together. They loved . . . completely . . . that was all they needed. Her life then was much simpler.

Real love is complicated. When love is a basic tenet, a solid foundation of your life, an unshakable strength that binds a committed relationship, you don't see or need anyone else, or anything else – 'things' are never missed, never needed. You are complete within each other. But, when love is missing, your world is filled with every 'thing' else, real love is the only thing your heart yearns for, craves, aches for. The worse thing about real love is that it's not something you can run to the nearest store and purchased off the shelf or even order online. That truth is something a born-to-the-manor multi-millionaire does not and cannot understand. It is incomprehensible. For the life of that person, they cannot understand why their partner wouldn't be deliriously happy when they've been handed an endless supply of money.

He's happy. Is he really?

Ally wondered if any millionaire would or could admit to not being extremely blessed or happy. They create many names or titles for their happiness instead.

Outward appearances can be deceiving. When Drake and she attended an event, he portrayed himself as the number one husband of the year. It was always comments like, "*My* wife is so beautiful;" she's so this and so that. When you are married to a millionaire, it is never about you; it's always about them. The wife is on his arm for one reason only: To make him look good or you would not even be in the building.

Drake would walk around the room with his head held high, shuffling his feet like he was the crowned King of Beverly Hills. Oh, if he only knew he really looked like the King of the Idiots. He threw hundred dollar bills around at waitresses as if the bills were quarters. Of course, the girls would smile and flirt a bit when making a hundred dollars every time they served him a cocktail. When Ally tried telling him it made him look like a fool, he said, "It's my damn money and you just need to shut up." At the same time, whenever a friend came by, he'd put his arm around me and call me his lovely wife.

Ally's days started to become longer and her nights longer and more restless. The Beverly Hills mansion seemed to get bigger. It can be strange about a house, how it can grow larger, colder and uninviting when things aren't what they should be. There's another old saying: "A house is not a home unless love lives there." That's certainly true.

Whenever she looked at the huge, elegant mansions along the palm-tree lined streets, she wondered who lived inside and if the mansions were as cold and lonely as her own.

Beverly Hills is very different from the South. When you drive through a nice little neighborhood in the South, there are no big steel gates blocking the entrance, or a Rolls-Royce parked in the driveways. There's a welcome mat at the front and back doors, nice family cars in the drive; children playing and laughing, and dogs running around in the yards playing fetch with the children. In the winter, you can smell wood fires and coffee perking; in the summer, the fragrance of barbecue and fresh baked bread drifts on the air. Warm and wonderful and inviting. Not so in Beverly Hills.

Ally didn't consider herself lucky, but a few of her friends did. They seemed to think she had so much more than they had. They thought she was being modest when she said, "It's not all that. You're not in my shoes."

They'd just laughed and say, "Oh, you know you have it all."

Well, if she did, then *all* was no longer a good word in her book. Her mother-in-law has it *all* and she was probably the most unhappy person Ally had ever met in her entire life. She almost felt sorry for her. Almost.

When married to a dominating multi-millionaire, don't consider any outside activities. A career? Oh, no, that certainly doesn't work either. When Ally was nine-years old, she knew she would become a writer. The big blue truck came through the neighborhood once a week, and she was excited each time. She climbed the two steps into the Book Mobile and stepped into a different world. She knew she could pick up any book and be transported far from home when she read it. She loved to read. She imagined herself as one of the characters in those stories. She told herself one day she, too, would write the stories that already swirled and danced in her mind. She, too, would take people far away on fabulous journeys.

Despite all the drastic changes in her life, Ally still had a great passion for writing, and found herself in the perfect place to do it – the place where imagination was rewarded and appreciated. She decided it was time to begin a long-delayed writing career and go on some happy journeys once again. It was certainly something she needed then: Inward journeys into full-blown imagination, an escape from her husband's cruel, cold and emotional behavior. She was excited about writing a book and

458

began a fantasy type story based upon a dream she'd had. It was filled with fairies and gnomes, and little people. After she thought about the entire storyline, it was really a cool idea. Living in Hollywood was perfect. It was exactly where she could mingle with people whose talent and creativity was encouraged and elevated to a fine art. When she felt the book was ready, she could talk to new friends about shopping her little book for a movie.

Once again, Ally became inspired. She wrote and wrote for several days. One day her husband noticed she was in her office at the computer, writing. She wasn't sun-tanning, or in the gym, or doing the usual Hollywood celebrity's wife thing. For some reason he was not too pleased.

He stopped in the doorway. "What are you up to behind that computer?"

Ally excitedly explained to Drake about her dream and that she was writing a book about it.

He looked at her and chuckled. His chuckle turned into laughter – loud laughter. "You!?" he said, "You write the great American novel? You're really funny, Ally."

"Well, no, it's not a novel right now, Drake, but a fairytale book."

"Oh, Ally, you are such a little girl. That's exactly what you need to be wasting your time on. What do you think you're going to do? You think you're going to sell it to one of our friends' big studios?"

"Well, maybe, if it's good enough."

He laughed louder. "Do me a favor, eh? Don't tell anyone about this, Ally." He walked out still laughing.

Ally's heart was broken. Why did he think she couldn't write? If she had the confidence to do it, shouldn't he be supportive? Most people would think he'd say the opposite under the circumstances because they knew those people. If it was worthy, she could try to sell the book, and it could be adapted to a movie one day. Even if it never was made into a movie, a lot of children would have a great adventure from her fairytale book. Her feelings were hurt. *He is just so mean.*

The days went on and she continued writing. Drake passed by her office door and give her dirty looks. Obviously, he wasn't proud at all that she was trying to accomplish her dreams.

Every now and then, he'd stop and yell. "How are the fairies doing?"

Her reply was sincere. "Really good. I'm almost at a hundred pages."

He literally made a snort sound through his nose. "Whatever."

Sje got up one morning to write, but couldn't find her document on the hard drive. It was gone. Her computer was blank. Her book was nowhere. Erased. Deleted. It was as if it had never existed. She stared at the empty screen for a few minutes and tried to stay calm. She *Knew* Drake had been jealous of her writing, but he had gone off the deep end . . . he had erased her story, her book, her dream. She rushed into his office in tears. "Why?"

He acted as if he didn't know what she was talking about.

"Why would you erase my story, Drake? It is mine – mine alone. Why would you do that to me?"

He laughed at me. "Practice, darling, lots of practice. That's what makes you good out here in this crowd. Now, you go and write it again. . . . maybe it will be better."

"Better? You said 'better.' Why? Did you read it?"

"Well, no, I don't have time for fairytale reading, Ally. I'm a real businessman doing real things, because I am real important."

She stared at him for a few seconds, turned and ran out of the room, crying. She told herself she was important, too. She wasn't going to let him stop her. She wrote it again, but saved it to a disk so she could outsmart him. Days later, her story was just about done, and once again it vanished from her computer. Somehow, he found her disk.

Okay, it was apparent to her now: She wasn't going to be allowed to write the great American novel or her dream about fairies anywhere around him. She went back to her usual job: Being his kept wife.

Drake seemed happier. "You're back in your place, by my side where you belong."

They continued to go to Hollywood parties. She continued to act happy.

One particular night they were at one of the biggest Hollywood parties. A few agents were there who really liked Ally's looks. The studio head said, "You know, guys, she would look real good on the screen. Maybe you should consider acting, Ally."

Can you imagine how that went over with Drake? Her husband made sure she never managed to get to acting classes or to any meetings. Her acting career was over before it began. At this point, she was exhausted in her attempts to be anything or anyone, and began to sink lower into nonexistence. Depression was her daily companion. To this day, she is surprised she didn't sink into drugs or the bottle like many of the other Hollywood wives. Zombies, but they look good on their husband's arm . . . bejeweled human ornaments. Her world began to feel like 'Hotel California' – people check in, but don't check out.

Drake went to parties without her, and she got so depressed that she became sick, very sick. She was in the bed one evening when he came upstairs. He had already been out with his friends for happy hour.

He leaned over the bed to kiss her, or so she thought. He pulled out a thick stack of cash and fanned it in her face. "Take a good look at this, darling. This is what it's all about. Now your rich husband is going out. Nighty-night." He laughed and slammed the door.

Ally wanted to die. Maybe she was already dead and in hell. She no longer felt alive; she didn't feel much at all anymore. He screened her calls, and timed whenever she left the house, which wasn't often unless it was to the beauty salon or shopping for clothes. The limo driver kept a written record of where she went and how long she was there. She wasn't allowed any close friends, because according to him, he was all she needed. She felt like a slave girl in one of those romance novels where the ship's captain steals the girl, locks her away, and only lets her come out for one thing. Drake evolved into a totally obsessive person and accused her of having affairs when she went out on the forty-five minute walks in the neighborhood.

Ally no longer knew what to do or say. No matter what she did, she broke one of Drake's unwritten rules and he would yell insults. She moved slowly and thought like a zombie. He wouldn't even let her go home for Christmas to see family. It was worse than the movie 'Sleeping with the Enemy,' because she couldn't even take swimming lessons. She knew and prayed that one day, just one day, he wouldn't be watching . . . and she'd be able to get away.

* * *

"Marriage is like a cage,
one sees the birds outside desperate to get in,
and those inside equally desperate to get out.
She's only a bird in a gilded cage."

Michel de Montaigne

Chapter 27

So, you *really* think it's a great idea to live in a cage as long as it's gilded in gold, encrusted with diamonds like some avidly pursued, hunted, captured and collected exotic bird? Do you really? Well, think again.

Remember the recurring theme of this story and repeat it to yourself, if you will. Repeat it over and over. It's Ally's mantra now. This is a Cinderella Tale. She is also wearing her newest pair of shoes, glittery red ones. She proudly keeps her head held high as she marches straight ahead on the yellow brick road to ask the Wizard to grant the deepest and sweetest gift of her heart. Along the way, she met an interesting and sometimes odd assortment of consorts and fellow travelers.

Drake himself has played every role along the way, with the notable exception of the cowardly lion. Drake was never cowardly; he was anything *but* that. As Ally recounted the next experience, bear in mind that Type A, egocentric, domineering multi-millionaire men generally come in two stripes. The first is the kind who collect harems, attempt to lure and jump virtually anything that's animal, vegetable, or mineral which happens to cross their path, and, for the most part, don't care a whit what their wives do because they're too busy doing their own thing with other women. Then there is the sort who are so microscopically obsessed and enthralled with every single, solitary, discrete and personally private aspect of their wives' lives that they maintain constant, laser-like focus only upon them and what they're doing at any given time. They are meticulous in their observations of their wives and what she and her circle of friends are involved in and whether or not it's an approved activity . . . things which fall within the tight penumbra or aura of what he finds acceptable.

Drake fell squarely and solidly into the latter category, and was in fact a cartoonish, a caricature, archetypal example of it.

One night, Drake and Ally stopped by a popular high-end club and bar in Atlanta for a drink. Drake proceeded her by a few steps, not in the stereotypically Asiatic fashion of the husband leading his wife by a measured number of steps, but simply because the club was busy, an elbow to elbow crowd, and Drake had zeroed in on an opening at the bar to order drinks. As she approached behind Drake, two men already seated at the bar, a giant frosty mug of keg beer in each hand, swiveled around on their stools to regard her appreciatively. In all fairness, it was not immediately evident under the circumstances that Drake and she were together.

"Look at the pretty lady," one man said to the other.

Ally had a flash of half-recognition, and thought they could be the two Williams brothers of televised wresting fame, Benny and Davey, although she wasn't entirely sure which one was which. It didn't matter.

Drake was wearing a Pink Rolex jacket which grabbed the wrestlers' attention as quite colorful. They stared at him. Perhaps to the wrestlers the pink jacket represented something other than a handmade garment created specifically-for-the-islands where they regularly went. That style and color was considered quite popular there.

Drake never paused to haggle over the impropriety of their comment. His reaction was immediate, swift, decisive and murderously savage. He spun around and lunged forward with all of the momentum he could muster with his 6-foot 5-inch muscular and athletically-agile frame. He grabbed the two oversized beer mugs and slammed them into the brothers' faces with thunderous effect. Glass shards and strong beer exploded in all directions, thoroughly dousing Ally as she stood there dumbfounded in her evening dress and coat. Blood splashed everywhere, and rivers of it sluiced down both the brothers' faces as they lay sprawled on the floor, legs splayed under their bar stools.

One brother, it could have been Benny, trembled and was clearly going into shock. Shiny slivers of glass protruded from a rather ugly-looking wound on his neck. People were screaming, shouting, pointing. The bartender quickly called 911 to summon an emergency ambulance.

Drake stood there, chest stuck out, fingers curled into fists, breathing in and out heavily in an adrenal inspired pant. As crazy as it may sound now, at the time Ally was gripped by a palpable sense of déjà vu. Curiously, it wasn't in regard to anything she had experienced. The image which forcibly seized her mind at that instant was the indelible image of Barlow, the vampire in the miniseries that was based on Stephen King's work 'Salem's Lot'. Her mind flashed to Barlow standing triumphantly over the little boy Mark's freshly slain parents, whose heads Barlow had just smashed together like oversized eggshells. It was a strange and ugly, yet true and accurate mental image.

The other brother, Davey, felt around on the floor and picked up a long, curved glass shard with his slippery fingers and came up slicing. Davey caught Drake a couple of times, first on the leg, then near his collarbone. To this day, Ally firmly believes *someone* was protecting Drake that night. She has absolutely no doubt that Davey's strike was intentional and aimed specifically for Drake's throat. Drake and Davey wrestled each other to the floor, punching and swearing.

As this was an elite section of downtown Atlanta, the ambulance arrived very shortly with a police escort. Officers managed to pull Drake off of Davey and separated them.

All three combatants were taken to the hospital in different ambulances. Ally rode with Drake. Even through her fogged haze of shock and disbelief, and given her knowledge of Drake's hyper-aggressively jealous nature, she knew the Lanzen's economic and political status and machine had already been put into motion. It resulted in the successful effort to keep Drake out of jail. Given his actions, the injuries he inflicted, and the comparatively low extent and non-urgent nature of his own injuries, a lesser affluent man would have spent the night in an uncomfortable cell.

For his part, Drake remained unrepentant and defiant. When asked by the authorities, he made it clear he didn't give a damn one way or the other. His point was proven and that was all that mattered. Ally was *his*, that was it, that was all, pure and simple – case closed before it opened.

Not for the first time her upbringing, her essentially caring nature and empathy for others caused her to wrack her brain to determine if she could have caused the incident, if she hadn't been minding her own business walking behind her husband, or if she had attracted attention during the half minute that she waited for him to order cocktails. She was looking forward to enjoying a couple of glasses of wine and a relaxing evening, listening to some jazz in a dimly-lit, posh, establishment. You know the kind of place; it's where quite a few well-known people can go for a drink with friends in a peaceful environment; where there's no riffraff scoping out the crowd or are there collecting celebrities' autographs, or trying to be discovered by a talent scout. Ally should have known a simple stop for a drink was too much to ask of the Fates.

Now whenever she reflected upon the events that transpired, it really gave her pause to reconsider details. Drake had walked up with pride and had smiled at the two famed wrestlers because he recognized them. Drake was friendly and spoke to several people as they approached the bar area. Everything was fine and normal until it reached the point that it was no longer time to be nice.

The two brothers seemed to be halfway drunk. As they turned to comment and ogle Ally, her husband simply thanked them for complimenting his wife. They had begun to laugh, commented about his pink jacket, perhaps there were too many obvious stares at her, perhaps they muttered something only Drake could hear. In total, it was more than the oversized ego of a man of Drake's size could handle.

472

Drake didn't waste words with a warning that they were being rude or were infringing upon his personal territory. He simply erupted, slamming the two huge body builders to the floor. It happened in seconds.

Considering all three men were well-known and Drake's family was of the extreme wealthy class, the local media were all over the story in a short-lived feeding frenzy of coverage. So were the brothers' attorneys. One brother required extensive plastic surgery to repair the damage Drake had caused. The other brother recovered from his minor injuries in a few days. Their reputation for toughness in the ring was damaged almost beyond repair by a non-wrestler.

Drake was lucky with minor cuts, though deep. The cuts were sutured and bandaged, and they were about to leave the hospital. She couldn't help but wonder if Drake needed more than just the few painkillers that were immediately prescribed and administered for his stitching procedure. What about some chemical compound with a twenty-to-thirty-letter, unpronounceable, extended and hyphenated name to tame his frenzied mind and spirit, something to control the timing of impulse firings across his brain's synapses – though she knew such hope was only fanciful. Spirits cannot be cleansed entirely by the contents of bottles. She thanked God that Drake had no other real chemical dependencies, other than alcohol; Drake's ongoing flirtation with cocaine was precisely that, an amusing diversion, a purely recreational fling. Drake's manic obsession and agitation and ferment were all quite natural, thank you. Although, she began to wonder if Drake's tendencies and inclinations exposed him to consequences that were a little more than natural. As anyone familiar with arsenic can attest, just because something is 'natural,' doesn't necessarily mean it's good for you.

A large settlement; nothing more was said or done, but to Ally, it was a big deal. She didn't recover from her husband's public temper tantrum quite as well. It was the first time she saw him in physical action, and she felt like she had just lived her own insane episode of Monday night wrestling.

She had never quite known anyone of this quick, purely impulsive and bizarre and crazed behavior. She was certainly no fan of her husband being a hero by almost killing two wrestlers to prove some boyish Robin Hood fantasy from a time of sword-fighting days. She knew of his childhood years, of playing in his so-called castle, of growing up pretending to defend his princess. Ally was not impressed. Embarrassed would be more accurate, not to mention that, according to Drake's parents, it had to be all Ally's fault somehow. The Lanzens came to the hospital. Mrs. Lanzen pulled Ally aside in the crowded hallway, asking about what happened after the bartender gave his statement to the police of what he had seen. She was adamant. There had to be much more drama to this incident. Mrs. Lanzen was extremely unhappy with the plain and simple truth of Drake's temper and violence.

As time went on, it passed and faded like some nightmare in most people's memory. But that incident was all too real for Ally. It faded somewhat into the distance without ever fading from her mind. She wasn't fond of going to many places with her husband, especially where there was a bar-like atmosphere. It became more obvious he could not contain his liquor or control his anger.

She hadn't enjoyed drinking much to begin with. A few glasses of wine to celebrate was enough for her anyplace, anytime. Drake seemed determined to drink until the bar was empty of all he could possibly consume.

Funny how a Southern gentleman could be on his best behavior and make the finest positive first impressions when dating, and say he really didn't care to drink and would rather offer you a glass of champagne and only have a small one so you wouldn't drink alone. Ah, the infinite control phase. He knew the entire time that he really couldn't have just one, that the illusion he was creating would instantly shatter into a million fragments if he drank more than one. Deliver me from date-night-only, white-knuckled sobriety.

And so it is . . . Southern gentlemen often just sit there, not really feeling well and even looking ill at ease, not daring to take a single sip. Yea, great one.

These are the same gentlemen who appear to have lots of natural class, they love to be seen with you in a beautiful evening gown, and love it when other men in the room watch and admire you, and feel proud you are with them. Best behavior always: they stand when you leave the table to go to the powder room, stand again when you return, hold your chair steady as you sit back down. It's as any Southern, well-trained and highly skilled gentleman would do. The perfect Rhett. The perfectly groomed graduate of the French Millionaire Boy's Club school. The perfect highly educated man . . . simply because their father donated gifts and endowments to Harvard.

No highly refined gentleman from the South would ever be seen out of character in public. No matter the circumstance or the ultimate cost, he must consider how he was reared, where he was reared, his family surname and the family's position in society for the past two or ten generations . . . *who* and *what* he is remains as crucial as his next breath.

*Ladies, all words and actions befo*re the marriage aside, hear and understand this: they catch their prey and put them in gilded cages. Need more be said?

"The dark prince takes many forms."

Unknown

CHAPTER 28

Life in that gilded mansion was agonizing. Days were spent either lying to her friends or to herself, telling them she was fine, merely haggard from walking fast a few miles every morning or working out at the gym, sometimes with a personal trainer, to stay fit. Lying to herself that tomorrow would be different, better, Drake would change, he'd care for her again as a person instead of a possession.

Many days she would feel so sorry for Drake as he struggled against his own second nature. When he was sober and good, he could be humble and compassionate towards everyone, he would go out of his way to do anything for anyone, he would quickly step up in some circumstances like an angel of mercy to help people. Watching Drake struggle, she recalled a hymn I sang in Sunday School as a child: "This Little Light of Mine, I'm Gonna Let It Shine." She could see there really was a small light glimmering in Drake's soul and she tried hard to bring that light into the open, to give it some air and positive fuel to help it grow and glow until it was bright enough for the world to see. It did shine during the early days of their marriage, then something happened by the time they moved to Beverly Hills that caused the light to flicker and almost die into a mere ember. She held tightly to a slim hope it would turn back around because Drake could be a wonderful man when he decided to be. Unfortunately, later on in Southern California, he didn't decide to be sympathetic too often. Perhaps it was because he had been born under a Scorpion moon and on the fourth night – worse of all, he had been born into a dark-seeded family. It was a sad truth that Drake never had much of a chance in this life to shine his inner light very far. The odds were against him. There was too much darkness called down around him from his first day on earth. Perhaps that was the power he reached out to grasp in his later years. For him to remain rich and powerful, he had to call upon and use those dark forces to every advantage he could muster. Ally could only watch and pray as the darker side of her prince overshadowed the good. It broke her heart to see it happening and for her to be unable to make it stop. Sadder still to realize Drake really wanted the darker side, wanted the power and the riches that the darker side delivered into his hand. The more he craved it and worked to acquire it, the more it was poured upon him from some mysterious source – it became a force unto itself.

There were times when it was obvious Drake believed he was a living god. Oh, how she dreaded those times. She had seen it before and refused to watch it again. She'd shudder and leave the room when she saw the darkness begin to manifest itself around him. Muscles in his handsome face would slowly draw tighter until his youthful appearance aged and wrinkled, becoming almost grotesque and shocking – her prince changed before her eyes. She never wanted to see that again. Yes, she ran from the room frightened.

Her once-beloved prince had found a way to conjure unusual power to himself. She likened it to seeing the ghosts that roamed Myrtles Plantation which was next door to where she'd spent her childhood and teenage years. As a child, she watched what remained of the earlier people's spirits gather into white mists to scoot along the ceilings or form into dense black shadows and hover in the corners, and then they'd follow her friends and her. She watched something happen with Drake that was different yet familiar enough that she never wanted to witness it again. It was still him in complete control of himself, yet he had changed.

In reality, she was doing her best to cope with Drake's changing daily personality, especially his constant microscopic scrutiny of her life. It was gradual, but at some unknown point in time, nothing fell under the pretense that Drake would allow her a shred of personal privacy. Her phone calls were monitored, in case a girlfriend said something hinting at an ulterior motive, some secret, some mystery. Shopping for clothes to wear to Drake's business required-attendance events only happened when she felt up to leaving the house – then someone usually went along. He scolded her like a child if she returned fifteen minutes later than expected. Attending those so-called high society events was another challenge. She put on a 'Happy Harriet Housewife' persona along with her makeup. She still wondered if anyone knew she was the most convincing actress in the building – probably not.

It's one thing for an actress to memorize lines in a script and perform one scene at a time. It's another thing entirely for someone to make it up as they go and perform perfectly for hours or days at a stretch. Friends and acquaintances never knew that was her real fulltime job. Mini vacations with friends aboard their private jets, flying to Vegas and staying at the MGM, flying to New York, attending parties in the homes of the biggest players in Hollywood, sitting in on private screening – all those events was her new career: To go, smile, speak little, look good and exude contentment. Everyone was relaxed and enjoyed themselves. She wasn't ever relaxed; she was working. Acting was her fulltime job and she was extremely good at it, too. No one ever questioned her about her relationship with Drake. Ally's acting career: Believable. Convincing. Oscar Winning.

She often wanted to evade the private detectives Drake kept on retainer, who were called every so often to track her down. It was never the same person, never the same car or day, but they never missed seeing her because she never really tried to hide. Why bother? She just wanted enough space to breathe, to
484

just go here or there like other people were allowed, to have lunch with friends without every word being recorded. The detectives reported to Drake, then Drake would scold her and tell her where she had gone, what she had purchased, who she had spoken with – he laughed if she objected, and he bragged about keeping tabs on her twenty-four hours a day, seven days a week. If she objected too much, he would try to gloss over his domineering trait by saying he was only protecting his most precious possession – Ally.

On rare occasions, she spent a few secret minutes writing at her computer or painting. If she was careful, she wouldn't be caught breaking Drake's rules, but some of the servants, his perpetual watchmen seemingly lurking around every corner and behind every potted palm, often did. She wasn't supposed to be talented enough to write or paint or think; she was only supposed to look good on Drake's arm when he wanted and where he wanted and how he wanted. She was his bejeweled ornament. He had already destroyed her computer disc of the fairytale she had written, and had destroyed the canvases she had painted of one of the wizards from the fairytale. Somehow, she knew in her heart that one day they would be recreated, at least she hoped they would be redone. Neither effort could be attempted while under Drake's roof.

Hidden microphones throughout the mansion, grounds and pool area captured every conversation; her cell and bathroom phones were bugged. Drake usually knew whose phone calls I'd received before one of the servants could tell him. I often suspected he had a hidden electronic devise in his office which identified every caller and recorded every conversation long before companies made such devises available. If one of her phone calls lasted longer than Drake thought it should, he would snatch the phone from her hand; cell phones were whirled into the swimming pool, or across the yard, or straight up into a tree, or simply smashed under his heel. Control of every word, every movement, every moment. That's all Drake demanded.

Sometimes she caught Maddox, Drake's personal assistant who did double duty as a butler, watching her. There was an element of sadness in his eyes; he seemed to know she was unhappy, crushed to the core, misery ran deep within her soul. Drake often insisted she take someone with her when shopping or having coffee with friends, to take either one of the maids as a chaperone or the butler Maddox. If Maddox went along, it was a relief. He would drift away to give her some breathing room alone or to chat with girlfriends.

Ally could never fully understand why someone as intelligent as Maddox worked as a butler; the job just didn't seem compatible with his abilities. Then, one day he said he had earned his MBA, his master's in business administration from USC, and hoped to learn practical application by working around and near Drake. Drake was an extremely successful businessman so she understood why Maddox would stick around as a personal assistant. He'd sit in on some of Drake's conferences, take notes and help Drake develop five-year business plans. Maddox met most of Drake's business contacts, seemed comfortable with them, and of course, he had the use of Drake's luxury cars. Perhaps he felt like a member of the entertainment business world's inner circle by staying.

Despite contributing and working side by side with Drake, Ally often heard Drake berating Maddox for thinking too much, for coming up with new ideas instead of parroting Drake's ideas, for showing too much ambition to further himself, for hoping to be anything more than a butler. Ally suspected he wanted to keep Maddox as a member of the serfdom sect in Drake's little kingdom. It could get rather ugly and embarrassing at times, especially when Drake reminded Maddox he was only one of the 'hired help.' That was another of Drake's changing personality traits, a new nasty habit: He belittled everyone he could, squashed their feelings under his foot, degraded any personal accomplishment. Recognition of talent or intelligence in anyone else must have been a terrible threat to Drake's precarious and fragile ego. She knew better than to remind Drake she had entered college at 16, had earned my degree by 19, and owned and managed a very profitable business in Atlanta while still in her early 20s. She had racked up an impressive resume' long before they ever met. She suspected he never would have married her if he remembered she was intelligent, that he couldn't fool her completely and constantly. However, a person had to be intelligent to follow any conversation with Drake Lanzen. He was highly ingenious, inventive, innovative, creative. It was a challenge to converse with him on any level. It's a known fact there's a fine line between intelligence and insanity. Many days Drake was determined to cross that line, to step into rarified air, to inhale the ether, and he was absolutely determined to drink too much. When he did, he'd swear he wasn't from this planet, but sent here on a mission of mercy to help dim-witted Earthlings to develop a higher level of intellect. How charitable. How disturbing.

As tight as he would hold Ally close with one hand, he attempted to shove many others away with the other. In one instance, Drake tried to separate her from those she held the dearest in her heart. He tried to convince her to send her two young daughters to an established, well-respected boarding school in France, saying it would be best for their education. That's when Ally scotched her heels, stood her ground. Her daughters came first, always had, always would. She warned

Drake if he even mentioned it again, she would leave in a heartbeat, taking her precious babies with her, that they would vanish, be out of his life forever. He finally apologized and agreed that the private academy the girls attended in Beverly Hills would provide an excellent education. He let the matter drop, but she knew he would have separated her beloved family if she hadn't objected long and loud.

Despite everything he said about trusting and loving her, Drake made it clear someone would either accompany or follow her to dress shops, to Starbucks, to the famed Old Hollywood's gathering place The Brown Derby, to Pink's, to Borders for books. Even small-minded sales clerks trying to make points with Drake would report her movements with a quick phone call. Drake never believed she actually had good, loyal friends, or that she met girlfriends for a latte where they would chat about upcoming events, about fashions or Hollywood husbands. Oh, those husbands. She learned things that would scare any young woman into staying as far away from Hollywood as possible, but they kept coming. They all thought they would be the next mega movie star and they'd never have to pay a heavy price for fame and fortune. Fantasyland existed.

Whatever Ally purchased, whomever she spoke with was always reported to Drake as if national security depended upon her activities. She felt as if every move and word were x-rayed and recorded. The short leash Drake had tied around her throat often strangled her, leaving her without words to contribute in a casual conversation. She felt stripped and naked – a shell, a shadow of what had once been a happy vivacious young woman. Doomed.

* * *

One of the maids signaled Maddox to step into a hallway off the main entrance. "Psst! C'mon, jest listen to what he's doin' now. One day, that dang fool is gonna lose it completely an' smack her one, hit her. If he do, oh, woe is me, he's gonna be sorry . . . 'cause that woman's gonna be gone in a New York minute, take them pretty girls of hers an' whoosh – they's all gonna be outta here. You jest watch."

"Hush, woman," Maddox ordered. Obviously, Drake had raised his voice loud enough to attract attention from the household staff. He was angry about something with Ally. Maddox shook his head and moved to the corner so he could see.

"Where the hell do you think you're going?" Drake yelled again. "Why the hell are you leaving the house dressed like that? You think you're Bo Derek? Think you're Pamela Anderson? Think you're some kind of movie star parading up and down the streets?"

Ally looked down at her favorite ensemble. "What? I don't think so, Drake. I've had this outfit for months now."

She was wearing a pale-toned, designer linen suit, her blouse tucked in, her slacks neatly pressed and creased, straw hat, gold coin-chained belt loosely draped around her hips, matching gold high heels. "I think I look okay for lunch with my girlfriends. I've worn this plenty of times before."

"Ha! Well, not today! Not ever again! You think you can traipse around Beverly Hills in something like that so people will stare at you. So they'd think you're a star or something?! Have your own fan club out there somewhere? You have people lined up somewhere waiting for your autograph? Want to play dress-up like 'I'm a big mega movie star' game? Well, I've had enough of your crap."

Drake yanked the straw hat off Ally's head, the long black ribbon entangling in her shoulder-length blonde hair, then he ripped the straw hat to pieces, threw them in the air and laughed at the shocked expression on her face.

"What's that?" he said gruffly, pointing to the belt around her waist.

"Uh, the Chanel coin belt. . . . the one you said I could buy."

Drake grabbed it, and almost knocked Ally off balance by pulling it hard enough that the delicate latch of the chain snapped, then he pulled the links apart and gold coins flew in all directions. Without a second's hesitation, Drake reached down and pulled her blouse out of her slacks so it looked as if she was wearing a gunny sack or something like a huge, baggy, maternity shirt.

"There! That's better. I don't want you out there on the street looking like you own the damn Rodeo Drive unless you're standing next to me. Do you get it? If you want to go out, you'll go dressed like I want, not like you're some movie star! You'll go out in public only as my wife. You understand me?"

Tears streamed down Ally's cheeks, but she nodded, turned and ran back up the stairs.

"Oh, that's it! Run like some scared little spoiled brat!" Drake yelled at her back as she darted up the stairs toward her room. Laughing, he headed back to his office, staggering a little from the amount of vodka he had already consumed before lunchtime.

Maddox put his arm out to stop the maid from rushing out into the foyer. "Wait until he's gone . . . unless you want to catch some of his flak."

"Oh, no-suh, don't want none of that."

"I didn't think so. Just wait until I'm sure it's over."

After Drake retreated behind his desk, the maid cautiously peeked around the corner, then silently stepped into the foyer to collect the gold coins and sweep up the straw debris. She had helped Ally pack for vacations in the Islands several times before and knew the belt was a rare piece from the Chanel collection that had cost more than a thousand dollars. It was destroyed, along with the one-of-a-kind straw hat. Neither could be replaced. And, she knew Ally would be depressed and heart-sick at losing a favorite outfit she had assembled herself. No personal shopper or professional stylist had collected and assembled those particular garments. The outfit reflected her style; casual yet elegant.

"Mister Drake done that jest to hurt her again," the maid whispered when Maddox stepped into the foyer. "He's tryin' to tear up Miz Ally's spirit jest like he done that there hat, but he can't. She's too tough for the likes o' him. Poor Miz Ally, I feels sorry for her all the time now."

Maddox cleared his throat. "Quiet woman; it's not our affair. You clean this up as quickly as possible. I'll have Cook send a tea tray up to Miz Ally's room."

Maddox turned on his heel and headed for the kitchen. It wasn't the first time, nor would it be the last that he would witness cruel and senseless acts against the little Southern blonde lady. Drake Lanzen's rope around his wife's throat was a strangle hold, suffocating; it was just a matter of time before Maddox suspected she would leave. Common sense had nothing to do with Drake Lanzen's intelligence, nothing whatsoever.

Maddox admired Ally's spirit and the fact Drake had tried but failed to destroy her free will. Although smaller in size, Ally was emotionally much stronger than her husband. Above all things, Maddox knew Ally was a true believer, a deeply spiritual woman who wanted to do good in the world and to help others.

The following day, Maddox held open the kitchen's delivery door as two maids carried arm loads of Bob Mackey dresses and other highly-priced designer garments to the dumpster in the alley behind the mansion. The closet was nearly empty.

Drake heard the maids clomping down the stairs and doors opening and closing. Curious, he followed the unusual sounds until he stepped into the kitchen. "Hey! What's going on here? What are you people doing?"

The eldest and braver maid tucked her chin close to her chest. "Jest doin' what Miz Ally done tole us to do: Throw these here things away. They's all tore up."

Drake merely stared at them and their armloads of clothing for a moment longer, shrugged his shoulders, turned around and walked back to his office. He didn't care one whit about the thrown-away garments or squandered money.

Several times a certain outfit or bathing suit or a hat would suddenly be missing. It would simply be gone from the walk-in closet or drawers. She would ask one of the household help about it and would only be told, "Mister Drake don't like it on you no more. He says it's too gaudy. That's what he tole us."

That's when Ally would know she had garnered someone's attention, someone had complimented her to Drake, someone had said how nice she looked at some event, or how lucky he was to have such a beautiful wife. One comment. One compliment. That was all it would take to set Drake off on a closet cleansing spree, to drab her down so no one would notice her at all, so she would blend into the woodwork. If she caught someone's eye while wearing something unique, that item vanished. If she thought a particular garment looked good, it vanished. Control. Always control. Diamonds, other rare gems, unique gifts, vacations – tangibles that people would instantly recognize had to have come from Drake's hand, from his magnanimous generosity toward his elegant and beautiful wife who was standing beside him – those were showered upon her without cease, as long as everyone knew *he* did it, that she had nothing to do with acquiring it. Drake did love Ally in his own way, and would have killed for her. She was never quite certain he hadn't already done so.

* * *

Drake had dated beautiful women most of his life; Vanna White was one, Marla Maples was another, a woman The Donald married at one time. Drake's good looks attracted offers by directors and producers to take a part in a movie. He wasn't interested at all. Acting in a movie was below him, a step down, in his opinion. Drake intended to own a studio, not merely work for one. He already kept company with most of the studio heads in Hollywood. One of Drake's closest friends was the son of the head of Universal Pictures.

It didn't matter than Ally, too, was considered beautiful by many people, and had been offered numerous movie roles. She spent most of her evenings alone. The butler Maddox watched her pour a glass of wine and kept track of her as she roamed the hallways and walked the grounds while Drake drank himself into a stupor and made international phone calls about one of his

496

businesses. Her evenings were spent either sitting on her balcony watching the city lights in the distance, or listening to her favorite music by The Eagles. One of her favorite songs on CD was 'You Can't Hide Your Lying Eyes.' She loved to hear Don Henley's 'Last Worthless Evening,' too. That was one song she always thought was written just for her. The lyrics really touched her mind: 'Rich old man and she doesn't have to worry, just dress up in the lace and go in style.' Ally couldn't help but grin and she'd notice Maddox would grin too. Perhaps they were like-minded about music, but there was never a 'boy across town' for her. No, she had taken her vows seriously, even if she had been half-drunk and half-drugged at the ceremony. Drake hadn't taken the vows seriously at all. Songs were a far cry from reality. Ally having an affair was simply out of the question and never considered. Anyone she even spoke to was in danger of losing their head – Drake, the dragon, was always on the prowl. She was limited to imagination and music. She'd play those songs while by the pool and wouldn't notice Maddox watching until her vision cleared, until she wiped away the tears. Sometimes, Maddox showed up almost silently, leading one of the kitchen helpers who was carrying a tray loaded with a pitcher of iced tea and a glass or something else that was cool and refreshing. They both enjoyed listening to the Eagles' music. Ally seemed to gather moral strength from the lyrics. Maddox would stand for a while, listening, nodding, enjoying the music and he would almost smile.

Of course being married to Drake Lanzen had many advantages. She was able to tap his massive money resources to host a lawn party for the local society that supported families of children who were fighting cancer. She bought dozens of Teddy Bears, rented clowns, others wore Bart Simpson and Ninja Turtle costumes, and she hired a specialty entertainment company to set up giant balloons that were absolutely safe so the frail children could jump and bounce as much as they could without being injured. There was lots of squealing and laughter as the children played.

A small band was set up on one side of the large lawn, and a photographer took a photo of each child sitting with their favorite character. We had enough ice cream and cake that even the parents couldn't eat any more. It was a wonderful afternoon and the brave little children left the mansion with big smiles on their faces. Ally enjoyed every minute and loved hearing the sick children's laughter.

Drake hated it. Hated she had spent one dime of his money on those children. And, so did his mother. Actually, she pitched a hissy fit, saying Ally had taken advantage of Drake and had spent his money on total foolishness. Ally had learned months earlier that 'Doodle' didn't have one sympathetic bone in her body. Her bad attitude didn't matter at all. She moaned and grumbled in public because she detested having to wait while children in wheelchairs were allowed to go through restaurant doors or shopping mall doorways before anyone else. Children in wheelchairs were referred to as 'door stoppers' by the infamous Mrs. Lanzen of Atlanta's upper crust. Ally could never get over that comment. It gave her chills that the woman was so cold-hearted. Every time she saw her own precious girls running and playing, she thanked God they were healthy and could run and play. Drake said he had once dated a woman who had a disabled child, a child whose brain had not developed beyond the age of three. He dated the woman only because his mother hated it. How disgusting.

By this time, Ally knew her life had to change simply because Drake was robbing her of it. If she stayed, she'd be absorbed into an all-consuming mechanism until even remnants of her spirit vanished. In scarce moments alone, she could barely envision a bleak future yet she could still hear the sweet murmurs of her long ago past. Stay or go – decision time.

She knew any future, if she stayed, would be a dull gray that was already fading to a blank slate. Even that blankness would eventually become invisible until she no longer existed. She was running out of choices: She could either take everything

Drake dished out, remain silent and join the zombie 'Stepford Wives' of Hollywood, or she could disappear from the mansion and Beverly Hills without warning.

Leaving was heart-wrenching to consider. Being a contributing part of Hollywood had been a lifetime goal. To be in the middle of the city yet be unable to partake of the perpetual excitement, or speak her mind or convey ideas to the creativity that emanated from the people she knew had been painful. To stay, she'd still be Drake's puppet, entangled in long ropes – not strings – unable to take a step in any direction without his approval. Staying as his wife meant she'd be overlooked by the majority of the power-people in their circle, ignored or considered as just another over-indulged housewife, more dull wallpaper; she'd slide into a mundane existence while secretly clinging desperately to the fringe.

Similar treatment had been doled out to stars and a few movers n' shakers, who had slammed into their personal wall and had lapsed into one form or another of substance abuse, either alcohol or drugs or both always brought on the same results to their families and friends and coworkers. Addicts had totally fouled movie schedules when they went off on binges and had cost studios hundreds of thousands of dollars a day. Publicists had a hard time keeping information out of the news. When the news did leak, the long-suffering addicts could read

500

supportive comments in the celebrity publications and in TV interviews, they could receive public pats on the back, they could enter and go through expensive rehab sessions, and they could come out the other side extremely frayed but intact. Then the balloon often burst: they'd not hear their phone ring, not see their name in print, not hear their name mentioned on TV, not be invited to screenings, even their agent could forget their name. They would struggle to regain a toehold on a temperamental industry's slippery slope. Despite what the celebrity had accomplished in the past, studio bean counters were the first in line to remind directors and producers how much a particular star's addiction had cost – the bottom line always ruled – people rarely mattered. Somehow, most temporary outcasts managed to survive. Eventually, their black ball status was forgiven by the mainstream and they'd be issued an invitation to join the ever-growing crowd of recovering addicts. Easily spotted, they usually stood together in little groups at parties, sipping their Shirley Temples. But at least they had a handful of comrades to commiserate with on a weekly basis.

There was no such faction for the likes of Ally, not someone who would willingly abandon Hollywood's money-god for pure personal freedom. Incomprehensible to the whole lot. She'd be labeled a leper, she'd never find a toehold, never get a hand up, never hear her phone ring, no one would remember her name, not even the other former lepers.

Decision: She could breathe, have a real life elsewhere, anywhere with genuine people who truly cared, or she could dive head first into the Black Hole that Drake had constructed. It would suck her in and pull the life out of her. She'd be twisted and crushed into his pre-determined shape. Its power to dismantle any object rivaled anything scientists had discovered in outer space. Reshaping would drain her of fortitude and imagination, her books never written, her canvasses never viewed, her personal history would be erased as if she had never taken a breath. Louisiana vampires ghosted into Ally's mind, wooing and tempting, telling her it would be so much easier to quit fighting, to drift along as one of the well-dressed and coiffed Hollywood mannequins without worries or thought. It was a last ditch effort by the blood drinkers to destroy what remained of her willpower to survive as an individual.

Instinctively, she knew not much time remained or all of her energy and ability to think clearly would evaporate.

As a counterpoint to the city's glittering false façade, came Granny Pearl's whisper. Her distinctive words drifted across the years and miles from the serene, unspoiled and unpolluted bayous of Ally's birth and formative years where the traditional values she had learned and lived by far outweighed the outrageous and pompous excesses of her current life. Distinctive and forceful, Granny Pearl's voice echoed in her room: "Fly away like a lighting bug." Its clarity scared Ally.

Among the noises in her head came another strong reminder, Sara the old black woman, the infamous oracle of New Orleans. She forced herself to relax, to close her eyes, to float backwards in time to recall details of that strange, long ago late afternoon. She took many deep breaths and remembered. In her mind's eye, old Sara sat in that nostril-burning dank and dark shanty only a short distance from the murky swamp, her stringy metal-gray hair touching her shoulders, her dark eyes peering at young Ally from a weather-worn face. A small candle flickered beside her, making the shanty's wooden walls seem to move and breathe as she rocked and rocked. How frightening for a teenager.

Sara's most serious warning pronounced itself loudly: "Guard your heart, child!" Oh, she was so guilty. She hadn't heeded the old woman's advice. She had given her heart to an arrogant man who not only never deserved it, but had abused it after she had laid it at his feet, once it was his. She had mistakenly trusted him to guard her heart. Since that time, he had tried every known way to crush Ally's spirit as often as he could, and had gradually taken total control of her entire life.

Old Sara had warned she would be trapped, sad, unhappy. *Oh, Lord, it had all come true, and I was warned to be watchful.*

The old black future teller had said she saw Ally in a large room, wearing fine clothes and "dripping in jewels," especially diamonds. Perhaps the large room she had seen was the mansion where Ally was now trapped.

She said, "You will have everything you ever wanted, but you will be trapped, sad. Somehow, you will know the call. You will hear it and know it. When you do, run. Run as fast as you can go. Just go quickly."

Oh, dear Lord. It was almost the same warning and advice Granny Pearl had given me when I was a child: "Heed my words: if you ever find yourself caught in a mousetrap, wiggle out as fast as you can and move like a lightning bug. . . . And don't look back. Never look back. Keep going forward."

Ally was caught tighter in something far more complicated than a mousetrap, that was for sure, and she was running out of options. She needed to move forward as soon as she could. Other things were going on behind the scenes which she dared not to disclose, at least for the time being. She learned years ago from her Aunt Faden and her wise oh-so-beloved Granny Pearl that it was always better, safer, saner, not to awaken the dead.

Running away was no longer relegated to a casual thought, a daydream, a 'what if,' mind game she could mentally play in solitude. It had become a serious contemplation and it was time to plead her case before the gods of Fate, those three great bearded gods she had envisioned in her younger years at Wildwind and Atlanta. She was positive they were still looking down from their cloudy perch and they knew what was happening. She, too, knew. She knew it was time to disappear from the Hills of Beverly.

"If you are going through hell, keep going."

Sir Winston Churchill

CHAPTER 29

Wise ones do not merely pick up their coat and walk out the door. They plan. They plan carefully, they consider the negatives, contingencies, distances, circumstances, and especially, exactly how they intend to survive after escaping. Carrying certain items out of the mansion grounds and secreting them in special places was important; such things as irreplaceable photos of her daughters, practical everyday clothing like blue jeans and tee-shirts to blend into crowds, and enough saved cash for gasoline and food. Credit card purchases would be instantly traced, so she needed cash, twenties, lots of twenties. She had survived on far less money in the past and didn't need or want Drake's credit cards or his flashy bundles of dollars. Attention was the last thing she wanted from waitresses or gas station attendants.

Everything was finally in place and had been for several days. One evening, Drake came in from a five-hour happy hour with his friends and bragged about his women again, of drinking, of gambling, then berated and insulted her for little reason.

Tonight.

Drake's alcohol level was way on up there, so it took him to bed early. She rolled further away onto her side of the California

King-size bed and turned back to look closely at her once gallant prince, who slept comfortably on the other side. *I'm going to leave now. I can no longer help you, believe in you, or live with you. Good-bye.*

There was something urgent in the air, as if some plan lay hidden behind the slightly snoring prince, who never really slept unless one eye was open. Even in the deepest sleep mode, he'd roar like a lion every time she got out of bed. It was as if he knew his fate was coming, so he seemed to sleep lighter lately. Tonight, the alcohol helped him to sleep deeply and almost peacefully without the usual nightmares.

Ally took a deep breath and held it as she inched her way to the edge and then slipped out from under the satin sheet. She stood motionless, shivering in the Santa Anna's blowing through the bedroom's open French doors.

She pivoted on one bare foot and the floor creaked a little. She froze. She had to get to the walk-in closet on the other side of the bedroom, but the floor creaked and squeaked with every step. She was forced to move slowly, one step at a time, each time expecting to hear Drake yell. It seemed to take forever to reach the other side of the room.

Once inside the giant closet, she gently closed the door and turned on the light. Her white flowing nightgown slid to the floor, and she quickly slipped into some workout pants, a pullover, socks, shoes, and then shoved a few ball caps and hoodies into a carry-on bag that held duplicate necessities and makeup she had hidden days before. She took a deep breath, said a prayer, turned out the light, and pushed the door open.

The floor creaked with every step. Why hadn't she ever noticed that before? If she awakened the beast now, there would be major trouble, but if she didn't go now Drake and his minions would keep her under watchful eyes the entire day, the week, the month, forever. It was now or never.

She had to get across the huge living room area, which was attached to the bedroom. She prayed their resident ghost didn't come to visit tonight, that she would ignore the chandelier instead of swinging it hard enough to make the crystals jangle. Ghosts could be uncooperative and unpredictable. The lady had lived here before and had died in this bedroom. When the nights were quiet and the Santa Anna's blew, she came. She must have loved the chandelier, and she liked to change the setting on the dimmer switch.

It could be quite scary for someone who didn't know she had lived here. The lady ghost couldn't recognize or understand that someone else owned her house. She always seemed angry to me, angry because her husband had sold the house after her death, she couldn't come home to visit him; when he remarried, he moved into another home with his new bride.

The resident ghost let her anger dispel here. Not very comforting because Ally could see and hear her. Of course, no one believed she was there, they thought the wind always blew the chandelier, even when the French doors were closed. Some people are determined to remain blind to truth.

Shallow breaths, I must take shallow breaths. She was almost dizzy from nerves and lack of oxygen.

Slowly, step-by-step, she reached the middle of the room. Drake rolled over, made a guttural noise, mumbled something in his sleep and stretched his long arm to her side of the bed, unconsciously searching for her.

Oh, God, please no. Oh, please don't let the sleeping giant awaken.

If he awakened and found her standing in the room, dressed, clutching a going-away bag in one hand, there would be no way to explain this. She would be forced to admit what was obvious – I was leaving in the middle of the night – yes, without telling him face-to-face. Of course, that conversation would have been impossible and unacceptable in his mind, but he would expect her to stammer and try. Consequences would be dire.

She froze again in place, waiting for him to resettle himself into a satin nest and drift into a deeper sleep once more. Slower than ever before, she took one step, waited, took another, and another, slowly making her way across the shiny wooden floor that creaked and popped.

She stopped and stared at the door. This door always made a noise whenever she tried to open it. She said a quick prayer and asked for The Carpenter to do a miracle, to fix the loud noise. Then she had to deal with another problem: the noisy door was usually locked, the key kept in the drawer by the prince's side of the bed. Why hadn't she remembered that earlier?

The resident ghost helped by not playing with the chandelier or slamming doors or turning up the lights. Ally gathered she was watching her leave the man sleeping where she had once slept in another time. Ally wondered if the ghost had been as miserable as she has been in this bedroom, this house. Perhaps she hadn't been miserable because she returned night after night.

Ally turned the knob. Nothing. *Oh, no! Open, damn door! Open! Let me out of here!*

It wouldn't open. It was stuck. It never sticks. The gods were playing tricks on her again. She held her breath and pulled. Nothing. Oh, no. Finally, she had no choice. She had to yank it open. It opened, making a terrible noise in the night's stillness.

She stood as if her shoes had been glued to the floor, waiting for a scream, for yelling, for cursing. Silence. She heard nothing, not even snoring. She didn't delay one second to glance at the sleeping giant. She whirled on a tiptoe and slid through the doorway, crossed the threshold, pivoted again to gently close and latch the door.

Ally ran down the hallway and skidded to a stop when she neared the butler's quarters. There was a small light shining beneath his door. He was still up reading, which he often did at night. She crept past his room.

Ahead was the elegant, white, elongated, curved stairway. She dreaded each step because the treads sometimes creaked and popped as bad as the bedroom floor. She was halfway down when she heard the cat. Burt ambled around the corner and called, thinking her presence meant it was time for a one o'clock treat. There was no way she'd leave her white Persian behind.

514

Burt strolled around the corner, climbed the stairs and curled around her ankles, as if telling her he was going wherever her feet went. He probably suspected she was going somewhere because he sniffed her packed bag, looked up, and tilted his head. She scooped him up, tucked him under one arm and headed for the front door.

Burt seemed all too happy to go for any ride at any time; he loved to travel. He liked to show off by sitting in the car windows. In the mornings, Burt was always the first one awake and up, arousing the household with his cat-singing, announcing to the butler that it was time for his breakfast.

Ally peeked around the corner to make sure no one was in the kitchen, scurried to the pantry, grabbed a carton of cat food, Burt's figure-eight harness and leash off the peg near the kitchen's delivery door, then scurried back to the main hallway. Burt was coming, that was that, no question, so he'd need food and gear, too. Simple.

Burt and she made it to the end of the entry. Staring at her was the huge wooden, hand-carved door; on the wall next to it was the security system control center with its secret code to disarm the system so she could open the door. Praying she remembered the code, she punched in the numbers with a slightly trembling finger and waited for a few seconds that seemed like hours. She could feel her heart pounding as she waited. A tiny beep. A click. The door unlocked. *Eureka!*

She opened the heavy door, grabbed car keys, gently pulled the door closed, then whirled around to run to the Mercedes in the curved area near the front. She tossed the bag into the backseat, almost tossed Burt on the passenger seat, put one foot inside the car before taking one last look at the house. It was still quiet, no lights had turned on. She took a deep breath and slid into the driver's seat, and quietly latched the door, planning to slam it later.

"Burt, baby, we're going to a place we've never been before."

Obviously, Burt could care less. He yawned, walked in a circle until he found the right spot, and curled up to nap in the front seat. She could hear him purring. He was happy just to be with her and going someplace. So was she.

As she drove down the long driveway, the headlights flashed on the distant black iron gates across the drive. She flipped open the magnet control device and punched the button to signal the gates to open. It was the last hurdle; the final physical obstacle blocking her freedom. She slowed slightly. Mentally, she imagined latches clanging, both gates inching along the rails embedded in the concrete. But when the car got there, the barrier was barely moving. Ally's heart jammed upward into her throat, she couldn't swallow or breathe. She was forced to slow more, then stepped on the brakes so the car barely crept forward, her grip on the steering wheel tightened as she waited for the metal giants to get out of my way.

Oh, hurry! Please, dear Lord, let me out of this hell on earth!

She whispered another prayer, held her breath, fingers clinched on the steering wheel until they burned and her knuckles popped. *Oh, how much long—*

A deafening blast hit the car on all sides, against the closed windows, the hood and rear. She screamed, flinched and ducked. Burt jumped straight up and dove headfirst onto the floor. The automatic timer had turned on the lawn sprinklers, and the car's sensors turned on the windshield wipers. Her hands shook as she gasped and tried to catch her breath.

As if dredged up from some weird movie's slow motion segment, the massive ornate gates finally cleared enough space for her to guide the car through the gap. She almost closed her eyes but didn't, braced to hear paint being gouged and scraped off both sides of her car, but somehow the vehicle threaded through the narrow slit. She accelerated, aimed the control device over her shoulder and pushed the button to close the gates.

She watched in the rearview mirror as she steered the car toward the road. The gates were slowly closing.

"Wha-hoo! I did it! Ya-ha!" and slapped my hand on the steering wheel. "Yay!"

Burt jumped off the floor, onto the seat, clawed his way to the top of the passenger seat and clung to the leather headrest with four sets of claws. He stared at her and yowled a protest, telling her she had scared him half to death again. "I'm sorry. It's all right, sweetie. We're outta there!"

She couldn't stop the riotous laughter she heard coming from her own throat. She had made it out of the gilded prison. She was out, but for how long. That didn't matter right now – she was free. She accelerated, craving immediate distance between that mansion's iron gates and her. Now she had to calm down, try to read scribbled notes and remember every landmark she had seen from the back seat of the limo, details from my girlfriends' conversations, and rare shopping trips alone when she could talk to salesclerks about the streets and distances. She dug around in her purse and brought out a small notebook. Drive several blocks, make several turns. She noticed Beverly Hills' streets were well-lit at one in the morning; light traffic going in the opposite direction, but no one on the sidewalks, a few bums sleeping off their latest drunk on park benches. Her prayers were answered: No reliable witnesses were around to tell police they had seen a Mercedes zipping past. Stay the speed limit; don't draw attention. Traffic signals blinked green or caution, never red. It all seemed blessed, nice, quiet – as if the gods were clearing her escape pathway.

Notebook again: Hang a left, drive until the freeway on-ramp, where she accelerated onto the freeway's freedom roadway – another milestone. A note: Drive straight through the scary four level interchange, remember to use the left lane to merge onto the San Bernardino Freeway, then follow the I-40 to the I-10.

* * *

*"It is a man's own mind, not his enemy or foe,
that lures him to evil ways."*

Buddha Dhammappada

Chapter 30

Time would tell how the prince would react when he discovered his princess wasn't where she was supposed to be, required to be, ordered to be. Unacceptable for her to ever be out of touch, out of reach when he wanted.

When Drake first awakened, he thought nothing of Ally's absence; she was probably on her usual morning walk. He headed straight to his shower and then dressed for his workday. He made his way downstairs and asked Maddox, the butler, if she was out for her walk. Maddox had already assumed she was.

Daily routine in the back of the house flowed smoothly until Maddox realized he hadn't seen the cat. Odd. Uh-oh. Burt hadn't followed him around the kitchen, insisting on being fed his breakfast before other human chores had been done.

Everything instantly changed at eight o'clock when Ally hadn't returned.

Drake put down his coffee cup and scanned the room, then yelled for Maddox. "She's not back yet. You know I don't like it. Stop whatever you're doing. I want you to search the house and grounds. She's here somewhere. . . reading or talking on that cell phone again."

Maddox summoned the entire household staff and ordered them to search every inch, and even sent one of them to cover Ally's walk route, to look for any trace of her. Drake's instinct told him something was very wrong. He went back upstairs and checked Ally's closet and jewelry cases. Everything looked intact, nothing was missing as far as he could tell. Something nagged on his mind, so he went back downstairs to ask Maddox about Burt the cat. He frowned at the answer, pivoted and quickly walked to the garage.

No Ally . . . no note . . . no cat . . . no car. *Damn!*

Stunned, Drake's stomach lurched and knotted as if he'd been punched by a tight fist. He was suddenly nauseated, terrified, almost paralyzed with fear, his knees weakened and he crouched for a moment in the darkened garage to collect his strength and thoughts. This was too much of an attack on his ego. No, no, no. This was impossible. Perhaps she had gone on a new shopping spree with friends, had just neglected to tell him her plans. Perhaps she was having a longer coffee session with girlfriends and they were gossiping about someone. Perhaps she was taking a longer session with her personal trainer at Sports Club L.A. No, not likely today . . . today was her usual appointment at the beauty salon, maybe the hairdresser or the spa. He couldn't remember. He hurried back into the house, grabbed his phone and hit the speed dial button for Ally's cell phone. No answer. It automatically rolled over to voice mail, and he shouted for her to call him back that very minute and to get herself back home – Now! He slammed down the phone and yelled for Maddox.

"Where the hell is she?" Drake asked when Maddox stepped into the doorway.

"I don't know, sir. I've sent our people out to search every place I could think of."

"Oh. Good. Okay. Then you take one part of this list and start calling the places, the dress shops, Starbucks, whatever, wherever she usually hangs out. Just call where she usually goes. I'm calling her closest girlfriends."

"Yes, sir; I'll do that, sir." Maddox headed back to the kitchen's menu planning area to use the telephone there. He bit his tongue to prevent a smile from touching his lips. If Miz Ally had made her escape as he suspected, she should have gone hours ago so Drake wouldn't find her easily. The woman was smart; she'd know not to go any place that was obvious, anywhere Drake would search.

Drake's list included the doctors' offices, dentists, then he called some of her family members in Louisiana. Nothing.

About thirty minutes later, Maddox said he had not found her and no one had seen her for a day or two.

Worried by the lack of information, Drake paced and ran his hand through his hair. No one had heard from Ally in the past twenty-four hours. Drake called her cell phone every fifteen minutes. No answer. After a while, he stopped leaving messages.

His hand shook as he poured more vodka into his coffee cup and carried it upstairs. He began to thoughtfully and thoroughly go through Ally's personal items in her bathroom. Her hair dryer and make-up were in the cabinet. He yanked open the closet door and stared at the garments. They all seemed to be there, but the zippered fabric duffle bag wasn't on the floor and some shoes were missing. He looked closer. How strange. Blue jeans were gone. She hardly ever wore blue jeans.

Drake hit the intercom button. "Maddox! Where's that cat of hers?"

The speaker buzzed a second later. "I'm sorry, sir, but Burt seems to have left the premises."

Damn! If this was Drake's new reality, he didn't like it one bit. He went back down to his office, called his secretary and had her cancel all of his appointments and told her to handle urgent business herself; she could report back later, telling her only, "Don't sell anything and don't buy anything. You're not able to handle that level."

Drake ignored the intercom system and just yelled. "Maddox! Get in here."

A minute later, the butler appeared in the doorway. "Nothing so far, sir."

"She's gone, isn't she." It wasn't a question. A tear spilled out of one eye and trailed down Drake's cheek. "None of this makes sense. Why would any woman in their right mind leave me, all this house, all this money? I've given her everything she ever wanted."

Maddox studied the upset man at the desk, who had been drinking for a couple of hours already. The man was breaking up, crying about losing his wife. Well, the man who considered himself 'Mister Wonderful' was rich, but a fool. Psychological abuse has always been just as damaging as physical abuse. Emotional scars never heal as fast as injuries that are inflicted on the surface. The mistreated must leave, *if* they have good sense, so it won't happen again and again. Sometimes, the abuser actually gets help to stop the behavior before they have driven away every person they love and hold dear. Most people learn that lesson long before they ever graduate from high school. Sadly, Drake Lanzen never attended class.

Drake glanced up. "Good, you're here, Maddox. Sit down . . . now!"

Maddox sat down in the chair opposite Drake and waited, knowing he was going to be blamed for something, for anything, for everything.

"You know something about this! I know you do. You're going to tell me right this minute, or you are going to be fired, sued, and I'll make sure you'll never work in California ever again! What do you know about all this?"

Maddox shook his head. "Absolutely nothing, sir. I didn't notice anything until I realized the cat wasn't in the kitchen."

"I don't believe you! You must have heard something. Where the hell is my wife?!"

Maddox took a deep breath and shook his head again. "I don't know, sir. Can I get you something?"

"You can get me the detectives who're sitting around on their asses and getting paid for doing nothing while raking in my retainer fees. Get them over here in the next few minutes. I want real investigators – not some overweight, elderly rent-a-cop. I want you to call in some physics, too. Call anyone else you might think of who can help. Do it. Do it quickly, too. Before you get started, bring me a full tray from the bar – you know what I want on the tray—bring some ice, too. Don't let me run out. It's going to be a long night and it may take a while to find her, but I sure as hell will."

The hunt had officially begun. When the prey finally was returned, punishment would not be pleasant.

Drake swiveled his desk chair around to look out the window. The sun was going down on the small town of Beverly Hills nestled in the L.A. basin. Drake knew Ally was not going to return on her own. The power of the alcohol had kicked into a higher gear, so he sat and brooded, went over every detail in his mind, every word Ally had spoken in the past week, every body language stance he believed he could interpret, if he had paid any attention to her at all.

Despite Drake's alcohol overload, embarrassment set in, crushed and almost destroyed his ego. He was forced to make calls he wasn't prepared to make. He picked up the phone, hit another speed dial button and spoke with his closest friend, a movie producer. It was time to say the words: Ally had gone.

"Who the hell does she think she is, Scarlett? I really don't give a damn if she comes back or not. Hmm. Almost sounds like Rhett Butler about another Southern girl, doesn't it? Hell, with all I have going for me, my good looks and all the money, maybe I'd be better off not being married. If I'm single, I can date all those bimbo starlets that keep hanging onto my sleeve wherever I go."

Maddox halted in the hallway with the tray from the bar. He had overheard Drake's comments about Miz Ally and muttered a few obscenities. Drake was such a fool.

Drake hung up, then hit another speed dial number and connected with the Ice Queen, his mother. "Doodle' thrived on melodrama and Ally vanishing was the epitome of high drama.

"Well, I told you that little beauty queen was no good for you – uncouth, uncivilized, never went to finishing school. Spending all that money on those tacky, drooling children in wheelchairs. So after that, what would you expect? Harrumph! Good riddance, if you ask me. She'll never inherit my diamonds and jewels, I can tell you that, son. Not even a dime or a dollar from me. She was just too independent and, and, well, just not good enough for you, dear. She certainly had some class for a country girl and was all looks, you know, and I'm not so sure about those Louisiana French Cajuns; a different breed of people, son. You know we're descended from English royalty. You could have had a cultured, magnificent bride like Di, the Princess of Wales. Pfft! You fell under the spell of her beauty, for heaven's sake, so what did you expect would happen?"

"Good-bye, mother." Click.

Drake refilled his glass. "Bitches everywhere."

By midnight, he had figured it out, and the sadness overwhelmed him. It turned into anger and desperation. Why had Ally left? He had provided everything he had decided she needed or wanted.

He slowly climbed the stairs to the master bedroom, and dropped to one knee and held Ally's photograph. "Oh, don't let anything happen to her. Please please please."

Drake got up and made it into his bathroom, washed his face, changed his shirt, then called Maddox. "Come up to pack a bag. I intend to find my wife even if it means going to hell and back. I intend to trace her every step. I'll find her, I swear!"

He began a serious drunken grieving process, trying to figure out exactly how Ally had managed to slip through his safety nets, his sticky webs and through his nimble hands. After all, he was a master magician. How did she do it? That mystery must be solved so it couldn't happen again after Ally was returned to her rightful place at his side.

Walking through every room of the now too massive, echo-filled, empty mansion, he would repeatedly slam his fist into his open palm – an old habit – swearing to find his lost princess and her white Persian cat, and someone would pay for this outrage, someone must have talked her into running away. There was no logical reason for her to leave the luxury he had provided. All he ever required in return was for her to do exactly what he said when he said it. That was all he ever wanted: Obedience and devotion. She was his princess, his life, the reason for his breathing and existing, but she would never know that. He was too prideful and arrogant to let Ally know just how special and beautiful she was. That was why he had chosen her for a wife.

He hated the way the producers and directors, the film crowd looked at Ally and glammed over her. When Ally walked into a room, it lit up. People stopped what they were doing just to watch her walk by and stared across the room, not at him, but all eyes were on his wife. Even if she had no makeup on or was wearing a ball cap and sweats. The gods had blessed her somehow with a hallo of pure golden magic.

A goddess. Hell, what was he talking about? From the moment he laid eyes on her, he was gone. History. Even women stared at her, the elderly, the young, children.

He put his head in his hands and memories came alive. He never gave Ally a chance to become Hollywood's brightest star because he knew she could have been Hollywood's biggest star. She was a natural, the classic Old Hollywood in a young way.

Now she was gone. Maybe she had been stolen by a Hollywood wolf, maybe by a close friend, maybe one of those long staring, evil-looking, grinning actors had already taken her to his den to devour her like a vampire.

He remembered there was one particular actor she seemed to have a fondness for, but no, his mind wouldn't let him go there. She was bought, paid for, and he had spent thousands on her, maybe millions, if he counted. That was the one thing that was so perplexing; money didn't faze his wife. She could live in a tee-pee and be happy.

* * *

Life is all about choices, when we come to a split in the road. Depending upon whether we go right or left, it really

533

doesn't matter. Neither one is a right or wrong decision. If we take what some consider the wrong road, it's only a lesson in life we're supposed to learn anyway. If we choose what some consider the right road, then life is good and we have earned and learned lessons, moving up for our rewards.

Looking back, Ally knew why she ended up on the wrong road with the choices she made. It was definitely the wrong road in many ways, but now that she had made that mistake, she thought she could help other women make better choices. She wanted to help awaken women who think they have the world by the tail just because they land a "rich and handsome prince" that they searched for most of their lives. The majority of important discoveries aren't made until it is too late. Years later, Ally thanked God she hadn't end up like some of the famous ones who had made the same mistake . . . ones who had millionaire husbands who would rather have their wives murdered or simply kill them themselves rather than to let them go. Those wives are only a piece of property . . . and those husbands don't ever depart easily with acquired property.

"More tears are shed over answered prayers
than unanswered ones."

Mother Teresa

Chapter 31

"Espiritu Santos"

Gold and silver streaked across the sky and glistened above the hills ahead. Ally reached for her sunglasses on the passenger seat, then stopped. Two floodlights had fizzled and burned out, but the billboard's words ahead were clear enough in the early light: Espiritu Santos. Lessons learned at Granny Pearl's knee whispered in her memory; loosely translated it meant 'a saintly man's spirit.' After what she'd lived through, she was ready for a double dose.

The freeway marker indicated availability of gasoline and a mini-market a quarter-mile ahead. She flipped off the cruise control, tapped the brakes and guided the slowing car down the exit and across a narrow, dusty road at the bottom. She eased to a stop at a gravel parking lot's entrance to look everything over before creeping closer. Only a battered pickup truck was at the side of the one-story, whitewashed building. She pulled under the gasoline station's canopy. A frayed cardboard 'open' sign wagged in the station's glass door.

"Hey, sweet baby, we're in luck. Someone's ready for business."

Burt opened his eyes and yawned, but didn't bother to get up to see for himself.

"Some co-pilot you are." Ally turned off the ignition and peeled her fingers away from the steering wheel. She flexed her stiff hands and fingers several times. "I need coffee. The car needs gas; we're almost on fumes. I guess you need food. Bet you expect tuna juice for breakfast. Well, we're roughing it; not a butler in sight. You're lucky I thought to bring you anything."

She lowered the driver's window for an instant, then a blast of warm air and grit hit her face. Sputtering, she got the window back up and lowered the passenger window two inches for ventilation. "You'll be okay for a few minutes."

Maps would have been great, but getting them earlier could have tipped off the staff mechanics. If she'd stepped into a travel agency, the security team that constantly followed her would have told Drake. She had to rely on memory. She drove straight to Wilshire Boulevard, up the 405 on-ramp onto the Santa Monica Freeway, and got out of the L.A. Basin by instinct much like a homing pigeon. When it merged into the San Bernardino Freeway, she saw the I-10 marker for the first time and relaxed a little. She'd gotten gasoline at an American Traveler truck stop, remembered driving past the Redlands off-ramp, recalled the 'Leaving California' sign somewhere near Blythe.

Only desert lay ahead, but she'd made it to Arizona. Now she needed specifics, a definite plan, not merely heading southeast on I-10. Once Drake realized she was gone, his detectives would head to Atlanta, New Orleans, or Saint Martinsville to interrogate anyone she'd ever spoken to.

"Okay, Burt, I'll be back in a few minutes. Don't leave without me, but I'm keeping the keys, just in case."

Burt opened one eye, blinked, and went back to sleep.

Ally's knees were stiff and her back ached a little, but after standing, stretching and twisting for half a minute she could walk without limping. She stepped inside the station's mini-mart where it was about 15 degrees cooler.

"Ah . . . coffee." The welcoming aroma of fresh brew pulled her straight past the food aisles to the coffee service area. A glass refrigerator case at the rear held cold drinks and ready-made sandwiches. She was startled when her stomach rumbled at the idea of food. A meal without Drake or distress was a rare thing.

"Mornin' " A man's smooth baritone rumbled from behind an age-darkened wooden counter at the door.

She whirled around, dropping the Styrofoam cup. Standing behind the counter was a grizzly bear size man, who was at least six-foot, seven or eight inches tall. He had broad shoulders, a firm jaw-line and piercing eyes beneath a sweat-stained, battered Stetson. She was shocked that she hadn't seen him before, especially since he consumed most of the space behind the counter. "Oh! I'm sorry. Good morning. Your coffee smells wonderful."

He merely nodded, lifted and pointed with his chin, indicating for her to help herself. She nodded back, grabbed another large container, filled it, added sugar substitute, snapped on a plastic lid, and picked up two packages of crackers.

Obviously, the man was a Native American. His classic weathered face would have been perfection for an artist's canvas in an Old West museum, or in a modern movie. He nodded again. His dagger-sharp eyes watched her every move.

"I need to fill up my gas tank, please. And, uh, I'm getting coffee and crackers, too."

He stared into her eyes, silent, with a half smile twitched at the corner of his mouth. She wasn't positive that he was laughing at her, but suspected he was. What was even more astounding was that she felt open, almost vulnerable under his gaze, as if he were reading her thoughts.

"Lost?"

"Lost? Me? Oh, no; just doing a bit of traveling and sightseeing, that's all."

The corner of his mouth twitched more, then a low-toned rumble similar to a hushed word or squelched laughter vibrated from somewhere deep in his chest. She knew he didn't believe anything she said. "You need a map. Look around, find a place to sleep here."

She forced a smile. "Maybe."

"Hmm, you stay. Rest now. No more run."

"Oh, I'm fine; a little tired, that's all. With the coffee, I can drive much further."

His flat, open hand swept across his eyes in a straight line. "Your eyes say no. Eyes don't lie." He moved swiftly and gracefully for a middle-aged man, lifted the drop-leaf countertop and, within two strides, was outside to pump gas into the Mercedes.

Ally didn't think she looked as tired as he claimed, but days, perhaps weeks of stress could be obvious even to strangers. She looked around and the name hit her again. Espirtu Santos. *Was he right? Do I need to be here for a while? No. Can't stop and rest.* She shook her head. Drake's pack of private detectives would descend upon her soon. *Get back on the road. Now.*

This had escalated far beyond a cat and mouse game, and she was the prey as usual. This lonely place wasn't a sanctuary. It was nothing more than a visible wide spot on a dirt road. She grabbed a highway map, and spread it out on the counter to study the state routes, county roads, paved and unpaved. '*Espirtu Santos*' wasn't even a dot on the interstate. *Quartzsite is huge compared to this place. Where the heck am I?*

She glanced outside, surprised to see the giant man washing the grime and wind-dried smushed bugs off her car's windshield. He finished and stepped back inside. "Your animal wears fur. He is warm enough now."

"Oh! Uh, yes, I know. That's Burt, my friend. My cat. I know he's getting warm, so I've got to hurry. Pardon me, uh, I hope I'm not being rude, but you remind me of a famous movie star. Will Samson. He did a lot of movies."

"Yeah. He was Creek. What you see written on my face is Ndee' West band of the White Mountain Apache. I am called Morgan."

Ally's eyes widened at the word Apache.

His grin was lopsided. "No, not Geronimo; he was another band, but still Apache. You know Natives, eh?"

"No, not really, but I love to learn. I'm a writer and I'm curious about everything. Are there any folklore stories about your Ndee' people?"

Morgan tilted his head and chuckled as if she had asked if he was a leprechaun. "Folklore?"

"Yes, I'm interested in folklore for a book I'm writing."

"If folklore is what you seek, you shall find treasures. Some you want and may keep. Maybe some you don't want to keep. It is your choice. I shall give you one now. Do you know why bats hang upside down?"

Ally could only shake her head.

"The bat was caught trying to seduce another creature's wife. He was thrown into the trees and his pointy-toed

543

moccasins got caught on a branch. He has been hanging that way ever since."

Ally blinked several times and giggled at the joke. "Oh! I get it. I get it! That's so funny and cool! I just love those kinds of stories. Thank you for sharing it with me."

"You are welcome." He shifted his weight and position on the tall stool behind the counter and looked out the window at the distant mountain range. "Perhaps you seek what is ahead like a Jumping Mouse that tries to see far ahead, to know what is beyond your present. You have much limit now." He turned back to face her. "I think you follow the path of the white jackrabbit."

Oh, cripes! Well, that makes sense. I am living like another Cinderella, so I should expect to run into things like a rabbit, like the white rabbit in Alice in Wonderland. "I figured there was a rabbit somewhere."

"You want Native folklore?"

"Yes. Stories would be great."

"I can tell you of the Red Tailed Hawk, the Frigate Birds, the Teaching Bird – some of our brothers say the turkey, others say the eagle who flew the highest in the heavens – the kestrel, our brother the bear, the coyote trickster, many animal spirits. . .
544

. you know some animals were once humans. Many, many legends . . . lessons the Great Spirit teaches us through animal spirits. You want to learn? It will take time."

"Time? How I wish. I don't have time for it now, but what about screech owls, barn owls, spotted owls?"

Morgan's expression froze and his eyes narrowed to mere slits. "No, woman; owls bad omen . . . they come to tell of death."

"Oh. I never knew that."

"It is also legend from our brothers the Lakota. We Ndee' used to war with many of those nations, but no more. There is much white people do not know about the First People, about Mother Earth, about Pollen Girl who comes to grow and strengthen crops and plants with power to heal us and the creatures The Creator made for us. White people fear what they do not know. They close their minds." He peered across the counter. "Hmm . . . but you are not one of them. Your heart is open to hear truth. That is good. Yes, you should go sit with the teachers and hear wisdom. I am only a man, but I can tell you need a sweat lodge with the women. Toxins inside need purging; bad medicine. I call my daughter to come show you where to go now."

He picked up the phone. Ally reached across the counter and grabbed his wrist. "No! No one can know I've been here. I'm leaving right now before there's trouble. How much do I owe you for the gas, coffee, crackers . . . what else?" She whirled around and placed several cookie packages on the counter, fumbled with her wallet and plopped cash on the counter. "Hurry! Please."

"Whoa, woman. You are running. I think someone will come after you."

Ally stared at him and took a deep breath. "Yes. They'll come. Fast. I need to leave."

"Ah. They have power over where you go and how you go?"

"Yes, yes. Very much power. Do you have a sack for all this?"

"Then we must break their power." He picked up the phone again and hit the speed dial button. "David. Come now, bring your brothers." Hung up.

"Oh, Morgan, you don't understand; men will come searching for me. They always do."

"Oh? They find you quickly?"

546

Ally sighed. "Yes, always."

A crooked smile flashed across the counter again. "We will fix that, so you go where you want, when you want. Okay?"

She nodded slightly. "That's more than okay, but only if you can really do it."

Morgan talked her into waiting. Ally paced, then soothed Burt's restlessness by letting him walk around and sniffing the different outdoor world. He was content to curl up on the passenger seat again after a few minutes. Ally paced again, checking her watch often. *I can't wait much longer.*

Pickup trucks from several directions slid into the parking lot, raising a dust cloud that enveloped her Mercedes. Six young men in blue jeans and t-shirts sauntered toward the office, nodded or tipped their hats to her as they moved easily across the rough gravel. Each had shoulder length, glistening blue-black hair beneath their cowboy hats. A few minutes later, they followed Morgan out the door toward her.

"This is my son David and his friends."

David nodded, "Ma'am. My buds and I are like an old-fashioned warrior clan here about . . . call ourselves an Auto Clan." The young men laughed and slapped each other on the back. "We figure you've been hunted long enough. Probably there's a GPS or a LoJack on your car somewhere. We'll find it and send it someplace else. How's that for a starter?"

Ally stared at him. "What?"

"Don't worry. We'll get it off and you can go wherever you want." He held out his hand. "Keys?"

Ally said a silent prayer that what she was about to do was right, then dropped her car keys, her only means of escape, into David's hand. Morgan explained details while Ally and Burt waited in the cooler air of *Espirtu Santos*.

Less than an hour later, David returned with her car and placed two electronic devises on the counter. "Just what we figured; GPS. Ol' Pete is heading to Colorado this afternoon with another batch of breeder sheep for that rancher he's dealing with. I'll put one on his truck, then we'll drive down to the truck stop and stick this other one on an eighteen-wheeler that's heading to Minneapolis or New England somewhere." His laughter filled the mini-market. "I love screwing with people's minds, and that ought to do a number on them 'cause they'll be chasing two signals that's going in different directions."

Ally pulled back onto the interstate an hour later and headed southeast into the brightening skies. "There's a lot of sand and rocks between us and the bayou, Burt, but we're finally going home."

Burt's long, snow white tail flipped a few times in agreement before he concentrated on getting a nap in the morning sunshine.

"Well, don't let me keep you awake." Ally grinned at the curled pile of fluff in the passenger seat. "What's ahead?"

Ally frowned through the windshield at the gray strip of asphalt that stretched to and beyond the hazy horizon. Uncertainty of what she would find when she returned to the deep South weighed heavily on her mind and her frown deepened. It wouldn't be the same after this length of time, after so many changes in her life – she had changed the most. However, one thing was a certainty: the bayou was far enough away from Beverly Hills' twinkling lights, far enough away that, if she could get there before being caught, she could hide among the same giant moss-draped trees which protected her as a child.

A smile crept onto her lips. This risk was worth it, worth Drake's wrath when he discovered she wasn't jogging in the neighborhood, wasn't doing his bidding, wasn't being tailed by his 'protectors,' as he called them. She had escaped. It had taken a long time for her to regain her courage and self-confidence to attempt another disappearance, but now she was on her way. There were friends who would help her play the ultimate game of 'hide and seek' just as they had as children playing together in the gardens of the old plantations. Although she hadn't contacted all of them in a while, she had managed to maintain communication with one special confidant despite Drake's efforts to cut her off from everyone she had ever known. Patty would be by her side the instant Ally called.

It seemed her destination was the same one thousands of people dreamt about: New Orleans and the surrounding bayous. The city was just the place to lose yourself in the wide open places where everyone sees what they want to see, and sees what they don't really want to see as well. New Orleans' ghosts and the few remaining vampires were on the loose in the streets every night. Ally laughed aloud. "There really are things that go bump in the night. Tourists just don't recognize them like we natives do."

Having oddities walk about was a normal condition in New Orleans' older sections just as it was for most of Louisiana, especially the cemeteries where long-time families maintained the 'little houses' built over some ancestors' graves. It wasn't all ghosts and goblins in the streets and woods, but the oldest plantations had the usual collection. Cajon and Creole people were used to seeing them among the beautiful trees, or strolling along the rivers, or riding on ferries. New Orleans was as close to Paris, France, as far as romance was concerned. Thinking about her favorite Cajon dishes with piles of fresh seafood from the Gulf made her mouth water. She decided to stop for a meal at the next gasoline fill-up, and to stretch her legs. She glanced at the sleeping cat lying against her hip, wondering what he'd do with a live crawfish and laughed.

Memories of her childhood and young adult years floated back across the years. What if a former boyfriend came out of the woodwork? What if she had taken a different road years ago, had not moved to Atlanta, had not started her limousine business, especially had not ever dated Drake? How her life would have changed if she had never married him, had not married into such a wealthy and prominent family? What a contrasting lifestyle she had lived compared to one she would have had if she had remained in St. Francisville, if she had turned into a bored and boring housewife, learned how to cook and even can vegetables that she grew in her own garden.

Ally burst out laughing so loud that Burt scrambled to the floor. "Don't worry, sweetie, I'm not going to do that again." Ally recalled her first attempt at using a pressure cooker and spending hours cleaning the mess it had made on and to the ceiling when it blew. "Maybe I'll try gardening. I won't be like Great Granny Violet with her two green thumbs, but I can learn to plant roses. I loved picking them and putting them in vases around the house. I love that fragrance."

It was enjoyable to recall her years living with her two beloved grandmothers and growing up like a real Cinderella princess under their loving care. It wasn't always roses like she'd hoped, but it was fine and strengthening of character. However, many things happened that she didn't care to discuss or remember in detail.

Ally realized she was not a simple country girl despite being reared in the farm area of Louisiana – she had blossomed in the bright lights of Beverly Hills and had relished the creative atmosphere. She would miss it terribly because she adored the stories people told of their latest projects, their novels, their movies. She also loved the stores and hotels that dotted the streets of that famous city. The old renovated buildings kept a certain magic about them of the 1930s and 1940s glamorous Old Hollywood stars who played their music and performed in the ballrooms and piano bars. There was a lingering echo of them walking where she had walked and dining where she had dined. It wasn't a surprise when she considered she had probably sat in the same chairs where famous stars had once sat, dined, laughed and celebrated their latest movie hit. She wondered if she had been able to stay in Hollywood just a little longer, if she could have become one of those famed stars. But, that had been impossible living with Drake. With a ruthless husband, who was a man with no sense of honor, a man of extreme wealth who could buy and sell people at a whim, only his own wants and desires were considered. His selfishness always dictated every aspect of her life. She knew she could never live her real dreams if she had to do it while under his microscope.

She glanced down at the white Persian lying next to her. "There's a time for staying and a time for leaving, but one day, when things are quiet, I'll be back." Ally nodded. "But next time, I'll bring my own bright light to shine when and how I want to shine. I'll bring my own talents and a movie to shoot, and one day I might even get a star on the sidewalk with my name on it. It's just a matter of time and me working to make up for all the lost time."

She knew Hollywood wasn't through with her and she wasn't through with Hollywood. There were many more candles to light and burn brightly, and many more to shine to guide her safely home. She needed to spend some quality time with loved ones while things blew over. She needed for her soul and confidence to heal.

Perhaps during that time, Drake would forget about her, would find another woman to tie down, to spend his energy ruining her life just like he had tried to ruin hers. In the meantime, she planned to find and settle in some place very quiet, obscure, well off the beaten path so Drake's detectives wouldn't find her. In the right place, she could write without interruption, or being yelled at for writing anything, or being told how stupid or horrible her stories were, that no one ever wanted to read about fairy princesses, or magic, or people living to a ripe old age until that person was filled with great wisdom. She felt the stories that filled her imagination ought to be shared with children and grandchildren, maybe the entire world. She'd grown up as a Cinderella and other girls could too. She had gone to the ball, but had ended up with the wrong prince. She needed to warn other girls about that danger.

Right now, she needed to concentrate on safety and getting as far away from her dark prince as possible. He wanted her back, to lock her away from the world, to keep her in mid-motion like a movie's freeze-frame. She glanced at the dashboard clock and knew his detectives would be on her trail by now. They would be following one or two trucks going in different directions and reporting to Drake about what was happening. She grinned, knowing that the conflicting reports would make

Drake mad and confused. He wouldn't know where to go, and she didn't care one whit.

Love is a tangled mess when you are with the wrong prince. It won't untangle until the right prince comes along who has a heart, thoughts and a caring soul like her own. She would know the moment he entered her life. They would be timeless. She would recognize him from the instant she saw him. He was there in her mind, locked in her deepest dreams. She had once glimpsed him in a crowded room, and her heart had leapt in her chest. She knew exactly who he was. The vision of him was locked forever in her mind. Timing then was all wrong. Perhaps one day.

"Somewhere . . . over the rainbow . . . way up high . . ."

Burt's eyes opened and he glared at her across the leather seat; his eyes widened when she disturbed his nap.

"Yes, I know it's odd, and no, I don't know why I'm singing that song. Oh, look."

A highway marker indicating gasoline, a restaurant, and a national motel chain was ahead. She flipped off the cruise control and guided the car toward the off-ramp and station to refill the tank. It was an excellent place to stop for a decent meal and good night's sleep. She got a room far away from the highway, and carried Burt and two overnight cases into the room. When she stepped out to walk to the restaurant, a male Cardinal, a 'redbird' as her Granny Pearl called them, flew down to perch on a nearby handrail. He tipped his head, watching her. She stopped to study him for a moment. It seemed he was there to remind her that real love wasn't far away, that it would follow her wherever she would be further down the line. He spread his brilliant scarlet wings and turned around so she could see all of his feathers. She felt he was telling her that she would find her true love on a bright red carpet similar to his red feathers. He took off and soared into the darkening sky toward the multitude of stars that were perfectly aligned in the clear desert sky. Ally smiled; confidence she'd made the right decision was returning and gaining strength by the minute.

A deep sleep without awakening several times during the night was a great healer for her tired body and soul. She showered, washed her long blonde hair, changed clothes and packed, wanting to get back on the road quickly. She looked around again and frowned. "This isn't funny. Did you move it someplace?" She scolded Burt because she couldn't find her shoe, so had to unpack the extra pair. She checked her watch. "We're out of time and out of here. C'mon."

The Mercedes merged into the scant southbound traffic on I-10 fifteen minutes later. She glared into the morning sunrise until she found her sunglasses, but happy to be on the pathway home. She caught herself singing once again. Burt stared at her for a long minute until she laughed at him. Why did she feel like Cinderella so much? She was running away from a dark prince, but had to ask herself if she would only end up waiting forever for the right prince to ride into her life on a white horse, to come to rescue her? Would it really take forever? Was she totally still a child, someone half-grown who still believed in fairy tales?

She sighed. "Yes, I guess I'm all those things. But, don't fairy tales get most of the rewards?"

Fairy tales are so much better than reality. She could feel the humidity begin to increase as she made her way further toward Louisiana, the landscape gradually changed from dusty brown and barren rocks to green pastures with grazing livestock. Her mind wandered back over the years and experiences, both as a child and as a married woman. Within a hundred miles, she crossed the state line and began humming a favorite song: Dream Dream Dream.

"After all, life is but a dream, especially when you're in the middle of a real live one." She glanced in the rearview mirror again, watching for any vehicle that seemed to have been there too long. "It's destiny that has me worried."

"...she knew that the looking-glass spoke the truth."

From *Snow White*

Chapter 32

Ally was home at last. She felt a lot like Dorothy coming home after her trip to the Land of Oz, with or without wearing ruby red slippers. Ally parked the car, rolled down the windows and sat in the driveway of her grandmothers' old plantation. She took several deep breaths, reminiscing to a time when she was young. She looked at the huge, moss-covered trees swaying in the breeze, their long fronds of Spanish moss waving as if welcoming her home again.

She looked toward her favorite old tree. It was half crooked over to the ground as if it was a very old and ancient soul that the ages had literally bent it down. It seemed tired, but still had many stories to tell. It was the great- grandfather of all the trees there. Lightning had struck it and had put many jagged marks on him. He almost had a distinctive face carved into the bark. It also looked as if a few more hits and bumps could have shouted out, as if Time itself told him, 'Hey, Ole Guy, we have many more bumps and years to go.'

Roots run deep in this old place. Ally supposed that if she was an underground varmint, she could see just how deep those roots went. She might be surprised if they didn't cover all the grounds and connect to all the other roots here on a much larger scale of something more important than what most people are aware of.

When Ally's imagination kicked in, it was always as large and brilliant as the bright blue sky. Imagining things was about all she did lately: think . . . think about everything. Right now all she could think about was being home. Finally.

She took a deep breath and passed through the 'threshold of time' when she opened the car door and took off her shoes, then ran straight into the garden – the 'threshold.' Family members had called it 'the threshold' for many decades. It was two large, old trees which had grown massive enough to overlap one another. Rose bushes and other flowering plants formed a living boundary around the garden. Whenever someone walked along the pathway beneath the beautiful shade trees, it was like strolling along a secret passageway and stepping back into times of old.

She smiled at same time as chill bumps erupted along her arms. She noticed the little iron garden bench where she used to sit as a child to watch for her fairy friends. She had patiently waited and watched to see if they would sparkle by or if a few lightning bugs would fly past her at sunset. Some lightning bugs always landed on her to make her all sparkles.

Ally smiled again and jogged over to the old iron bench. Its paint had faded with time, but she happily sat down, closed her eyes, then quieted her mind and spirit to once more drift back across time. Ah, to be that innocent little girl once again. The one who came to the garden dressed up in her Cinderella play dress to await her True Prince to arrive. She had held many tea parties in the garden, her tea dishes shining and ready, filled to the brim with fresh squeezed lemonade to give the Prince a cool drink because he might be warm when he rode into the garden on his white horse to accompany her into the future. Maybe . . . just maybe.

She took another deep breath. The many fragrances of blooming roses and peonies drifted in the breeze. She caught a glimpse of something that swiftly moved past her. Could it be an old friend? Could it be a fairy friend or a mouse scampering by? Perhaps it was an old fairy friend or two that had recognized her. She closed her eyes and heard a voice in the distance, calling her. "Ally, oh, Ally. Are you still in that garden, child? It's getting late. The bad bugs will be coming out soon and eat you alive. Get home, Ally."

Suddenly, a tear came streaming down her cheek. Now it was the hard part. Now she would have to leave her secret hiding place and garden, and face the house. The house, her home, had been sold, and those owners had sold it to the state as a historic site. Now it was a tourist attraction.

She had to get up off the bench and stand in the middle of the long drive that led up to the old homeplace. The massive trees growing on both sides slope over the gravel drive and paved the beautiful drive with moss. She stood and stared down the drive, her mind traveling back in time to days long before she was born, back to a time when horse-drawn carriages drove through this gate and down this path. She envisioned her great grandmother and great grandfather holding hands as they rode in a beautiful carriage on their way to town, or returning from town after attending some fancy party at another plantation, or after having dinner at a friend's home. She imagined her great grandmother wearing a lavender silk dress and a beautiful hat with a fancy, wide, silk ribbon tied to one side of her cheek, her long blondish-brown hair flowing down and tied in a bow to the side. Her great grandfather would have been just as refined looking as her great grandmother. He would have worn a fancy hat and a smile on his face, and dressed in nice trousers and white shirt. They would return home for the evening to have their tea before retiring to their rooms for bed. A slower time. A quieter time. A happier time.

Ally slowly walked closer and closer to the house, and noticed the columns were as white as they were when she lived there. The home was immaculate. She climbed up the wide porch steps and looked at the shutters on either side of the plantation's tall windows. She noticed the cool breeze as several ceiling fans spun around and around overheard on the big covered porch. Even the old rocking chairs were slightly rocking, as if her whole family were in them, watching Ally come back home. Her misty, teary-eyed face showed that she missed them terribly. She hoped they would answer the door and come rushing out to grab her in big hugs just as they did when she had been left on the porch as a small babe in the winter's cold on that February morning so long ago. She had been dressed properly in a big basket that was covered only in a pink, satin-trimmed blanket. She had been wearing two pink booties. The wind took one off her foot and sent it sailing into the sky where it disappeared in no man's land. She hoped it landed in some faraway place near her true betrothed prince because he, too, would have been a babe. Perhaps he found it, perhaps he may have it still, perhaps he had grown up to search for the one person it would fit – her, of course, just like in a tale about another slipper from another place in the distant past.

Ally knocked on the door as her father had done long ago to see who would answer. Only she stayed; she didn't run as he had. The door quickly opened and an older lady on the other side opened the door wider, indicating Ally should step inside. The woman frowned slightly when she noticed this tourist had teary eyes.

"May I come in? I grew up here and I've come back one last time to . . . to just look around."

The lady stepped aside. "Of course."

Alley looked directly at the staircase and climbed up, sniffing the air, memories of smelling the food her grannies cooked in the kitchen. She smelled fresh baked bread, and somehow smelled blackberry jam bubbling in giant pots to be canned, even though it was all in her mind, in her memory. She held on tight to the railing which she slid down on Christmas morning in a hurry to see what Santa had put under the tree. Now she hurried up the stairs and passed her gram's bedroom without going in, then her great gram's room without even looking inside, and finally reached her room, surprised to discover it had been turned into a child's nursery for appearance sake. She remembered exactly where the dollhouse stood that was delivered one Christmas by a tall, nameless stranger; tiny people lived in that dollhouse. She looked where her giant four-poster bed once was and imagined her red tricycle, and her bears and dolls that came to her tea parties, and most of all her bunny collection on a tall shelf. Bunnies were her best friends. It was easier to talk to them, her play ones than the real ones, but bunnies always listened to her made-up stories.

Her window was open. A large tree limb grew just outside her window and invited her to step out onto the narrow ledge to sit a spell on the limb. It was something she almost always did when a child.

She also saw herself sitting on her bed, crying and waiting for the parents who had dropped her off here so many years before ... and wondered why they never returned for her.

All the happy time memories made her smile. Some memories weren't so happy. She remembered taking her Great Grandmother Violet's fancy shoes from the attic to play dress-up Cinderella. Ally didn't know they were her Gram's bejeweled shoes she had planned to wear for her marriage ceremony. Taking them from the trunk in the attic got her into so much trouble. Eventually, the special shoes were given to her as a gift to be married in as well, which suited her to a 't' – because they were beautiful. However, before they could be used, her betrothed was also killed. It was a duplicate tragedy exactly like her Gram Violet endured when her betrothed was killed a half-century earlier. Neither Violent nor Ally ever wore the fancy shoes. Then, one shoe was lost forever in the automobile crash that killed Ally's fiancé. The room held many sad memories yet so many happy ones as well.

Ally made her way to the window and stared out into the forest. She remembered special places where she played and thought about the giant she once saw out there. She wondered if he still lived in the forest along with the rest of the strange creatures of the night.

The sudden ringing of her cell phone was startling. It snapped her mind back into harsh reality. Time to close down memory lane and come back to earth, to leave this place once and for all before her heart broke.

Ally ignored the phone call, ran down the steps and passed the docent lady in a flash. "Thank you for letting me inside. Bye," and slammed the door behind her.

She ran past the garden and bench, through the threshold and got back into her car. She turned her little Mercedes around and sped as fast as she could down the driveway and out the gates, turning onto the city's main highway. Without thinking about it, she headed straight to her Great Aunt Faden's house. Ally needed to know if Aunt Faden was still alive, if her mind was clear enough, if she remembered Ally enough to brew some tea and talk for a spell. Ally hoped she'd be lucky enough for Aunt

Faden to read tea leaves for her one more time. Ally needed to see what she must do now with so many problems facing her that needed to be resolved: her broken marriage and running away from home and an angry wealthy husband. After seeing her childhood home and precious memories turned into a tourist attraction, she felt more alone than ever. She felt like a lost child of the night once again. She needed guidance from someone she loved and trusted.

Aunt Faden had to be extremely old by now, almost ninety-four. Everyone in that bloodline lived long lives. Ally had not spoken to her in several years, but the last time she had heard from her half-sister, Aunt Faden was still 'alive and kicking,' as they say in the South and still had her wits about her.

Aunt Faden was a strange and unusual lady, even to most people around these parts, only because she could tell the future. So many people misunderstood this gift. Fortune telling was wrong, according to both of Ally's grannies, but they didn't perceive Aunt Faden herself as all that wrong even though they didn't like what she did. Most people in Louisiana did a little fortune telling, at least most of them in Ally's family. They didn't call it 'fortune telling' though. They called it what it really was: "In the Know." The Knowing, the gift. You were either born with it or not. Aunt Faden just happened to get a double dose. She was not only born with the Knowing, but with an extra dab of this and of that. Either way she had many of the gifts and was not ashamed to use them. She used her gifts to help anyone who needed to know something they didn't know, yet really did know it in their heart – most of them just didn't want to face what they already knew. . . . they just wanted someone like Faden to confirm it for them.

A lot of people in the South call it 'hoodoo.' That was as far as from the truth as you can get. It was just a name in the South, such as Voodoo, which seems to be real, if you believe in such a thing. We all stayed far away from New Orleans and Algiers where that kind of nonsense went on. Aunt Faden didn't kill chickens, or drink the blood, nor did she cut off chicken feet and put them in a pot of bones, and she didn't strip down naked in the woods to sacrifice animals and babies. Aunt Faden didn't worship the devil either. She read her Bible, went to church, and was a professional nurse at a hospital.

But, Aunt Faden did live in the swamp, a way-back swamp, in a big, wooden house painted bright red. She just liked the color red as the Chinese still do. She believed it brought good energy, love and happiness. Well, she was happy, even though her love story hadn't ended well.

To reach her home, people had to park their car on a levee and use a small motor boat to float across the water. She liked her privacy because the rotten scoundrels and kids on Halloween liked to call her a witch. They didn't know the facts. They'd roll her house in toilet paper, throw eggs against the walls, and play tricks on her. She put all that to a stop.

Visitors by the dozen believed she had special powers and would line up at her door to wait for hours for a turn. To have her privacy, she only saw a few people and only told a few fortunes. She would only do that for the ones who were friends and family members, those people who wanted to see future things for the good – never for people who wanted her to cast a witch's spell. This all came about because back in the day, when Aunt Faden was young, a few incidents happened that tagged her in the community as a witch. The rumors started. All things, incidents, weren't of her doing. She only told folks what she saw could happen. If for some reason it did happen, they claimed it was because she was a witch. From then on, she was tagged as a witch.

Aunt Faden was Ally's great aunt, her beloved Grandmother Pearl's sister. Ally never saw Faden do anything to a family member except cook great chocolate pies and cakes. Once Ally found a snake curled up in one of the kitchen drawers, but it was only because they were in the swamp. There are snakes out there, spiders, lizards, egrets, gators, and other animals. By the way, do you know that Native Americans believe snake medicine can cure cancer? Maybe.

Aunt Faden was more of an elderly wise tale woman, who grew herbs and knew healing medicines from plants and old remedies.

Creases formed on Ally's forehead when she considered that information probably added to the rumors about Faden being a witch. Ally laughed aloud. Well, there she was in the swamp decked out in an ensemble right out of the shops on Rodeo Drive: a California style straw hat, gold slippers, black Chanel crock pants, a black shear blouse with gold stripes, and a hip-hugging gold Chanel belt. She didn't look as if she was about to take a boat ride into the swamp to a big, old, red house to see her aunt that everyone claimed was a witch.

Laughing to herself, Ally was actually happy to still have a family member who was alive, old and wise. She was making it across the swamp without a problem. Crickets were singing loudly as they always did. Clouds in the distance began to rumble a bit and a small clap of thunder roared as if to announce that a storm was brewing somewhere.

"Oh, God, this is only happening because I'm going to visit with my aunt."

The closer she got, the stormy it looked and the darker it turned. "Weird. I just said my aunt's not a witch and here comes a storm,"

This storm was from another source, the same source generated when Ally's cell phone began to ring. Without even glancing at the screen, she knew who was trying to locate her – her dear husband, who was worst than a witch. He was a warlock not from a nice place. She called him 'the dark prince.' He was the one brewing up the storm. One thing was for certain; he knew little about Aunt Faden and it would be impossible for him to ever find Ally in these swampy waters.

Aunt Faden was on the front porch rocking when Ally's boat arrived. As she got closer, she could tell Faden was almost blind. The small, elderly woman stood without looking in Ally's direction. "Let me guess. . . . Oh, my! Could it be you child? Is it my little Cinder girl?"

"Yes, it's me, Auntie. It's me, Ally."

"Oh, my," Faden said. "I knew you would come again and I knew it would be soon. I have had some strange dreams about you, child. I sent out my calling to you and here you are."

Ally tied the boat to one of the stilts under the house and climbed the steps.

"Come on up here so I can grab you and just hold on to you for a moment. Come on sit a spell. Please tell me you're staying the night, please. So much to catch up on and it's so lonely out here. To be honest, I'm about tired out, little Ally. We must talk."

"Yes, I'm here for those reasons," Ally said, "to visit, to see my beloved aunt and check on you. I only came back to see the old home, and you, and my sister.

"I've been in Los Angeles all this time, married. Things have gone so wrong, just so wrong."

"I know, dear. I see it, you know, as I always have. I see the troubles and what you must have gone through and know you need answers now.

"Danger, child, ahead, but have beat it. Here you are. They are not going to like getting out here. Too many alligators," Faden said, then laughed. Snuff dripped down her wrinkled chin.

"Hearing you laugh warms my heart."

"Good. I have cornbread cooking and those peas you used to love," Faden said. "I don't cook much anymore, you know, just a few bites here and there, enough to survive off of."

Ally frowned. "Yes, Aunt Faden, you are quite slimmed down."

"Well, Ally, you never know. I just might get married again."

They both laughed at that thought.

"You are well, Ally?"

"Yes and no. I'm stressed Aunt Faden and ran away from my marriage. I couldn't stay in that dungeon. I was being treated like, well, you know, like . . ."

"Like a princess locked away at sea by some old ship's captain?"

"No, that would have been a luxury compared to what I've lived through. It was more like a fairytale nightmare. That would describe it much better."

"Well, beware, my dear, of marrying the prince especially when you don't know from whence he came. If you want to know and to see, we can go inside for a look."

"Oh! Yes! I would love to if, and only if, you're up to it, Aunt Faden."

"My dear," she grabbed tightly to Ally's arm, "it is not that I am up to anything. It is not so causal as this. It is absolutely detrimental to you that you know just what you are dealing with. You are young, innocent, pure of heart. I don't think you understand what nest you fell in. It is much more than a simple rabbit hole that you used to play with. Come, child; teatime and the rabbits are welcome to the tea party, if you choose to bring them."

Ally knew by Aunt Faden's urgency that it was going to be more than a thunderstorm that was brewing outside once their tea brewed. The storms were coming in, the cell phone no longer worked and there was no telephone in Aunt Faden's swamp house. It was just them, and the alligators, snakes, spiders and Aunt Faden fortune telling tea and more time.

Faden raised her cup. "Shall we drink? Here's to the best of luck. We are going to need it, especially with the storm coming, trying to cloud my judgment. That's okay. I have cloaked it." She laughed loudly.

Ally frowned. If her Aunt Faden was a real practicing witch, she certainly didn't want to believe it.

"I also made the bowl of clear water so we can see," Faden said when she placed a large bowl on the table. "Here's our water. Drink your tea. I will get my cards. Now we can put this fairytale nightmare you described to an end or see what the old dark prince is up to."

Faden sat back down and finished her tea. She swirled the dregs around the bottom of the cup, then peered at them for a long moment. "Ally, dear, the tea leaves show much travel for you, much travel, rocks and caverns, and high up places. You have to go high into mountains with lots of people. Hide out for a spell, a good year. You must not return to that castle, that huge home in Hollywood. Leave it all behind.

"You are pure of heart. He wants that power . . .

Faden looked up. "I see you have some protection amulets. Good moves. He has lost your scent – like a wolf, he is seeking you out. Things are throwing him off your track, but he suspects you have no place to go. It senses, it tells him to come here, thinking this is your home, so you would return here. He is nearer than you think, but it is okay. He cannot pick you here or suspect you are here. He wants to keep you.

The old woman lifted a necklace over her head, smiled at the silver object in her palm and placed it in Ally's hand. There was a glass amulet in the very center, surrounded by jewels. Ally was momentarily blinded by the light reflecting off of the looking glass shaped stone. "This will help you to Know, to see far beyond what you can see now. Wear it

Faden pushed the teacup aside and pulled the bowl of clear water closer. "Put your finger in the water, dear."

Ally hesitated for a moment before placing a fingertip in the center. Ripples moved back and forth for a few seconds as Faden stared into the water's depth.

"No one is to have you, but him. It is obsession love. A love, but not true love. You never loved him because you could not see his heart. It was dark. You could not get past that darkness, and you have been desperately trying to escape him. He tricked you. That is why you could not see for a while.

"A spell or something like it; you were under it until he proceeded to marry you. After that the spell was broken, then you immediate saw him as soon as a marriage chain was wrapped around you both, an ancient chain given to you at a castle as you two were going to be married. If the marriage chain broke, the marriage and spell he had over you would break. If it stayed in place, it meant he would lose you. I see it being placed around you two by a couple you didn't know; it passed down to you. As it was being placed around you during the ceremony, it broke.

"You believed this was only superstition, but he knew it was true. You had too much tainted champagne, the drink also held something dangerous. You couldn't understand or remember anything until morning. As soon as you awakened, you were sad and disenchanted because the enchanted chain had broken. You had slept with it and had awakened with the chain in your hand, not understanding the power of it. He was still sleeping and you were able to sneak away for a week, to find a trusted friend you loved once. You told him the strange tale, but it still would be many moons before you were totally free. You had no other option than to return to him and stay with him for a while.

"One day, the stars aligned once more in your favor so you ran, you escaped. Now you are free. The spell is broken. This does not mean he will not hunt for you for a very long time. He will see you one more time. He has something he had made for you. On the bottom of it is a golden key that fits into something you will discover that may bring you a lifetime of happiness. It was placed there long ago, but it is invisible to the human eye, nor can it be felt.

"You will be famous and sitting in a quaint little book store far away across big water, maybe France or England. A man will bring you a crystal slipper, if it is he, then you will be back under a spell of his kind."

Faden's voice grew softer, slower, yet more serious. "You will be brought a crystal shoe. There are two. Everyone has two slippers. One is from a man who you are destined to be with forever. It is written in the stars, your true prince . . . and the other one is *him*.

"You lost the crystal shoe . . . when you were very young on the ocean . . . you played. You always return to the ocean, looking for it, not knowing what you are looking for. You seek your golden key and crystal slipper.

"There is a name . . . written in the sand. It is the name of your true love. When you find this name written in a mysterious place, it will be the name of the one you belong to, . . . then the hard part begins.

"Your other half . . . . must receive this story somehow, . . . and he must deliver the crystal slipper to you. There are many clues along the way. A map of treasures you must go through. Some will be trickery. Only one will be real. The rest will always leave you because you are truly destined for the one true prince."

Faden looked up and smiled. "The true one who can deliver the crystal slipper with the right golden key."

"But Aunt Faden,... Aunt Faden?"

Faden was sadly gone. Now it was up to Ally to take this journey alone, to discover the true prince who held the mysterious small slipper the size of her palm which kept the golden key, visible or not.

Ally stepped out into the stormy night sky. She could still feel Faden's spirit on the wind. She smiled.

"We are with you, child, now go."

Ally looked up. There was no one there. Suddenly, she saw a burst of bright light appear in the dark sky, she smiled. Faden was now home. Three stars shone brightly in the night rain. The three women of her life were watching over her once more: her fairy God mother, her grandmother, and her aunt Faden.

Ally looked down at her treasured necklace and smiled. She closed her eyes and squeezed the necklace. Suddenly, she heard another voice.; it was him: The Timeless One...

The End.

About The Author

Alexandria Altman grew up in a wonderful small town in Louisiana. She credits her family and God for an amazing life filled with real life fairy tales and enchantment beyond her wildest dreams.

Today, Alex spends her time writing and helping those in need. She is active in many charities, including Johnny's Angels and Johnny's Sea World: two charities that are dear and near to the author's heart.

Of her process, Alexandria says, "I dream my Books, and then I write and deliver the messages to the world."

When asked if she could leave her readers with anything else, Altman simply replied, "Life is good if you live it well."

Acknowledgements

I want to thank my content editor, J. R. Williamson-Sorrell, for all of her hard work and for caring for this very special project. She worked hard to help make this book possible. Thank you, J. R.

I want to give special Thanks To My Publisher and Friend, Jarrad Hewett. Without him, I would have made a different turn with this Novel. His uncanny ability to work 25 hours a day, 7 days a week without sleep has made it possible for this Book to be the best it could ever be. His dedication has simply amazed me. There are no words, Jarrad, to thank you enough for what you have done for this novel. You are Amazing; Thank You.

I want to thank my good friend Donna Bennett for being there all along with all her support. Donna is one of the busiest women I know. Her work as the International Peace Ambassador is a blessing to us all. It is because of people like her that this world is moving more and more towards "happily ever after." Thank You, Donna, for all your Support, and for inviting me to the ball...LOL.

I want to Thank My friend, actor and director John C. Depp for his support. John, you are such a Positive Influence and Inspirational friend. Thank you for always being aware of other peoples gifts and for so bravely sharing your own. Thank You John for your Inspiration...and endorsement and Poem to add to this book, I am truly grateful because you are so loved by many...

God, I want to thank You for your kindnesss. Without You, my books would not exist. You are my inspiration for everything.

To Doug and all my family, thank you for allowing me the time to finish this long awaited Novel. I love you all.

Finally, to my friends: If I listed you all, it would be another Book. You Know who you are.

I hope each and every one of you also have a Cinderella story...

May all of your dreams come true.

Goodnight... until the clock strikes midnight...

I must go to the ball.

- Alexandria Altman

Alex

my Cinderella,

beautiful and fragile as a rose,

life has prepared you the most beautiful surprise ...

I am no prince,

I've no glass slippers to offer,

only my sincere Love...

my beautiful and beloved Cinderella,

life put us in the same way ....

By: J.D.